From the reviews for *Girlfriend in a Coma*:

'A richly associative novel... you'd have to be cold as ice not to be truly engaged and stirred.'   *Independent*

'We really should pay attention to Coupland. His eye is so firmly on the ball he's virtually clairvoyant. And the second reading is even more fun than the first. Enjoy.'
NICHOLAS LEZARD, *Guardian*

'An unforgettable novel: elegant, scary, witty'
VICTORIA GLENDINNING, *Daily Telegraph*

'Visually brilliant, fresh like new paint. I was absolutely knocked over by it.'   TOM PAULIN, *Late Review*

'A great wake-up call to young Americans everywhere'
MARK LAWSON

'Coupland remains America's most notable youth-culture novelist... *Girlfriend in a Coma* shifts his generation-defining focus to people of his own age (the hero finishes high school in 1979), while weaving an affecting tale of tragedy, childbirth, the supernatural and mornings spent waking up to New Order's "Bizarre Love Triangle".'
JOHN HARRIS, *Select*

`The novel's wit and moral force are unshakeable. As in the moving *Life After God*, Coupland offers something far more substantial than self-pity or reflexive irony. His novels are perfect time-capsules, replete with gloriously funny dialogue and unnervingly accurate commentary on his own (now ageing) generation. For these wasters, phoneys and sad sacks, Coupland offers a much-needed call to higher consciousness.'   BEN FARRINGTON, *Literary Review*

'Coupland's novels have named, defined and explored the parts of American youth culture that other commentators haven't reached... He possesses an uncanny gift of foresight and a great style. In *Girlfriend in a Coma* Coupland tackles the big ones: pre-millennium tension, growing old, identity, loss... It's strange, familiar, infectiously readable and at the end it goes completely berserk. Which is what you want, really.'   *Bizarre*

DOUGLAS COUPLAND

GIRLFRIEND IN A COMA

HARPER PERENNIAL

Harper Perennial
An imprint of HarperCollinsPublishers
77-85 Fulham Palace Road
Hammersmith London W6 8JB

Harper Perennial is an imprint of HarperCollins Publishers

www.harpercollins.co.uk/harperperennial
www.coupland.com

This edition published by Harper Perennial 2004

1

First published in Great Britain by Flamingo 1998

A catalogue record for this book
is available in the British Library

ISBN 978-0-00-788153-6

Set in Postscript Linotype Galliard
Printed and bound in Great Britain by Clays Ltd, St Ives plc

GIRLFRIEND
IN A COMA

PART 1

1 | ALL IDEAS ARE TRUE

I'm Jared, a ghost.

On Friday, October 14, 1978, I was playing football with my high school team, the Sentinel Spartans. It was an away-game at another school, Handsworth, in North Vancouver. Early on in the game I was thrown a pass and as I turned to catch it I couldn't help noticing how clean and blue the sky was, like a freshly squeegeed window. At that point I blacked out. I apparently fumbled the pass and I have no memory of what happened afterwards, but I did learn that the coaches canceled the game which was dumb because we were cleaning up and for all anybody knew, it was probably just a severe relapse of mono from two years earlier.

But between that fumbled pass and a few hours later when I woke up in Lions Gate Hospital, I was diagnosed with leukemia—cancer of the bone marrow and hence the blood. Just three months later I died, on January 14, 1979. It was a lightning-speed progression for this particular disease. Before I died I lost all my hair and my skin turned the color of an unwashed white car. If I could do it all over again, I'd have hidden the mirrors from about Week Six onward.

My life was happy and full and short; Earth was kind to me and my bout with cancer was my Great Experience. Unless, of course, we include my sex binge with Cheryl Anderson the week her parents were renovating and the whole family moved into The Maples motel for five days. That aside, I believe that unless a person passes through some Great Experience, that person's life will have been for naught. Such an experience doesn't have to be explosive or murderous or include Cheryl

Anderson; often a quiet life of loneliness can be its own Great Experience. And I will also say this: hospitals are girl magnets. My room there quickly became a veritable parade float of flowers, cookies, knit goods and girls who had quite obviously (and fetchingly) spent hours grooming. Such is the demented nature of the universe that I was too weak to properly respond to my being hit on by carloads of Betties and Veronicas—all except for the cheeky Cheryl Anderson who gave me 'manual release' the day I lost my eye-brows, followed by a flood of tears and the snapping of Polaroids in which I wear a knit toque. Gush gush.

But back to right now—here, where I am, here at world's end.

Yes, the world is over. It's still *here* but it's . . . *over*. I'm at the End of the World. Dust in the wind. The end of the world as we know it. Just another brick in the wall. It sounds glamorous but it's not. It's dreary and quiet and the air always smells like there's a tire fire half a mile up wind.

Let me describe the real estate that remains one year after the world ended: It is above all a silent place with no engines or voices or music. Theater screens fray and unravel like overworn shirts. Endless cars and trucks and minivans sit on road shoulders harboring cargoes of rotted skeletons behind the wheel. Homes across the world collapse and fall inward on themselves; pianos, couches and microwaves tumble through floors and expose money and love notes hidden within the floorboards. Most foods and medicines have time-expired. The outer world is eroded by rain, and confused by lightning. Fires still burn, of course, and the weather now tends to extremes.

Suburban streets such as those where I grew up are dissolving inside rangy and shaggy overgrown plants; vines unfurl across roads now undriven by Camaros. Tennis rackets silently un-string inside dark dry closets. Ten million pictures fall from ten million walls. Road signs blister and rust. Hungry dogs roam in packs.

To visit earth now you would see thousands of years of grandeur and machinery all falling asleep. Cathedrals fall as

4

readily as banks; car assembly lines as readily as supermarkets. Lightless sunken submarines lumber to the ocean's bottom to spend the next billion years collecting silt. In cities the snow sits unplowed; jukeboxes sit silent; chalkboards stand forever unerased. Computer databases lie untapped while power cables float from aluminum towers like long thin hairs.

But how did I end up here? And how long am I to stay here? To learn this, we need to learn about my friends. They were here, too—at the end of the world. This is the place my old friends came to inhabit as well—my friends who grew old while I got to remain forever young.

Question: would I do it the same way all over again? Absolutely—because I learned something along the way. Most people don't learn things along the way. Or if they do, they conveniently forget those things when it suits their need. Most people, given a second chance, fuck it up completely. It's one of those laws of the universe that you can't shake. People, I have noticed, only seem to learn once they get their third chance—after losing and wasting vast sums of time, money, youth, and energy—you name it. But still they learn, which is the better thing in the end.

So here follows the story of friends of mine who finally learned their lesson: Karen, Richard, Pam, Hamilton, Wendy and Linus. Richard's the best talker of the group so in the beginning the story is mostly his. Karen would have been better but then Karen wasn't around Earth much in the beginning. *C'est la vie*. But then Richard's story only takes us so far. The story gets bigger than him. It includes them all. And in the end it becomes *my* story. But we'll get to that.

Destiny is what we work toward. The future doesn't exist yet. Fate is for losers.

18–25–32 . . . *Hike!*

2 | EVERY IDEA IN THE WORLD IS WRONG

Karen and I deflowered each other atop Grouse Mountain, among the cedars beside a ski slope, atop crystal snow shards beneath penlight stars. It was a December night so cold and clear that the air felt like the air of the Moon—lung-burning; mentholated and pure; a hint of ozone, zinc, ski wax, and Karen's strawberry shampoo.

Here is where I go back to the first small crack in the shell of time, to when I was happiest. Myself and the others, empty pagan teenagers lusting atop a black mountain overlooking a shimmering city below, a city so new that it dreamed only of what the embryo knows, a shimmering light of civil peace and hope for the future. And there I am now, up on the mountain: *What did you see, Karen? Why weren't we allowed to know? Why you—why us?*

That night—December 15, 1979—Karen had been so ravenous, demanding that we connect full-tilt. She said to me, "So, Richard, are we ever gonna do it or what?" She unzipped her bib overalls on a steep, breast-shaped mogul, then hauled me into the woods, where she yanked me down into the scraping snow, a snow too icy for snow angels. I felt so young, and she looked so mature. She pulled me with unfamiliar urgency, as though an invasion were about to occur that would send us off to war. And so there we lay, pumping like lions, the insides of our heads like hot slot machines clanging out silver dollars, rubies, and sugar candies. As if time was soon to end, what little time remained must be squandered quickly, savoring the delicate, fluttering pulses of cool, dry cherry blossoms passing back and forth between our bodies.

Afterward, cold snow trickled into our pants, then into our orifices, chilling and congealing those parts so recently warm while we zipped up and schussed down the ski runs to the chairlifts. "Hey, Richard, you pussy—it's a rat race!"

Karen and I were flushed, slightly embarrassed, processing all these new bodily sensations while feeling transformed—and then we rose up again, up the mountain on a bobbing chairlift that stalled halfway up the slope. And it was there that the arc lights also blinked, then skittered, then blackened. In the pitch dark, Karen and I sat bouncing, stuck, suspended above raw nature, our faces blue jeans-blue from the Moon. Karen lit a Number 7 cigarette, her bony cheeks inflamed with blood, burning pink in the Bic lighter's heat, like a doll inside a burning doll house. My arm draped her shoulder; we both felt safe, as if we were a complete solar system unto ourselves, dangling in the sky, warm heated planets inside a universe of stars.

I asked Karen, who was also trying to gauge the impact of what we'd just done together in the woods, if she was happy. This is never, as I have since learned, a good question to ask of anyone. But Karen smiled, giggled, and blew silky smoke into the deep blue darkness. I thought of jewels being tossed off an ocean liner over the Marianas Trench, gone forever. Then she turned her head away from me and looked into the forest that lay to the right, trees visible to us both as only a darker shade of black. I could tell something was now wrong with her, as though she were a book I was reading with pages tantalizingly removed. Her small teeth bit her lower lip and her eyebrows lowered.

She jittered with a delicate jolt, as if she'd tried to start her Honda Civic with her house key.

The realization dribbled into my own head: Karen had been off kilter all afternoon and into the evening, fixating over dumb things like the olive-colored dial telephone in my parents' kitchen or a bouquet of crummy gladiolas on the kitchen table, saying, "Oh, isn't that just the most beautiful . . ." then trailing off. She had also been looking at the sky and the clouds all day, not just glancing, but stopping and standing and staring, as if they were on a movie screen.

Karen's back arched just faintly, and her face stiffened just so. I said, "What's up, Pumpkin—regrets? You know how I feel about you."

And she said, "Duh, Richard. I love you, too . . . goonhead. Nothing's wrong, really, Beb. I'm just cold. And I want the lights to come back on. Soon." She called me "Beb," a snotty contraction of "Babe."

The absence of light frightened her. She pulled up my wool ski cap and kissed my waxy, cold ear. So I held her tighter and once more asked her what was the matter, because she still wasn't okay.

She said, "I've been having the weirdest dreams lately, Richard. So *real* . . . I guess it sounds kind of loser-ish, me saying that, doesn't it? Best forgotten." Karen shook her head and blew out a puff of tobacco smoke that spider-webbed against the dark night. She stared at the chairlift's stalag towers, unable to light the slopes with man-made sun. She changed the subject: "Did you see Donna Kilbruck's pants tonight? God—so tight—she had walrus-crotch. The horror. It, too, best forgotten."

"Hey, Beb, don't change the subject. Tell me," I said, with an unexpected curtness. I was mad at myself; I was growing up and was at the stage where smart-ass one-liners were no longer in and of themselves adequately meaningful to sustain a conversation. Karen and I rarely had conversations of true depth. The closest we ever got to hearing each other's deeper thoughts was during stoned group philosophizing sessions—which is to say not much at all. But then we were young and glibness was our armor. We yearned for better thoughts. I vowed to try to bring myself closer to her. "C'mon. Please—tell me."

Karen said, "Nope. Sorry, Beb. It's too complicated to explain. . . ." Again I felt excluded. Minutes before I had been so totally one with her. A wind scraped by, our bodies shivered, and then she said, "Well maybe it wasn't a *dream*. You promise not to laugh."

"Huh? Yes. Of course I promise."

"Well, I was asleep when it happened—but it was more realistic than any dream. Maybe a kind of vision."

"Go on."

"It wasn't like a dream at all, more like movie clips—like a TV ad for a movie, but with still photos, too, but just barely developed, like a blur that becomes a face when I develop them in the photo lab at school. I think it was supposed to be the future."

I could kick myself now for having said what I said, an ill-timed stab at being funny: "So how was the future? Vietnam conquers Earth? Aliens for dinner? Pods for everybody? Maybe that explains your being a space cadet all day." I thought I was being witty here—a real center box on *Hollywood Squares*. But Karen's falling face showed that I'd grossly misjudged. She looked spooked and let down.

"Okay, Richard. I see. I *knew* I shouldn't have trusted you with that. That's one mistake I won't be making again." She looked away. Chills.

I felt like a farmer watching his field flattened by hail. "No. *Shit*. Karen. Please. I'm a shit. Big-mouth strikes again. I didn't mean that. You know I didn't. I was being a jerk. I don't like it when I'm like that. Shit. I was only trying to be funny. Please tell me. C'mon. I want to hear about your vision. *Please*."

"Your groveling has been noted, Richard." She flicked away her cigarette; her tone indicated probation. She was silent a while. We were beyond chilly, quite cold now. Our eyes adjusted to the dark. She continued: "It had texture. For example, I could feel plants and clothes and things when I touched them. Especially last night. It was set in our house on Rabbit Lane, but everything had gone to seed. The trees and grass . . . and the people, too. You, Pam . . . really dirty and grungy."

Suddenly, she had clarity. "These things *are* all in the

future." She sniffed back a moist bead of goo dripping from her nose. "The air seemed smoky. There weren't any flying cars or outer-space clothing. But cars *were* different, all smooth and round. I drove in one. It had a new brand name ... Airbag? Yes—*Airbag*. It was on the dashboard."

"You didn't happen to pick up a *Wall Street Journal* and notice any big market trends in the future—or any stock prices—or anything like that, did you?"

She nogged herself on her forehead. "I get shown the future and all I paid attention to is cars, haircuts, and . . ." She rolled her eyes. "I'm blanking, Richard, I can't help you there. Stop being crass. Wait—yes—yes: Russia isn't an enemy anymore. And sex is—fatal. *Ta-da!*"

The ski-lift chair jiggled—engines up the hill were sending rumbles. Karen continued trancing: "Earlier this week, I saw the future and there were these machines that had something to do with money—people seemed to be more . . . *electronic*. People still did things the regular way, too, like they had to pump gas and . . . and . . . oh, *shit*, I can't believe this, I see the future and it sounds just like *now*. I can't even remember how it was different. People looked better. Thinner? Better clothes? Like joggers?"

"And . . . ?"

"Okay, you're right. Details are kinda patchy—but there's bad news, too. It's a good news/bad news thing." She paused and said, "There's a . . . darkness to the future." She paused and bit her lip. "That's what's scaring me now."

"What kind of darkness?" That night, I had worn only jeans, no long johns. I shivered.

"The future's *not* a good place, Richard. I think it's maybe cruel. I saw that last night. We were all there. I could see us— we weren't being tortured or anything—we were all still alive and all . . . *older* . . . middle-aged or something, but . . . 'meaning' had vanished. And yet we didn't know it. We were meaningless."

"What do you mean, 'meaningless'?"

"Okay. Life didn't seem depressing or empty to us, but we

10

could only discern that it was as if we were on the outside looking in. And then I looked around for other people—to see if their lives seemed this way, too—but all the other people had left. It was just us, with our meaningless lives. Then I looked at us up close—Pam, Hamilton, you, Linus, Wendy— and you all seemed normal, but your eyes were without souls . . . like a salmon lying on a dock, one eye flat on the hot wood, the other looking straight to heaven. I think I need to stop now."

"No—don't!"

"I wanted to help us, Richard, but I didn't know how to save us, how to get our souls back. I couldn't see a solution. I was the only one who knew what was missing, but I didn't know what I could do about it."

Karen sounded as though she were about to cry. I was quiet and had no idea what to say; I put my arm around her. Below us on the left I could see skiers gathered in the dark, toking up and passing wineskins while hooting.

Karen spoke again: "Oh! I just remembered! Jared was there last night! In the vision—he *was*! So maybe it's *not* a real vision of the future, but a vision of what might be—a warning, like the ghost of Christmas Future."

"Well, maybe." I didn't like hearing Jared's name, though I didn't let on. The chairlift then lurched forward a few feet, the lights flickered on, then stopped. The world was dark stillness again.

"But you know what, Richard?"

"What?"

She caught herself. "Nothing. Oh, never mind, Beb. I think I'm tired of talking about this." She reached into her jacket. "Here. I want you to hold onto this envelope for me. Don't open it. Just hold onto it for me overnight. Give it back to me tomorrow."

"Huh?" I looked at the Snoopy envelope with the word "Richard" Magic Markered on its front in her maddeningly girlish, rounded-sloped, daisy-adorned handwriting. Her handwriting was actually the subject of an argument the two

11

of us had a month previously. I'd asked her why she couldn't write "normally." Idiot!

Karen watched me look at the handwriting. "Normal enough for you, Richard, you daring nonconformist, you?" I stashed the envelope in my down jacket's pocket and then the chairlift jumped into motion again.

"Remember—tomorrow you give it back to me, no questions asked."

"It's a done deal." I kissed her.

The chairlift started with another lurch, causing Karen to drop her pack of Number 7's from her lap. She cursed, and instantly the mountain was again electrically lit with energy from the great dams of northern British Columbia. The skiers on the slopes below whooped, as though whooping for energy itself; our moment was lost. Karen said, "Look—there's Wendy and Pam." She deafened me by shouting instructions to Wendy to meet at the Grouse Nest in half an hour; she asked Pam to rescue her dropped pack of cigarettes, now many chairs behind us.

Our intimacy reduced, we quickly and soundlessly chairlifted up the Blueberry Chair's slope while Karen discussed plans for the rest of the night. "Look, there's Donna Kilbruck now. Arf Arf!"

I thought of Jared.

Jared was a friend of ours, as well as my best friend while growing up. In high school, Jared and I had drifted apart, as can happen with friends made early in life. He became a football star and our lives increasingly had less and less in common. He was also the biggest male slut I've ever known. Girls would hurl themselves at him and he was always there to catch. While Jared was definitely inside the winner's circle humping himself silly, I, on the other hand, seemed to be on a vague loser track. We still got along fine, but it felt comfortable only back in our own neighborhood and away from the high school's intricate popularity rituals. Jared's family lived around the corner from mine, up on St. James Place. One hot afternoon during a game at Handsworth Secondary, Jared simply keeled over and was

12

wheeled off to Lions Gate Hospital. A week later, he'd lost his gold curls; two months later, he weighed less than a scarecrow; three months later he was . . . gone.

Did we ever really recover from the loss? I'm not sure. I had been, in a way, Jared's "official friend," so many of the consoling stares and words came my way, which I hated. All of the girls who once mooned over Jared began mooning over me — Jared's sex energy still filled the air — but I wasn't about to take advantage of the opportunity and emulate his life of sluttery. I acted stoic when in fact I was angry and scared and sad. Jared had thought of us as best friends before he died, but we really weren't. I'd made other friends. I felt guilty, disloyal. The next year was spent not talking about Jared, pretending that everything was proceeding as normal, when it wasn't.

IF IT SLEEPS IT'S ALIVE

I was quiet in the gondola descending the mountain while Karen was lightly bantering with Wendy and Pam. Our skis were strapped together and faintly clacked. Karen and I were transformed from the two who had gondola'ed up just hours earlier. Lilting and swooping across the gondola's middle tower, we looked at the lights of Vancouver before the 1980s had its way with the city—an innocent, vulnerable, spun-glass kingdom. We tried to spot our houses, which twinkled across the Capilano River inside our sober, sterile mountain suburb.

I felt faraway as I then looked underneath the gondola at the white angel-food snowpack and the black granite that poked out from within it. I had the sensation that I was from some other world and had fallen onto Earth like a meteorite. Instead of being an earthling I had crash-landed here—*Ka-thunkkk!*—and my life on Earth was an accident. First-time gondola riders and fraidy-cats tittered and screamed as our gondolas swooned downward. I looked at Karen, with her head resting atop her ski poles. She had the extra pulse of beauty people have when they know they're being fondly admired.

The gondola moored at the base; we clomped to my Datsun B-210, where we removed the plastic anchors of our ski boots and luxuriated in the freedom of recently freed toes. We hopped into the car and drove to a party we had been warned might be a *house-wrecker*—up to a winding suburban street on the mountain of West Vancouver. It was a party where a now forgotten teen of questionable popularity had been left minding the house while parents gambled away in Las Vegas.

And indeed the party was a grand house-wrecker—larger than any of us had seen to date. We arrived around 10:00 p.m., and the Datsun was one of dozens of cars parked up and down Eyremont Drive. Teenagers leaped out of cedar hedges and spruce shrubberies like protons, their beer boxes clutched under knobby jean-jacketed arms, bottles inside carrying imprisoned genies offering just one last wish.

From all directions came the sound of excited voices and smashing bottles. Silhouettes of teens sparkled atop broken bottles lit by street-lights. Several of us were just arriving from Grouse Mountain. I heard a hiss—my friend, Hamilton—my own personal patron saint of badly folded maps, damp matches, low-grade pornography, bad perms, tetracycline, and borrowed cigarettes. He beckoned me from inside a hedge of laurels just ahead of the parked car, hissing, '*Richard, drag your butt in here.*"

I complied, and inside I found a branchy wigwam rife with headache-inducing Mexican pot of the weakest caliber. Roughly ten of Hamilton's drug buddies were toking furiously. In no mood for a headache, I said, "Jesus, Ham—it smells like an egg fart inside a subway car. Come out and meet me and the girls. Where's Linus?"

"Down at the party. I'll be out in a minute. *Dean, please, pass me those Zig-Zags.*"

Back at the car, Karen, Pam, and Wendy were discussing Karen's new diet. I said, "Karen, you're not *still* hell-bent on starvation, are you?"

Karen had been obsessed with Hawaii and dieting. 'Richard, *Beb*, I've just *got* to be a size five by next week or I won't fit into my new Hawaii swimsuit."

Pam, wafer-thin, asked, "Are you *still* taking diet pills? My mom gives them to me all the time. I refuse."

"Pam," Karen replied, "you *know* I was raised on pills; Mom's a walking pharmacy. But if I take even *one* speeder, I spazz out and climb the walls with my teeth." She paused to sweep hair from her eyes. "Most drugs, even vitamins, send me to the Moon. But downers are okay. I take them to cool out. Mom gave me my own bottle." To all of us, this sounded glamorous and wanton.

Wendy, trying to be cooler than she really felt, said, 'That'd be just so loser-ish—you know, OD'ing on vitamins," and her quip was met with polite stares.

Pam broke the silence. She was then trying to break into the world of modeling, and she said, "Oh—I was at a shoot yesterday—do you want to know what models sound like when they talk?" We agreed enthusiastically. "Like this," she said, "like Pebbles Flintstone: '*Koo goo koo baa baa baa diet pills goo koo koo.*' Promise me that if I ever start talking like that, just pull the plug."

Slaphappy Hamilton, beanstalk-tall, black-booted, bolo-corded, with hands as big as frying pans, appeared from behind, saying, "Richard: It's im*per*ative we check the party right now, man. The house is just getting de*moli*shed. Hey there, Pammie . . ."

Pam stuck out her tongue. He and Pammie had been blowing hot and cold for three years; that night, they were in a cold spell. Hamilton turned back to me: "If we don't rescue Linus, he'll be cat food by midnight. It's berserk down there. Besides, Mr. Liver here wants a drink." Hamilton squeezed the side of his stomach; below us something lurched and crashed.

Pam asked the sky, "*Why* do I have to like aloof jerks who couldn't care less if I exist? Please, O gods of love, send me a winner next time."

We all discussed skiing for a while, and I felt myself pulling back, again looking at Karen, Wendy, and Pam. As a trio, they resembled three different-looking sisters, but sisters nonetheless. They called themselves Charlie's Angels, but then, so did many other trios of girlfriends at that time.

Personalities.

I sometimes wonder what can be said of people when they are young, whether the full expression of their personalities is truly discernible. Do we even offer hints? Do murderers seem like murderers at eighteen? Do stockbrokers? Waiters? Million-

16

aires? An egg hatches. What will emerge—a cygnet? a croco-
dile? a turtle?

Wendy: wide shoulders earned on the swim team, a friendly,
earnest, square, slightly mannish face capped with a chocolate-
brown wedge cut. Hamilton and I once tried to pin down
Wendy's looks, and Hamilton wasn't far wrong when he said
she looked like she was twenty-seventh in line to the British
throne. At our family Christmas party every year, when intro-
ducing ourselves to the older crowd, Wendy always said, "I'm
the smart one." And she was.

Pam (Pamela, Pammie, Pameloid): thin as water streaming
from a tap, a perfect oval face, a face like a tourist attraction
crowned with a wispy corn-silk Farrah perm. Glamour vixen
Pammie: eyes always looking a bit farther than your own:
"*Whatcha lookin' at, Pam?*" "*Oh—just. Something. Up there.
In the clouds.*"

Karen: small face with straight brown hair parted in the
center. Moss-green eyes. As comfortable with boys as with
girls. A guy's gal. Skiing? Touch football? Wounded animal
needs mending? Call Karen.

As a trio, their six arms were perennially crossed over either
brown leather or down jackets, hands clasping purses full of
high-tar cigarettes; Dmetre ski sweaters reeking of Charlie per-
fume, sugarless gum, and sweet-smelling hair. Clean and free
and sexy and strong.

Karen asked for a drink and Wendy said, "Are you sure you
want to drink, Karen? I mean you're looking kinda frail. All
you've eaten today is a Ritz cracker and half a can of Tab.
Let's go to my place and get something."

Pammie said, "Don't say that—don't tempt me—because
I'll be the one who ends up eating too much." She paused:
"Is there much in your fridge?"

Karen ignored them. She climbed into my Datsun to put a
new lace in her runners just as I walked to the car to get my
sweater. I saw Karen slip two pills from her makeup compact
into her mouth. She caught *me* catching her. So she stuck out
her tongue jokingly. "It's *Valley of the Dolls*, I *know*, Richard—

17

but let's see *you* in a size-five bikini." I could feel myself trying to mold my face into a nonjudgmental scrunch; I lost.

"Christ, it's only *Val*ium. It's totally legal. My mom gave them to me." She was slightly angry at my having caught her. I think it made her seem less in control.

I said, "Karen, I think you look great; you've got a great body, you're perfect the way you are. And I should know . . ." I winked, but I think it looked dirty, not friendly. "You're nuts to even *think* about dieting."

"Richard, that's *sweet*, you're the bestest, bestest boyfriend on Earth, and I really do appreciate it. But listen: It's a *girl* thing. Drop it, okay?" At least she was smiling. She leaned over the seat and gave me a quick kiss before I went back to the makeshift bar Pam had set up on the top of her car's hood. "Roll up your window and shut the door," Karen said to me, a Valium underneath her tongue, "God may be watching." It was the last thing she said to me for almost twenty years.

Pam cradled a bottle of Smirnoff vodka, and she and Wendy began pouring itty-bitty drinks into stolen McDonald's paper cups, with Tab as a mixer.

Wendy was talking about her Friday meeting with the school guidance counselor. She was considering applying for the accelerated pre-med program at UBC, but she couldn't decide if she'd be missing out on all the college fun: "You know, drunken piss-ups, drug orgies, unchained sex, and afterward writing fake letters to *Penthouse Forum*."

Pam was in no mood to discuss careers. "Hey, let's booze-and-cruise tonight, eh, Wendy? This housewrecking crap is such a guy thing." We looked down at the house; from the racket it generated, we thought the house would implode, as if in a horror movie.

Hamilton said, "What's that, Pammie? You're just scared of those North Van chicks in their white jeans. *Admit* it." In 1979 white jeans among partying females were the tell-tale code that the wearer was up for "a scrap."

"What . . . and like you're *not* scared, Hamilton?"

18

Wendy said, "Touché, Pamela," then looked at me. "Are you going down there, Richard?"

"*Umm*—I'd rather not. But Linus is down there. Ham and I told him to meet us at the party and we can't just leave him among the pagans. As we speak, he's probably sitting inside a boiling cauldron reading a World Book Encyclopedia."

Pam fondled the amulet on the chain around her neck, which Karen told me contained a curl of Hamilton's pubic hair. Wendy chugged her cocktail completely and said to Pam, "ABC." I asked what that meant, to which the two of them chimed, "Another Bloody Cocktail! Now go rescue Linus, you wee laddies. We three are gonna stay up here and guzzle *hooch*."

And so Hamilton and I went down the steep driveway—reluctantly, with forced bravado and a patch of giggles behind us—down into the pale yellow rancher then being smashed by angry, dreadful children, ungrateful monsters, sharks in bloodied water, lashing out at this generic home, their incubator—a variation on their own homes—homes for the prayerless, homes that imbued their teen occupants with rigid sameness and predictability while offering no alternative.

An uprooted ficus tree straddled the billiard table, its soil and some beer making a mud puddle onto which a six-ball now rested; a sliding glass door was smashed, touting a hole wider than a fist where blood dripped down onto the carpet; the TV-room walls were Dalmatian-spotted with boot-kicked holes and dents; the remaining billiard balls had been tossed through the holes and shattered on the patio. The toilet had overflowed in the worst way imaginable; vomit had been seemingly flung, then sprinkled, onto the most unlikely surfaces. 'It's like an inmate riot at a maximum security prison," Hamilton said. Only the stereo, with its ability to generate ambiance, had been spared, playing more and more loudly as drunken teenagers skulked around in their jean jackets and leather coats, walking amok, erupting spontaneously into beery rages, crashing chairs and pulling down the light fixtures from stippled ceilings. The girls, those tough North Van girls in the fabled white pants, sat in the master bedroom uninterested in the crashings. The bedroom was now converted into a smoking room, its occupants trying on silk blouses and orange lipsticks and combing their hair with pastel combs. Some of them sat on the kitchen counters hotknifing hash with heirloom silver, showing only marginal concern when a particularly loud crash was heard.

We continued walking. Hamilton and I had never been to a party of this caliber of violence before, and we didn't dare say we were frightened. We skulked about, hands in pockets. "Precisely *what* is it that's giving me the niggling feeling we're headed backward as a species?" Hamilton said. He was then almost slugged in the sternum by a partygoer offended by too many syllables. Shortly, he said, "Right. Well. Where's the pisser then?" only to learn that the other toilet was in shards. Out the window, people were skeeting records across the pool, lobbing empty beer bottles at these bat-like targets.

Walking by what was somebody's bedroom, we found Linus—monkey-postured, stubble-chinned, and wiping his nose with the back of his ink-stained hand—poring over an atlas, oblivious to the toxic trashing about him. "Oh. Hey— you guys wanna go get, umm, *food* or something?" he asked.

We considered. The unthinkable consequences to the poor kid who lived there was too depressing. Hamilton said, "Cops'll be here soon, kids. Let's booze-and-cruise. Come on, Linus."

Suddenly, out of a window a lime-green lightning bolt cut the sky above the patio; seconds later, a La-Z-Boy recliner went to sleep at the pool's bottom.

Linus walked behind us, lighting a cigarette and placing a book or two back into a bookshelf that had been tipped over. "Did you guys know that Africa has over sixty countries?" he asked, while Hamilton bellowed, "Be gone, you imbecilic avalanche of hooligans!" and led us up the driveway. We cut over a topsoil landscaped mound and into a neighboring yard. On the road above, police cruisers' cherries pulsed American reds, whites, and blues. At my Datsun, Wendy and Pam stood over Karen.

"Richard," Wendy said, "Karen's totally out of it. Not even two drinks and she's almost passed right out. Not her style. Pam, go get a blanket. You should get her home, Richard. Hi, Linus. How was the, um, *party?*"

"Smashing," said Hamilton, cutting in.

A jolt passed through me: Karen had only two drinks? She looked okay, but something was *off*. No vomit, no anything; she was weak and pale. Talking to her didn't work; she was almost asleep and was making no effort to say anything or communicate with her eyes. I tried to sound casual to quell panic: "Let's take her back down to her house. Her folks are out of town, so we can put her to bed, watch TV, and keep our eyes on her. It's probably nothing."

"Probably that *moronic* diet," said Wendy. "She probably just needs to sleep after skiing on several days' worth of empty stomach."

"There's a new *Saturday Night Live* on," said Pam. Wendy and I lifted Karen into the Datsun, her clammy skin offering no shivers. Our small convoy of cars fled to Karen's house, one house below my own. There, I carried Karen into her bedroom, removed her coat and shoes, and tucked her into bed. She still felt clammy, so I put another blanket over her. She seemed okay. Wiped out, but the day had been long.

We sat in the living room, turning on *Saturday Night Live* just as the show was beginning. Wendy burned some popcorn in the kitchen, and we sat in beanbag chairs watching the first few minutes of skits. Hamilton was feeling upstaged by TV, and he tried to steal our attention with tales of boils, cysts and lame knock-knock jokes. We told him to shut up.

Linus lay on the sidelines staring at a blood-red poinsettia beside the presents underneath the Christmas tree. He was telling us about its petals' veins, marveling at the cell structure of the stems and leaves. He explained how you could say that roots are like electrical wiring and that photosynthesis was the most self-contained and efficient solar energy system possible.

"Will somebody tell Johnny Appleseed to *fermez-la-*

bouche?" said Hamilton. Pammie maneuvered her way toward Hamilton. Tastemaster Wendy, going through a snobby I-don't-watch-TV phase, was doing a tabulation of the number of owls Karen's mother had accumulated—"Owls, owls, owls—no surface left owl-free. There's even a small macramé owl above the phone in the hall alcove. Thirty of them and you could make a macramé jumpsuit like the one Ann Margret wore in *Tommy* just before she rolled around in the pile of baked beans."

"Wendy, *what* are you talking about?" asked Pam from the kitchen.

"Why is Mrs. McNeil obsessed with owls? What do they represent to her? What dark secret lurks inside them? What need do they satisfy in her?"

"They're pill stashes," said Hamilton. "The brass owl on the mantelpiece contains two hundred decayed Milltowns."

I excused myself and went to check on Karen. I heard Wendy shout, "Eighty-six," as part of her owl tabulation. I saw Karen had turned white as milk. Her head was propped upward, green eyes vacant, looking at heaven.

My brain collapsed. My arms and legs stung as though they were growing quills; my mouth dried as though stuffed with straw. "She's . . . not . . . breathing!" I shouted. "She's not *breathing*!" The gang in the living room was confused, saying, "*Wha* . . . ?" as they came over.

Pam said, "Shit. Oh *fuck*. Oh God. Wendy? You're on the swim team. Do mouth-to-mouth." Wendy dropped down to Karen on the bed and gave the kiss of life while Hamilton called the ambulance from the hallway phone. Pam said, "*Oh, no, it's another Jared*," to which Hamilton raged, screaming, "Don't even think that fucking thought! Don't even *think* of thinking it."

Jared. Oh *God*. This could be *forever*. This could go well beyond *real*. My eyes moistened and my throat hurt. We stood around feeling desperate and alarmingly useless, muttering *shits* and bobbing our heads uselessly. The bedside plastic dome lamp on her side table was turned on, throwing cheap yellow

22

light on us and the mural on Karen's wall – an aging photo mural of the Moon with Earth in the background. I saw her swim medals and a Snoopy trophy saying: *World's Best Daughter*. There were lipsticks; lip smackers; two shirts that hadn't been chosen for wear that day laid out on the chest of drawers; a beer stein filled with pennies; high school yearbooks; a thesaurus and hair brushes.

The paramedics swooped through the front door with the gurney. Karen's lumpen body was lifted onto it like a clump of Play-Doh. The driver said, "Drinking?" We said vodka. "Any drugs involved?" Pam, Wendy, and Hamilton didn't know about the Valiums, but I did. "Two tranquilizers. I think they were Valium."

"Overdose maybe?"

"No." I'd seen her take just the two.

"Any pot?"

"No. Smell her if you don't believe it."

A respirator was being stuck down Karen's throat.

"Parents?"

"Down in Birch Bay."

"How long without breathing?"

"It's hard to say. A few minutes? She was wide-awake just thirty minutes ago."

"You the boyfriend?"

"Yeah."

"You ride in the car with us."

We shot out into the hallway, then onto the front walk and on to the driveway. My parents walked toward us from my house, faces pulsing colors from the ambulance lights, the panic in their eyes subsiding only slightly when they saw that it wasn't me on the stretcher.

"Hamilton, fill them in," I said. "We have to leave." Then Karen and I were in the ambulance, launched off toward Lions Gate Hospital. I took one last look through the rear windows at the neighborhood where Karen and I and Hamilton and Linus and Pammie had all grown up—cool and dry and quiet as a vault.

Karen's dad's burnt orange Chevy LUV . . . leaded gas fumes . . . two pills . . . trimmed hedges.

Our ambulance drove up Rabbit Lane to Stevens Drive and onto the highway to the hospital, and how was I to know that time was now different?

4 | IT'S ALL FAKE

That first week of Karen's coma was the hardest. We couldn't have known then that the portrait of Karen that began that cold December night inside her Rabbit Lane bedroom was one that would remain unchanged for so long: ever-shrinking hands reduced to talons; clear plastic IV drips like boil-in-bag dinners gone badly wrong; an iceberg-blue respirator tube connected to the core of the Earth hissing sick threats of doom spoken backward in another language; hair always straight, combed nightly, going gray with the years, and limp as unwatered houseplants.

Mr. and Mrs. McNeil tore up from Birch Bay near dawn. Their Buick Centurion's right front wheel nudged over the yellow-painted curb beneath the Emergency's port cochere. Already inside sat my parents, Hamilton, Pammie, Wendy, and Linus, all of us worn out from worry and fear. The McNeils had faces like burning houses. I could see they'd both been quite drunk earlier and were now throbbing in a headache phase. They refused to speak with any of us younger folk at first, assuming that we were all entirely to blame for Karen's state, Mrs. McNeil's accusing red eyes saying more than any shouted curse. The McNeils spoke with my parents, their neighbors and more-or-less friends of twenty years. At sunrise, Dr. Menger emerged to lead the four of them into the room where Karen was lying.

"Thalamus ... *mumble* ... fluids; brain stem ... *mumble* ... cranial nerve ... hypoxic-ischemic encephalopathy ... breathing ..."

"Is she *alive*? Is she dead?" asked Mrs. McNeil.

"She's alive, Mrs. McNeil."

"Can she *think*?" she continued.

"I can't tell you. If this continues, Karen will have sleep and wake cycles and may even *dream*. But thinking . . . I have no idea."

"What if she's trapped inside her body?" asked Mr. McNeil. "What if she's—" Mr. McNeil, George, was fumbling for words, "—*in there* hearing everything we say. What if she's screaming from the inside and she can't tell us that she's stuck?"

"That's not the case, sir. *Please*."

Meanwhile, Linus was glurping and snorkeling through a cup of vending machine hot chocolate. Hamilton called him an asswipe for being so disrespectful, but Linus said slowly, "Well, Karen *likes* chocolate. I think she'd want me to have it." There was a pause and a straw poll of eyes indicating this was the conventional wisdom. Hamilton calmed himself but remained in a piss-vinegar mood.

"Richard," barked Mr. McNeil, rounding a corner with the other older folk, "Dr. Menger said Karen took two pills. Did you give them to her?"

I was alert: "No. She had them in her compact. They were Valiums. I've seen her take them before. Mrs. McNeil gives them to her."

Mr. McNeil turned to his wife, Lois, who nodded her head and motioned her hand gently, confirming that she was the pusher. Mr. McNeil's posture slackened.

I said, "Karen wants to look good for your trip to Hawaii. She's trying to lose weight."

My use of the present tense shook them. "It's only five days from now," said Wendy. "She'll be fine by then, *right*?"

Nobody responded. Mrs McNeil, whispering like a calculating starlet, asked Wendy, "Were . . . were you girls drinking? . . . Wendy? . . . Pammie?"

Wendy was direct: "Mrs. McNeil, Karen couldn't have had more than a drink and a half. Weak stuff, too—Tab and a drop of vodka. Honest. It was mostly Tab. One moment she was standing there wondering if she'd lost her watermelon lip smacker, the next she was on the grass beside the road moaning. We tried to make her throw up, but there couldn't have been more than half a French fry inside her, tops. She was trying to lose weight really fierce. For Hawaii."

"I see, Wendy."

Dr. Menger cut in with the results of the blood-alcohol test, which confirmed next to no alcohol in her system. "Virtually clean," he said. "Point-oh-one."

Almost clean. But *not* clean. Dirty. Tainted. Soiled and corrupted. Shitted. Malaised. Poxed and pussed. Made unclean by her sick teenaged friends who wreck houses.

And we sat there in silence far into the next day, six friends, wretches of transgression, feeling deserving of punishment, sipping lame paper cones of Foremost eggnog brought to us by a nurse leaving night shift, anticipating our burdens, and castigating ourselves with silence. Sunday morning. Already news would be traveling throughout the school community— the early risers off to skate or ski. Karen's mental state would be glamorously linked to the house-wrecker, as though the damaged house had been the actual cause of her ails. And drugs.

I developed a cramp and went to the bathroom. There I found a stall, took a deep breath, and remembered the envelope in my jacket. I opened the envelope. On binder paper it read:

December 15 . . . 6 Days to Hawaii!!!

Note: Call Pammie about beads for cornrowing hair. Also, arrange streaking.

Hi Beb. Karen here.
If you're reading this you're either a) the World's Biggest Sleazebag and I hate you for peeking at this or b) there's been some very bad news and it's a day later. I hope that neither of these is true!!

27

Why am I writing this? I'm asking myself that. I feel like I'm buying insurance before getting on a plane.

I've been having these visions this week. I may even have told you about them. Whatever. *Normally my dreams are no wilder than, say, riding horses or swimming or arguing with Mom (and I win!!), but these new things I saw—they're* not *dreams.*

On TV when somebody sees the bank robber's face they get shot or taken hostage, right. I have this feeling I'm going to be taken hostage—I saw more than I was supposed to have seen. I don't know how it's going to happen. These voices—they're arguing—one even sounds like Jared—and these voices are arguing while I get to see bits of (this sounds so bad*) the Future!!*

It's dark there—in the Future, I mean. It's not a good place. Everybody looks so old and the neighborhood looks like shit (pardon my French!!).

I'm writing this note because I'm scared. It's corny. I'm stupid. I feel like sleeping for a thousand years—that way I'll never have to be around for this weird new future.

Tell Mom and Dad that I'll miss them. And say good-bye to the gang. Also Richard, could I ask you a favor? Could you wait for me? I'll be back from wherever it is I'm going. I don't know when, but I will.

I don't think my heart is clean, but neither is it soiled. I can't remember the last time I even lied. I'm off to Christmas shop at Park Royal with Wendy and Pammie. Tonight I'm skiing with you. *I'll rip this up tomorrow when you return it to me UNOPENED. God's looking.*

xox
Karen

I thought it best not to show Mr. and Mrs. McNeil the letter at that moment; it could only confuse without offering consolation. I stuffed it back in the vest pocket of my ski jacket and sat and thought of the times I'd used this very bathroom before, back when Jared was in the hospital and before he left us and this world, atom by atom.

I thought of Karen in the intensive care unit and I felt as though I was a jinx of a friend. I stood up and achingly returned to the waiting room. An hour later when the corridors seemed empty enough, we snuck in to see Karen. The machinery of her new life was fully set in motion—the IVs, the respirator, tubes, and wave monitors. An orderly shooed us out of the room, and we shambled toward the exit, the world no longer quite an arena of dreams—it was just an arena.

The West Vancouver police interviewed each of us that afternoon, down at the station on Marine Drive at Thirteenth. Understandably, they wanted the story from each of us individually to weed out discrepancies. But there were none. The housewrecker was quickly glazed over, the culprits still lolling about in the cells below us. Afterward at the White Spot restaurant down the road, we hunkered without hunger over cheeseburgers. The only pattern we could see in Karen's behavior on Saturday was that she *had* been behaving ... *differently* that day. I showed everybody the letter, and we became chilled.

"We were shopping at Park Royal yesterday," said Pammie, "all Karen could notice were weird little things like the color of mandarin oranges. We tried Christmas shopping, but instead she just rubbed her hands over fabrics. At the bus stop at Taco Don's, she ate one of Wendy's Mexi-Fries. I think that was all she had to eat before skiing. Poor thing. I'd have passed out, too, if I'd been her."

Wendy said, "We should have forced her to eat."

"Don't take yourself over the coals," I said. "There's something else going on here. We all know it."

"I agree. She *was* acting sort of spazzed yesterday," said Pam. "Tiny stuff. Preoccupied—and not just by that diet, either."

"I think we should show her parents the letter," Hamilton said. We agreed to do so later that day. Our table went silent.

*   *   *

29

That same evening, after feeble naps, we returned to Lions Gate Hospital, but Karen was unchanged. Not a limb, not a hair, not an eyelash. A chill fell upon us: Karen was not transforming the way she ought to. Leaving her room, I placed pink and blue carnations in a bud vase at her bedside; outside by our cars, we agreed that we would assemble at the school's smokehole the next morning so we could enter the building together, providing a casually united front.

At home, my parents, being neither heavy moralizers nor stringent disciplinarians, continued life as usual. Meatloaf, green beans, baked potatoes, and an episode of *M*A*S*H*. Years ago my cousin Eileen had once been out cold for two days after smacking her head in a swimming pool's shallow end; her successful later career as a med school student made Mom and Dad less worried about comas than they might have been otherwise.

But none of us slept that Sunday night. Instead, we made an electronic cat's cradle of phone calls between each other's houses, all of us wearing house robes, hunched over kitchen chairs with only stove lights burning, whispering, unknowingly mimicking the purgatorial hiss of Karen's respirator.

The next morning, as agreed, we sluggishly convened down in the parking lot beside the smokehole five minutes before first bell, our eyes reddened, hair already stinking of smoke, our then-stylish corduroy wide-leg pants flapping in a wet, chilly Pacific wind.

Our entrance into English class—Wendy and Linus and me—caused a not unsurprising teen zing as Karen's seat in front of me was pregnantly empty. Yet the three of us kept our down jackets on, chins buried within their waffled nylon quilting, not as an act of defiance but as one of insulation, to shield us from the stares, the passed notes and hungry sideways glances. Philip Eng and Scott Litman gave us goggled incredulity; Andrea Porter offered kittenish gossip-hungry leers. Unspoken voices surrounded us: *Look: it's the Karen killers. I hear they wrecked the Carters' house. Drugs, too: prescription*

30

drugs. Pissed to the gills! We all saw it coming, what with Jared kicking it last year. They're jinxed—they bring death to those around them. Look at their faces: I've never seen their badness before—I . . . I can't wait to talk to them. Stars! Killers right here in our own English class!

When the session bell rang, the three of us skittered down the booming north hallway to reconvene outside by the Datsun. Hamilton and Pammie were already there, smoking and looking prickly. Their experiences had been similar to our own.

"Well, that was a real *lulu*, kids," Hamilton said, saying what we all felt. "No shitting *way* am I going back into that freak show." The five of us had already realized we were never going to finish school in a normal way. Pam said, "Canyon," then we hopped into our cars.

We had a few cigarettes and Linus had bargain-basement dime-bag skunkweed pot, which was all we needed for that moment. So we zoomed off to the canyon forest below Rabbit Lane. There, we parked the cars, walked down into the canyon's windless soggy greens where the tall trees above shielded us from the wet harsh weather, and we were calmed.

5

NO SEX NO MONEY
NO FREE WILL

Again, personalities.

I have always noticed in high school yearbooks the similarity of all the graduate write-ups—how, after only a few pages, the identities of all the unsullied young faces blur, how one person melts into another and another: *Susan likes to eat at Wendy's; Donald was on the basketball team; Norman is vain about his varsity sweater; Gillian broke her arm on Spring Retreat; Brian is a car nut; Sue wants to live in Hawaii; Don wants to make a million and be a ski bum; Noreen wants to live in Europe; Gordon wants to be a radio deejay in Australia.* At what point in our lives do we stop blurring? When do we become crisp individuals? What must we do in order to end these fuzzy identities—to clarify just who it is we really are?

What have I said about myself so far? Not much, as is obvious. Until Jared vanished, I had thought my life average. You might look at me and ask me to baby-sit your children or coach them in baseball. I believed my mind was clean. My ambitions were undefined, but I assumed I would make my way in the world. I tried to be pleasant and likable. I don't think that's bad, but I was left every day with the sensation that I wasn't doing a good job at being . . . *me*. Not fraudulent, merely . . . not doing a good job at being *me*.

I remembered people from back in my early twenties, friends who would adopt a persona—the chic Euro-person; the embittered Grunge Thing; Stevie Nicks—and after years of practicing, they suddenly *became* those personas. What had I become? I don't remember even trying to fake a persona.

And after Karen left, I felt permanently jinxed; I was pulling away from the center. I darkened. My life had the beginnings of a story. I was no longer just like everybody else; the sensation felt wobbly, like jittering across a creek on slippery rocks with wet shoes, the current running ever faster.

The high school yearbook for the class of 1980 bore a special page honoring Karen. It showed Karen's grad photo, taken the month before her coma, inset above a foggy picture of trees with the following words below:

Memories . . .

KAREN ANN MCNEIL

To Karen Ann, who left us on December 15th,
still dreaming of larger worlds than ours. Hey,
Karen—we miss you and we're always thinking of
you.

THE CLASS OF 1980

David Bowie freak/Future legal secretary living
in Hawaii

"Bumhead"/chatterbox/Smiles for all/
"Ferrrrr-get it!"/Oh, those Mondays!/Let us ask
ourselves, girls, do we have enough sweaters?/Lost
a shoe at the Elton John concert/*duh*, ... /
walking to the portable in the rain/Eggie (right!)/

Greatest love in life? The Fonz: Heyyyy!
(Sorry Richard!)

**Senior volleyball, senior grass hockey,
yearbook committee
Photography Club, Ski Team**

Eggie was the nickname of Karen's white egg-shaped Honda Civic, speedily renamed by Hamilton as "the Ovary"—one of those nicknames that clings like a burr. Students most likely remembered Karen as the girl who was always gallivanting through the student parking lot, shuttling a load of laughing girls off to McDonald's for lunches of tea, saccharine, and half a small bag of fries.

The yearbook of the previous year had the following:

IN MEMORIAM:

JARED ANDERSON HANSEN

"Jare" was 1978's best sportsman, a good student and a fine friend to all. He left us in his prime, but we can maybe find peace in knowing that when we knock on heaven's door, Jared will be there to answer. Good-bye, Jared; we think you made the team.

"Ladies Man" (. . . ahem!)/senior football/senior basketball/brewskies/thin ice at Elveden Lake/ fix your muffler!/Jethro Tull/Elvis Costello/ Santana/That night at Burnside park/first to wear puka shells/tipping the canoe with Julie Rasmussen

. . . Hey old man, take a look at my life
. . . I'm a lot like you were

My own yearbook caption, as well as those of my immediate friends, was perhaps more interesting than most, as Wendy was on the yearbook staff—as was Hamilton's arch-enemy Scott Phelps, who adored Pam from afar:

RICHARD DOORLAND

Richard was too busy racing his Datsun with Hamster to hand in his questionnaire. As the only guy who ever picked up litter at the smokehole, we salute you. We'll still have a hard time forgetting those fetal pig dissections and the blowtorch in metal shop. Look out for radar traps and good luck in the future, Rick!

34

Suntanning up at Cypress/"I hate to be the bad guy, but . . ."/senior football/bondo patches on the Datsun/stereo man/free Steve Miller tickets/ nice teeth, fella!

Hamilton's was less sedate.

HAMILTON REESE

Hamster thought he was being really funny handing in his grad questionnaire with a big lipstick kiss and a rude word on it. Ha ha. Thank you for five years of tormenting people weaker than yourself, you weed. We hope to see you working at the Texaco station in 1999.

Initiation day terror/pyro/"Omigawd . . . what's that in the Jell-O?"/never bothered to join one single club/swipes your sandwich if you're not looking/Ciao, babe

WENDY CHERNIN

"Brainiac" helped make many a day pass more sweetly. When not inventing a cancer cure or designing space capsules, Wendy was dressing up for Graffiti Days and hanging out at White Spot. Word has it she made DNA out of those bending white straws. Bye, Wendy, and we all expect you to be the first cool chick in space.

"Are you eating that cookie?"/"Thank God It's Monday"/nail polish in math class/swim team/ choir/"What's the cube root of Revlon?"

PAMELA SINCLAIR

"Pam the Glam." "Pamster." She's so good looking that . . . we can't keep our eyes off her! Hey, Pammie—thanks for being so beautiful and making our volleyball and basketball teams winners. Don't know *what* you see in Hamil— (just kidding!) and we expect you to be in Hollywood some day.

Supertramp/Charlie perfume/That little blue comb in the rear pocket/Smokin' in the Boys' Room/Gain two pounds and make us happy/ Always looking out the window . . . clouds!

ALBERT LINUS

We dare not say anything about Linus, since he might wire a laser beam satellite to blow up our houses. Not a talkative fellow, Linus (we always thought Linus was his first name!) spent his years partying with other sci-fi's inside the fume hood and rigging the computer dating system so as to land Jaclyn Smith as his grad date. Good luck, Linus: We see much zinc in your future.

"What planet are we on?"/same shirt two weeks in a row/"Umm . . ."/Photography Club/ Kleenex/dustbunnies/lint

I'd known Karen all my life, her family's post-and-beam rancher lying just below our house (mock Tudor) on Rabbit Lane. Through elementary school we'd been friends and by high school we were one of those couples that nobody remembers ever *not* being a couple.

Karen: Her yearbook description was correct in saying she had a smile for everyone. And she *did* laugh all the time—not a nervous titter, but a gnarling Komedy Klub guffaw that could occasionally make us the unwanted floorshow in quiet restaurants. She was an avid photographer, flash-bulbing away at school, at Park Royal mall, at parties, or in the wild: seagulls, bare trees, mountain mists, and water ripples—yearbook stuff. Yet when any one of us searched for stray photos of Karen, we looked almost in vain, rifling through boxloads of our teen-filled snaps, finding the most meager rewards: a left arm here; half a head there; legs cut off at the thighs. We realized that Karen must have gingerly yet effectively pursued a life-long campaign to avoid being photographed. Her preoccupation with the deficiencies her mother kept telling her she had: *Your nose is too plump; your hair's too straight; you're pretty enough but no beauty*. Her graduation photo became almost the sole exception, one solitary image we were able to remember her by. Over time, the photo gradually leeched away our real memories of Karen—ultimately becoming the "Official Version": oval face with long brown hair parted in the middle, dripping off her head like sleek water (a style Karen called "Bumhead"); a neck she considered too scrawny sheathed beneath a sweater's cowl; and small, nice features with no one feature eclipsing any other. Karen is gently looking out—not toward us, the viewers, but to her left—to that place where she went on December 15? Maybe.

What *did* Karen see that December night? What pictures of tomorrow could so disturb her that she would flee into a refuge of bottomless sleep? What images would frighten her out of her body, making her leave our world? Why would she leave *me*? C'mon, Karen—Beb, Sugar Pops, Starbaby—we all know life's hard . . . we found *that* one out pretty quick. *You* told me we were all going to be dead-but-alive zombies in the future. That's what you said. Fair's fair: Tell us what you *meant*, Karen. I want an *answer*. Wake up, wake up, okay? We'll go to a place that's quiet and dry and talk about precious things. We'll drive downtown and have an Orange Julius. Hey!—we'll drive to the States for a steak dinner the size of a mattress. We'll drive to Europe and drink champagne, and we'll stop in Greenland for ice cubes along the way. *Knock-knock*. Who's there? It's me, Karen. No joke, no punchline—*c'est moi*. Will you come out? Or will you let me in?

6 | LONELINESS IS FUN

Karen's family:

When we are young, we assume adults behave according to a strict adult code. Only years later does it dawn on us that Mr. Phillips down the road was a manic depressive wife beater; that Mrs. Owen's liver was bloated like a diseased water balloon; that Mr. Pulaski perved out on all his kids and that's why they beat him up one night and left him facedown in a ditch on Good Friday. In this same tradition, Karen's mother, Lois, exhibited behavior that was, to younger eyes, downright random but adult. Nevertheless, that was Lois.

A minor example springs to mind. When I was young, lunching *chez* McNeil, Lois boiled water for Kraft macaroni, banged pots and colanders like crazed jungle tom-toms ("She wants us to know how much work she's doing," whispered Karen.). Then, right in front of Karen and me, Lois whisked away the crumpled cheese sauce packet like a victorious toreador, flipping it into the cupboard, saying, "We'll save *that* for a more special occasion." Quietly, Karen and I would eat the semi-cooked noodles in margarine while exchanging glances. Beverage? Tap water. Napkins? "Oh, just use your pants, Richard. You're a boy."

Karen, it might be surmised, had grown up with a bizarre relationship with food. Lois, a former Miss Canada runner-up (1958), saw food as alien, alive, requiring passports, visas, and security guards before allowing entry into the mouth. Fads came and went. One week she might be a vegan, the next week it was "Starch only!" Karen was dragged, holus-bolus, into Lois's cockamamie nutritional vogues. During one particularly fevered patch of vegetarianism in the seventies, I made the mistake of saying I'd been to Benihana's steak house; a brisk, half-hour anti-meat jeremiad followed. When Karen interrupted, she was met with icicle stares from Lois: "Really Karen, if you'd just eat, you might become at*trac*tive and then I wouldn't have to worry so much about your future." To me, Lois said, "Karen's in her 'awkward stage.' Now about that steak house, Richard . . ."

George, Karen's dad, owned a body shop where he spent sixteen hours a day, seven days a week, all year, choosing to dine in Lois-free restaurants. He was essentially nonexistent, and this absence bred a good cop/bad cop mythology: Mrs McNeil, the fevered shrew who drove the quiet, honorable George out of his own home. Neither of them could be described as "happy."

"Oh, I *wish* I knew what Mom's secret was," Karen would moan. "There's obviously a biggie. But how to ask?"

Lois grew up in Northern BC, and by dint of her looks, her cultivated smile, and her fathomless misguided snobbery was hypersensitized to those in life who didn't work hard enough (in her eyes) to earn their keep. Little digs: "My husband works with his hands—unlike *other* parents around here who've never had a callus in their lives." This referred, of course, to my accountant father who, like most others in the neighbor-hood, made an okay, but only okay, living as the middlest of middle classes. People across the city believed our hillside neighborhood to be the cradle of never-ending martini-clogged soirées and bawdy wife-swaps. The truth would have bored them silly, as it was middle-class dull to the point of scientific measurability. My mother, while barbecuing one fine summer evening in 1976, said prophetically that this neighbor-hood was "like the land that God forgot." Yes.

The first month of Karen's coma was a write-off—strange yet drab, hope dripping away bit by bit, making us unaware of its loss. We were all of us poleaxed with the flu—a good thing in that we didn't have to attend school for the final week before Christmas.

39

We shambled around to each other's houses and yakked on the phone a good deal. Hamilton phoned on Friday night: "Of course," he said, "we're beacons of gossip at school now." I had to admit we were. "They're ghouls," he said, pausing to honk his nose, adding, "God, my brain feels like a furry clump of dog shit." There were voices in the background at Hamilton's: "My Dad's marshaled up his sap tonight. He's dating a young twinkie in the payroll department. *Aggh.* My future stepmother is spoon-dancing with Daddy-O as I speak. Well—they'll have a litter of golden little brats together." The background music crooned Brazil-Sixty-Six. "You really should see her, Richard. She's not a mother—she's a golden retriever. You just wait until she turns into a slut. Won't *that* be jolly." A sigh: "Must go, Toots—*owww!* My head. Is. In. Pain. Bye."

Click.

A few minutes later, Wendy phoned to say Linus was at her house and they were languidly barn-raising a gingerbread house. "It was supposed to be a Hobbit cottage, but it ended up looking more like Hitler's bunker. Linus's flu is gone. He's going down to see Karen in a minute. Anything to send?"

"No."

Linus became our proxy visitor, but he returned to us with maddeningly obscure information. He never noticed straightforward data like whether or not Karen's eyes were open or how her skin color was; he was interested in the inanimate, in frameworks and systems that weren't easily apparent. Accordingly, he began recounting the visit in frustratingly pointless detail.

"You know the IV she has? What do they *put* in there? How can they squeeze all of her food into a watery liquid? I mean, doesn't it seem like it should be a lot *thicker*? With fiber or *pulp* at least?"

"There's a food tube that goes directly to her stomach," Wendy said. "I guess she's involuntarily quitting smoking, too. Her poor body."

Hamilton was straightforward: "Did you see *Karen* or were you there doing your science project? Can you tell us how she *was*?"

"Okay, okay . . . so the food goes in one tube and out another. There didn't seem to be any problems there. Except when you think about how her body is like an earthworm, kind of, a big food-to-compost converter . . ."

I took offense to the direction this was going. "Linus! Does she look okay? Does she *move*?"

"Well, um, actually, *yeah*. Her eyes were open and her eyeballs, her pupils I mean, followed my hand when I moved it over her face."

"What? She's awake?"

"No. Her eyeballs are open, but I think she's still sleeping. She has a little radio beside her bed. It was playing a disco song. Sister Sledge?" Linus seemed pleased at having remembered such a nontechnical detail.

We finally visited Karen two days before Christmas, dazed like bejeezus on Robitussin and decongestants, and we kept far away from her bed. Linus was right: Karen's eyes did follow hand motion—inspiring news. When Dr. Menger came down the hall, we excitedly informed him of the miraculous event. He looked worried and beckoned us into the cafeteria, telling us to sit.

"It doesn't give me any pleasure to tell you, kids, but your friend Karen is in what's known as a persistent vegetative state. Karen is completely unaware of either herself or her environment. She has sleep cycles and awake cycles. She has no control over her bowel or bladder functions. She has no voluntary responses to sound, light, motion, and no understanding of language. I really must tell you that recovery is rare. So rare as to be big news for the newspapers when it ever occurs. There's really not much else I can tell you."

"But my hand!" Pammie squealed. "Karen's eyes watch your hand if you move it around in front of her face."

"That's misleading," Dr. Menger said. "That's misleading and sad. It's a common involuntary reflex response to motion. There's no high brain function linked to the act."

So much for hope, I thought as we all drove to Pammie's house. "Oh, God, I haven't done any Christmas shopping,"

I said. "Let's not give each other presents, okay?" Everyone listlessly agreed. My own family members that year received chocolate bars and magazines from a Mac's convenience store, all badly wrapped in kitchen tin foil and handed over free of enthusiasm.

New Year's Eve that year, a minty fresh new decade, consisted of Hamilton half-heartedly letting off a brick of stale leftover Halloween firecrackers inside the Hitler's Bunker followed by two beers and games of Pong. Ugh.

The year became 1980.

A daily pattern of hospital visits emerged with us of the inner circle, as well as the McNeils visiting daily. Lois McNeil was still grumpy at Pammie and Wendy over the dreaded vodka-Tab cocktails, so the two would skittishly beetle down the corridor at the slightest hint of Lois. Mr. McNeil, though, was on our side, saying, "Christ, Lois, they're kids and they weren't doing harm. Nobody forced Karen to drink, and even *then* that's probably not the full cause."

Mrs. McNeil would be pursed-lipped, with Mr. McNeil saying, "It may well have been *your* two pills that caused this, so don't act so bleeding innocent." (*Thank you*, Mr. McNeil.) "I can see she didn't inherit her drug tolerance from *you*." Ow!

But as the days slipped by after Christmas holidays, visits dropped off a bit, always with good excuses; by the end of January, it was only Karen's parents and me visiting, Mr. McNeil going daily from the body shop. Softly, he said he couldn't imagine ever not going. We became the two regular visitors.

"I never had a real chance to talk to her, Richard. You know that?" he would say. "Always working. Always assuming there'd be time later. I feel closer to her now than I did during all her birthdays—and she'll never even know."

"Not *never*, Mr. McNeil."

"No—you're right. Not never."

It was in February a few weeks after school had resumed that I came home and saw Dad's car in the driveway at four o'clock in the afternoon, two hours earlier than usual. For someone as strongly habit-bound as my father, this could only bode big news, good or bad. I entered the kitchen, heard Mom on the phone in the living room and Dad rustling the newspaper. I came into the room and cautiously asked, "What's up?"

"Richard," she said in a warm, yet neutral voice designed to pre-empt shock, "Karen's pregnant."

From the top of my skull, flames burned downward; once again, I felt my skin grow quills, my forehead antlers. My stomach jumped off a cliff and my legs became stone. The pill . . . was she on it? I never asked. First shot lucky. The Sperminator. "*Oh.*"

Dad said, "The hospital called us this morning. We had lunch with the McNeils today."

Mom added, "There's no problem with us, Richard. Please remember that. Apparently there's no problem with the baby, either. This has happened before—women being pregnant during comas. You know we love Karen like our own daughter."

My mind was steam-whistling.

"There are many cases of coma patients giving birth, Richard," my father said. "*Richard?*"

"Yes. *Yes.* Just give me a moment here . . ." *Fire; a throat that will not breathe: that joke isn't funny anymore.*

"What about *Karen?*" I asked.

"Apparently in this sort of—*situation*—Richard," Mom said, "the mother is just fine. Birth will be by Cesarean section next September."

My mind flashed to abortion and as quickly flashed away. No. This child must be born.

"Richard," Dad said, "if news of this gets out, the media will eat you the way a snake eats rats. Karen and you will both be sideshow freaks."

"You must ensure, Richard," Mom stressed, "that nobody—not even your friends—find out about this. We're

43

absolutely firm on this. In a few months when she starts to show, we'll have to tell people she's having breathing troubles and is unable to take visitors for a while."

"But what if she wakes up?" I asked. Sad stares shot down that question. I then asked, "Who's going to take care of the baby?" I had pictures in my head of holding a swaddled youth. The word "diapers" sprang to mind unconvincingly.

"Mrs. McNeil"—(*oh God*)—"has eagerly volunteered to take charge. We're equally happy to help out, but she seems adamant. We'll pitch in what we can to cover costs and so will you, too, Richard, once you start your working life. You're a father. You're to live up to your obligations as best you can. But as far as the world is concerned, the baby will be Mrs. McNeil's 'niece' or 'nephew' to be taken care of after a family tragedy on her side."

"It'll be called McNeil?"

"Yes. Does that bother you?" my dad asked.

"I, uhhh . . ." I was too dazed to reply coherently.

My parents' tone followed their calm natures. They became silent statues when confronted by large events. I hadn't even begun to digest the news; as with most events in life, ramifications would have a delayed onset.

"What about the baby—will it have a proper brain? Will it have a normal personality?" I asked.

Mom said, "That's a long way off, dear. We'll think about that when the time comes."

THINKING ABOUT THE FUTURE
MEANS YOU WANT SOMETHING

And so the time came.

The seventies were over. With them left a sweetness, a gentleness. No longer could modern citizens pretend to be naïve. We were now jaded; the world was spinning more quickly. Karen's Honda Civic was sold. Her clothing, makeup, childhood toys, and diaries were boxed and stored in a musty basement beneath the rear stairs of her parents' house. Memories of Karen slipped away from those who knew her. She was no longer a person, only an idea—somebody asleep in a room somewhere. Where is she? Oh . . . *somewhere*, we think.

The remains of high school flowed by like a wide, slow, pulsing river of cool chocolate milk. December and January's fiery baptism of peers had come and gone, but classmates still offered sad looks, accusatory stares, or wordless hee-haws. The five of us had become down-jacketed, disheveled curiosities— young necks craned to view the killers as we headed to the parking lot, bystanders doubtlessly assuming we were off to break into the rathskeller of a country club, swig bourbon, and dribble messages on the walls with the blood of dogs.

During schooldays, I preferred to cut class and sit down below the cedars above the fire station smoking and wasting time on the grass whittling twigs, thinking of the baby and of Karen and the things she saw. What did it mean?

As I sat there assembling the puzzle, Hamilton ignited chunks of stolen laboratory sodium with rainwater while Pam combed and combed and combed her hair with a sky blue plastic comb. The last days of high school in particular were a hazy waste of time. I'd crossed a line—I didn't care any longer.

School became an activity I *used* to do. Wendy and Linus, though, veered the opposite way, losing themselves in science, memorizing equations for Teflon, gravity, and the Moon's orbit. Come June, both graduated with honors, but *he* who was once a promising student—me—barely squeaked by with an undeniable *tsk-tsk* of the faculty, who saw their once-golden Richard thrown away on a life of cigarettes, scrubbing Buicks at the Oasis car wash, and dead-end tomcatting with Hamilton Reese.

On graduation day in early June, Karen entered her third trimester, and was transferred into maternity. I was there for the move that afternoon, in my graduation outfit, a then-stylish baby-blue tux. I had just had my hair feathered in the style of the times and thought I cut quite a pretty picture as I entered the hospital room. Mr. McNeil wolf-whistled and said to Karen, "Karen, here's your prince, honey."

The nurse allowed me to lift Karen onto the transfer gurney. How bony and light she felt!—as though I were picking up kindling wood. I hadn't held her since that night on the ski slopes. Her eyes were open at that moment; our retinas met, yet we didn't connect. I felt as if I were looking into the eyes of an aquarium fish—no, a *photo* of an aquarium fish. Her tummy bulged out like a goiter on a crone's neck.

A short while later, I pulled my Datsun up to a grad party on Chartwell Drive—rock walls, hedges, and dwarf shrubs. The sun shone brightly. It occurred to me I'd been asleep at the wheel since the hospital, yet I hadn't crashed the car. Turning off the car's ignition, it hit me that Karen would probably never wake up; her eyes had been—*dead*. My hopes for her then switched from cheerleaderish bluster into loss and remorse. I sank in my car seat there on the roadside, sucking in the air, heaving my chest, hiding from arriving party-goers. I'd nearly run out of air; my stomach felt like two hundred sit-ups when there was a gentle tap on the door. It opened just a crack and there stood Wendy, in a strange yellow dress she'd made herself, her hair tangled like brassy telephone cords.

She was crouched down so that people driving by wouldn't see her. My mouth fumbled; she looked at me calmly and said: "Karen was supposed to be here, Richard." I nodded and she and I looked up at the car's ceiling with its nicotine smudges and Hamilton's boot scrapes, umbrella punctures and cigarette burns.

She said, "Jared, too," and sat cross-legged on the roadside gravel, her gown crumpled on the stones, and with those stones she built sad little totems that quickly toppled. "Jared was supposed to be here, too." Wendy took a breath and relaxed her shoulders, then I relaxed, too. "I was in love with him," she said.

"Yeah, I think everybody kind of knew you were hot for him, but I mean, really, Wen—take a number and stand in line. He was humping half the girls in class."

"I've never told anyone this—I mean about me loving Jared. Not even my mom. Funny. Now that the words are out of my mouth—outside my body—they feel different to me." She knocked over her small rock pile.

I said, "They would have been the center of everything tonight, wouldn't they? They would have been the *stars*."

Muscle cars swooshed up and down the road. From the party house rose shrieks and patches of Bob Seger. I was calm. I reclaimed my normal breathing and sat up.

"You want to go in?" asked Wendy.

"Not really."

"Let's go for a walk instead. We'll catch up with everybody later at the hotel."

We drove down to the Capilano River canyon, then entered its pathways and didn't say much, which was best. On the lower branches of a maple we found a robin's nest with a crop of three chicks inside. Their necks were weak, their heads scrawny. They were waiting for mom-bird to cough up some worms. Jesus-loves-you sun-beams pulsed through the trees, and the chicks were illuminated from the inside. They glowed like Christmas tree lights—their veins, their pinfeathers, their eyes, their tiny raptor beaks. And then the

47

sun lit up Wendy's dress and I caught my breath.

"Richard, there's something you're not telling me. Am I right, Richard?"

"Yeah."

"Can I guess? If I guess right, you can confirm it—fair?"

"Okay."

"Karen's pregnant."

I turned to her. "Yeah."

"How far along?"

"Six months."

"I *was* right." She picked a maple leaf. She looked through it. "How are *you* feeling?"

I threw a stick. "I'm too young to be a father. I'm too young to be *anything*. I'm seventeen. I haven't even left home yet. It seems unreal. You won't tell anyone, right?"

"Sealed lips." She wiped a twig from her dress. "It'll be like having part of Karen back. I miss her. We never talk about these things. But I miss her. Do you?"

"Yeah."

"But we don't ever say it out loud, do we?"

"I guess not," was all I could reply. "I don't like the silence, either." I didn't realize then that so much of being adult is reconciling ourselves with the awkwardness and strangeness of our own feelings. Youth is the time of life lived for some imaginary audience.

The forest colors smudged together. The sky was darkening into the color of a deep clean lake. I picked some late-blooming rhododendron flowers; the last magic light of the fallen sun cut through the petals in tropical purple brilliance.

We drove the Datsun to the hospital to see Karen. Wendy placed her ear to Karen's stomach; I placed the rhododendrons in the bud vase still beside the bed. After that we left the hospital to drive down-town for our grad party at the Hotel Vancouver.

That summer I worked full-time at a Chevron station, barely conscious of the pumps or customers, most of whom must surely have taken me for an idiot. That summer remains a fuzzy dot of sunburned necks, beer bottles clinking in the Datsun's trunk, huckleberry picking with Wendy and Pam, and beach-side bonfires.

End of an era.

At the hospital, anyone inquiring about Karen was to be told that she was stable. No visitors. Nobody questioned the switch. By summer, Karen's only daily visitors were me and George. Wendy, with her clean scientific voice, helped talk me through the willies. Hamilton, Linus, and Pam had trickled away. I wasn't mad at them for this diminuendo. Truth be told, Karen never *did* change from one week to the next; cruelly, there was only so much that could be seen or said.

I'd think of Karen often, too. Our first and only time together had been so wonderful. I replayed it over and over in my head, savoring each nuance, her skin like milk atop the snow, the smell of the snow, her underwear's frilled cotton, cold and dry. I never told her I loved her. Schmaltzy, but these things *rankle*; they count. By summer's end, I'd finally decided that I didn't even *know* Karen too well—who *was* she on the inside? This only fueled her mystery. At night, when such moments tended to strike, I'd have a self-indulgent little cry, walk around the yard, then come inside where my parents would be cheerfully watching the national news. I'd go sit with them, putting a good face on everything.

By late August, waiting for the birth, I felt as though I was breathing the air inside a capsized boat—steamy, biological and ominous—an activity that could only continue for a little while longer. George, as ever, visited his daughter each day. I showed up less frequently, often in midweek. George and I never talked much; when we did, we'd end up saying the same old vapid niceties that somehow made Karen's coma time seem even longer. He'd also lapse into a mist of maudlin boo-hoos. He'd remember Karen singing 'Oklahoma' in the school play. "She was a pretty girl, wasn't she, Richard?"

"She still *is*, George."

"Remember the time she played guitar for our anniversary party?"

"I do."

"Such a pretty girl." Then he would sigh and sing a show tune from *Oklahoma!* "*When I take you out tonight with me— honey this is what you're going to see—*"

"How's business?" I asked, moving away from this gooey patch.

Lois, on the other hand, while not having completely written Karen off as dead, was certainly the more pragmatic of the two. She had read the statistics on coma patients and the persistent vegetative state. She knew that with each succeeding day, chances for an awakening approached absolute zero.

At the pregnancy's start, Lois treated me about one notch friendlier than she might a sperm donor, but Lois realized that in order to build her custody case for the baby, she would have to try harder to be nice, which must have been torture for her.

And as time went on I became increasingly angry at Lois for Shanghaiing the baby. Not that there were many other alternatives, but still—she just barged right in and swiped my kid. It was only through discussions with my father, who painted some all-too-clear pictures for me, that I understood that Lois keeping the baby was the best solution—for the time being.

We met in the hospital corridors. "Oh, hello, Richard. Well. Another day, isn't it? Another day older and another day wiser." Camel hair coat, white gloves. Her small talk was rather limited; she was not a particularly creative woman, new attitude or not. What drops of creative fuel she possessed must have been expended on her hideous accumulation of owl knick-knacks. Bumping into her in the hospital's hallways or down on Rabbit Lane, I would brace myself for her curious overtures at warmth. "Richard, you're certainly not looking sick at all. I'd heard you were fluey." (Awkward pause.) "Hmmm. That's a very handsome color on you, you should wear it more often."

(Awkward pause.) "Well. She's in there. Everything looks fine." (Lois never again referred to Karen by her own name. Karen had been downgraded to "*she*.") Lois removed her gloves. "And your parents?"

Lois was definitely changing for the better, though I didn't entirely trust her motives. Lois wanted the *baby*—as though it were her own. I'm sure she wanted to be right there with the obstetrician, ripping the baby from the womb, herself cutting the cord with her dentures, then taxiing off with her loot, leaving Karen behind in her eternal repose, as though that daughter could be checked off her list, allowing Lois to start on her next project, a new child to raise occupying Karen's old slot.

I still felt as though the secret of the pregnancy was mine to bear alone. Aside from Wendy, there was no one that I could tell who really knew me, which only added to my own feeling of unreality. The two families were taking such pains to appear casually pragmatic: *no emotion*. My head felt like a watermelon the moment before being whacked with a baseball bat. Kids at seventeen? I could be a grandfather at thirty-four. What kind of role model could I possibly be for my kid? What help would I be with Lois efficiently covering the mother front and nobody expecting anything from me?

My parents seemed serene about the whole birth, digging through the garage for mildewed boxes of baby goodies for Lois. My parents visited Karen once a month. Mom also made effort-filled visits to Lois next door every week or so. Mom would gird herself the moment she rang Lois's doorbell, activating the McNeils' astoundingly nervous bichon frise into a frenzy of sterile yapping.

"Hello, Lois."

"Oh, Carol, hello, please come in. My, you *do* look tired. Careful, I just bought that owl figurine, and it's fragile—here, let me move it out of your way. Well, what have you brought— more clothes for the baby? Stack them next to the other boxes. You're really outdoing yourself; you shouldn't go to so much trouble. Careful! That owl—I'll just move it into the other

51

room. Don't move a muscle. My—the dog never barks like this. And what else—coffee? I suppose you'd probably like some. Why don't I go make some, stay right there. Oh, Carol, please—remove your shoes if you could. I have guests coming over tonight."

"Thank you, Lois."

The child was to be born via C-section, September 2, Karen's birthday. The night before, rain stomped the roof like hooves, yet the night air was warm and inviting. I stepped outside onto the rear patio underneath the eaves and sat on a lawn chair. I had been unable to sleep; in order to konk me out I had taken a plump, green chloral hydrate left over from my wisdom teeth extraction a few months earlier. There, under the drum of rain in a lawn chair, I experienced what was to be the only vision of my life. It was this:

My head was the nucleus of a sparking, dazzling, steak-sizzling halo. I rose, I floated from under the eaves, up off the patio, being yanked up into space, toward the Moon. There I met Karen walking on the Moon's dark side, lit only by stars. Karen was so clean, wearing her ski jacket, brown cords, and red clogs, holding her purse. There was wind in her hair, even there on the Moon. She took a drag from her cigarette and said to me in a voice I'd lost for so long, "Hey, there, Richard. How ya doin', Beb? Just look at *me!* One day we were all walking across the surface of the Moon, then we discovered a way home. Didn't we?"

I said yes.

She said, "I'm not *gone*, you know."

I said, "I know."

"Take care of Megan, Richard."

"I will."

"It's lonely here."

"I'm lonely, too. I miss you."

"Good-bye, Richard. It's not forever."

"Karen, where *are* you?"

She tossed her cigarette into a dusty gray crater the size of an aluminum ball-barbecue and said, as though I'd asked her the answer to a simple algebra equation, "Well, d*uh*! Until we meet again, Beb." Then she leaped over a crater to disappear behind its edge.

There was a flash of aqua-colored sparks. I rubbed my head. My vision was over.

I returned to the patio; rain still drummed.

The Moon.

Home.

Energized, still not sleepy from the pill, I put on boots and walked down to the McNeils', making my way through the backyard trees. I came down to where I could see Karen's old room—her light still burning. I came up closer, hidden behind a laburnum tree. I saw baby clothing stacked up against Karen's wall mural of the Moon. Mrs. McNeil came into the room carrying a box, stopped, heaved down the box, sat on top, and sighed with all her body. I'd never seen her in a pose of exhaustion before.

She turned out the lights as she left. It was dark; the rain fell. A car purred through silent suburbia, past basements, stereos, and street-lights yellow over the rainy pavement. There I stood.

Then I returned to my house, undressed, and went to sleep. I was awakened by my mother at 6:30 to drive to Lions Gate Hospital with her and Dad.

EARTHLY SADNESS

From the moment our daughter emerged, around 8:20 p.m., seven pounds four ounces, there was no point trying to pretend she was Mrs. McNeil's "niece." She was a kinder, softer, feminized version almost entirely of me, as though I'd divided by mitosis. Good Lord, where were *Karen*'s genes in all this?

Karen went through the birth with nary an indicating flicker of higher brain function—something we'd all secretly been praying for. How could a woman go through something as major as birth yet not know it? For Mrs. McNeil, Karen was forgotten almost altogether as she pressed her nose up against the glass wall of the nursery window, then cooed at the baby, her legs doing involuntary cha-cha's. "So big! So pink! And *look* at her thrashing away . . . hello, my little goo-goo ballerina. So perfect. *Nothing* like a Cesarean for a perfectly shaped baby's head."

Mom and I stood there, agog at seeing Lois fog-horning a blast of such sugary sentiment in the baby's direction. But then ours *was* an adorable baby, no doubt about it—adorable and *mine*. She might even live to see the year 2100. She might save the world. I tapped the window, said, "*Goo*." She looked at me and then I was hers. It was that fast.

Afterward Lois decided that we should all celebrate the birth, and through some sick contortion of fate, she chose the restaurant at the top of Grouse Mountain, only a snowball's throw away from where my daughter had been conceived.

"Has it really been just nine months?" I asked my mother in hushed tones as the gondola lilted over the center tower, my first time up the mountain since the previous December.

"Yup."

"It feels like nine years."

"You're young."

"Can you believe it?" I asked. I looked at the small lights that were our houses below.

"It is wonderful, isn't it? It's going to be such fun," my mom said.

We surveyed Cleveland Dam and the cool black reservoir behind it. Once more I searched for our house amid the seine of amber twinklings below. Mom asked me quietly so that the others couldn't hear, "Do you ever miss Karen, Richard?"

"Yeah. Always."

"I thought so. Oh, look, there's our house."

A tinny squawk on the PA system informed us we were set to berth at the top station. Once inside the restaurant, the high altitude and a glass of contraband white wine made me muzzy. At dinner I felt more like a fertility totem than a father; my role as father seemed a mere footnote. The baby was toasted, but I was not; to have made too big a deal of *me* would also be making too big a deal of unspoken issues such as teenage sex and illegitimacy.

Dad asked, "Has anybody thought about names yet?"

I blurted out, "Megan. I mean, I think Megan's a good name."

Lois looked at me, smiled, and said, "Yes, I think Megan is a perfect name," then she gave me the first genuinely warm smile I'd ever had from her. Later, when she'd gone to the ladies' room, George told us, "We had a miscarriage about ten years ago. It was a girl. Lois had already decided on Megan. Did you know that, Richard?"

"No. The name came to me in a . . . dream last night." Best not to mention the word "vision."

"Well, it's a happy coincidence. A beautiful Welsh name it is. A toast!"

And so our daughter became Megan Karen McNeil.

*   *   *

The first few months with Megan flew by for me, but not for Lois, who endured almost continuous crying, shrieking, wailing, and bawling without, to her credit, any complaint. Mom said that Megan must have come as a godsend to a decidedly anal woman with not much else to do other than collect owl knickknacks and play unchallenging mind games with her bichon frise.

Sperm donor though I was, I was also a proud papa, though limited in my ways to express this pride. I resisted the impulse to tout her doubtlessly infinite wonderfulness until we had completed at least a one-year embargo on "the news."

Every so often Lois wheeled Megan up to our house, where Megan gurgled, plopped, squelched, and shrieked like any baby. Thus my own mother was able to experience the flush of grandmotherhood dauntingly early and always seemed a tad relieved when Megan's stroller was wheeled away.

That September I enrolled in a business program at Capilano College, still muddy-brained about Megan and Karen and glad to have a productive way to occupy my waking hours. Our adult lives, good or bad, chugged ahead full-steam. No more traipsing through wilderness whenever we wanted. No classes to cut. Instead, there was rent, utilities, and taxes. Adolescent wishes of jobs in Hawaii or becoming a professional ski bum were replaced by newer, glossier pictures of giddy unregulated sex and adventurous metropolitan living. Wendy, to nobody's surprise, was intent on becoming a doctor, and off she went across town to the University of British Columbia. Pam continued her modeling work. Linus wanted to mess around with sparks, gases, and liquids, and he did this at the University of Toronto.

Hamilton and I were the ones without goals. "Imagine you're a forty-year-old, Richard," Hamilton said to me around this time, while working as a salesman at a Radio Shack in Lynn Valley, "and suddenly somebody comes up to you saying, 'Hi, I'd like you to meet Kevin. Kevin is eighteen and will be making all of your career decisions for you.' *I'd* be flipped

56

out. Wouldn't you? But that's what life is all about—some eighteen-year-old kid making your big decisions for you that stick for a lifetime." He shuddered.

Shortly before Christmas, the five of us were dressed for rainy day hiking and exploring around the train tracks above Eagle Harbour. Track-walking was an activity we all enjoyed, as it combined the thrill of law-breaking with the beauty of the natural ocean views around us. An added bonus was the possible pulp-fiction thrill of finding a corpse hidden in the bordering shrubs.

Our feet crunched on the stones beneath the trestles. Linus was dawdling, discussing creosote molecules with Wendy. Hamilton barked orders for them to hurry: "Come on, kids, Pammie wore flats instead of heels for today. We don't want to make her regret that choice." We were about to walk through a two-mile-long tunnel; the prospect was always seductively frightening, even with nine-volt flashlights.

Once inside the tunnel, the silence roared; I've sometimes wondered why silence seems so loud. About a mile inside, Hamilton said, "Stop and turn out your lights," and we did. We stood and inhaled the darkness. Our only light source became a Bic lighter held by Pam, at which point Hamilton said, "One, two, three . . . *Flame on*, kids." Instantly, the four of them semicircled around me, arms folded, lopsided stances with pursed lips betraying frostiness indeed. Only Wendy looked tentative; she'd known all along.

"Okay, pops," said Pam. "What's going on? You could have told *us* at least. We're pissed at you, Richard . . . *Dad*."

Hamilton said, "Don't try to weasel out of this one, Dickie."

Even Linus was in on the anger: "We, uh, saw the kid, Richard. Megan, I mean. We ran into Lois at Park Royal. It was just *so* obvious. Unless you've been fooling around with Lois, that is, which I doubt. So what happened?"

I was caught. Fair enough. "Okay, *gang*. So I'll fess up, *okay? Yes*, it's Karen's and my kid." ("*We knew it, we knew it!*") "Megan's birthday's September second—Karen's birthday, too. She's fully normal, but Karen's the same. She didn't wake up or anything during the birth. She probably never will."

The five of us breathing sounded as though we were in a bathyscaphe thousands of feet beneath the ocean surface, looking for those jewels Karen had once thrown from the ocean liner's deck. I sighed—then the truth just coughed out of me like a bubble jellyfishing upward from the deep sea, flattened by extreme pressures, but becoming larger and more full as it nears the surface. I'd been worrying so much about the press and about not wanting Karen to be a freak show. And the family had its own way of trying me: Lois's bossiness and George's lack of interest in Megan. The relief for me was great, as though I had been choking and then Heimlich'ed up a drumstick. My chest relaxed; my muscles slackened. To be able to discuss what I felt for Karen and Megan to people who would listen. My friends didn't speak until I was finished.

"You know, Megan looks so much like you it's scary, Richard," said Pam. "She's you in a wig."

"As if I don't know."

"She's cute," said Pam. "I held her. Linus did, too."

"Yeah," said Linus. "She's sweet. I think I nearly dropped her. She spewed chuck all over my calculator, my TI-55—I'm very sentimental about that machine."

We were all sitting on the rails. Hamilton lit a cigarette. He said, "Well, let's have a bit of pity on her. Fancy having Richard's face and Lois as a substitute mother. Life *is* cruel."

I wanted to make amends: Godparents?

"Does that mean diapers?" asked Hamilton, scrunching his face. I replied, "Yes, Hamilton, it does. Acres and acres of shit. It's the deal." We sat and talked a bit, just our five voices surrounded by black. There was a quiet patch. Then Linus leaned down, stuck his ear to the track, and whispered, "*Train.*"

There was no way we could run to the entrance; the five of us hit the ground and rolled into the stony ditches on either side, willing ourselves to shrink. Within seconds, a Pacific Great Western train exploded above in an H-bomb roar—108 freight cars loaded with plywood supernova'ed up above us inside the granite walls. The train radiated intermittent light from which I was able to see directly in front of my nose, pressed to the ground, an empty wine bottle, a six-year-old yellowed newspaper, a sock, and a balled-up Huggies diaper. These objects flashed briefly and vanished like fleeting shivers of shame that are soon forgotten, never again to see the light of day. It felt strange to see these castaway things deep inside the Earth, never to return to the surface.

The train passed above us for five minutes. What if we were to die right there? What had our lives been? What had our ambitions been? What had we been seeking? Money? No—none of us seemed financially motivated. Happiness? We were so young that we didn't even know what unhappiness could be. Freedom? Perhaps. An overriding principle of our lives then was that infinite freedom creates a society of unique, fascinating individuals. Failure at this would mean failure of our societal duty. We were young; obviously we wanted meaning from life. I felt a craving for duty, but to what?

Meanwhile, the creosote on the railway ties stank and burned my nose, and my elbow rested in dirt. Small tornadoes of litter scraped my face and I closed my eyes. I tried to curl up and close my body to protect myself from the train's roar—the noise of the center of the Earth.

Dreams have no negative. This is to say that if, during the day, you think about how much you *don't* want to visit Mexico, your dreams at night will promptly take you to Mexico City. Your body will ignore the "no" and only pay attention to the main subject. I think we thought daily of avoiding tribulations—and of avoiding loss.

The train passed. Our ears throbbed with the silence. We stood up and somberly walked out to the tunnel's entrance and into the rain. We climbed into Linus's van and drove over to see Megan. I hoped Lois would be gracious and permit four new godparents to share in Megan's adoration.

Linus asked, "Three months old—does she speak yet?"

"No, goofball," said Hamilton, "she's too busy generating random numbers to speak."

I nodded. "I *do* hate to say this, but poor little Megan really is going to grow up to resemble me wearing a Bumhead wig."

"I didn't know you and Karen were, uh, *doing it*," said Hamilton. "I mean, if you were, it was one heckuva secret."

"Go figure," I said, then we drove off, everybody yacking and—except for me—catching up on life. I was remembering Karen saying, "*Are we gonna do it or what?*" Remembering the delicate birds and butterflies and flowers that passed between our bodies. I was remembering her determination that last day that she was awake. Would she have been like that always? Or had she known time was running out? Was she trying to squish as much into a day as she could?

That month I had read a science fiction story, *Childhood's End*. In it, the children of Earth conglomerate to form a master race that dreams together, that collectively moves planets. This made me wonder, what if the children of Earth instead fragmented, checked out, had their dreams erased and became vacant? What if instead of unity there was atomization and amnesia and comas? This was the picture posited by Karen: She saw something in her mind—in between the smaller bikini and the itty-bitty bits of Valium, in between putting on a down coat or a ski boot one cold winter day, or maybe turning a TV channel or rounding a corner in her Honda. She saw a picture, however fragmentary, that told her that tomorrow was not a place she wanted to visit—that the future is not a place in which to be. This is what haunted me—the thought that maybe she was right.

EVEN MORE REAL THAN YOU

Half a year after giving birth to Megan, Karen was moved permanently to a room of her own in a local nursing home then called Inglewood Lodge. On her bedside table sat moisturizers, costume jewelry, a wooden hair brush, Kleenex in a pink ruffled box, birthday cards rigorously kept up to date, framed family photos, stuffed animals (one Garfield cat, two teddy bears, one polar bear), books for visitors—*The Best of Life* and *Jonathan Livingston Seagull*—plus a dieffenbachia vine that eventually colonized the entire room. Her radio was frequently left on for hours at a time.

Karen's "day" would technically begin near midnight when her body would be turned over by lifting her up from her "intermittent pressure" anti-bedsore mattress. At this same time, her garments would be inspected to see if they required changing. Karen would be rolled over two more times between midnight and 6:00 a.m.; as well, her mouth would be brushed with a soft toothbrush then swabbed with a flavored sponge; Vaseline would be applied to her lips.

Twice a week in the morning Karen would have a proper bath, during which time she would have "range of motion" exercises—shoulder, arm, extensors, abductors, and all joints flexed by a nurse's aide. On other days she had sponge baths and motion exercises.

During Karen's awake cycles, food from inside a suspended bag would be gravity-fed into her stomach through a J-tube (jiugiostomy tube) that was permanently attached to a valve near her belly button.

After being clothed in special front-only garments, Karen

would be placed into a geriatric wheelchair with a buttocks pad and a device to hold her head up straight. She would attend all breakfasts, lunches, and dinners held at the lodge, as well as special events such as films and birthday parties and even a church service that was usually, but not always, held on Sunday. In between meals Karen sat in her chair in her room, and her position was frequently moved by staff.

Karen was atypical in that she had few of the normal afflictions of the comatose: pneumonia, bowel obstructions from lack of fiber, urinary tract infections, blood clots in the legs, seizures, ruptured stomach, skin breakdowns, and skin infections from lack of blood circulation.

With Karen there was no "plug to pull," as the common expression goes. There were only degrees of heroics through which the family would be willing to go through in order to hang on to life. An example of this might be antibiotics to help with pneumonia. George wanted full heroics, but Lois refused to have an opinion on the issue. Many parents of coma patients divorce after years of anguish, self-recrimination, lawyers, social workers, family meetings, doctors, nurses, and bills. George and Lois remained together.

"Comas are rare phenomena," Linus told me once. "They're a byproduct of modern living, with almost no known coma patients existing prior to World War Two. People simply died. Comas are as modern as polyester, jet travel, and microchips."

In the years since the incident, Karen had withered and shrunk to skin and bones, and her body appeared more like a yellow leather hide stretched over bone drums. To an outsider, Karen could seem awfully gruesome. Her hair had thinned and had begun graying by age twenty-three. She was breathing without a respirator and her almost inaudible air intake was the only evidence of life-force. Sturdy splints and rods were in place to keep her body from contracting fetally into itself, yet the one medical oddity about her case was that instead of "going fetal," as her leg braces anticipated, she remained supple and relaxed. Not a few research doctors and students from

UBC had come to study Karen in her permanently relaxed state.

In the spring of 1981, Hamilton showed up at my apartment with a cut lip, a black eye, and a seething disposition. "That douche bag Klaus whacked me with a tripod. Pam can keep him." I asked who Klaus was: "Pammie's new beefy plaything." The next day Pam phoned me to say good-bye; she was moving to New York with Klaus. "He's not a very talented photographer, Rick, but he *is* sweet." For the next decade, I only saw Pam on magazine covers and heard from her via breathy little phone calls from exalted places: "Hi Rick. I'm in a G3 flying over Juneau (*crackle crackle*). Oh bugger, I just spilled the coke box in my lap. Oliver, what time does the hunt start? No . . . that was the jacket in Madrid. Hi . . . Richard . . . where were we?"

Hamilton spent a few years with a surveying crew in the wilds of northern BC, thus beginning his romance with dynamite blasting, a natural extension of a pyromaniacal bent that began in the first grade with black ants, barbecue starter, Hamburger Helper boxes, and a large magnifying glass. By 1985, he earned his geology degree and his blaster's ticket, and for years thereafter he was clam-happy, roaming the province, felling mountains and hammering cliffs into gravel.

Linus became an electrical engineer, which surprised nobody. After graduation, he worked for two years at an engineering firm down-town. We saw him rarely. His life seemed dull. An adult too early.

Virtuous Wendy studied emergency medicine at UBC. Such is the life of the med student that we saw Wendy only when she came up for air throughout the decade, underslept, vague, with cherry-stained eye-balls, rumple-clothed, and a preoccupied, crow-footed face. At lunch with her one day, Hamilton and I learned the rigors of medicine—thirty-six-hour days, gorgon floor nurses, and flesh-eating bacteria lying in wait around every corner. "God, I feel like a carton of time-expired milk all the time. But I love the work."

Hamilton pulled a bottle of Visine from his pocket and told Wendy to lean back. "There," he said, dribbling it into each eye, "I don't like to see you looking so beat. Your eyes feel better?"

"Yes. Thanks, Ham."

"Keep the bottle. I bought it for you. Want to go for a walk on the beach at Ambleside?"

"I'd love to, Ham, but I'm on night shift. Have to be there in fifteen minutes."

Me, I had to go work at the Vancouver Stock Exchange—lucrative, but so dull that words to describe it escape me.

Megan, she knew from the start that I was her father, but knowledge of Karen was another issue. There was no right or wrong decision in this matter. Our final decision not to tell her about Karen was tough on us. Should we have told her Karen was dead? A lie. Should we have said she's on a long holiday? Dumb. Should we have told her that Karen's ill? "The only problem there," my dad said, "is that she'll want to see her, of course. To a young child, the sight of Karen, love her as much as we do, might be more than shocking—cruel even."

In the end, we figured that by age seven Megan would be adequately mature to see Karen. In the interim we told Megan Karen was sick, that it would be some while before we could go visit. Megan asked the inevitable questions soon: "What was Mom like, Dad? You know, my *real* Mom." This distinction, while natural, made Lois's toes curl under each time Megan used it. "Is Mom dead?" "Is my mom pretty?" "Does Mom like horses?" "If Mom came to visit, could she help me clean my room?"

In 1986, Megan started school with unfettered glee. She bounced out of bed each morning and hurled herself through the kitchen door before Lois had the chance to dole out either a lecture or a berating. No extracurricular activity was too time consuming; no school project or music lesson too long.

And Megan had indeed started out in life resembling me in a Bumhead wig—her hair grew straight as rain and that was

64

just fine—but fate took pity on her. As her baby fat melted away, Karen's infinitely prettier features emerged from within. We all mentally exhaled a relieved "whew!"

Occasionally, I'd pick Megan up at school to drive her home: *Ding dong, hello Lois* . . . "You know, Richard, I just don't understand why she enjoys school so much. She has a lovely house here with stacks of toys, plus I have worthwhile activities planned for almost all of her waking hours, so she has no reason to go gallivanting up to your house. No offense, but your house has nothing in it for a baby. Not one single thing. I had coffee up there last week and it was the most I could do to locate even a bouncing ball—and *then* it turns out to be Charlie's [our golden lab]. I'm going to have to be much more strict from now on. Or figure out a much more elaborate containment system. Come inside, Megan. We have flash cards to do. Good-bye Richard, and please, cut your hair, because I know shorter hair is now in style and you're a father now." Door closed; muffled yaps; Megan squalling as French language flash cards are produced. Poor baby.

Shortly after enrolling in first grade, Megan's classmates— having heard it from their parents who heard it at the Super-Valu who heard it from wherever—these vicious little oiks told Megan, then six, that her mother was a "vegetable." As little brutes will do, they howled grocery lists at her across the gravel playing field: "*Lettuce. Corn. Green beans, carrots—Megan's mother is a carrot.*" And so forth. On the day of the 1987 stock crash, just moments after it sank in that I'd lost most of my assets, Megan's school principal phoned my office around noon—Lois was out, so he called me. He said that Megan was in "a state."

I drove from downtown to fetch my daughter and then we cruised aimlessly around the neighborhood, the crisply changing leaves that hinted of wine amid the lengthening shadows of fall. The radio was off. "What's up Sweetie Pie?"

"Dad, everyone's saying my *real* mother's a carrot."

"Well she's *not* a carrot. That's impossible."

"Lettuce?"

65

"Megan! Of course she's *not* a lettuce—nor any other vegetable. Your mother is *not* a vegetable, Megan."

"Then why does everybody call her a carrot?"

"Because kids are cruel, Megan. They say stupid untrue things and have no idea what they're really saying."

"Did *I* used to be a carrot?"

We came to a stop sign at Hadden Drive. "Megan, stop . . ."

Megan opened the door and dashed out into the trees beside the golf course. Shit. I left the car running at the stop sign, door wide open, and chased after her. Fortunately, I knew my way through the surrounding trees as well as any child, having spent so much time there myself when young. "Megan, come back."

"*Kleek. Kleek. Kleek.*"

What was this strange noise she was making? I followed the sound over a series of logs, over a dewy patch of psilocybin mushrooms, then into a glade where as teenagers we'd spent many a Friday and Saturday night. Megan was sitting fetal beside an old rotted log that had probably been felled back in the 1920s.

"*Kleek. Kleek. Kleek.*"

"Megan, *there* you are." I stopped to catch my breath and looked around at the dry cool dent in the forest floor, untouched by undergrowth as the shade canopy above was too dense. Between the yearly layers of pine, fir, and cedar sheddings lay bits of uncountable cigarette packs, weather-yellowed pornography, candy wrappers, condoms, dead flashlight batteries, and clusters of stolen Mercedes hood ornaments.

"*Kleek.*"

"Megan, what's that sound you're making?"

"*Kleek.*"

Two could play at this game. I said, "*Kleeg Kleeg.*"

Megan rolled her eyes. "Daddy, you're not doing it right."

"*Kleeg. Kleeg.*"

"Daddy, that's *not* what carrots sound like. They sound like this: *Kleek. Kleek. Kleek.*"

"How silly of me. I forgot."

There was a quiet moment and I thought of the summer Jared and I stole a golf cart from an elderly twosome and drove it through the woods, bailing out just before it ran over a small cliff. We never got caught.

"Megan, for God's sake, stop the carrot stuff. You know it's not true."

"Where's my real mom?" She was getting teary.

"Okay, Megan. I'll *tell* you, okay."

"Okay." Her posture slackened and she relaxed visibly.

I caught my breath. "Your mom was eighteen when she became sick. She has the same birthday as you."

"Really?"

"Really."

I told Megan about her mother—everything—and afterward we walked out of the forest and back to the car, still running, still waiting to drive us away.

Of course, Megan wanted to see Karen—the sooner the better. We went that night. My mother and the staff at Inglewood spruced Karen up as best they could. Once inside Inglewood, I greeted the staff as I'd done hundreds of times before, and all the while my stomach felt lightweight and bilious. We slowly marched down the echoing hallway into Karen's room, where a small radio played Blondie's "Heart of Glass," then a song by the Smiths. Her bed had a blue chenille spread. "It's okay, Megan," I said. "There's no need to be afraid. We all love you."

Karen, even dolled up by Mom, was a heartbreaking sight. They tried to make Karen as natural as possible with foundation plus a dab of blush, with a trim of her hair, all crowned with an Alice-band. She wore a lavender cardigan. Not having seen Karen dolled up since 1979, I felt a pang of intense loneliness. For Megan, the initial shock of seeing her mother seemed to wear off quickly. She gave no initial reaction. I stood still while Megan approached Karen's bedside. She placed her hand on her mother's forehead and with her other hand stroked Karen's hair and touched her hollow cheeks. She smudged her fingers on Karen's eyelids. "She's wearing makeup," Megan said.

"Sleeping people don't wear makeup." She moistened her fingers to try to wipe clean Karen's cheeks and forehead, erasing Mom's makeover effort. Having accomplished this, she jumped up onto the bed and lay down beside Karen. Karen was inside a sleep cycle, her mouth rasping. Megan looked closely at her face. "How long has she been like this?"

"Since December 15, 1979."

"Who visits her?"

"George does," I said, "every day. And I come here once a week on Sunday."

"Hmm."

Megan looked at her mother. "She doesn't scare me, you know."

"Well, she shouldn't."

Megan ran her fingers over Karen's face again, then said to me, "Can I come with you on Sunday from now on, Dad?"

"Deal."

"Do I look more like you or Mom?"

"Your mother," I said with relief.

Megan looked at Karen's face right up close, as though trying to locate the watermark on a forged banknote. She gave out a puff of air indicating satisfaction, and then lay down beside her and rested. I went outside for fresh air, flummoxed by Megan's casual acceptance. I stared into a coffee cup as I thought of how life ought to have been as opposed to what it became. After that day, Megan drove with me to Inglewood Lodge on Sundays.

In the 1980s, Hamilton and I would party often. One morning in particular I was awakened by Hamilton tweezing unmetabolized coke from my nostrils. Life was big.

I recovered somewhat from the 1987 stock crash and continued treadmilling within the city's financial district selling low-tide stocks. This was around the time where I started to drink. My compatriots were machine-bronzed fiftysomethings decorated with gold nugget rings and pin-curly hairdos lying into telephone headsets at 5:00 a.m. *Lord*—the scammy little push-me-pull-you's we enacted over the phones from within our bleak putty-colored office cubicles.

A minor scandal about a spurious core sample knocked me out of the Stock Exchange. With my savings, I bought a Kleenex-box house in North Van where I lived alone, seeing Megan only rarely—*baaad* father. I took that first house, spackled, sanded, and painted it, then flipped it for a twenty-five-thousand-dollar profit. This became a pattern: I'd buy the worst house on a good block, work and drink like a demon on weekends to whip it into shape, then flip it for a reasonable profit. My behavior wasn't greed, it was . . . it was me doing anything but speaking honestly with myself—countless silent moments hastily varnished with vodka and thoughts of renovations. I was visiting Karen twice, thrice a week. At Inglewood, I drank vodka and orange juice from a carton.

10 | ONE DAY YOU WILL SPEAK WITH YOURSELF

After some years I realized I'd landed myself a major drinking problem—a device for coping with life's endlessly long days. I truly wondered if I was in some kind of coma myself, shambling through life with an IV drip filled with Scotch. My twenties were vanishing and the only good thing I had going for me was a daughter who I hardly ever saw. For her sake I bucked up a bit in the early 1990s and began to sell residential properties with a modicum of success—my years of renovating claptraps left me with a good instinct for the true value of a house.

I also began doing things I couldn't have imagined doing while sober: I'd often lose my car when I went out at night— forget where I parked it, then call all the towing firms the next day to see if they had it. I woke up one morning to see I'd peed onto the wall. For the most part, I maintained a good front while inner deterioration grew. My breath stank permanently like wine left inside a stemmed glass overnight.

And time ticked on.

Pam sent me a card from Athens:

> DINNER WITH DAVID BOWIE. GLAMORAMA.
> DRANK ABSINTHE FOR THE FIRST TIME, P.

Linus, one day in 1990, without telling anybody, left the city. He drove to Lethbridge in Alberta, parked his VW Bug on the side of a ridge, the Continental Divide, donned his knapsack, and went walking through the stubble and chaff on the fields, across the prairies, flushing out the partridge and pheasants, slouching eastward, then south as winter approached, never again to return to his VW. He spent the next few years gadabouting the southern United States, growing his beard, doing spare jobs for food, and sending a postcard from here or there in his microscopic print:

DEAR RICHARD, THIS IS LAS VEGAS. VIVA. IT'S WINTER NOW. I'M WORKING AT AN ITALIAN RESTAURANT AS A WAITER. IT'S OKAY. THERE'S NOT MUCH TO DO HERE. THERE'S A TARGET RANGE NEARBY, SO I'M LEARNING TO SHOOT. IT SOUNDS DUMB, BUT IT'S SOMETHING TO LEARN. THANK YOU FOR YOUR KIND LETTER PLUS THE SNAPSHOTS OF HOME. I APPRECIATE YOUR BEING CONCERNED FOR ME, BUT I ASSURE YOU I'M OKAY. YOU ASKED WHY I'M DOING THIS AND THAT'S A REASONABLE QUESTION. I THINK I COULDN'T SEE ME HITTING INTO THE EVERYDAY WORLD ANY LONGER. I FOUND MYSELF DOING ELECTRICAL WORK DAY IN/DAY OUT AND REALIZED I WOULD HAVE TO DO THIS THE REST OF MY LIFE AND IT SPOOKED ME. I DON'T KNOW IF THERE'S SOME ALTERNATIVE OUT THERE, BUT I SPEND MOST OF MY TIME WONDERING WHAT IT MIGHT BE. I SUPPOSE THERE'S ALWAYS CRIME, BUT THAT'S NOT GOOD WHEN YOU'RE OLDER. THERE'S DRUGS, BUT YOU KNOW, I'VE NEVER SEEN ANYBODY WHO'S BEEN IMPROVED BY DRUGS. LIFE SEEMS BOTH TOO LONG AND TOO SHORT. THIS BEING SAID, I HAD A GOOD DAY TODAY. THE CLOUDS WERE PRETTY AND I BOUGHT A SACK OF CLOTHES AT THE GOODWILL STORE FOR FIVE BUCKS. PAMMIE WAS ON THE COVER OF *ELLE*. PLEASE WRITE IF YOU CAN. CARE OF THE POST OFFICE, LAS VEGAS. YOUR FRIEND, ALBERT LINUS.

In 1989, Hamilton married Cleo, a hiker he met while triangulating land up north near Cassiar. They moved into a small townhouse near Lonsdale Quay and became ultra-domestic, hosting theme dinner parties (*"Provence!"*), allowing themselves to pudge out a few pounds (*"Dove Bars . . . dare we?"*), and spending their weekends wallpapering (*"Love to play baseball but the den molding just arrived today."*). Hamilton seemed to have settled down and lost much of his sarcastic edge. He left my radar for a while, even though he lived nearby.

In 1991, Wendy became a specialist in emergency medicine. Also, her mother died of liver cancer that year, so Wendy returned home to the old neighborhood to live with and take care of her father, Ivor, a trollish grump with never a kind word for his daughter or anybody else. Wendy was occupied, but her life really wasn't much of a life. I know she'd wanted to fall in love during med school, but it never happened, and I know she was unhappy about this.

This was also the year that Pam began vanishing from magazines, until she finally went completely AWOL at year's end, nary a lipstick-smudged postcard to any of us. Hurt feelings, yes, but we knew there had to be a reason. Hamilton, in a less generous mood, said, "She in rehab. Don't glamorize it. Serves the cow right."

"In what way does it serve her right, Ham?" I asked. We were in Hamilton and Cleo's nest at the bottom of Lonsdale: matching pine furniture, wacky animal fridge magnets, and white wine. Cleo positively glowed every time Ham took a swipe at Pammie.

"In what way?" I asked again. He didn't know in what way. He harrumphed and said he had to make a phone call. "Aren't *I* Mr. Pissy tonight." Cleo looked miffed.

In mid-1992, Pam returned home to her folks' place—shaky, fearful, thin, and eerily gorgeous. The modeling lifestyle had wiped her out. We were sitting on her parents' front patio. "You know, it was fun, Richard. I grant you that. But it's over now. There's only a small fraction of 'me' left. I used to think there was an infinite supply of 'me.' Wrong-o. I have to be calm now. My small seed needs to grow and become a whole person again. I blew it all—a whole decade raking in dough and not one effing penny."

"Where'd it go?" I asked.

"Clothes. Dinners. Drugs. More drugs. Bad investments— a mall in Oklahoma that never got built; a retirement community in Oregon that bankrupted." She was spitting out the words. "Shit. At least I'm allowed to smoke." The trees way above us rustled. A crow cawed. "And it's not even the drugs I miss, Richard. I miss the *action*. I miss feeling like queen of the roulette table. The black cars. Shallow shit, but I miss it. I miss feeling fabulous." A big silence, then: "Lois lets me baby-sit Megan sometimes. She's a fun kid. And gorgeous. She reminds me of Karen."

"Thanks."

"When I first saw Megan as a baby I thought she might as well go she-male and become your twin. By the way, my dear, *you* look like *crap*."

"Thanks again Pam." I was making impatient gestures—I had to go pick up Megan from ice skating.

"Richard, you're not leaving—not now, are you? Is it because I pointed out your boozy skin condition?"

"I have to, Pam. I . . ." Pam's composure waited. She was on the cusp of tears. I sat next to her and asked what was wrong. She sniffled and stared into her two clasped hands.

"It's just that I'm . . . I'm . . ."

"What, Pam? What?"

A whisper: "Lonely."

"I know. Me, too."

I held her as she sniffled. "How's Hamilton? You see him much? Is he happy?"

"I think so."

"Oh, *pooh*." She was still wearing the pubic-hair locket. I asked her to come along with me to pick up Megan and she did.

*　　*　　*

73

As fate would have it, Pam shortly ran into Hamilton and Cleo at a record store in Park Royal; they clicked instantly and they left the shop together, forgetting Cleo entirely. In those first few moments poor Cleo saw Pam and Hamilton together she knew she was out of the picture. Cleo had never seen that expression on Hamilton's face before: incredulous, worshipful, witty, lustful, and adoring—all of this *love* laser-beamed straight at Pam.

Hamilton's marriage didn't just wobble, it crashed like a dynamited casino. In six months it was legally over, too: Cleo got the townhouse; Hamilton boomeranged into his parents' rent-free house, just a mere three-minute stroll to Pam's. At dinner at my parents' one night I saw the two of them mosey-ing down Rabbit Lane. Every three steps a kiss. Every five steps a caress. Hamilton in love.

It was great fun to have Pam among us again, with her tattletales of sex, drugs, and cannibalism. Her reputation in the fashion industry was shot, but this didn't bother her at all. "Much better for me to be here in Deadsville with chums. All very matey, isn't it?" I asked her if she had a plan yet. She said she was going to start doing TV and film makeup for some of the many US studios shooting in their Vancouver branch plants. It turned out to be the best idea any of us ever had.

And what of Karen? Neither alive nor dead after all these years, ever dimming from the world's mind—rasping, blinded, and pretzeled in a wheelchair, a chenille half-shirt covering the outer, exposed part of her body. She moves her head, her eyes flicker, and for three seconds she sees the sky and the clouds— she is briefly among the living, but no one is there to witness. She returns to the dark side of the Moon. We still don't know what she saw that December night, nor may we ever.

By the early 1990s, Karen's awakening had become a billion-to-one shot, but it was still a shot. No, Karen didn't "contri-bute" anything to society, but how many people really *do*? Perhaps she *did* contribute: She provided a platform on which people could hope. She provided the idea that some frail essence from a now long-vanished era still existed, that the brutality and extremes of the modern world were not the way the world ought to be—a world of gentle Pacific rains, down-filled jackets, bitter red wine in goatskins, and naïve charms.

11 | DESTINY IS CORNY

After four years of drifting, Linus returned in late 1992. In that time he'd become more remote than ever. "Reading his facial expressions is an exercise in Kremlinology," Hamilton said. "Direct inquiry's no help: *Gee, Linus, you're so remote these days—gee, what's the reason?*" Discussion was awkward indeed, and in the end it was simply avoided. His years away were treated as though he'd popped out to get a pack of cigarettes and returned a few minutes later.

Wendy met Linus for dinner a week after his low-key return. Afterward, she told me Linus had "gone inside himself, and hasn't quite emerged yet. He talked about sand dunes, ice, chocolate bars, and hitchhiking—the sorts of things that would be a big deal if you were a hobo. Chalk marks and stuff."

I was envious of Linus's venture into nothingdom, but also ticked off that he hadn't had a revelation in all of his wanderings. I still lived, as did Hamilton, with the belief that meaning could pop into my life at any moment. I was getting—*we* were getting—no younger, yet for some reason not particularly wiser.

Linus's parents had moved to the waterfront on Bellevue two years earlier—no spare bedroom. A homesick Linus rented a bungalow four houses down from his old house on Moyne Drive, paying the rent with earnings as a freelance electrical contractor. Generators were his specialty. It seemed an anticlimactic sequel to his romantic solo wanderings.

Wendy, eager for any excuse to not have to be around her aging churlish feed-me-my-gruel father, visited Linus every night after her shift at Lions Gate Emergency. One night at a

Halloween party in North Van, Wendy curled herself into Linus's lap and smiled love's smile. "Good for them!" we all said. Wendy began spending less time at the hospital; she resumed kibitzing about with our old crowd.

I bumped into Wendy on Moyne Drive one afternoon. Seemingly dancing on air, she held a Safeway paper bag. I asked her what it was, and she opened it to show me. "It's a pile of sulfur that Albert gave me."

"Albert? Oh—that's right—it's Linus's real first name."

"Isn't he *sweet*?"

Wendy soon moved in with Linus and that summer the two were married, as were Pam and Hamilton. A week after the ceremony it was a rainy day and Wendy and I were sitting on cardboard boxes in the living room, rain thumping the rooftop. I asked Wendy why she and Linus had never gotten together before. She said, "All my life I've had this problem of being lonely all day. Then one night loneliness began creeping into my dreams. I thought I was jinxed or spooked or voodoo'ed into a life of eternal loneliness. Then Linus told me that he had the same problem. Oh, the *relief* I felt! It dawned on me that maybe we were the same in other ways."

Pam said, "They both had solitary natures, neither needs to explain themselves to the other. Added bonus? They're comfy with each other. So who'dathunk?"

That fall I began living in Linus's house, too. I'd lost my driver's license, which made me take taxis in whose comfortable interiors I could drink even more. Drinking made me a shameful salesman; I was broke and needed a cheap place to crash. Linus rented me a basement room—a small room with one lamp and a window that overlooked the tool shed.

"I think," Linus said on moving day, "you drink because you want to kill time until Karen wakes up. Correct?"

I told him to mind his own business, although he was probably right. "But I don't think it's just one thing." We discussed my drinking problem as though it were a cold.

I was the last of our crew to return to the neighborhood. Hamilton began living at Pam's house. Our situation felt wildly regressive. The Loser's Circle. Pam asked me one day on a forest walk if we were all winners or losers. "Where do we fit in, Richard? We're all working. We all have jobs but . . . there's something missing."

"We're empty, maybe," I said. Some birds screeched.

"I don't think so. But no kids—that must mean something. Oh—stupid me. I mean there's Megan, of course. Hopefully, I'll have a little brute some day. It's like that thing you told me—the line from that post card Linus wrote you: *Why does life feel so long and so short at the same time?* Why *is* that?" Rain was starting to spit.

"I think we live in this world, but we don't *change* the world. No, but that's wrong. We're born; there *must* be a logic—some sort of plan larger than ourselves."

We walked farther. We had all awakened X number of years past our youth feeling sleazy and harsh. Choices still existed, but they were no longer infinite. Fun had become a scrim, concealing the hysteria that lay behind it. We had quietly settled into a premature autumn of life—no gentle mellowing or Indian summer of immense beauty, just a sudden frost, a harsh winter with snows that accumulate, never to melt.

In my head I wanted to *thaw* the snow. I wanted to *reorder* this world. I did *not* want to be old before my time.

The two of us arrived at a long, clear stretch of the path. Pam said, "Watch this." She began to catwalk down an invisible runway. "Calvin Klein. Milan. Fall Collection, 1990. What's in my head as I walk the catwalk? I'm worried my legs look too scrawny. Will there be free coke afterward? The supermodel's mind, eh?"

We forded a stream and entered a mossy patch lit by a shaft of sun cutting through the rain.

That night, I went on a bender for no real reason except that there was nobody home and nobody was reachable on the phone. I was rehashing the day's conversation with Pam and I felt the loneliest I'd ever felt, because I was getting old and I was alone and I saw no chance of this ever changing.

I remember nothing that happened after I opened the

evening's second vodka bottle (no pretense of flavor or finesse ... just getting it in). I awoke the next morning, my head flopped inside the toilet bowl like a pile of meat at the butcher's. I'd vomited onto, then *into* my stereo, I'd cut the chain on my exercise bike and shitted all over my sheets, some of which were rubbed onto the wall. No memory at all.

Wendy found me and talked to me while I was still on the floor. Linus came in. Wendy said, "You can't go on like this, Richard." Linus ran the bath and he and Wendy placed me in it. The two of them cleaned my room for me as I sat in the bath, still slightly drunk—a blank, angry hangover beginning to thunder inside my cranium. They stuffed me into Wendy's 4-Runner and took me to the hospital. That was the end. "But I want to pass out," I shouted at Wendy.

"No you don't," she calmly replied.

"I want to be where Karen is."

"No you don't."

"I *do*."

"You're not allowed there."

"I *am*."

"Grow up," Linus said. "Be a man."

On New Year's Eve, 1992, the five of us were sitting in Linus's under-heated igloo of a kitchen around a Formica table playing a lazy poker game, trying to make each other feel noble about the fact that our lives had the collective aura of a fumbled lateral pass.

Rain was pelting the windows; we were using candles, not electric light. Hamilton, His Grumpiness, was saddled with a leg cast after falling thirty feet off a cliff up Howe Sound the month before. As well, he'd been recently nabbed "borrowing" some blasting materials from the company's warehouse and was asked to resign rather than be fired. His life was, if not in tatters, certainly ripped.

I asked, "Ham—what on Earth were you going to do with blasting caps and plastic explosives? Bomb the mall?"

"*No*, Richard, I was going to drive up to the interior to

blow up rock formations. It's my art form. How am I going to develop my talent if I don't take artistic risks? My palette is dynamite, rock is my canvas. *Piss*. What am I going to do *now*?"

Linus was also in a grumpy mood, which was interesting in itself as he never seemed to *have* moods. Pam was riding her "monthly train to hell," and Wendy was underslept after having been on call the whole of Christmas week. I had a bizarre headache from having inhaled too much helium from a clown-shaped canister given to me as a gag gift from Hamilton. As well, I'd been guzzling zero-alcohol eggnog; my stomach felt fur-lined. My not drinking was a challenging bore.

Hamilton was theorizing about work. "Well kids, in order for the system to work, there must be glittering prizes. *Another card, Richard, and not from the bottom, I'm watching.* A highly competitive society must have simple rules and terrible consequences for not obeying the rules. *I fold.* There *must* be losers on the edge to serve as cautionary tales for those in the center. Nobody likes to see the losers—*Wendy's deal*—losers are the dark side of society and they frighten people into submission. *I* must *have more plonk. Linus? I must have more of that yellow swill! Now! Mush!*"

Linus gave Hamilton a sneer. Pam said, "Hamilton, fetch it yourself, you one-legged pig. And once you're there, fetch me some, too." Cards remained on the table. Wendy arranged her chips into tiny Angkor Wat towers, the same way she'd arranged stones on grad night. The evening's theme continued: an intense scrutiny of everything we had become up until now—relentless self-criticism—adding, subtracting, looking at the lives of others. It reassured us to hear that other people's lives were proving to be as unstable as our own. I put forth the question, "Do animals have leisure time? I mean, do they ever go 'hang out'? Or is everything they do connected to food and shelter?"

"There are hawks," Linus said, "who ride the thermals in the mountains without moving a wing for hours. Not even dive-bombing for rodents—just riding the wind."

80

"Dogs have leisure," said Pam. "Chasing sticks. Having tussles on the carpet. Great fun."

"I don't know," said Wendy. "Hawks are always alert for food. Dogs chasing sticks is pack mentality reinforcement. Besides, animals don't even *have* time. Only humans have time. It's what makes us different." Wendy dealt like a croupier goddess, massaging the whole deck rather than shuffling—a treat to watch.

Linus sipped his drink and said, "You know, from what I've seen, at twenty you know you're not going to be a rock star. *Threes are wild this round.* By twenty-five, you know you're not going to be a dentist or a professional." Wendy pecked Linus on the cheek. "And by thirty, a darkness starts moving in—you wonder if you're ever going to be fulfilled, let alone wealthy or successful. *Pam, are you folding? Wake up, girl.* By thirty-five, you know, basically, what you're going to be doing the rest of your life; you become resigned to your fate. God, do I have a shitty hand. My cards, I mean."

Pam said, "Hamilton, my plonk? *Oink?*"

Pam had at least accomplished her dream of being a model. Hamilton—what dream had he made real? He stumped to the table with the bottle. "Oinks to *you*, Pamela."

The game lapsed into banter, which is all we really wanted. If we'd been serious, we'd all have owed Linus ten million dollars long ago. Linus always won. Card-counting during his stint in Las Vegas?

"I read about this study," Wendy said. "The researchers learned that no matter how hard you tried, the most you could possibly change your personality—your self—was five percent."

"God, how depressing," said Pam.

"Crap," said Hamilton. "No way."

Wendy's fact made me queasy. The news reminded me of how unhappy I was with who I was at that point. I wanted nothing more than to transform *100* percent.

A few minutes later, Linus interrupted his poker-faced silence: "What I notice," he said, "is that everybody's kind of

81

accusing everybody else of *acting* these days. Know what I mean? Kind of, uh, not being *genuine*." He looked at his Kahlua coffee. ("A teenager's drink," Hamilton had heckled.) "Nobody believes the identities we've made for ourselves. I feel like everybody in the world is fake now—as though people had true cores once, but hucked them away and replaced them with something more attractive but also hollow. Play your card, Wendy—" We pokered for a while, all feeling odd at Linus's lengthy barrage of insight.

"Amen, Reverend," said Hamilton. "Three jacks and the kitty is mine. Richikins, your deal. Or are you really Richikins? Prove to me that you're *you*, you impostor."

"Hamilton, you talk funny," barked Linus in a voice so new it startled us. "You talk in little TV bits. You're never sincere. You're never nice. You used to be a little bit nice once. I don't think you've ever had a real conversation in your life." We were all still: "When you were young, you were funny, but now you're not young and you're not even boring. You're just kind of scary. When was the last time you had a real conversation with *anybody*?"

Hamilton scratched an itch beneath his leg plaster. "I don't need this shit."

"Well? When was the last time?"

Hamilton looked to Pam for backup, but Pam had placed her cards down on the table to investigate the elegant waxy sheen of the Queen of Diamonds. "I . . ." Hamilton was off guard. "Pam and I have conversations all the time. Don't we, Pam?"

Pam kept looking at her cards. "I'm not in this particular pissing contest, fellas."

"Thanks a *lot*, honey. So what are you driving at, Linus— that I'm a phony because I enjoy 'light conversation'? You ought to look into a mirror at yourself sometime. A real lulu *you* are."

"I look in the mirror every day, Hamilton. I'm saying that you're shutting the last door that might save you—kindness and honesty. You have thirty-five more years to go; life's all downhill from now on."

82

"What the . . . ?" Hamilton lifted himself up and reached for his crutches that leaned over by a pile of boots and a kitty litter box in the corner.

"Cor fricking *blimey*. No one needs this." (Hamilton was in his phase of only renting British VHS tapes, thus Anglicizing his diction.) "I'm getting out of preacher-man's house, and then I'm gonna hobble home. Pam? Are you coming or are you going to stay here to be *real* with Jesus and our chums here?"

Pam looked him in the face. "Yes. I'm going to stay a while."

"Very well, *luvvie*. I'll toddle off now." Wendy helped Hamilton with his crutches. He walked out the door and into the rain, where he shouted "Feck off" to all of us and grunted back to Pam's house, then most likely into a Demerol fog. We sat around the table and quietly packed up the chips and cards.

"He'll forget all this ever happened," Pam said. "He's not the sort of person who changes." She picked up three glasses at once with her fingertips. "And would somebody please tell me why fucked-up guys are sexy? I'm lost."

I said, "Hey, Linus. What was all *that* about?"

He said, "I just don't know. I had to say it. I'm worried. I'm worried that we're never going to change. I'm worried that we might not even be *able* to change. Do you ever worry about that?"

I said, "Yes."

The next morning all was forgotten.

While walking over to Hamilton's, I bumped into Megan. She was with two other thirteen-year-old girlfriends and one boyfriend, all puffing away on ciggies, the boy wearing baggy pants and the girls wearing clones of each other's fashions, groomed to the point of almost biological sameness (just as Karen and Pam and Wendy had once been). I said, "Where you off to today, Meg?"

"Out."

"Where*abouts* out?"

"Good deeds, Dad. We're delivering Easter baskets to crack

babies." Her friends sniggered. I realized that for the first time Megan was embarrassed to be seen with me. I understood, but nevertheless the barb stung.

"Don't forget dinner at Grandma and Grandpa's tonight."

She rolled her eyes, her friends looked the other way, and she said, "Right, Dad."

Torturous teen. To think I once believed teen-rearing would be so easy; like most parents, I thought I had the "magic touch" that would make my own teenager be my pal instead of my enemy. No such luck.

THE FUTURE IS MORE EXTREME THAN YOU THINK

Our film careers began one soggy Tuesday morning in early 1993, the daffodils still asleep within the grass, the clouds like soaked dishrags squeezing out gray wet glop. Pam, then doing makeup and styling for the exploding local film and TV industry, had arranged for Hamilton, Linus, and me to visit her on location at a "Movie of the Week" being shot just up the hill from Rabbit Lane—a film of the mom-loses-tot-gets-tot-back genre we soon came to know all too well.

The January housing market was dead; I took a few more days off to play cards and waste time. Linus, a consultant, could take off whatever hours he wanted. We decided to walk up the hill to Pam's shoot while Hamilton drove. We shortcutted through the golf course and had a golf-ball fight, which landed Linus in the espresso-colored water traps up to his knees. "A dissolute lifestyle has its rewards," said Linus, peeling a bulrush frond from his shins, a leech cuddling into his calf.

We arrived at the location on Southborough Drive bemucked, resembling extras and feeling like outsiders. Hamilton's Javelin kachunk'ed onto the road's shoulder and soon we three bumbled pointlessly amid the necklace of white vans and utility trucks that border any film location. We found Pam. "Go grab a bite at the catering truck. Wait for me there."

"Where are the *stars*?" Linus asked.

"What were you expecting, kids," Pam said, "chorus-line girls carrying enormous foam boulders? Roman centurions riding along in golf carts? I'll tell you the official credo of film: *Hurry up and wait*. See you in five."

We ate cold pasta, watched thick white lighting cables being hauled into a front doorway, and became thoroughly bored. "This blows," Hamilton said. "Let's amscray."

We were set to amscray when Tina Lowry, an old classmate of mine, called, "Richard! Richard Doorland, is that *you*? It's me. *Tina*." Tina, like most people in the film and TV industry, had that slightly on-the-run-can't-talk-long look on her face. A tiny patch of blue sky allowed sun to sparkle the light meter that hung around her neck.

"Tina. You're here?"

"Heya, Richard, what are you doing on set? Crew? Extras?"

"No. I just live nearby. A friend of ours, Pam, is doing makeup here. Are you directing or something?"

"Not yet. I'm a production assistant here—a PA. We're scum on the food chain, but the job rocks. You know Pam?"

"We grew up just down the hill. Hamilton here," I indicated the soggy beanpole to my right, "is her meat puppet."

She gawped at Hamilton. "I use to cut out the pictures of her in *Vogue* and stuff. I wanted to *be* her so badly and now I'm working with her. It's trippy. What are you doing these days, Richard?"

"You mean right now—right here?"

"No, like in your life—and stuff."

I'd learned it was easier to say "nothing" than to mention real estate. "Nothing. Taking it easy." I awaited the usual strained, "Ohhh . . ." signaling embarrassment. Tina surprised me.

"You need work?"

"Uh, sure . . . maybe . . . doing what?"

"We'll find something for you. We're short-staffed and need bodies quick. I'll help you with union stuff. Phone me." A horn honked. "Gotta go." Like most film people, she vanished in a little cloud of cartoon dust.

Once again, for the first time in what seemed like a decade, the city was a place of enchantment for me. Voilà! Hamilton, Linus, and I became location scouts, and for two cigarette-packed weeks, we rollicked about the city and countryside in Hamilton's Javelin running over trash cans, drag racing yuppies, and "tailgating hair triggers," those agitated souls Hamilton seemed to locate with such ease: "Gronks itching to kill, barflies with pickled brain stems, meatheads fresh from the gym – how easily inflamed they are." We found every location required by the director within minutes, mainly as a result of my having sold real estate and growing up here. We felt useful.

Scott, a production guy from Los Angeles, told us that "they film everything here because Vancouver's unique: You can morph it into any North American city or green space with little effort and even less expense, but at the same time the city has its own distinct feel. See that motel over there? That was 'Pittsburgh' in a Movie of the Week."

Scott, like us, had never trained to be in film. Like everybody in the local industry, he arrived from another realm. Mathematicians, lawyers, dental assistants, ex-hippies—all of these people winging it. The energy was addictive.

Life became very *cha-cha-cha*. "My oh my," Hamilton would preen verbally, "aren't *we* just the niftiest, coolest, hippiest, grooviest, sexiest, most with-it, and most happening people we know?"

"Yes, Hamilton," we would reply as androids. "You certainly are."

Then came word that Fox was filming a series pilot in Vancouver, one of dozens filmed here annually. Phone calls were made and shortly Pam, Hamilton, Linus, and I wound up working on a new show in which conspiracies, be they alien, governmental, paranormal, or clerical, impacted on the lives of everyday people. These visitations would in turn be investigated by a male detective who has belief in the paranormal and a female detective who has her doubts. It was a simple formula, but one that resonated with us.

TV pilots are crap shoots. We enjoyed our location scouting as much as we could, making hay while the sun shone and we located dank, dense, evergreen versions of Florida, California, Wisconsin, and Pennsylvania. "It's a good thing not too many botanists watch this show," Linus said with grating frequency. "Or weathermen, for that matter." As it rains a fair deal in Vancouver, so it rained a great deal on the show. Critics applauded the show's rainy "noir" atmosphere. Whenever this issue was raised, Pam merrily twittered, "Giggle giggle."

After a few weeks, Tina introduced Hamilton and Linus to the world of special effects at an FX house across town called Monster Machine. Their eyes lit up; within a week, they left Fox to score jobs with Monster Machine, entering a sub-world of flash pods, latex limbs, buckets o' blood, and blue screening. Their combined explosive and electrical knowledge was impossible to refuse. Me? I stayed on the set of my weekly paranormal drama. It hadn't become a hit yet, but I liked its vibe and it was the most polite set I'd worked on.

Soon enough Pam stopped doing makeup work and joined Hamilton and Linus at the special effects firm; the three became known locally as quality special effects people. Their specialties were latex body molds and convincing explosions. Pooling their skills, they helped create aliens, zombies, vampires, Mafia-shot corpses, humans in all states of decay, mummification, terror, and explosion. They traveled frequently, usually to California to take courses with the masters, and returned to Canada with Ziploc bags full of smuggled, tissue-wrapped, German ceramic eyeballs. "Aren't they *wunderbar*?" squeaked Pam in my car driving back from the airport.

Pam was so happy. The "Whatever Happened to . . ." magazine articles ended, replaced by "Hot New Comeback!" articles. An ex-model turned special effects artist was an irresistible combination for the media. Added bonus: "I've conquered a drug problem!" Magazine and TV stories about her flourished.

A strong memory of that early period of TV production was of bodies: bodies on gurneys, bodies in boxes, bits of bodies, bodies bleeding, dummy bodies, alien bodies, bodies embedded with artificial components, bodies slated to vanish, bodies popping out of bodies, bodies just returned from the beyond, and bodies set to explode. A few of these bodies were used on my own show, but I'd also see "a galore of bodies" (Linus's term) while visiting Monster Machine, where they were experts in the trick-wiring of both latex dummies and real people, making their subjects explode, cough up blood, shimmy, or radiate green light on cue.

I popped in for a visit one rainy day after they'd been working there a year and found the two intently wiring a man's girdle with explosives and fake blood, an outfit that was to be worn in a police thriller then shooting downtown, one in which everybody shoots everybody in the climax. "Hey Richard," Linus said. "Check this out. We put the blood into these little ravioli cubes and then attach them to an outward bursting charge."

"Truly a gore-fest," Hamilton proudly added, coiling multi-colored wire into an FM blast-detonator and discharging a gelatinous glob onto a plywood sheet. "Lunch?"

"Bagel run," Linus said.

We were headed out the door when Hamilton's pager beeped and Linus suddenly had to pee. Left alone, I wandered around the studio and saw a door that was slightly ajar. I opened it, thinking I might find a studio. What I found instead must have been a corpse storage room, a room unlike any I could have imagined—men and women, children and aliens; whole, cut in two, doused in blood; arms and legs stacked like timber; glass bottles of eyes and shelves of noses. The light was dim and the air was stifled and dusty. In the center of the room sat a pile of used bodies, which appeared to have fulfilled their cinematic destiny and were now slated for selective demo-lition—pink latex aliens, moist and flabby. I walked over to the pile, fascinated with this unlit bonfire.

I circled the room and a wire tugged my sweater. I heard a *thunk* behind me and saw a dummy that I probably ought not to have seen: a plastic female body almost identical to Karen—bony, taut, skeletal, and yellowed, made of polyurethane foam, with long straight brown Orlon hair parted in the middle. The fallen corpse was now leaning against a wall near an electrical subunit, as though freeze-dried. I heard Hamilton's voice in the corridor: "Hey Linus, where's Richikins?" He walked past the door, saw me, and smiled, thinking I'd be enjoying the local attraction. He came around to where I stood, looked at the dummy, looked at me, and said, "Uh-*oh*. Sorry Richard. We used this one in a movie last month—this movie about people who survive a plane crash but who never get rescued."

"Yeah."

"We should have boxed it."

"Shit, Hamilton. Did you have to use a *chenille* shirt on it?"

"Well, it *does* look authentic."

I sighed; they'd meant no harm. I walked over to inspect the corpse, with its taxidermy glass eyes and dusty plastic hair. A fish inside my stomach wriggled and thrashed, and I looked away. Hamilton quietly sandwiched the body inside the pile of aliens. We ate lunch and afterward I drove to Inglewood. I wanted to see the real Karen, who only differed slightly from the plastic female replica I'd just seen.

The years progressed and I began to notice ideas inside my head changing, as well as detecting new sensations in my heart—my soul? The fact was that our work continually exposed us, day in, day out, to a constant assembly line of paranoia, extreme beliefs, and spiritual simplifications. The routine nature of these ideas had begun to activate parts of me that previously remained untouched. Like most people I'd known, I was unconcerned with what happens to "me" after I die. Implicit was a vague notion that I would somehow continue in another form and that was that. But then new doubts surfaced: Would I continue on? And how?

Linus asked good questions whenever I fell into one of my reflective states. On-set one day, he asked me, "Richard, let me ask you this—What is the difference between the future and the afterlife?"

"Is this what you were thinking about down in Las Vegas?" I asked.

"Maybe. But answer the question."

"The difference is that . . ." I was temporarily stumped.

"Yes?"

"The difference," I said, "is that the afterworld is all about infinity; the future is only about changes on this world—fashion and machines and architecture." We were working on a TV movie about angels coming down to Earth to help housewives. The sunlight was hurting my eyes even though I was wearing dark glasses.

"So," Linus asked, "when you die, do you still get to watch TV and read magazines and see what's happening on Earth? Or do you go someplace where that's not an issue?"

"I'm not sure. It would really bug me not to know what the city would look like in a hundred years. Or what my favorite stars would look like fifty years from now."

"Hmmm." The "star" of the angel movie walked by and asked Linus for moisturizer for her elbows. "I'm in special effects," he replied, "I can give you a dab of bloody red goo to rub into them." The "star" walked away miffed, no sense of irony.

I began to think about other issues—about leadership, about who was in charge of the world and who was *not*. Like many people, repeated exposure to paranormal situations caused me to develop those niggling little feelings that certain truths were being withheld. UFOs seemed silly, but then there was that little bit of me that said *maybe*.

"Look at it this way," Linus said before getting up to arrange a drooping wing, "you have to take all these little bits of nothing that we're given—aliens, conspirators, angels, big government—and from them you have to construct a useful picture of the afterlife. Or the future. Either way, is it enough? All these cheesy movies of the week we help make—TV movies with long-dead fighter pilots reemerging into the modern world; strange children writing binary messages seized by the government; cannibalism; vanishings; kidnapped college students; burnt people returned to life; loggers who've seen God; green blood; disembodied souls being enticed back into a body—" His pager beeped. "*Mañana*. Gotta go."

I sat there in the sun. The catering truck was cleaning up with clangs and slams. The sunlight and heat was intense. I felt like I was inside a beam shooting down from a flying saucer—a beam that would make me float up into the sky and into heaven, where I would then receive answers.

13 | REJECT EVERY IDEA

When I discovered that Hamilton and Pam were doing heroin, I first assumed it was a practical joke, because the drug had by then become a local cliché, the Port of Vancouver having in recent years become a salad bar of cheap Asian drugs. The two had rented a small 1950s house at the end of Moyne Drive, a spit away from Karen's family's house and Linus and Wendy's. During a March wrap party, I found two syringes, soiled cotton balls, and so forth in the trash can of their en-suite bathroom—plus rubber tubing lying on the counter. It wasn't a joke; they'd just been too lazy or out of it to clean up. I became angry at them for being so medically stupid and dangerously and pointlessly trendy.

Hamilton had walked into the bedroom while I was still flipping out over the discovery. I confronted him without even thinking. "Let me get this straight, Hamilton. You were at a party, and in between handfuls of Doritos someone said, 'Hey—wanna do some smack?' And you said, 'Sure! Stick the needle right here'? At least this explains why you and Pam have been so blasé lately—as well as the long-sleeve shirts."

Hamilton was serene. He gave a tender little sigh and stared me down. "Life is only so exciting, Richard. And it soon becomes a drag. This cool cat plans to enjoy his ninth life. Heroin's not a meaning, but it *does* make life feel as though life still has possibilities. I'm getting old; it's becoming harder and harder to be a unique individual."

"Life is a *drag*? What—are you a *teen*ager now? '*Bummer, man*.' I mean, how *passé*, Hamilton. Heroin. How totally ten minutes ago. A *drag*?" A city-wide rash of China White ODs made me feel protective and prudish.

Hamilton pursed his lips; I could see he was preparing to shut down on me shortly. "Curious to see you being a prig, Richikins. Excusez-moi if I've committed a lifestyle violation."

"Since when is life a *drag*, Hamilton? Things are going well. Things have never been so good."

He made a *pfffft* noise and shot me a patronizing glance that made me feel eight years old, like I'd felt when I hid my mother's cigarettes to make her stop smoking. He sat on the bed. "Don't you understand, Richard? There's nothing at the center of what we do."

"I—"

"No center. It doesn't exist. All of us—look at our lives: We have an acceptable level of affluence. We have entertainment. We have a relative freedom from fear. But there's nothing else." I felt I was getting the bad news I'd been trying to avoid for so long.

"But didn'—"

He cut me off. "*Shhh.* At least Pam and I accept things as they are. And I wish you'd let us do that. We get our job done. We pay our taxes. We never forget people's birthdays. So just let us be." He stood up. "Good night, Reverend. Ta *ta.*" He floated out of the room and yet again I had that sick feeling that accompanies a recently bruised friendship. I thought of all my recent years of AA abstention—weeks on end with my head feeling like a rotten pumpkin—all to combat doubts, to kill time, to wait for something that might never happen, some revelation that a center *did* exist. I felt very lost there in the bedroom. I walked the four miles home.

Home was a small, recently purchased two-bedroom condo in North Vancouver—a ragtag old seventies condo with slatted cedar walls and Plexiglas bubble skylights. It had, according to Linus, an elusive "sex-in-the-hot-tub, cum-on-the-ultrasuede" character. I loved my little condo merely for its calmness and coolness and the view of the mountains out back; it was the first place I'd ever lived in that actually felt like my own. I was glad to be home.

Around eight o'clock the next evening my doorbell rang: Pam, white-faced and bushed after PA-ing a TV movie filming nearby. "Ghost Mom returns to Earth to help her family fight land developers." She sat pooped but birdlike on the couch. She shushed me and crossed her arms. She looked at the floor.

"What?" I asked, trying to be casual.

Silence. "It's happening again, Richard."

'What is?"

"You know. I *know* you know. Stuff. *Junk*."

"How long now?"

"A few months? It's manageable. Nothing hardcore yet. But it's getting bigger. It always does." She stood by the window.

"Are you—?"

"*Shhh!*" She huffed out a carbon dioxide sprite into the glass and continued: "I've escaped before, Richard, we all know that. Maybe I can again. I'm still a *little* bit fabulous."

"Okay. Can you function while you're on it? I mean, doesn't it zonk you out?"

"Au contraire, it makes us zingy."

"Zingy?"

"You look sad, Richard. Don't be. You'll do me a favor?" A pause. "Sure."

"We've never judged you. Don't judge *us*. We enjoy liking you. It should stay that way."

"It *could* stay that way."

"*Shush*."

We talked a bit, then went into the kitchen where she drank an Orange Crush. We talked more, mostly in circles. Then Pam chugged her pop and hopped through the rain and into her car, driving back to Hamilton in a half-hearted Transylvanian drag race.

Megan was going through teen dramas at that time. In 1996, at age sixteen, she was a little girl in so many ways. She read her fantasy books and her eyes lit up when she talked about magic. I thought she was a wise, cool kid who could obtain better marks in school if she'd only try. She dressed weirdly, but then big deal. She'd dyed her hair nighttime black (with mouse brown roots) and used the black nail polish exclusively. Her skin was morgue-white. She had piercings up and down her ears, nose, and heaven only knows where else. She spent weeks sequestered behind her locked bedroom door, a nonstop boom box pumping out endless rotations of albums by the Cure. It seemed a typical enough rebellion.

Megan and Lois had a particularly vivid relationship. Lois considered Megan's friends losers—responsible for her rebellion. And Megan baited Lois to no end, as, for example, the time Megan and her friend Jenny Tyrell staged a phone conversation when they knew Lois was eavesdropping on the extension.

"How many cocaine straws do you think you could get out of a yellow McDonald's straw, Jenn?"

"I dunno. Three?"

"No. I think it's more like two and a half. I've got a whole pile here in my room. I'll cut some while we talk—I can see what looks like the best length." Lois stormed into Megan's bedroom at that point only to hear Megan crow.

Lois ranted, "You think you're so *clever*, don't you? Who gives you the money to pay for all your things?"

"*I* do. I sell your ugly little owl figurines one by one to collectors, *Grandma*."

Shrieks.

Once a teenager decides to be bad, the cycle is hard to break. Megan's phase kept spiraling downward. And the drug issue was scaring me. I don't think Megan did as much as Lois suggested, but it was worrisome nonetheless. Drugs were so different than when I was young. Pot was once a few giggles, munchies, spaciness for a few hours, then a headache. Modern drugs—previously unknown acid molecules, dimethyl tryptamine, crack—were a parent's most fearful imaginings made compact and simple.

In early 1997 came a small crisis. Megan and Lois had an extreme scream-fest over a black cotton sock that had made its way into Lois's white laundry cycle. Megan vanished. That night, Megan was found by a jogger passed out on a Burnside Park bench.

The police constable said she'd been drinking heavily. "There was an empty rum bottle there. We went through her purse to try to locate an address; we found a large amount of pot and some psilocybin mushrooms."

The cops let Megan off with a warning. When they left, Lois said, "She can't stay here. This is it. I love her, but she's lost to me."

I understood. The next day I suggested to Megan, hung over and groggy, that she move into my spare bedroom, and she grudgingly accepted the offer. George, Lois, and the dog had gone away for the day, so the house was quiet. We grabbed a few posters and some knickknacks to make her new space her own. She spent most of her time at my house, too. She'd been suspended from Sentinel high school so often that having her around the house became the norm on weekdays.

"What is it this time?"

"I told my English teacher to go fuck up a rope."

Or:

"What is it this time?"

"I wore a black lace shroud to gym class."

"That's all?"

"I lit a cigarette after I walked in. I blew smoke rings."

We enrolled Megan in an alternative school in North Van; she seemed to do half decent. We were glad she was making progress until we learned the real reason she continued attending: the school was a close walk to the house of her charming new boyfriend, Skitter, whom I met by accident when I went to the school to drop off some documents. He and Megan were off for lunch (drugs) somewhere over on Lonsdale.

"You must be, like, the old man. Huh?" Muttonchop sideburns. Dice tattoo. Beady eyes looking out from a hopped-up '71 Satellite Sebring. A real *doozy* of a boyfriend.

"I'm Megan's father, yes." Lord, I felt old. "And you are . . . ?"

"Skitter, man."

"Skitter," screamed Megan, "just take off, okay?" She was in the passenger seat and refused to look at me. "*Boot* it."

"Hey man—gotta go." And with that, Skitter's car farted itself out of the parking lot.

Skitter was every parent's worst fears of a daughter's dream date. He lived in a moss-roofed 1963 cereal box in darkest Lynn Valley atop an unmown lawn sparked with gasoline burns and neglected auto parts. A disassembled black Trans-Am on blocks rested in the carport. One could almost hear the neighbors' groans of shame at Skitter's house. A few times Megan called me on his cell phone: "You don't understand, Dad. Skitter's *different*."

14 IN THE FUTURE EVERYTHING WILL COST MONEY

October 31, 1997—Halloween Friday was a day of profound omens and endless coincidence, but with no guidebooks to help in discerning a higher meaning. It was a day when the world became one enormous omen-making, luck-producing factory. Later, I would learn that coincidences are the most planned things in the world. Later, I would learn that every single moment is a coincidence.

My enchanted day began just after I woke up from a sexy dream, like ones I'd had as a teenager, to my favorite song, "Bizarre Love Triangle," then playing on the clock radio.

I was shaving and glanced through the bathroom window just as a swallow flew directly at me, hit the pane, and fell earthward, seemingly dead. It regained consciousness just moments before the neighbor's tortoiseshell cat pounced. Minutes later, I saw that a spider had spun her web across my kitchen sink. I fed her a nub of hamburger meat and she tweezed the meat away with her crane-like limbs.

I dialed Tina about the day's work, but before her phone rang, Tina was already on the line—no ring. ("*Isn't that the funniest thing . . .*") I was helping Tina out on a TV thriller movie she was doing—one about an Iowa high school football team that develops a collective mind that may well be used to further the forces of evil.

On the sidewalk outside my house, I found a twenty-dollar bill. In my car (that morning, covered with fresh raccoon paw prints), I turned on the radio and learned that a murder had occurred a block away from my house; the radio then played my next three favorite songs.

At a stoplight, I looked at my odometer for the first time in months to see it revolve from 29,999 to 30,000. I looked up, there were two men on the corner with thalidomide arms staring at me.

Arriving at work, I found the best parking spot. Exiting the car, a woman passed by with a stroller-load of screaming twins. She winked, smiled, and said, "Ain't life grand?" At the lot's edge, workers were pouring a concrete slab. They asked if I wanted to trace my initials in the concrete, and so I did. Just as I was doing this, an electrical circuit box on a telephone pole coughed itself open in a shimmy of sparks.

Coincidences, omens, and luck relentlessly continued. Our film crew was on location in the agricultural flatlands of Chilliwack, a ninety-minute drive away. On the drive there, we witnessed not one but two spectacular car crashes on the other side of the freeway. A few miles on, a pair of hawks circled the freeway chasing a pigeon.

While driving, I won twenty-five dollars on a scratch-and-win lottery ticket that had been laying on the dash for weeks. Then we learned that all three people in my car had the same birthday.

A mile before we arrived at the location, a rogue cow sat stupidly in the thin road's center. We stopped and got out of the car; we saw a rainbow, and the cow ran away. The moment we arrived on location a hailstorm began. My cell phone rang and it was Megan calling to tell me she loved me.

The next call was George phoning from Lions Gate, where Karen had been transferred the previous week with a slight respiratory problem. Apparently she was well again and would be returning to Inglewood some time next week.

While we waited for the hail to melt, we had a rock-throwing contest to try to hit a telephone pole across the field—I hit the pole on my first try.

The day just wouldn't quit. I was being swept down a river of grace and wonder. The weather turned dry and crisp with Indian summer sparkle. The crew were hoping we'd wrap early so they'd have time to gussy themselves up for a Halloween party in North Vancouver later that night over at Hillary Markham's, a prop lady living near the Cleveland Dam.

The coincidences continued: I found a gold ring in the grass at the side of the field. One of the actors, the coach character, was an old high school friend, Scott, who told me that a girl we knew in high school had just died of stomach cancer.

A fumbled football landed in the ditch, and as I went to pick it up, three snakes slithered around the ball and then melted into the reeds. To the right of the ball grew a sequoia-like marijuana plant, which I traded to a coworker named Barton in lieu of money for his stereo system that I'd been wanting to buy.

In my jacket's breast pocket I found the house key I thought I'd lost the month before. I began to feel almost drunk with karma. The shoot went swimmingly; we finished almost two hours earlier than scheduled. I returned to town with Tina and two other staffers. I popped by the studio and borrowed a silver Apollo astronaut's suit used several episodes earlier. I drove home to change and relax before the party.

After a quick nap, I started to dress. I was in such a fine mood—such a day! I couldn't have known that putting on my silver jacket in my quiet house that crisp October afternoon was going to be the last truly calm moment I would ever have—the last silently normal moment of my life.

Before going to the party I drove up to Linus's house. He'd placed various rather terrifying monsters around his yard and arranged lighting so that after the trick-or-treaters had finished and were walking down the driveway, the monsters would flare up. I stayed to watch the festivities and a few trick-or-treaters. The first were two sweet little kids and their dad. One of the kids was barely six. Linus gave them each a Crunch bar, and as they scurried away, he lit up the monsters and the kids began to wail in fear. Linus hadn't anticipated this. The father yelled, "What are you, some kind of freak? Jesus, these are just little kids!'

Pang of conscience; monster floodlighting switched off. (*"Oops!"*) The monsters tucked away.

Linus left his bowl of candy outside the door and fetched his costume, a cardboard U-Haul box painted black. I asked him what he was and he said he was going as the Borg. I just don't get Trekkies.

The Halloween party began just after dark and was a smashing good time. Everybody arrived dressed up as an aspect of their subconscious: a Wonder Woman, a hobo, a cat, a Hell's Angel. These costumes reminded me of a cartoon I'd seen years before, one in which an Acme Hat Company delivery truck crosses a tall bridge. While doing so, it unleashes hundreds of hats that float to the ground and land on the characters, who suddenly become whichever hat had landed on their heads: pilgrims, Valkyries, toreadors, gangsters, and ballerinas. Wendy was working at the hospital's emergency room that night. I wondered what her hat might be: Joan of Arc's armored hood? Florence Nightingale's white nursing hat?

My astronaut's costume was a smash. I don't think I'd ever had as many people, male or female, hit on me the way they did that night—its silver skin seemed to truly ooze sex. I began wondering about ways to further the astronaut look in daily life. A crew cut? An orange Corvette Stringray?

But Hamilton and Pam were the ones who stole the show with their costumes that night. Pam walked in the door wearing two large red cardboard hearts—one on her back and one on her front. ("I'm a cinnamon candy!") Behind her was Hamilton, who zombie-walked through the door making the party go silent. Pam and Linus had done a remarkable job of transforming him into a rotting zombie with gobbets of flesh hanging down his arms and legs, his skin a map of olive green, ochre lesions and eruptions of vile mashed-potato goo. Black plague sores dotted his body like island outlines on a map of Southeast Asia. After waiting a moment for his costume to make full impact, Hamilton chirped up: "I'm a Leaker!"

We all said, "Wha—?"

"A Leaker. You don't know what a Leaker is?"

No's all around.

"Oh, I must tell you. Oh—wait a second—" He reached for his eye. "Oops! My eye just fell out." Everybody screamed in good-natured horror as Hamilton squished his left eye shut and held up a glass eye. The music turned down slightly. He pretended to reinsert the eye and said, "There. That's better. Now, a cocktail, methinks. Mr. Liver is thirstier than usual." A tray of martinis came by; Hamilton grabbed one and plopped in the eyeball.

The party started up again and Hamilton and Pam joined Linus, Tina Lowry, and me. Tina said, "Not fair, Hamilton. You have to tell us what a *Leaker* is."

"With pleasure," Hamilton said. "I first discovered Leakers maybe fifteen years ago—back when I was living down in that Gastown apartment building. Eighty-one? Eighty-two? I forget. Anyway, my neighbors were mostly a mixture of poor arty types and senior citizens on fixed incomes."

"Get to the *Leakers*, Hamilton!" Tina said.

"Okay. All right, already. Well, what would happen is this: I lived there for two years, and each August during the annual heat wave, a senior citizen on an upper floor would pay his rent, lock all of his doors and windows, watch TV, and promptly die. But because they were old or didn't have friends or what have you, nobody noticed them from one month to the next. And so—"

"I don't think I want to hear this," Tina said.

"And so—one morning I was walking over the cobblestones, returning from a pierogi breakfast at Gunther's Deli, and there were not one but *three* fire trucks out front of the building, as well as cop cars and two inhalator trucks. The firemen were wearing ventilator masks normally used for toxic spills, they had hatchets and crowbars, and they were carrying piles of construction debris they chucked into a specialized van."

"Oh, *God*—" said Tina, holding her stomach.

"That's right," said Hamilton. "Unit 403. Mrs. Kitchen. The people in the suite below were reporting something black

103

making a stain on the ceiling right above their TV set. The landlord went upstairs to investigate. There was no answer, and so he opened the door and was whomped on the nose by the absolute worst smell in the known universe—shit and piss and vomit, but a thousand times worse. The firemen arrived and had to remove every single object in the apartment and burn the rubbish. Even the Formica kitchen counter and the dry-wall were impregnated with the smell. The suite below had to be gutted, too. That's where Pamela here comes in."

We looked at Pam in her cinnamon heart costume. She curtsied. Hamilton continued: "The police brought in smell experts from the university. They told us this weird fact, that odors are like a game of tug-o-war. If one smell is pulling one way, there's always another smell to pull it in the exact opposite way. And apparently the opposite smell of dead people is artificial cinnamon."

To a chorus of ooh's, Hamilton went on. "For weeks afterward, the building was replete with sickening sweet fumes of cinnamon candy. The odor vanished after a while, but the next year I returned from working up north and the cinnamon smell was there again. I asked my next door neighbor, Dawn, if there'd been another Leaker, and she said, 'Yup. Suite 508. Mr. Huong.' So next time you smell cinnamon . . .'"

A few minutes later, Tina and a few wardrobe people were all quite sozzled; I was drinking club soda. We became increasingly silly; Suzy from payroll and I went off to neck like teenagers in the backyard between the tool shed and the composter. Once there, we escalated through all levels of intimacy rather quickly until finally we were just ourselves. The sky was black and starlit, with a pale blue Japanese fishbone cloud tickling the moon. And so we reclined. We were cold, but so what?

We watched the sky silently, as though a gentle wind was blowing through our minds. It was then, just past midnight, when my pager beeped and shooed away our intimacy. We dressed and went inside. I dialed the number. It was Wendy calling from the hospital to tell me Karen was having difficulty. "Her readouts are going all wonky. Her heart's beating irregularly and her brain print looks like a seismograph."

I couldn't imagine the world without Karen. "Should I come down right now?"

"No. Sleep. Wait until morning. I know that sounds heartless, but we'll know more then. Lois and George aren't coming either."

I began to cry. Wendy said, "You want me to come pick you guys up?"

"No. Everybody's tanked. You missed a fun party."

"Don't do anything drastic, Richard." She meant *don't drink*.

"I'll be there in the morning," I said. "I need to go be alone."

"I'm here. You have my pager number."

But I did drink—I grabbed an almost full twenty-sixer of J&B and walked out of the party and over to the dam, which was silent. The water was turned off as the water levels were so low just before the fall rains. The dam was white like aluminum under the moon, clean and fat and strong. I walked across it, sipping from the bottle, and having crossed the dam, I had the notion that I would walk to Rabbit Lane through the canyon's pathways and once there, dump my butt on either Lois and George's front stoop or on Linus and Wendy's. I hadn't been drinking for years; the Scotch took only a few baby sips to transport me into that other place I wanted to go.

I stumbled down a steep path with the world around me, the trees and air hushed as though waiting to jump out at me and yell, "Surprise!" Pearly blue clouds lit my shoes, which snagged on tree roots; my hands crushed delicate fall leaves. My mouth misted the air with chuffs of steam that vanished instantly, like a thought of a thought of a thought. Inside my head I saw the ghosts of old logging trains that once passed by here. The land was still—even now, ninety years later— beginning to heal, unaware of the sterile, suburban tracts above, the driveways and flowers and dishwashers and bird feeders. What seemed like tall trees paled from within the mighty ancient lumber stumps from which they grew.

A few swigs later, I was down by the salmon hatcheries, a fish-growing facility built in the seventies to help the Pacific salmon spawn. Like the dam upriver, the hatcheries were aluminum white in the moon. They were rectangular shaped concrete mazes, thigh-deep with cold water. They resembled office towers laid on their sides. Juvenile salmon skulked through the concrete maze like bored guests at an amusement park.

Another swig and I was soon down below the salmon hatcheries, alone as the sunlight began leaking into the sky at dawn. With no water flowing down from the dam, the river had become a beaded string of dark ponds. I hobbled on the riverbed boulders, my balance gone. The Scotch bottle broke. And in that breaking, I looked to a pool behind a rock, a large deep river pool. There I saw a thousand salmon waiting to spawn, unable to swim upriver, trapped together, this clump of eggplant-purple salmon whose only wish, whose only *yearning*, was to go home. These salmon mulled within the stilled pool—a deep dark voluptuous brain—fluttering at the edges like black apple blossoms. The fish were dreaming of sex and the death that comes afterward.

The whisky caught me. I had to vomit, so I turned around and retched into a pile of stones. I hopscotched on the rocks a bit farther down the river and tripped and fell, knocking my head on a boulder. Woozy, I laid down on my stomach, my head propped and looking into the water. The sky was brightening, and I rubbed my skull.

I looked at the pale blue sky. I saw trees the color of Karen's eyes. A seagull screeched, a heron jumped up, and water trickled down. I remembered an old thought: When I was young, my father always ensured that the family would visit the killer whales in the Stanley Park Aquarium once every year. It was his way of letting us know that our city lay beside the ocean and we lived where we did only by Nature's good grace. The aquarium wasn't as crowded then as it became in later years; one could easily ask the whale tenders if one could touch the whales—their bright white leather spots, their black dorsals packed with steel, and their teeth of sharpened ivory drills circling meaty, clean pink tongues the size of a tabletop, swallowing buckets of platinum fish at one go. A decade later, when it became my own turn to take Megan to visit the whales, I discovered that Megan had already decided penning whales in a zoo was cruel—animal prison. She became an avid follower of any newspaper information about whales being captured or released, which struck a chord in me. One of my own stray childhood fears had been to wonder what a whale might feel like had it been born and bred in captivity, then released into the wild—into its ancestral sea—its limited world instantly blowing up when cast into the unknowable depths, seeing strange fish and tasting new waters, not even having a concept of depth, not knowing the language of any whale pods it might meet. It was my fear of a world that would expand suddenly, violently, and without rules or laws: bubbles and seaweed and storms and frightening volumes of dark blue that never end. I mention this as I consider what happened next in my life and as I consider the changes that followed.

A bird trilled above. I blinked and paused, and then I cried, because I knew that at that same moment three miles away in a crypt-like hospital room Karen was blinking, too—that after 6,719 days of sleep, she had just awakened.

PART TWO

15 | NO IMPERIAL CHILDREN

Imagine that for an unknown reason you have begun to rapidly lose your memory. You now no longer know what month it is, say, or what type of car you drive, or the season or the food in your refrigerator or the names of the flowers. Quickly, quickly your memory freezes—a tiny perfect iceberg, all memories frozen, *locked*. Your family. Your sex. Your name—all of it: turned into a silent ice block. You are free of memory: You now look at the world with the eyes of an embryo, not knowing, only seeing and only hearing. Then suddenly the ice melts, your memory begins returning. The ice is in a pond—it thaws and the water warms and the water lilies grow from your memories and fish swim within them. You are you.

And so here we have Karen, asleep for seventeen years, ten months, and seventeen days. Above Karen stands a nurse who changes her J-tube. This nurse has been changing J-tubes for a dozen years. She looks down at Karen and feels nothing and thinks of other things—her choir practice that night, a wool coat she saw on sale at the Bay.

The nurse remembers that Karen will most likely die shortly from her pneumonia—no heroics. *Really?* She seems to have recovered rather well from the illness that brought her in. She pauses and looks more closely at Karen: poor thing—nearly killed off this time. Back to Inglewood and then what? Better dead than alive. No love, no past, no future, no present, no sex. A sad thing. Half a person. Yet even now, almost seventeen years later, prettiness is evident from Karen's bones. What she has missed in life! The nurse looks away from Karen's face and resumes J-tube procedure.

111

Then the nurse hears a voice, gentle, husky, girlish, and direct, like pumice rubbing on pumice: "*Hello.*"

The nurse looks up. Karen rasps *hello* once more. The nurse sees Karen's eyes—clean and green as moss, crinkled with crusted sleep in the corners. She sees Karen's turkey-giblet neck keel sideways on the bed. Karen is immobile, but she speaks: "*That tickles.*"

The nurse says, "Oh my! Oh . . . *my!*" and then dashes from the room. She runs to fetch the doctor on duty—Wendy, Dr. Chernin.

Nurse, comes the thought.

Karen thinks: *That was a nurse. I am in a hospital. I . . . Wait: who am—I? I am Karen . . . Where am I? What time is it?* Karen loses her grogginess quickly, though; she feels her brain now starting to rev and then backfire like a rib-ticklish Camaro. The last thing Karen remembers is being with Wendy and Pam outside a party on Eyremont Drive—a house-wrecker, a stupid party. She had gone skiing with Richard just before that. They had made love. She remembered giggling with the girls, having a drink, and thinking of maybe telling them about her and Richard. And then she remembers nothing. Why nothing? Karen understands that if she's in a hospital, she must have passed out, maybe, and badly at that. *What did I have—two Valiums? Vodka? Surely not just this . . . God, what a hangover. Mom to deal with. Oh, God.*

Darkness. Darkness headed her way. A dream? She remembers her fear of darkness and her wish that she might sleep forever so as to avoid it—an idle wish gone badly wrong.

She closes her eyes against the early sun now beaming through the window and then opens her eyes and looks down at her body. *Oh God—where's my body?—I can't feel my legs. I can't move—I—*

She screams weakly and then coughs and can no longer scream. Another nurse enters the room, eyes agog, and Karen hacks out more words: "*Water. Please, water.*"

*　　*　　*

Back at the party house of Hillary Markham, most of the guests have gone home. Hillary, still flying on a cocktail of upwardly lifting substances, surveys the comical remains of her party—costume remnants, pumpkin fragments, and dozens of stale, lipsticked wineglasses and bottles of skunked beer. Teddy Liu and Tracy are asleep on the couch; Linus is on the guest room floor along with Hillary's two cats.

Hillary goes into her bedroom and sees a few coats still lying on the bed, at which points she hears two *thunk* sounds. Walking into her bathroom, she finds Hamilton lying on the floor, bone-white, jaws agape; Pam is in the bathtub, head leaning sideways, hair flowing over the tub's rim. She is as white as Hamilton. There's not even time for panic. *What to do? What to do? Teddy! Teddy Liu—paramedic!* She runs into the living room and screams and kicks awake Teddy from sleep inside his race-car driver's costume. Within a minute, Hamilton and Pam have been hooked up to drips going into their arms containing Narcan, an anti-opiate drug, and D5W solution. Breathing apparatuses are installed, and they lurch off to Lions Gate Hospital.

Almost immediately, the two emerge from their all-too-deep sleep. "You stupid bastard, Teddy," Hamilton shouts. "That was the best fucking high I've ever had. Why the hell did you go and fuck it up?"

"Sticks and stones."

"Teddy—where *are* we?" Pam moans.

"You're both on the way to Lions Gate," Teddy says.

"Oh, shit," says Pam. "It was feeling so good."

"Linus, is that you?" asks Pam.

"Yup."

"Tell these bastards to sod off."

Karen's nurse knows that Karen is somebody close to Dr. Wendy Chernin—family? She notifies the nursing desk about Karen, then speeds down to Emergency where Dr. Chernin is on call. "Dr. Chernin," she puffs, "your friend!"

Wendy, preoccupied with two gurneys rattling into Emergency, says, "I know, I *know*."

The nurse is confused: "But . . ."

Wendy, the paramedics, and the two bodies on gurneys zip by, followed by a stringy-looking young man the nurse recognizes from a Christmas party as Dr. Chernin's husband. As well, there's a teenage girl dressed all in black, perhaps as a witch for Halloween, eyes darkened out like the old glamour days of Alice Cooper.

The first gurney carries a serene blond woman, a bluish shade of white underneath an asphyxiator; the face looks familiar— magazines? TV? The nurse has seen celebrities here before. No big deal. On the other gurney lies a thirtyish man with some dreadful skin disease. AIDS? He is the sickest-looking admitted patient this nurse has ever seen. He is also screaming at the top of his lungs, telling everybody to fuck off and demanding more heroin. The nurse asks the paramedic what has happened, and she receives a reply—one that is, by 1997, all too common: "China White. OD'd at a Halloween party." The nurse now understands that the sick-looking man is wearing makeup. A dreadful costume.

The gurney moves on and the stringy-looking man, Dr. Chernin's husband, speaks to the young witch: "Megan, what are you doing *here*? How in hell did you know about *this*?"

Megan says, "I only came down here to help Jenny Tyrell get a morning-after pill. She drove me. And then I just saw you guys come in. So—what is it? What's wrong?"

"They're toasted on heroin," Linus says.

"Oh, wow. Hey! Aunt Wendy, Wendy quick, tell me, are they gonna *die*? For real? That China White—"

"Megan, we'll talk later." Wendy turns around and talks to an orderly.

Linus tries to imagine the world without Ham and Pam. He feels sick and his stomach burns. He remembers visiting Jared nearly twenty years ago, and he thinks of Karen in Inglewood all these years, her blank eyes focused on death and nothingness. Poor Richard, having to live with that forever. The hospital is a place where lives come to an end. This is a place that erases hope. He admires Wendy so much for having the guts to work in such a place, for being an emergency specialist.

How long had they been shooting up? Idiots. Fuck 'em. Pam and Ham clank into Intensive Care. They are injected, pumped, and probed; new IV's are inserted, more Narcan administered. Wendy is frustrated because there is no single test to administer to heroin OD's that can tell her where she stands. No CAT scans, white blood cell counts, or T4s—she never really knows: '*Is this person lost?*'

The heads are moved back and forth—the "Doll's Eye" procedure—to check the neurological system.

The poorly breathing bodies are briefly put into the ventilator. They are fine and will be sleeping for a few hours. The worst is over and Wendy emerges. *They'll make it,* Wendy says. And then she, Megan, and Linus sit in the lobby trying to relax after the close call. The thought of losing two more lifelong friends is more frightening than they could have imagined. Cold air puffs in from outside and they shiver. Wendy feels as if she has an icicle embedded in her spine from the small of her back and into her brain. She is now off duty for the night. Meanwhile, the nurse from Karen's floor approaches the trio and says, "Dr. Chernin, I *really* have to tell you . . ."

"Yes?" Wendy tries to hide her weariness and relaxes her chest. "I'm out of line. What did you need?"

"I thought you should know that your friend is talking now."

"Talking? She should be out cold for the next four hours—and then some. We gave them seda—"

"No. No. Not *those* friends. That . . . *old* friend of yours. The one in a coma. She's up in 7-E. Karen."

Wendy turns around to Linus and Megan and their bodies curdle; small hairs on the necks prickle; their arms become weightless. They have entered a mesmerizing and frightening realm. The nurse says, "You must know the girl—she's been in a coma for fifteen years now. Karen."

"Seventeen," says Linus instantly. Megan feels like vomiting.

"She said hello to me twice. Her eyes were clear and intelligent. She's all there, all right."

115

Wendy looks at her friends; glances are exchanged. Linus's brain empties as though passing through a trapdoor in the floor. Within moments, the three race down the ozone putty corridor and then endure a long, tense elevator ride. Nobody speaks, and a few breaths later they arrive in Karen's room, now buzzing with staff. Karen is crying. Someone is about to give her a sedative, and Wendy grabs the needle and throws it into the trash. "No. Don't *do* that. Jesus. That's how she ended up here in the first place. No drugs of *any* sort. None. Ever. Everybody—out . . . *out*!" Everybody clears the room save for her, Megan, and Linus. Wendy says, "Karen. It's me. Wendy. I'm here, honey."

Karen raises her eyes, her hysteria dwindling: "Wendy? Is that *you*, Wendy?"

Wendy walks forward, kneels down, and puts her left arm on Karen's shoulder. She then wipes her eyes with the other hand. "Hey, Karen? Yeah—it's me, Wendy. I'm here, girl." Wendy has been a doctor long enough to know that Karen's awakening is a miracle. She tries to keep her composure as she has done throughout her life, but now she isn't sure she can do it.

"Wendy—what happened to me—my body—I can't move. I can't see any of it. What the hell's happened?"

"You've been asleep for a long time, Karen. A coma. Don't worry. You'll get your body back. Soon." Wendy is hoping that her face doesn't betray this last lie.

"Oh, Wendy. I'm glad you're . . ." Karen closes her eyes. Several breaths later, she reopens them. Her eyes dart sideways. "Is that Linus?" Karen's voice is rasping, like beard stubble rubbing on paper. Linus comes over and sits beside Wendy.

"Hey there, Karen. Welcome home." He kisses her forehead. Karen lies there and looks into the eyes of her friends. They are older. Much older. This is not right.

"My body," Karen says. "Where's my *body*?" She cries once more. "I'm a fucking pretzel."

"Shhh," Wendy says. "You've been gone a long time. You *will* get your body back. You will. I'm a doctor now. We missed you, honey. We missed you so badly."

Karen looks about, her eyes darting. She asks Linus how old she is now. "You're thirty-four, Kare."

"Thirty-*four*. Oh, *God*."

Linus says, "Don't worry, Kare—your twenties suck. Believe me, be glad you missed them."

"Linus, what *year* is it?"

"It's 1997. Saturday, November the first, 1997, 6:05 a.m."

"Oh. Oh, *God*. Oh, *my*! My family—how's my family?"

"All fine. Alive and well."

"And Richard?"

"Pretty good. In good shape. He's visited you once a week all these years."

She focuses on Megan, standing by the door. "And *you*—you by the door. I—I think I know you."

"No," Megan says. Megan feels bashful for one of the few times in her life.

"Come here," Karen says, because there is something about this teenager that Karen has been told—by whom? She remembers the Moon. She remembers talking to Richard on the Moon. Bullshit. Nonsense. "Come here. Please." Megan meekly shuffles forward, nearly paralyzed with hope, anticipation, sickness, and fear. Karen looks over Megan calmly. "You're related to me—aren't you?" Megan nods. "A sister?"

"No."

Karen is now understanding just how long she's been gone. She focuses on Megan as though she were a difficult algebra equation. Her brows knit. "What's your name?"

"Megan."

Karen thinks out loud: "Mom had a daughter once—a miscarriage. 1970? The name was Megan."

Megan buckles. She walks to the bed and hops onto its metal ricketiness and lies down beside her mother as she did the first time she met her. She places her face directly before Karen's and they look at each other, retina to retina, brain to brain. *Who is this creature?* Karen is now calm about this scenario. She knows that answers will come. She says to Megan,

117

"You're very pretty, you know," to which Megan sniffles, saying, "I am *not*."

Karen asks, "And I've never seen makeup like yours, either. Concert last night?"

"I wear it all the time. If you want I'll take it off. I really will." She gouges her palms into the eyes.

"Stop," croaks Karen. "Stop."

Megan is trembling. "I took your makeup off once, too," Megan says. "The first time I ever saw you. I was seven."

Karen is silent. She pauses and looks at the ceiling and sighs and meditates: *This must surely be a sister, but she says she isn't. And she looks like Richard.* "How's Mom and Dad?"

The floodgates open: "I—I've been a . . . a . . . real *shit* to them. I'm a horrible person. And you're awake. Mom—my real Mom."

Karen is unable to move her neck, but her eyes are focused deeply on the boo-hooing teenager clutched against her right side. "I never thought you'd wake up. And now you *have* and I see I've just been *horrible* to *everybody*." Megan uses her tears to wipe off her eyeliner and kohl. Her eye sockets are a mess.

"*Shhhh . . .*" whispers Karen. "It's over now. All over. I'm here." Karen thinks over the outburst. *Mom?* "Megan, did you call me *Mom*?"

"Yeah. Because you *are*. My mom, I mean."

Karen is faint: "What are talking abou—Oh, *man*." The night with Richard on Grouse Mountain? This is not possible.

"I've wanted to talk to you all these years. Did you like punk rock? It's coming back in now."

This last comment distracts Karen. Suddenly, Megan is off on a tangent discussing the Buzzcocks and Blondie. Karen, meanwhile, assembles pieces. She notices the absence of a mirror in the room. Hair that has fallen into her face tells her she has gone gray. In spite of her bedridden condition and seventeen-year-old mind, she knows that *she* is going to have to be the mature one here.

As she thinks this, Wendy is taking pulses and doing medical thingies. Outside in the corridor, employees are quietly milling

118

about. News is spreading quickly. A friend of a patient down in the lobby has phoned the city desk of a local paper. Wendy has asked staff to clear away from the room.

Karen says, "And Wendy . . . there's something wrong. I can tell. Wendy. Wait—what are all of you *doing* here? I mean, it's Sunday morning. How did you *know* I was—that *this* was going to happen?"

"We didn't," Wendy says, recognizing the morning's coincidences. "We had no idea."

Megan butts in, as though imparting hot gossip, "Hamilton and Pammie OD'd on heroin last night. They're down in Intensive Care. They're, like, com*plete* heroin addicts now. Linus was at a party with them. Wendy fixed them up an hour ago."

"*Thank* you, Megan," Wendy says.

Karen thinks. "They're doing *her*oin? At thirty-four? That's so old. That's *my* age."

"Heroin's big these days," says Linus.

"Ugh."

All of the dramatic things Wendy and Linus had once planned on saying upon Karen's reawakening have vanished— *poof*. Instead, they discuss the commonplace. "Hey, Wendy— do I still *smoke*?"

"Not anymore, hon." Then Wendy says, more to herself than to anyone present, "You *know*, I just can't understand the coincidences—Ham and Pam, Megan, Linus, and then *you*. That leaves Richard, I suppose. No doubt he'll be traipsing in soon."

Karen looks at her arm, bony, defleshed, and prisoner-of-war—useless looking. "Shit. Just *look* at me, Wendy. I was gonna go to Hawaii. Whatta disaster. I look like a praying mantis." Karen is now oddly objective about her body—her *self*. She looks up at Wendy. And then she yawns. "Hey there, Wendy—I saw you watch me yawn. Don't sweat it. I'm going to be falling asleep soon. But it'll only be *normal* sleep. I won't be going into deep freeze ever again." She blinks. How does she know this?

119

Wendy asks again how Karen feels. "Woozy—and thirsty, too. Is there lemonade here? I get really thirsty here in 1997. There's a tube in my belly button!" A small kerfuffle explodes in the corridor and Gatorade and a straw are produced from somebody's lunch bag. "My tongue," she says. "It feels like a box of kitty litter. Linus, can you go get my parents? I don't want them to hear about this over the phone. Can you do that?"

"Sure."

"Good. When they arrive, and if I'm asleep, don't wake me up." She pauses. "That sounds sick. Just ask them to wait. I'll be back."

Megan gives Karen a peck on the cheek, then resumes lying against her mother.

Wendy tallies all of Karen's vital signs now. Everything, is about as normal as can be given the extraordinary conditions. Megan is resting like a papoose against Karen's back. "Look— I got your fingernails," Megan says. "And your hair, too. Well, it's gray now. We'll dye it together. My friend Jenny's really good."

"Why are you dressed in all black?" Karen asks.

Megan now feels immature. She doesn't want to tell her mother that she views herself as Death—the cause of so much darkness. "It's a phase. It's over now."

Linus is on a chair beside the bed, happy. Linus thinks the world is a cruel place, and in his mind he is thinking of the deserts he used to walk through, the endless crappy little small towns and the meanness of the world, and yet here, from nowhere really, blooms a flower. Such moments are so rare, as rare as the ruby plucked from a salmon's guts that he remembers from childhood. That ruby—it had been only a piece of taillight plastic found when gutting the salmon on the docks up at Pender Harbour, but to Linus it was a ruby.

Karen attempts to stay awake and savor her new consciousness. She is glad to have friends nearby and her magical daughter talking beside her. The staff have been shooed away, and among the four in the room, a tension exists—a sense of giddiness shared by all, giddiness from having witnessed an emotional reawakening not unlike the thawing of Niagara Falls, the sheaths of ice calving off the shale in thick, glorious blocks. The people in the room feel enchanted—*chosen*.

"We're going to have to move you as soon as possible, Karen. The media's changed quite a bit since 1980 and we don't want them vulturing around you." Wendy makes a phone call. "*Yes. Full. Normal. Immediately. Yeah. Yeah. Thirty minutes.* Just try to do it. Thanks.'

Richard is no longer drunk. He is a silver-clad astronaut climbing up a dirt bank, the soil rich and crumbly and moist as canned dog food. He reaches Capilano Road above and then lumbers at a pronounced clip through the roads and the subdivisions, counting the colorful dead fireworks and fragments of pumpkin craniums at his feet. Above him, the sun rises under a sky the color of a navel orange—a color one would like to *eat*. Tangy. Richard walks along Edgemont Boulevard to Delbrook, then down across the Westview overpass. A taxi driver going off duty slows and asks if he needs a lift, and soon he is at the hospital's front, where the local news vans are parked. Richard's costume in itself has become another unusual sight on what has already been an extraordinary day. He sees a camera crew and press people making a silent scrum toward the elevators. A nurse who has known Richard for over a decade admits him into the elevator. Somebody asks, "Hey, who's *he*?"

"It's the boyfriend. Hey, you—*boyfriend*—what can you tell us?"

Richard exits the elevator on Karen's floor. The nurses recognize him anxiously and hold their breath as he walks down the corridor, silver, powerful and serene, breathing deeply, as an astronaut might well do on a foreign planet. He hears his breath from inside his chest. He walks in the room and sees Wendy and Linus there. They smile and politely leave the room. Richard kisses Karen on the lips.

"Hey, Beb. I'm back," Karen says.

"Hi, honey. Welcome home," Richard says. "I missed you always." He lowers himself onto his knees before her and kisses her again.

Silence. They stare into each other's eyes with all the intensity of two people in the flush of first love. "They haven't allowed me to look in a mirror, Richard. I know I look like a rat's ass."

"You're beautiful."

"Flatterer. So much for Hawaii."

"I see you met our daughter."

Megan props herself up on an elbow beside her mother. "Hey, Dad."

"Hey, sugar-cakes."

An awkward silence ensues. "This is whacked," Megan says. "Come on. Get up. Hop onboard. There's just enough room."

Richard unzips and removes the top of his astronaut's outfit, which peels away from his body down to his belly button like a chrome banana skin. He climbs onto the bed and Karen becomes a human hot-meat sandwich, a witch on one side, an astronaut on the other. Karen feels as if they are all in a row boat, floating, going someplace new. This is a dream, but it's not. Richard feels as though he has found a vein of gold inside his heart, a klondike of feelings he had thought long buried.

Karen says, "You smell sweaty, Richard."

Richard says, "I walked over here from Cleveland Dam." A pause. "It's a long story."

"We're all tired now, aren't we, gang?" Karen says. "Wanna sleep?"

And they *do* want to sleep as they realize that they're all tired from walking, from hoping, from waiting, from losing faith and from finding it once more. Richard has his arm under Karen's head. "Yeah, let's go to sleep. It's been so long. And we're tired."

"Look at us," Megan whispers to both Karen and Richard with a happiness she once long ago reserved exclusively for small animals, birthday cake, and roller coasters: "We're a real family. At last. And for*ever*. And I'm not Death anymore, am I, Dad?"

Richard whispers back, "No, but you never were."

And the three drift toward sleep.

"And what's with the costumes?" Karen asks almost inaudibly before falling asleep.

"Costumes? *What* costumes?" Megan and Richard answer in stereo, drifting along with Karen in their boat that will not tip.

16 | THE FUTURE AND THE AFTERLIFE ARE DIFFERENT THINGS ALTOGETHER

Stereo.

Floors away, Hamilton and Pam are now entering new thought cycles. While their brains are too taxed to generate pictures, they are, however, able to hear words, sounds, and music. A choir. Noises as though from heaven: sweet and seductive and lush. Words. Anyone looking at their Intensive Care'd bodies would never know of the concerts akimbo within their minds. *Oranges and lemons, say the bells of Saint Clement* . . .

And then, only after this music peaks, do pictures begin to appear—a slide show: a Houston freeway empty save for a car parked here and there; a rain of mud falling on the houses of suburban Tokyo; African veldts on fire; Indian rivers like thick stews, churning corpses and silks oceanward; a time/temperature sign on a Florida Chrysler dealership flashing 00:00/140°.

A nurse on duty, meanwhile, watches the two patients. Something is wrong. Off. Not right. And then the nurse notices it: the two patients are detoxifying in stereo. Their heads twist or nod in sympathy. They jerk together—a rehearsed dance of death. She calls another nurse, who records the action on her brother's VCR-cam that she had meant to return later that afternoon.

A minute or two later, the intensity of Hamilton and Pam's synchronized show begins to involve spastic arm motions and leg jerks—they are frightened of what they see and are warding off perils. Their life signals leap and jag, copies of each other.

And then the dance is over. The patients resume their own individual sleeps, and the videotape is saved for later.

*   *   *

This was not supposed to happen.

Lois navigates the Buick as though it were a cumbersome pleasure craft. Hand in glove, she changes gears. George weeps uncontrollably beside her. The implications of today's hospital visit are so fraught with meaning that the two find themselves unable to communicate save for minor grunts. (*Seatbelt on? Yes. Okay.*) Their hopes have leapfrogged too far ahead of them, and how could their hopes *not* do so? Just two hours ago they might never have imagined feeling as extreme as they feel now. Linus rang the doorbell shortly after nine. George, puttering in the kitchen, was sipping coffee, wondering which azalea he might prune in the afternoon; Lois lay upstairs in bed, half asleep, idly deciding whether to clean out the Christmas decorations. And then came Linus. They had thought that Karen might be dead—the lung condition. Instead, "*Karen's awake, Mr. and Mrs. McNeil, and she's talking normally and everything. She asked for you. I think she wants you to go there.*"

George and Lois had reacted with whitening faces, knotted tongues, and the clotted taste of blood in their throats—each for different reasons. George, receiving the one thing he had truly ever wanted in life, and Lois because she feels a wallop of guilt for having ignored Karen across the many years—having given up all hope and lying to George about having visited her. And Lois remembers that she was the one who wanted to "pull the plug"; Lois is the one who just yesterday asked the hospital for "no heroics—*Just let her go this time.*"

Suddenly, Lois has to imagine herself as a citizen of a world containing hope, and it frightens her; it makes her dizzy. And she realizes she may have *two* daughters who hate her now, instead of just one. There is a flood inside her head, like the broken trees and mud and cracked boulders she once saw burbling down a mountain as a child in northern British Columbia.

After Linus had delivered the news, George slumped down on a stool below a macramé owl and cried. Lois rubbed his shoulders and told Linus that they would dress properly and be at the hospital shortly. A phone call to Wendy confirmed Karen's awakening.

"Daddy?"

George heard the words and fell into the phone.

"Is that you, Daddy? It's me. Karen."

George is unable to breathe. Lois fears a heart attack.

"It's me. I'm here. I'm confused. My stomach itches."

Lois grabs the receiver from George. "Karen?"

'Mom?"

"I—hi, honey."

"Hi, Mom."

"You okay?"

"I can't really move. Come down. I'm hungry."

"George, stop crying. Karen? We're coming down right now."

"Are you at Rabbit Lane?"

"Same as always. George, do be quiet. Say hello to Karen, for God's sake."

"Hi."

"Hi, Daddy."

George is in floods again. Lois yanks away the receiver: "Hang in there, Karen. We'll be there right away."

Megan is nowhere to be seen. *She's at Richard's*. Lois throws on a twin-set and pearls and spackles the ridges time has eroded into her face. George bumbles into his one "good suit" and has a small jerk as he remembers that *this* was the suit he bought for Karen's funeral.

Upon leaving the house, a Valium-enriched Lois is pleased that she has kept her figure and her hair is shiny. Time has hardly touched her. These are tiny, fleeting thoughts.

The Saturday itself is cold and clear. Their breath steams. Most of the leaves have fallen and Lois rolls down the window and thinks of Karen as the hospital comes ever closer.

Lois has always kept her feelings on her comatose daughter to herself. George has only seen Lois shed tears once. There was one night maybe ten years ago when she and George had

126

been watching TV. There was a news program on, a show about a crazy man down in Texas who had poisoned a famous historical tree. The citizens of the town were trying to save the tree's life, pumping water through the soil to wash away the poison, but the tree was confused. The tree lost its ability to detect seasons. It became lost in time and would shed leaves and then resprout them in fall and then in winter. Its leaves fluttered and fell earthward one last time, and the tree died in the end. Lois felt herself losing her breath as she watched this. She went into the kitchen, stood by the cutting board, and tried to compose her thoughts, but the tears broke through and she fell to the floor, a pond of tears in her right hand. The kitchen was dark and the linoleum cold, but George came in, said, "Hush, dear," and held her. They sat together on the kitchen floor, the TV playing in the background.

A stop sign.

Lois thinks of Karen—of how much of herself she had seen in Karen but never let her know. Karen, so smart. So full of beans. Lois remembers how she felt after the coma had begun—dry and hollow like the empty plastic flower tubs in the garage. Lois thinks of the three miscarriages she has had, especially Megan the First, born in 1970, who died at birth, taking some small but essential part of Lois away with her. The experience made Lois feel like a car with no ignition key.

And Lois thinks of Richard—such a dolt at the beginning when Megan was born. Then he became a drunk. And he switched careers again and again. No stability. Yet only recently has Richard come to feel like true family and seems to have leveled out. He isn't so daft these days. He tries to make adult decisions. He is sensible. "No, George," she had said last month, "he's doesn't have all his ducks in a row yet, but he's on the right path. Or let's hope."

Local TV cameras and lighting men throng inside the hospital lobby and the visitors' parking lot. There are trucks with satellite links, news reporters having makeup applied—a sedate but purposeful circus. George and Lois know the cause of this scene, and they instinctively scurry into a side entrance that George has sometimes used over the years. They slip down corridors and bump into a nurse who beams with pleasure at seeing them. She escorts them to Karen's new room. "It's such a miracle," says the nurse. "Never have I . . . well, I'm sure you *know* what I mean."

At the room there are people milling around outside the door. George and Lois see Wendy and beeline her way. Wendy smiles: "She's having a small nap right now. Not a coma. Simply a nap. Richard and Megan are in there sleeping with her, but don't worry about that. It's good for her. She needs to be held. I've given orders nobody except family be admitted. You saw the posse downstairs."

Karen awakens from her nap soundlessly. She hears Wendy on a phone over by the door. She sees and feels Richard and Megan on either side of her, their breath, their heat. How did this happen? Why am I here now? Seventeen years. *Ooh.* Has the world changed *much*? Has the world changed or have I changed? Richard is no longer cute—he's . . . handsome, and hairy now, so much broader than he was . . . last *night*? He's a man now. Larger. A man. Good looking, but—a *man*, not a teen. He smells differently than he did last night—no—the same yet more intense. Megan, too. A daughter? A dream! *But only last night I was young and alive.* Megan smells like fresh white corn, fresh from the cob, a sweet scent of youth. Karen wonders if Megan and Richard are friends. Does Megan like Mom? Maybe. Probably not. Mom makes it so hard for people to like her. Why does she do that? *My stomach hurts*, she thinks. And it tickles, too. *Cramping.* Hunger. A tube into my stomach. *Gross.* Have I had periods over the years? Now? Will I be able to eat solids? I'm not even a baby now. *I'm a fetus.* Why is my head so clear, so lucid?

Karen tries to move an arm and the effort is torture. Her nose itches, but her tendons are too unexercised for her to reach and scratch. Her body is in complete but dreadfully

128

creaky shape. Her jaw hurts and she feels like a chopped-down tree. *I'm so far gone. My body! Wait—this is too much. I can't worry about this now.* She is immobile but alert, and she is curious. She shuts her eyes and opens them and finds all that she sees hard to believe. She doesn't want to talk to strangers. She wants it to be Sunday morning. She wants it to be just any other day. Just imagine—all the other people in the world have been awake for seventeen years!

Wendy leaves the room; there's noise outside the door; she comes back with a phone—no cord—and seeing that Karen's awake, asks her to say hi to Mom and Dad, which seems odd as she only just saw them last night. After the call, she quizzed Wendy: "What year is it again, Wendy?"

"1997."

"Oh. Oh *my*."

"Karen, I want to ask you a favor." Wendy's voice was hedgy. "Hamilton and Pam are really sick, but they'll be okay soon enough. They need something to give them hope."

"They're hopeless?"

"In a way. They're without hope. It's in their heads. Can I bring them up here with you? It'll help them."

"Are they really doing drugs?"

Doing drugs—what an old-fashioned word. "Yes. Pathetic as it sounds. Drugs are different these days. You'll learn it all soon. How do you feel?"

"Fantastically awake. They OD'd?"

"Yup."

"Bring them in—I want to have lots of people around me. But only people I know."

"Your mom won't be too thrilled."

"I'll deal with her." She smacks her lips. "Can I have a sip of water?" Wendy rushes over and holds a glass. Karen notices her wedding ring. "Thanks. How long have you and Linus been married?"

George and Lois nudge the door open soundlessly. The room is dim. The parents are startled to see Megan and Richard

129

there on the bed with her—unorthodox, but then hospitals aren't the same citadels of reflex cruelty and loneliness they once were. Richard is snoring and Megan is breathing warmly. And there is Karen. Her eyes are open and smiling. "Hi, Mom. Hi, Dad," she says under her breath. "*Shhhhh* . . . the kids are asleep." Her jaw aches.

Her voice! She's back! George blubbers while smooching Karen's cheeks, oblivious to the scene he creates. "Hi Dad." George is lost to emotion, as Karen smiles and raises happy eyebrows over George's shoulders toward Lois. Karen winks. It is hard for Karen to be sentimental, because in her mind she has only had a quick nap since 1979.

Richard awakens just then. "Hi, George. Oh. *Excuse me.* Here. *Oh.* Let me move out of the way and down off this thing. Lois. Hi—" Richard clambers off, the top part of his silver astronaut suit dragging behind him like a beaver tail. George hugs Richard. Lois, meanwhile, has stayed away from the bed. Her purse is clutched to her chest. She comes nearer. She locks eyeballs with her daughter.

"Hey, *Mom*," Karen says.

There is a silence. "Hello, Karen." Another silence. "Welcome back." Lois gives Karen a small kiss.

George and Richard shut up. Karen sees that time has done little to alter her mother. Some gray hair here, a wrinkle there—the posture and voice are timeless. "You look as good as ever, Mom," Karen says.

"Thank you, Dear." Lois has not visited Karen for almost a year now. She is finding it hard to overlook Karen's deterioration. "Can you eat now, Sweetie? Are you hungry?" The old food games have begun already. "I brought an owl figurine to cheer you up."

"Thanks." It's as if seventeen years have never happened.

Megan touches her mother, holds her neck and rubs it with her hands. Karen's gray hair is limp and sad and has been cut with blunt scissors; Megan holds it to her nose and the hair smells dusty and sweet. All her life Megan has felt jinxed, that

130

people around her would come to bad ends. Richard, too, has felt the same way for years, though neither of them knew it of the other. Megan has been dressing in black for so long now, and has been chasing an early death; it seemed only fitting—the drugs, the fearsome boyfriends, and the fast cars. Why would anybody miss her? Richard—whoops *Dad*—might miss her, but then he'd most likely go drink himself into the center of the Earth to forget her. That's unfair. He *did* quit drinking for real. But then didn't he fob her off on Lois and George? *Lois*—glad to have me out of her hair. George? George is nice, but he's always liked Karen better.

Megan soon accompanies Richard, Lois, George, Wendy, and Linus into another room. The hallways have been cleared. Wheels squeak. It's quiet.

The group arrives at a new, larger room. Inside, Uncle Hamilton and Aunt Pam are already there, conked out in separate beds, resembling dead extras in a sci-fi movie. *Drugged out losers*, Megan thinks, but then she reminds herself that she really has no right to condemn on that front. Where does this judgmental streak come from? Megan decides she's going to go straight edge: She's never going to do a drug ever again. Even aspirin. She is going to be the mother that Karen never had. She is going to protect her—keep her smart, make her whole. And then Megan remembers why she is even *at* the hospital: last night with Skitter on the mattress in Yale's basement, a pot dealer friend of Skitter. She'd told Linus that the morning-after pill was for her friend, Jenny, but it wasn't. Megan knows that she is pregnant. It was meant to be.

"*I want them all in the same room because they'll all give each other incentive to get well.*"

Pam and Hamilton hear Wendy's voice and open their fogged eyes to see white curtains. They hear background snatches of other voices. Hamilton's throat hacks up a clump of blood-phlegm; Wendy, standing beside him, says poker-faced, "Welcome back to prime time, douche bag."

"Wendy? *Ooh.* Ahh. I feel like a paper sack of burning dog shit. What *time* is it?"

"Time to change your life, you screwed-up junkie."

"Hamilton—are you *there?*" calls Pam.

"Assuming we're not dead, yes, dear. What time is it, Wendy? Where *are* we? What are we doing here?" Lifting his head feels like lifting a swarm of hornets.

"It's Saturday, *kids.* And *you* are both in the hospital. You're here for emergency supernumerary mammectomies."

"Super *what?*"

"We're removing your third nipples."

"*What?* Ow! Don't talk like that, Wendy."

"Hospital humor. It's my style—oh and don't give me that little wounded look: '*Ooh, I'm so surprised.*' You came one eyelash close to death, you bastard." She walks over and looks into Hamilton's eyes and then slaps him gently.

"Ow, *shit*, Wendy, whaddya do *that* for? You screwed up a fantastic high. I was on a roll last night."

"*Why?* You were almost *dead* last night, scuzz bucket." Wendy approaches Pam in the bed to the left and pecks her on the forehead. "You both scared the hell out of us. You're too old to be so pathetic doing junk. I don't need to be friends with junkie losers. And having said that, I want you to sit up and have a look across the room."

Pam says, "My head hurts, I—"

"Just *look*, you two losers."

With two push-button controls, Wendy elevates Pam and Hamilton's backrests, then opens the curtains, allowing them to see Richard and Karen across the room; Richard is holding Karen's arm, wagging it back and forth, and the two of them are making faces. Karen is wearing a shirt Lois brought along with her—the same Levi's shirt she wore in high school: rough cotton, embroidered parakeets.

George and Lois and Megan are parked on stools, and Lois looks furious, first at Wendy and then at Hamilton: "Wendy, I don't think there's anything useful to come of having two . . . *drug addicts* in the room. They're the worst possible influence, and just *look* at Hamilton. What a dreadful sight to wake up to after seventeen years. There must be some sort of rule about this."

"Lois," Wendy says, "I had to pull a whack of strings to get them all in here. You think this was *easy*?"

"But they're so . . . *ugh*."

"Once more, Lois, it will be *good* for them to be together. They all need support."

"Oh, God. This *is* a hallucination," says Hamilton.

"Hi, Hamilton," Karen says. "Who'd you take to the prom?"

Pam, not fully clicked in to the tableau across the room, pipes up and hears the voice—Karen is back from McDonald's. "Karen? You're *here*!"

"Hi kids," says Karen. "How was grad? I missed it. As you know."

"Oh, oh—you wouldn't *believe* it; Hamilton took Cindy *Webber*. A computer date. I went with Raymond Merlis."

"No!"

"Yes, and—"

"I did *not* have a computer date," Hamilton interjects.

133

"Oh shut your gob. No one would take you."

"Did Raymond remove Keith for the night?" Keith is their name for the single strand of wiry hair growing from a mole on Raymond Merlis's face.

Instantly, Pam and Karen relapse into their older, younger selves, like exotic birds chattering in a mango tree. Pam tries to step out of bed and stumbles toward Karen, but her body aches and she's unable to stand up. Her knees buckle. The activated granulated charcoal given to her earlier seems to have sunk like ball bearings into her lower colon. Hamilton, meanwhile, is nauseated and feels as though he's lying on a dock in choppy weather. He vomits Halloween chocolate and dead martinis into a bedside bucket while his muscles spasm and he feels the onset of scorch-and-burn diarrhea.

"Just so you know, Kare," Pam says, "Keith came, too."

"Wendy," Lois barks. "This is revolting. They're sick. I really must protest."

"Sickness is part of life, Lois."

"Mi scusa, everybody—" Pam begins to sweat and clam; her anxiety is escalating. Hamilton is already desperate for a fix, Pam not quite so, but soon she will be. "You can't say we're dull."

In the background Lois is saying, "Very well then, *Doctor* Chernin. I'm going to call my lawyer. George? Call my lawyer."

"Lois, be quiet," says George.

Karen has been awake a few days and has had some rare time alone with her thoughts. The first two days were such a circus that she had to ask Wendy to lock everybody out of the room save for Mom, Dad, Richard, and Megan.

Pam and Ham are now gone; she has the room to herself. She looks down at her body—bones marinated in liquid and only vaguely responsive to her will. She has already gained three pounds and she thinks this is a sick joke. She lifts her hand to where her breasts once were; she touches what is now mere parchment and bone, emits a squeak, and sighs.

She surveys her hospital room, her world, almost identical to the room she had during her appendix removal in third grade. Where has she *been* for seventeen years? What other world did she visit? She is furious with herself for not remembering. Her coma was dreamless, but she *knows* she went *to* some place real. Not the place you go when you die—some other place. She thinks back to the previous week, the week before the coma, and she remembers being chased by darkness. Darkness? *What?* Some of it returns to her. She was trying to find a way to cheat the darkness. And she lost in the end. *Shit.*

She tries to raise her arm but the sensation is as though she is trying to lift a telephone pole. Megan, her "surprise daughter," will be in soon to help her with stretching exercises. Megan and Lois and Richard are taking shifts. Her tendons apparently need to tenderize before muscle can rebuild. She feels as though she's an item on a menu.

Why has she been kept alive? She can't imagine the point of it. She's happy to be awake but is secretly appalled at the thought of the money and human effort it must have taken to keep her going for so long.

What has happened to the world? What has happened to the people in her world?

She's been awake just a little bit of time, but much is apparent. Richard: He's so different yet he still holds her the way he used to—bodies retain memories long after the mind forgets them. His face is so ravaged. Drinking? How did *that* happen? And Ham and Pam on *heroin?* Such a punch line. It's as though Karen walked through a door in 1979 and directly entered a health guidance class showing a film on the unmentioned perils of aging.

Wendy, working hard—too hard, it seems. She's not much in love with Linus—obvious to anybody—nor is Linus much in love with Wendy. His soul is full of glue. Karen seems to have understood everyone's life immediately; the others think she is too out of it—too clued out about the modern world—but Karen sees all. She remembers the innocent pointless aims of their youths (*Hawaii! Ski bum at Whistler!*) and sees that

135

they were never acted upon. But at the same time, larger aims were never defined. Her friends have become who they've become by default. Their dreams are forgotten, or were never formulated to begin with.

Her friends are not particularly happy—not with their lives. Pam had rolled her eyes when Karen asked her if she was happy.

"No."

"Fulfilled?"

"No."

"Creative?"

"A little."

Through the monsters they design and the TV shows they work on, they give vent to the loss they feel inside. Expressions of pettiness, loss, and corruption. She asked not to see any more of their FX photos. Yuck. The photos sit on a stack beside flowers from the mayor as well as from various studios and film production companies wishing to purchase rights to her life story.

On top of it all, the world itself has changed. Karen must try and absorb seventeen years of global changes. That can wait. And she thinks she'll go crazy if one more person tells her that the Berlin Wall came down and AIDS exists in the world.

One week later, Wendy still can't comprehend Karen's return to the living and her complete retention of *all* her brain power. Wendy knows the medical statistics. To others, Karen's awakening is a lottery win—a prize behind Door Number 3, a pair of snowmobiles. But to Wendy, Karen is a river running backward, a rose that blooms under moonlight—something transcendent, an epiphany.

Wendy thinks of Karen's long rehab road to reach the point where she will be able to perform simple everyday functions once more. Brittle bones; atrophied ligaments. Yet her face is already fully animated, and she smiles as clearly as always. Already her arms are now skittishly mobile, storky chopsticks reaching for gum and the squeeze bottle of water. Checks and balances. Karen is a time capsule—a creature from another era reborn, a lotus seed asleep for ten thousand years that springs to life as clear and true as though born yesterday.

Wendy is concerned about swamping Karen with too much information or too much novelty. As a doctor, she can limit certain things. Richard has been coming in with the annual volumes of the *World Book Encyclopedia* and teaching Karen about the new years leading up to 1997. He is already at 1989: the fall of the Berlin Wall, the AIDS quilt—Karen must be so amazed at this. And then there's crack. Cloning. Life on Mars. Velcro. Charles and Diana. MAC cosmetics. Imagine learning so much stuff at once.

Karen and Pam have spent some hours sifting through style magazines together; Wendy beamed with pleasure at the sight—so much like the old days. Good gossipy jags: "Oh, and Karen, food is amazing these days. It suddenly got good around 1988," Pam says, making Karen eager to try all the new food trends—Tex-Mex, Cajun, Vietnamese, Thai, Nouvelle, Japanese, Fusion, and California cuisine—"sushi, gourmet pizzas, tofu hot dogs, fajitas, flavored ice teas, and fat-free *everything*."

Lingering in the back of Wendy's mind, though, is the phenomenon of Hamilton and Pam having stereo heroin nightmares. The nurse showed Wendy the tape of stereo dreaming as well as parallel stalagmite brain readouts. So now Wendy has two medical mysteries on her hands at the same time. Best to keep the video hush. Pam and Hamilton are unaware it even exists. Best to scoot Karen home immediately—away from public intrusion.

Megan enjoys visiting her mother at the hospital, where she helps her flex her arms and legs and fingers. She has never been able to help others, and the sensation is as though she had opened her bedroom door and found an enormous new house on the other side full of beautiful objects and rooms to explore.

Megan is relieved that Karen has a good sense of humor and, though older, is technically the same age. "Megan, tell me, all the young girls I see on TV these days dress kind of, um . . ."

"Slutty?"

"Your word, not mine."

"It's Lois's word." Megan giggles. "Lois is from another era where girls had to be doormats. Nowadays we dress for strength. Didn't you?"

Karen ponders her adolescence: "No. I think we felt equal to guys but never more forceful than them."

"I guess that's a switch. Soon we'll have you going to the gym."

"I think I'm a bit far gone for that."

"Crap—*Mom*." Megan loves saying Mom with extra vim, as each mention is a small stab at Lois.

Yes, Karen is happy to see that Megan is rebellious—and that she talks back to Lois. Karen had never dared. Megan is also angry—at Richard and at her parents and at the world. And Karen is angry with Richard for being so shiftless in helping raise Megan. That's something to be dealt with in the future. Karen is mad and lost and found and bewildered. The new world lies before her eyes like an opened chest of treasure, a flock of birds over Africa, a thousand TVs all playing at once.

Wendy thinks:

Karen, unsurprisingly, is front-page news the world over; a medical oddity, a feature-section story, tabloid grist. Yet the only photo the media have is Karen's old high school photo. The media have been unable to snap a new picture of Karen; such a photo has become the golden fleece of journalism. There have been attempts to bribe relatives—Wendy herself was approached by a French photographer, Linus by the Germans. Such *cheek*. And to think that Karen never wanted to be photographed even at the best of times—it would be too cruel to exhibit her in such a frail, emaciated state.

Friends and family want to protect Karen and her innocence

from the modern world, the changes that have occurred since her sleep began. Her innocence is the benchmark of their jadedness and corruption. The world is hard now. The world doesn't like simplicity or relaxation.

The world also wants photos of Megan—the girl who met her dead mother. Dozens of photos of Megan abound, courtesy of her school-mates. She is the "Lost Child," the "Child of Corpse Born."

In particular, the US news networks have been fearsome in demanding interviews at top dollar and wide exposure. "Maybe in the future, Richard, but not now." What Karen *doesn't* tell Richard is that she feels the onset of some previously withheld news on the brink of making itself clear. From where? What? A message from the other side—from the place she went to for all those years. She needs to wait for the right moment to use it correctly.

18   EXTREME BODY FAILURE

Less than two weeks after awakening, Karen is taken home to Rabbit Lane. She has gained two more pounds; Lois changes her diapers and inspects her waste as though Karen were a Chinese Empress, reading meaning into her waste's patterns like tea leaves on a cup's bottom. "Mom, do that somewhere else, *pleeeze*."

"Dr. Menger says you can start on solids next week."

"Gee."

"No need to be sarcastic, young lady."

Once home, Karen is both relieved and annoyed by the absent signs of time's passage, by the same owls, furniture, knickknacks and carpets that adorn the house. Only Megan's room, once Karen's, gives evidence of time's march: posters of strange young pop stars engineered to disturb parents, unfamiliar and annoyingly provocative garments strewn hither and yon plus a plaque on the door made in wood shop: 'Megan's Space.'

Richard spends an inordinate amount of time in Karen's new room, which was previously George's never-used den. At night he sleeps on the floor beside Karen's bed, and sometimes on the bed with Karen. Thus the geography of their lives has become the same as when they were teenagers. The two of them quickly develop baby talk words between themselves and when they aren't together they begin to experience a sweet ache. Their conversation devolves into a secret patois and the two are wonderfully aware that they are in love.

"I look like a telethon child," she tells Richard. "My body may be interesting to others as a science project but that's all. I'm not sexy."

"Well *I'm* head over heels for *you*," says Richard.

"Toot toot, Beb," Karen says.

"*Ick*," says Megan, overhearing them speak, beginning to feel pangs of jealousy. Megan is allowed to be helpful, and enjoys being so, but between Lois and Richard, she feels the way she imagines a Best Supporting Actress must feel when she loses her Oscar. Megan and Karen have many chats, but they aren't as deep or intimate as her chats with Richard. Karen saves all her intimacy for Richard. How can she jimmy her way inside Karen's heart? Fashion? How pathetic. Dyeing Karen's hair was fun, and the new hairdo is at least serviceable. But that was just a few hours. She must try harder. Food? *Lois* has taken complete charge of both Karen's nutrition and her hospital functions. Lois is blissed out. Even a few days earlier, when a coyote from the canyon made off with the bison friche, Lois took the event with almost cheerful equanimity. "Nature's way. *Sigh*. Here, Karen—freshly squeezed orange juice—no pips, either."

Karen jokes with Richard that her bedroom is a jail cell with Lois as warden. "It's her dream situation, Richard. I'm her dietary lab rat. No chance of escape." She bites her knuckles. "There must be something karma-ish about this. I might as well be a newborn."

"We'll break you out of here soon enough."

"As if."

"Don't be so negative."

Richard is happier than he's ever been, juggling Karen and his TV work. Hamilton and Pam are happy enough, too, juggling work with Narcotics Anonymous meetings and clinic visits. They live in a bedroom cocoon of un-rewound VCR tapes, rancid yogurt containers, empty prescription bottles, color-coded vitamin jars, half-eaten meals, lipsticked napkins, stained blankets, and half-read magazines and books. Wendy oversees their recovery.

Richard, looking at all of their lives from a distance, sees the recurring pattern here, the one mentioned on a rainy poker night months ago—a pattern in which the five of his friends

141

seem destined always to return to their quiet little neighborhood. Karen notices this, too. What she *doesn't* tell Richard, though, is that in a strange way her old friends aren't really adults—they *look* like adults but inside they're not really. They're stunted; lacking something. And they all seem to be working too hard. The whole *world* seems to be working too hard. Karen seems to remember leisure and free time as being important aspects of life, but these qualities seem utterly absent from the world she now sees in both real life and on TV. Work work work work work work work.

Look at this! Look at this! People are always showing Karen new electronic doodads. They talk about their machines as though they possess a charmed religious quality—as it these machines are supposed to compensate for their owner's inner failings. Granted, these new things are wonders—e-mail, faxes and cordless phones—but then still . . . *big deal*.

"Hamilton, but what about *you*—are you new and improved and faster and better, too? I mean, as a result of your fax machine?"

"It's swim or drown, Kare. You'll get used to them."

"Oh, *will* I?"

"It's not up for debate. We lost. Machines won."

After life has calmed down somewhat—after the initial flushes of wonder have pulsed and gone, Richard waits until he and Karen have the house alone—a cold gray overcast afternoon day hinting at snow but unwilling to deliver.

"Karen," he gently asks, "do you remember the letter you gave me?"

"Letter?"

"Yeah. The envelope. That night up Grouse. I was supposed to give it to you the next day unless something happened—which it obviously did."

"Yeah." She mulls this over. "I remember. You never mentioned it. I thought you'd left it unopened, that it was forgotten."

Richard pulls Karen's letter from its envelope where it has

lived for nearly two decades, removed every so often for confirmation of its existence. "Here." He hands it to Karen.

December 15 . . . 6 Days to Hawaii!!!

*Note: Call Pammie about beads for cornrowing hair.
Also, arrange* streaking.

   Hi Beb. Karen here.
   *If you're reading this you're either a) the World's
Biggest Sleazebag and I hate you for peeking at this or b)
there's been some very bad news and it's a day later. I
hope that neither of these is true!!*
   *Why am I writing this? I'm asking myself that. I feel
like I'm buying insurance before getting on a plane.*
   *I've been having these visions this week. I may even have
told you about them.* Whatever. *Normally my dreams are
no wilder than, say, riding horses or swimming or
arguing with Mom (and I win!!) but these new things I
saw—they're* not *dreams.*
   *On TV when somebody sees the bank robber's face they
get shot or taken hostage, right? I hate this feeling I'm
going to be taken hostage—I saw more than I was
supposed to have seen. I don't know how it's going to
happen. These voices—they're arguing—one even sounds
like Jared—and these voices are arguing while I get to see
bits of (this sounds so* bad*) the Future!!*
   *It's dark there—in the Future, I mean. It's not a good
place. Everybody looks so old and the neighborhood looks
like shit (pardon my French!!)*
   *I'm writing this note because I'm scared. It's corny. I'm
stupid. I feel like sleeping for a thousand years—that way
I'll never have to be around for this weird new future.*
   *Tell Mom and Dad that I'll miss them. And say
good-bye to the gang. Also Richard, could I ask you a
favor? Could you wait for me? I'll be back from wherever
it is I'm going. I don't know when, but I* will.

I don't think my heart is clean, but neither is it soiled.
I can't remember the last time I even lied. I'm off to
Christmas shop at Park Royal with Wendy and Pammie.
Tonight I'm skiing with you. I'll rip this up tomorrow
when you return it to me UNOPENED. God's looking.

xox
Karen

Solid evidence confirms her fears. "I wrote this. Yes. Didn't
I?"

"Okay . . ."

"And what I say in it is real. It exists. Yes." There's a defiant
note to her voice.

"I don't doubt you, Karen, not at all." Silence falls between
them. Karen fidgets with a Tetris game Megan gave her to
help improve her dexterity. Richard looks at her averted eyes.
He asks quietly, "What is it—who are they—*them*—
whoever?"

"I'd rather not if that's okay. My ankles hurt."

"You *know* who they are?"

She looks up: "I do; I don't. I tried to run away and I got
caught. They're not going to let me get away again."

"What do you mean, 'get away'? And who's *they*."

Karen wishes she could be more forthcoming. At that
moment Megan bounds into the room, bumping into a chair
as she does so. "*Ouch*. Hi kids. Ready for some stretching
Mom?"

Karen is all too glad to have her talk with Richard end.
"Sure. Let's go." Richard's stomach flutters; he feels like he's
being shipped off to war.

Mom.

Lois.

Owls—nothing has changed. Or maybe not. Lois seems
slightly hardened, probably the result of Megan's shenanigans.
Lois isn't quite as vain as she once was. The outfits are there

144

but gone is the constant preening. George—Dad—comes home early from the shop. He sits beside Karen's bed, dewy-eyed.

Karen likes 1997 people because they're never boring—all these new words they have—the backlogs of gossip, of current events and of history.

"What was it *like*?" George and everybody else keeps asking, "What's it *like* to wake up?"

Like? Like nothing. Honestly. Like she woke up and it was seventeen years later—and her body was gone.

But her answers are consistently lame to deflect them away from darker ideas that are returning to her memory. Her day-to-day memory is fine. Some people from UBC gave her some psychological memory tests. Her memory is as good as the day she passed out. She even remembers the page number of her last algebra assignment. But the darkness? It's taking its time.

She knows people are expecting more from her. A certain nobility is demanded—extreme wisdom through extreme suffering. People tread lightly around her.

"I'm not made of uncooked spaghetti, everyone. Jesus—come a little bit closer, okay? I promise I won't splinter."

One afternoon Wendy is having a coffee on Lonsdale with Pam. Wendy has decided she needs to know what Pam saw during the stereo dream. "Pam, remember when you OD'd last Halloween. I've always wondered what you were seeing inside your head. Your brain readouts looked like wheat blowing in the wind. Do you remember?"

"Oh yeah. It was wild. I don't think I've thought about it much since then." She puts more sugar into her cup. "It was like a bootleg video of natural disasters and it even had a theme song. Remember when we used to do choir? *Oranges and lemons, say the bells of Saint Clement* . . ."

"Go on."

"There was this empty freeway. Texas. Very clear about that. And mud. Like a monsoon—in Japan. Again, no mistaking that. There were fields in Africa—all up in flames. And then this gross one—these rivers in Bangladesh or India—just full of bodies and fabric. The last thing was a big digital clock sign—Florida. Definitely Florida. The time was 00:00 and it was 140 degrees out." Pam puts down her cup. "Wow. I can't believe I remembered all that. But I did. *Me* with a brain like a damp paper towel."

"It sounds beautiful in an eerie way."

"It *was*. And it was *real*—it was no movie. That's for sure."

Later that afternoon Wendy contrives a reason to visit Monster Machine—dropping off some long-ago borrowed books to Hamilton. "Got time for a quick coffee?"

"For you, the *Moon*."

A few minutes later in the staff coffee room during a lull enhanced by canned music that Hamilton describes as "Eleanor Rigby played on a didgeridoo," Wendy brings up Hamilton's Halloween overdose, and like Pam, he remembers it vividly yet is surprised he hasn't thought of it since. "Texas— a freeway—all quiet, like a sci-fi film. Oh, and music—a children's choir singing 'Oranges and Lemons'. What else—mud. Lots of mud. Slopping onto Tokyo. Some fields in Africa burning. Bodies in a river in India . . ." Hamilton's eyes aren't fixed on Wendy but are distant and reminiscing. "And the time and temperature in Florida. Dade County? Zero o'clock and 140 degrees Fahrenheit. There."

Wendy is immobilized with shock. "Wendy—what's up? You look like you've seen our most recent monster creation— come on—I'll show you."

They stumble into the main shop full of urethane and fiber-glass odors. Hamilton leads Wendy to a decapitated torso with a hand sticking out from the neck. Wendy nods approval but her mind is elsewhere.

The news cameras and TV trucks left a while ago, having given up attempts at garnering photos. Linus snaps some black-and-white head shots of Karen and her recently dyed and styled hair. From this selection, one photo is chosen, copied and

146

given out to the press at large. Nobody in the family has given interviews.

Karen's body, hidden by day under a Canucks hockey jersey, is slowly returning to life—fingers, then hands and then forearms; ankles, feet and then the knees. Richard and Megan and a trained therapist oversee many hours each day of bending, rotating and stretching Karen's sad little body, porking up as it may be. Richard helps Karen re-learn to write her signature and he's shocked at how difficult the effort is for Karen. Her round girlish signature of yore is now an angular nursery school blotch.

Lois makes sure Karen eats; her stomach, essentially unused to solids for nearly two decades, can accept only the tiniest amounts of food, but Lois, always happy to merge science and dining, is happy to see the amounts rising gram by gram and Karen's body filling out.

Richard has bought an extraordinarily expensive Norwegian wheelchair equipped with a hammock-like sling that allows the passenger, Karen, to travel across bumpy surfaces such as forest paths, and so outside the two of them trek. It's too late in the year for tourists; their only intrusion is a quick greeting from a strolling neighbor; passing dogs lick Karen's face. The chair's sling makes Karen feel utterly dependent and while Richard tries to yank the chair up a rocky patch, Karen's eyes tear; she misses nature.

"Richard, just give it a rest a second," she says. She collects her breath. "Just look at the trees. So alive. So pure. So blameless and strong." Light dapples the leaves of the undergrowth; Karen shivers.

"What is it, Kare?"

"Richard, look at my body. I'm—I'm *nothing* anymore. I'm a monster—some monster cooked up by Hamilton and Linus. I'm a teenager trapped in an old crone's body. I've never even lived, barely. What if you get tired of taking care of me all the time?"

Richard stills the chair and lifts Karen out of it, then cradles

147

her in his lap while looking at the canyon and river and tall fir trees below. Karen calms down and apologizes: "Time out. That was uncool."

"Cool? Karen, *please. Cool* is not an issue. Coolness is for eighteen-year-olds." He rethinks that statement in light of her mental age. "Well, you know what I mean." He holds her close to him. "Karen, I hear your voice and it's like having jewels rustling across my heart." He pitter-pats her chest with his fingers; Karen loves touching and she loves Richard's sentimental blurts. "Me . . . a poet? Yikes."

Karen leans her head on Richard's shoulder; it still takes so much effort to lift it. "You're being sentimental," she says. She feels odd being so intimate with an *older* man. Mentally her taste is what a teenager might choose: a first year college guy; a steady North Van guy who plays hockey on weekends. She has had to radically redefine her vision of sex. And Richard, lying there every night, holding her and spooning with her. She has felt him go hard a few times and sensed him pulling away in silent awkwardness, pretending to be asleep. But in his sleep he is hard and he *does* press against her and between her legs. She finds herself enjoying this—wanting this—but she is unable to imagine herself making love again. She hasn't even been able to ask Wendy about the medical side of all this, but she knows she'll soon be doing so.

Richard is in love with Karen, and she with him, but their connection to each other needs to progress or perish. She is angry that she may never again be with Richard as they were up on the mountain.

Richard finds himself wanting Karen and it feels perverted. He, too, is embarrassed to ask advice from anybody. More times than he can remember he has been aroused by Karen during the night. Lois and George have been understanding of the two of them sleeping together. They understand the healing effect of skin on skin. But how far should it go? What would Karen say if he asked her? What would she think? *Perv.*

"Do you remember that night up on the mountain, Richard?"

"Yeah."

"I remember it, too." Karen cocks her ear to listen to the river. "I dragged you into that. I was pushy."

"I didn't mind."

"I thought maybe you'd think I was a slut or something."

"Oh, I rather doubt *that*."

"Well, I *did* think of it that way. I avoided your eyes afterward. On the chairlift. And at the party afterward—up in the car. I felt bad. I feel bad now." A heron swoops by and Richard makes a gesture to lift Karen into her chair, but Karen says, "No. Not right now. I need to ask you something."

Richard says *sure*.

"I need to know if—if I was—" Karen's voice squeaks here then becomes a whisper. "If I was any good or not."

"Oh Karen, honey!" He bends down and kisses her sallow cheek and rubs her neck, skeletal still, like bones being reduced in a kitchen pot. "Of course you were. That's one of my happiest memories."

Karen starts breathing in staccato. Richard speaks in a soothing monotone to relax her: "See those paths over there?" he says, pointing to lines within the forest where the trees grow along thin road-width glades. "Those used to be logging roads, a long time ago. Linus told me he'd read through old maps and found out that a train had run right through the spaces now occupied by our houses. Sometimes I think of the ghosts of trains flowing nightly through my head. I mean, up here we have our world of driveways and lawns and microwaves and garages. Down there inside the trees . . . it's eternity."

"You know, Richard . . ."

"What?"

"That night up Grouse—"

"Yeah?"

"It's—well it's the only time I'm ever going to have. I don't think I can live with that."

"I don't get it. I mean . . ."

"Richard, just shut *up* for a moment. Listen to what I'm *feeling*."

149

There is a silence and then, *boom!*—with all her effort Karen lifts herself out of Richard's arms in a manner that attempts to be graceful but which ends up looking undignified. She crumples on the muddy soil. Richard is frightened she might be broken.

Karen's weakness is utterly at odds with the landscape's rigor. She tries to crawl away with her arms, inching forth like a worm, soil smudging her face and sleeves, her face grim and determined. With her mouth she tries to drink the sky; her sweater and shirt and jeans are cold and wet, and her fingers clasp and rip a fern. Richard lets Karen move a fair distance and then walks alongside her and then lies down on the soil beside her. She is shivering; he gives her his coat and says, "That's not true at all." He then lifts her and carries her home and leaves the wheelchair where it sits. He can come fetch it later. If.

'Two strong arms," says Karen.

Richard says, "Yes," and kisses her.

DREAMING EVEN THOUGH
YOU'RE WIDE AWAKE

Pam's detox has not been as shaky as Hamilton's—cramping mostly, eternal period pain, constipation, and dizzy headaches. Today the two are chauffeuring Karen around on a tour of the city, showing her new and modern things. The sun has emerged—cold and bleached, weak and low on the horizon out beyond Burnaby and Mount Baker; sunglasses are required by all. Karen is buried within an ivory-colored sheepskin coat of Pam's. "*Très* glam, Kare, you sexy detox kitten. *Meow.*"

Hamilton has strapped Karen into the front seat with extra nylon harnesses for legs and chest, carefully checked Karen's neck brace, and promised Richard that he'll drive under the speed limit at all times. He notices Karen's mood this morning: beautiful, lively, and loquacious. There is good reason for this. The night before Karen and Richard made awkward but delicate love and afterward he asked her to marry him and she accepted. *Well, Richard, I'm thirty-four and I can count the number of times I've done it on two fingers.*

By now Karen has taken many drives with her family and friends and has seen the changes progress has wreaked. She's seen the city of Vancouver multiply and bathe itself in freighter loads of offshore money. Blue glass towers through which Canada geese fly in V-formation, traffic jams of Range Rovers, Chinese road signs, and children with cell phones. Karen rather likes the new city and she rather likes the small things in life that are new: blue nail polish, hygiene products, better pasta.

Karen wishes she could shop in the department stores, but a recent excursion to the Park Royal mall caused such a pandemonium they decided not to repeat the experience. The

151

theoretical purpose of today's road trip is to buy a copy of *Royalty* magazine. Karen wants to see pictures of Princess Diana. She can't believe she missed out on the entire fable—the wedding, the kids, the flings, the divorce, and finally her rebirth as a private citizen—and then, the *end*. Diana's life is one of the few things that makes her jealous that she's been away. "Pam, it's just like in high school when we felt like everybody was out there partying but us."

"But, Karen, I don't remember feeling that way."

A sigh. "God, you good-looking people drive me nuts."

Hamilton is grouchy this morning, Pam is withdrawn, and Karen is preoccupied by what she sees outside and what's inside her head. Three people sitting in the same car but not really together.

'Look," Karen says, "an old Datsun B-210. Like Richard's back in school."

"Don't see many of those around these days," Hamilton says. Karen asks, "Is Vietnam making cars now, too?"

The Jeep comes to a stop sign and Karen's sunglasses slip off. Hamilton replaces them and continues driving. "Hey Kare,' he asks, "how do you feel being here now? After so long. I mean, not just what's new and different, but what does *now* feel like?"

"*Um*—"

"Is that too annoying a question? I mean, you've been out of the coma for a while now. You must be used to it, right? Kick me if I'm yanking your chain too hard."

"No. I mean yes. I mean *wait*, Ham—let me think."

They pass a clique of high-schoolers. Their fashions seem alien yet attractive to Karen. She would have enjoyed wearing these new styles. *Sigh*.

"Pammie asked me, too. I told her, *imagine walking a million miles . . . in heels*, and she kind of got it."

"Hey, Karen, don't shit me. That's crap. *I* could have told *you* that. There's other stuff. You know there is. How does it *feel*? I mean, seventeen *years*. Spill. And if you don't spill I'll spend the next hour telling you about the Berlin Wall coming down and AIDS."

Only Hamilton can speak to her like this. *Brat.* He's always been able to go way off the edge with Karen. She likes him for this. "Well, *okay*, Hamilton. As one bullshitter to another. Very well." The Jeep is on the highway now, headed west toward Horseshoe Bay. The day is becoming pale blue and clean and cold. The ocean far down below the highway is a flat anvil blue.

"Okay. You know what, Hamilton? There's a *hardness* I'm seeing in modern people. Those little moments of goofiness that used to make the day pass seem to have gone. Life's so serious now. Maybe it's just because I'm with an older gang now." She lifts her scrawny arms and nibbles her finger and the act is a large effort on her part. "I mean, nobody even has *hobbies* these days. Not that I can see. Husbands and wives both work. Kids are farmed out to schools and video games. Nobody seems to be able to endure simply being by them*selves*, either—but at the same time they're isolated. People work much more, only to go home and surf the Internet and send e-mail rather than calling or writing a note or visiting each other. They work, watch TV, and sleep. I see these things. The whole world is only about work: *work work work get get get* . . . racing ahead . . . getting sacked from work . . . going online . . . knowing computer languages . . . winning contracts. I mean, it's just *not* what I would have imagined the world might be if you'd asked me seventeen years ago. People are frazzled and angry, desperate about money, and, at best, indifferent to the future."

She grabs her breath. "So you ask me how do *I* feel? I feel lazy. And slow. And antique. And I'm scared of all these machines. I shouldn't be, but I am. I'm not sure I *completely* like the new world."

Hamilton's jaws clench and Karen sees this. "I know—you want me to say how great everything is now, but I can't. It's pretty clear to me that life now isn't what it ought to have become."

They drive past the Cypress exit, the Westmount exit, and the Caulfield exit. Pam coughs in the backseat, a cough like two thick steaks flapping against each other, and Hamilton reacts: "Jesus, Pam—honk those things into a Baggie and maybe we can fry them up for dinner."

"Ha."

More mountains and ocean. "I think I know what you mean," Hamilton says. "If you look at the world as a whole, we have to admit life's good here where we live. But in an evil *Twilight Zone* kind of way there's nothing *else* to choose. In the old days there was always a Bohemia or a creative underworld to join if the mainstream life wasn't your bag—or a life of crime, or even religion. And now there's only the *system*. All other options have evaporated. For most people it's the System or what . . . *death*? There's nothing. There's no way out now." A pulp mill up the fjord of Howe Sound stains the sky with an ash-white glaze. Hamilton asks, "What about the people you know—Richard, Wendy, Pam, and me? What changes have you noticed in all of us?"

"You mean friends and family?"

"Yeah."

Karen tells him only the palatable half of the story. "The thing I'm noticing is that nobody's really *changed* in seventeen years; they're simply amplified versions of themselves. Mom is as . . . er . . . *regulatory* as ever. Dad's nice but weird. Richard is still earnest and a cutie-pie and he tries so hard. *You're* still a brat. Pam's quietly beautiful. Linus is still on Mars. Wendy may be a doctor and everything, but in her head she's still handing in essays and getting A's. Everybody's become, *yeah*— more like them*selves*."

The car hums, and they look at the mountains and the city. "Remember when we went to Future Shop to buy a camera?" Karen asks. The others nod. "Did you see the categories they had there for their products? 'Simulation'; 'Productivity'; 'Games.' I mean, what kind of world *is* this? And please tell me what's happened to *time*? Nobody *has* time anymore. What's the deal? Shit. Now I'm in a bad mood." Lowering the window allows into the Jeep the faint industrial fart smell of a pulp mill. Karen retreats behind her sunglasses. She *doesn't* tell Hamilton that she had expected people to be grown up at the age of thirty-four. Instead, they seem at best insular and without a central core, which might give purpose to their lives.

Hamilton talks: "And what of your lovely daughter, Megan?"

Karen smiles: "Isn't she the coolest, Ham? So strong. So sure of herself. Imagine being so *together* at seventeen—wow." She pauses: "Well, in a way I *am* seventeen. So maybe I *can* be as cool as her, too. Yes."

"I think you're going to have to be older," Pam says from the backseat, talking through a yawn. "People are expecting you to be wise after all that sleep. To most people you're not seventeen anymore—you're one thousand years old."

It's true. People treat Karen as though she can sense not only color, smells, and sound, but something else—something rich and sublime and far beyond color. She has this subtle feeling people are a touch jealous of this. What frustrates her, too, is that she *knows* she's seen things, but these things are locked away and unreachable.

Megan now has morning sickness and wonders how much longer she can keep her secret. She avoids nearly all her old friends and lives at Richard's condo, essentially alone, since Richard spends most of his time with Karen or at work. She likes the solitude; she's too young to understand the throbbing weight of loneliness. She has tossed out most of her old Goth clothing and now favors a pared-down, somewhat athletic look. She has also dropped out of school and works part-time with Linus; she'd like to work there full-time someday once her baby is in day care.

For lack of peers, Megan is reduced to having to speak with adults. Megan can't believe that she actually wants to speak with Lois. A good rousing fight would be fun. Karen ("*Bio-Mom*") is great, if not slightly clued out (*Well, she* did *miss two decades*). But there remains an awkwardness between them. A jealousy? Emotionally, they are both the same age; both need attention from Richard, Lois, and the others. Yet on some deeper level they just don't connect. They're too much the same and each poses a form of competition to the other. They're wary.

Blond walnuts; a blush; a smile before she closed the door.

It's a rainy day: Karen and Wendy sit in Wendy's kitchen discussing a small party soon to be held on the day after Christmas—a party celebrating Karen and Richard's engagement. The ceremony is to be small: immediate friends and family only. No dates allowed; no strangers. There isn't too much to plan, so it's fun for Karen and Wendy to arrange things. Wendy's life is so stressful; she enjoys having a girly-girl break. A dress? That's Pam's department. Food? Endive with cream cheese, prosciutto and melon. "What happened to food?" Karen asks. "Food used to come in a box or a can. Now there's dozens of everything and it's all so fresh."

Their coffee cups run low. *God bless NutraSweet.* There is a pause at the end of their chat, a pause that indicates that a change in conversational gears is now possible.

"Wendy," Karen asks while looking out the window at some of Linus's old monsters standing beside the garage, "have you ever noticed—Wait." Another pause. "Have you ever noticed our lives are maybe . . ."

"Maybe *what*?" Wendy's tone of voice almost says, *Please don't. Please don't talk about this.*

"Well, I mean, I know my waking up was like a million-to-one shot. And I can't explain that, but even still—"

"But even still *what*?"

"Well, we all seem to have more . . . not coinc*idences*—more like spooky things in our lives than most people do. I mean, *don't* we?"

Wendy's reply is dry and therapeutic: "When did you start feeling this?"

"The day I woke up. That's a good start: We all ended up at the hospital that day. What are the odds of *that*? And I'm noticing that we all ended up returning to the same old neighborhood like so much undeliverable mail. I bet we probably couldn't escape Rabbit Lane even if we tried."

Wendy's unsure where to go with this. "So you think this all means something more, do you? Something big?"

"Yeah." Karen pours more coffee, eager to do such a mundane task with her new stronger arms. The liquid shakes. "Then there's these visions I've had."

"Oh?"

"Wendy, listen up. I'm serious. You're a doctor. Listen." Karen tells Wendy of the images she saw, how she believes it was no accident that she went into a coma in 1979. Karen then asks, "Haven't you *ever* seen anything weird that wasn't real life, but wasn't a dream either?"

Wendy enters and form of trance. "I . . ." She pauses. "I saw Jared. Years ago. He came and talked to me. Back when I was lonely, back before Linus and I were married. He'd told me I wouldn't be lonely forever. He said he was doing what he could. He was real; he was *there*. I was in love with him back in high school. You knew that, right? Even now I'm still in love with Jared. In my own way. Of course, I love Linus, too. Oh, these feelings are com*plex*."

"We *all* knew about you and Jared," Karen says. "The worst kept crush in school. But he was such a dog, Wen—I mean, he'd hump anything in a bra like he was a Great Dane going at the sofa."

"But Jared *wasn't* just a crush. I was in *love* with him. I've never doubted that. Ever." Wendy remembers what had really happened—the sleepover with Jared's older sister, Laura, walking into the sauna while looking for soap, opening the door to find Jared naked, eyes closed, his butt roasting on the cedar. She remembers the brief second (a second and a half?) before Jared knew she was there, the smell of salt air in her lungs and Jared's skin melting like cake frosting, his balls like two blond walnuts, his member turgid, and the embarrassment afterward, slamming the door shut. She remembers avoiding Jared's eyes for weeks afterward, blushing if she even saw him far down the school's corridors. And then came October 14, 1978, the day Jared snuck up behind Wendy and whispered, *See you after the game. Meet me in the parking lot. I've got a bag of candy to give you.* And then came the collapse on the football field followed by the thousand passionate nights that never were to come Wendy's way. And she's never told anybody, because who would believe it? Because she is only Wendy: dutiful, sexless, brainy, and almost a tragedy (in her father's eyes) had Linus not happened along. Romantic beauty is for others. She wonders if she entered medicine only so that she might see naked men's bodies with impunity. This thought frightens her.

"Do you still ever speak with him?"

"No. He's gone. I don't know if it was even really him. It was probably in my head. I work too hard. I don't get enough free time. I still try to talk to him sometimes, but he's never returned. Real or not, I miss him."

"To me, Jared feels like just a year ago," Karen says. "But for *you*, Jared's gone for almost twenty years. And the feeling has never gone away?"

"Never."

The phone rings, but Wendy doesn't answer. There's a silence between the two. Wendy says, "Off the record? I think, yeah, all our vision stuff means something. But who's to say what? There's no pattern, no direction, no relationship."

"Let's just keep our eyes open, agreed?"

"Agreed."

20 | . . . AND AFTER AMERICA?

Ten days before Christmas, Lois and George approach Karen, who sits by the living room TV watching a tape of *The Thornbirds*. Karen intuits that their approach will be taxing in some way.

"We'd like you to do that TV interview, dear."

I knew it. "Which one?"

"I don't like that tone of voice, Karen. We're only thinking about the best interests of you and Megan."

"Explain *that* to me, please." She remotes off the TV.

"They're offering a good deal of money, dear," George says. "You could certainly use it. Megan, too."

"You could put her through college on it," Lois adds.

"Oh, puh-*leeeze*. I think we should all know by now that Megan is not and is unlikely to ever be college material."

Thus begins an hour-long tussle, after which Karen finally agrees to do a network TV interview for an astronomical sum of money, to be taped in three days—on the condition that the money be put into trust for Megan until the age of twenty-one. "And you're not allowed to tell her how much, because I can just imagine her killing time until she gets a big bundle to blow."

Almost instantly, lawyers are phoned, moneys are negotiated, and people from both American coasts descend on Karen's doorstep for a Thursday shoot. As Karen's friends are intimate with almost every aspect of TV production, they mastermind lighting schemes and color effects and are bossy with their imported colleagues as they protect Karen. Pam instructs Karen on posture (where possible), deportment, breathing, pacing, makeup, and styling. Their competence is a wonder to Karen; for the first time, she understands that her friends have actual skills. Richard and Hamilton "danger-proof" the Christmas tree while Linus stands lost in his own world, mentally rearranging the furniture to best visual advantage.

My friends know how to put a good face on a bad situation, Karen thinks.

"I wouldn't be nervous, Kare," Pam says while applying a Christian Dior 425 foundation. "TV isn't about information. It's about emotion. People will be hearing your words, sure, but first they'll be checking out your skin and hairdo."

"Then I'm up shit creek."

"Piffle. You've got good skin and bones and people will probably feel cheated if you don't look a bit weird. Which lipstick do you want?"

"Do I really have to do this, Pam?"

"What, makeup? God *yes*. Even the healthiest people on TV look like corpses without it. The less they look at your skin, the better they'll hear what you're saying."

This makes sense to Karen. She calms down, lets Pam do her work, and watches out the front window as a newscaster who looks surprisingly like Lois has her hair brushed and dictates notes to minions. Lois, standing on the lawn, raptly watches.

Karen recalls her conversation with Richard, who was unsure why she, a photo hater at the best of times, would participate in such an intrusive procedure. *Well, it's not going to atone for two decades away from Megan, but it's something practical I can do to help her. It makes me feel motherly. And Megan wants to be interviewed, too.*

A few minutes later, Lois, obviously thrilled, says, "Karen, this is Gloria."

Gloria walks in, wearing a red suit and flashing teeth like baby corn, teeth so perfect she looks as though she has three rows, not two. A white, paper makeup bib sticks out from her collar. "I'm so happy to meet you *Karen*. Are you relaxed?" The woman's hand almost crushes Karen's fingers. Before

160

Karen can reply, Gloria is saying, "That's ter*rific*. It's probably best we don't talk too much right now. It makes for a better show if I meet you the same time the world meets you. Paula said she had a lovely pre-interview with you." A smile. Gloria's eyes: *blink blink blink*. An assistant asks if Paula called. Yes, Paula called. Gloria is out of the room, but her voice is audible. "Aren't these owls just the dearest things!" Karen can hear Lois blush with pleasure.

Technicians—who couldn't look more bored even were they to try—hook up cables, manipulate light meters, set up reflectors, and link a satellite feed from one of three vans. Karen feels like she's in a movie in which scientists discover alien life-forms inside a suburban house. Her hearing vanishes; suddenly, she is deaf. She turns her head and sees Richard and Linus at the dining room table chatting with Megan. Wendy is on the back patio playing with a neighbor's cat. George is out of sight in the front hallway.

And suddenly she is lost in a blast of white light. Her eyelids shut, her arms jitter, and her face bleeds water. "Christ!" says Pam. She, Richard, and Linus come over; Karen's face is running like a river. "Karen." Richard taps her shoulder gently. "Karen!"

She now remembers where it was she went. She was up in the stars and then she descended to Earth, shimmering and blue, into the swirls of clouds over the Atlantic, flying and swooping, joining the birds and feeling like a bright color. And then she was pulled upward again—a hand, a clasp behind her shoulders where her wings ought to have been. She was pulled up in the stars. Once there, she turned around and saw the Moon, and then the hand dropped her there—inside a crater. She was dressed for warmth, but this is outer space and why should it matter?

"I remember," Karen says. "Yes, I remember." In her head, she walks into a crater and kicks some dust, which falls downward at one-sixth Earth gravity. "And it's going to happen. It's going to happen here."

She blinks and can hear again.

"Karen, you're scaring the crap out of me," Pam says. "What happened? Are you okay?"

Her eyes open. "It's going to happen here."

"What is? What's going to happen, honey?"

Karen snaps out of it. "Oh. Pam—what did I . . . ?—I spaced out there."

"From a cosmetician's viewpoint, you did more than space out, Karen."

Pam reworks Karen's face, gooey with sweat and foundation. "Is it fixable?"

"Of course. Relax. Richard—can you get Karen a glass of water?" Richard scuttles to the kitchen and returns with a glass. When he hands it over, Karen says thanks, but refuses to look him in the eye. A few moments later, she looks to her right and sees both Richard and Wendy looking concerned. A technician shouts out, asking if everybody's ready to tape; and so the taping begins.

> We now bring you a girl, or rather, a young
> woman, who's been very much on the world's
> mind these past few months. On a cold
> December evening back in 1979, Karen Ann
> McNeil, a pretty and popular Vancouver, Canada,
> teenager, was at a party. There, she drank two
> weak vodka cocktails and took two Valiums—
> pills she used to calm her metabolism after a
> two-month crash diet. The price she paid for this
> youthful folly? Karen spent the next seventeen
> years in a coma, during which time she gave no
> evidence of higher brain functions or other
> promising signs. Then, miraculously, after a
> bronchial infection earlier this fall, Karen awoke
> on the morning of November first. Her brain
> functions were fully normal, as was her memory.
> She could even remember her homework
> assignments from the week before the coma.

162

And what sort of world did Karen wake up to? A dramatically different world—one without the Berlin Wall and one with AIDS, computers, and radicchio. She also woke up into a world where she now has a daughter, Megan, born nine months after Karen entered her coma.

I met with Karen recently at her home on a mountain suburb of Vancouver. I found her sparkling with words and, I have to admit, I was a bit shocked at her appearance. Karen left her coma weighing eighty-two pounds. By interview time, she was up to ninety-three, but seventeen years have left her body ravaged by diminished muscle capacity. Fortunately, her mind and face are as animated as they were that fateful December night seventeen years ago . . .

"What about your body—how do you feel now that it's"—pause—"so *different* than the way it was in 1979?" Gloria has been drilling for tears and is annoyed at the lack of a geyser. She mistakes Karen's disbelieving pauses at Gloria's rude intrusions for emotion. "Do you *miss* your body?"

"I'm *fine* with my body, Gloria. It returns more to normal every day. There are people out there in far worse straits than me. I can stick it."

The interview isn't going well at all. Karen realizes that Gloria wants to present a plucky, back-from-the-brink-of-death woman, eager to sing the praises of the new and changed world. Instead, Karen seems not all happy and not too thrilled with modern life. And she won't cry.

"What's the biggest change in the world you've noticed so far, Karen? What strikes you as the deepest change?"

Behind Karen stands the Christmas tree, cheerful and twinkling. She is alone in the room with just the TV people, Pam as makeup, and Richard as emotional support. The others she asked to leave, so as not to pressure her with her answers.

Karen speaks: "You know what it is, Gloria? It's how confident everybody comes across these days. Everybody looks like they're raring to go all the time. People look confident even when they're buying chewing gum or walking the dog."

"You like that then?"

"There's more. You take these same confident-looking people and ask them a few key questions and suddenly you realize that they're despairing about the world—that the confidence is a mask."

"What kind of questions?"

"What do you think life will be like in ten years? Are you straining to find some kind of meaning? Does growing old frighten you?"

"Hmmm. We're a culture searching for meaning. Yes." Gloria doesn't like this avenue. Her face morphs into a new position. Suddenly, Gloria's smiling. "You have a daughter now, Karen: Megan." Conspiratorial leer. "We need to know—how does it feel to wake up and discover you have a seventeen-year-old?"

"Feel? It's a pleasure. And a surprise. Imagine waking up one morning and suddenly there's a teenager there saying, 'Hi, Mom.' In a way, I feel like a sister. I ask myself, If I were back in high school, is Megan somebody I'd be friends with."

"And?"

"I don't think I would. She'd be too confident to follow the crowd. She'd be offbeat, and I'd wish I could just talk to her and see what's in her head."

"And Megan's father—do you still see him?"

"Absolutely. We're engaged." Karen smiles at Richard over Gloria's shoulder. Gloria gives an appropriate smile reaction, then says, "*Cut!*"

Gloria unclips her mike and bolts toward a door where the minions cower. "Why the hell didn't we know about this? Who researched this—Anthea? Get her on the phone now. No—she's in 213, not 310. We're going to have to retake the intro. Is the weather going to hold?"

There's panic for the next ten minutes, and then Gloria

164

returns. "*Speed and—*" *Clack!* "*Rolling—*" Gloria turns into "Gloria" instantly, like a plugged-in appliance. "Karen, so you're engaged now?"

"Indeed I am."

"Will we be able to meet . . . *him?*"

"I think not. He's far more private than I am."

"What's his name?"

"Richard."

"So Richard waited all these years for you? All these decades, your one love waited?"

Karen pauses. Her eyes begin to mist up—*damnit!* She fell into Gloria's trap of tears. "Yes"—sniffle—"he did." Now her eyes flood. Gloria heaves a relieved breath and knows this will be a dynamite kicker.

"Gloria," calls a technician, "we lost the sound on that one. We have to redo the take."

Gloria mutters a curse and the process begins again in a startlingly machine-like process: "Karen, so you're engaged now?" Gloria bats the eyes: *blink blink blink.*

"Yes."

"Will we be able to meet . . . *him?*"

"No."

"What's his name?"

"That's private."

"Very well. So your boyfriend waited all these years for you? All these decades your one love waited?"

Karen pauses. "Yeah. He did." No tears. Gloria is furious.

> How many of us have a love so true it spans
> eternity? A purity of need so clear it can remain
> strong in the face of all that the world throws at
> us? This is Karen Ann McNeil, the woman who
> fell to Earth, the woman for whom the people in
> her life never gave up waiting.

"What about your friends, Karen? How do you feel to see them all aged seventeen years overnight? Do you still hang out with them?"

"They're my life, really. They and my family. If they weren't here, I don't think I could handle the world." Karen is disgusted with the platitudes she's dishing out. She sounds to herself like a Miss America contestant allowed out of the sound-proof booth and given thirty seconds to answer questions that will, to a large degree, define future directions of her life.

Gloria looks peeved. *We need more drama.* A woman named Randy comes over; she and Gloria have a hushed discussion over notes on Gloria's crisp red lap. Pam powders Karen's face. "How's it going, Kare?"

"I think I'm a dud. And they're furious about losing the crying scene."

Karen thinks over what Pam blurted out in the car the other day—about how people expect her to be a thousand years old now, not just thirty-four. She knows this is what Gloria wants to get at.

"Karen—" Gloria returns. "Let's just do a few more questions. This must be tiring for you."

"It's my pleasure. When are you interviewing Megan?"

"After you," says Gloria. "And then we'll do the two of you together. Everything is out of sequence, but we patch it all together in post-production." Gloria's face looks harsh, unwilling to spare any niceness energy until production noises are made. The board claps and once again she becomes "Gloria."

"Karen." Gloria puts on her serious look, cradles her chin atop her hands, and looks deeply at Karen. "The world is curious—and I *know* this is a simple question, but I need to ask it—how does it *feel* to be a modern Rip Van Winkle? Almost twenty years asleep. My *my*. What's it like inside your head? What's it like to be *you* right now?"

"You know what I feel? I feel useless in this modern world. I'm unable to do anything but lie around. I feel like I'm the only person on Earth who relaxes anymore. And then I think about all the bad stuff that's about to happen and I feel sorry for the world because it's nearly over."

Cut!

166

Assistants run over. "Karen, what on *Earth* was that?"

Karen blinks and looks out the window at the sky, competing for attention with the camera lights. "I'm not sure. It just came out." Richard slips around a corner and motions for Wendy to come over. He tells her what happened.

"Karen," Gloria says, "let's try that one again. Maybe we can ask about the, er, bad stuff with another question. Agreed?"

"Sure. It's your show."

Rolling . . .

"Karen." Gloria again looks deeply at Karen and repeats word-perfectly, "The world is curious—and I *know* this is a simple question but I need to ask it—how does it *feel* to be a modern Rip Van Winkle? Twenty years asleep. My *my*. What's it like inside your head? What's it like to be *you* right now?"

"I feel useless as tits on a board. I sit around all day doing dick-all while everybody else runs around like crazed cartoon characters."

A semi-defeated silence follows. Gloria asks, "Anything else?"

"Seeing as your asking, yes. The world's going to be over soon."

Cut!

"Karen, I—Excuse me a second." Gloria darts outside. An assistant, Jason, comes in to play good cop. He's a slow walker; his eyes have seen something. He doesn't discount the odd and he sees a possible miracle where others see dreck. "Karen," he says, motioning the film crew to keep rolling, "when you say the world's over, what, exactly, do you *mean*?"

"What I said. I . . ." There is a pause and a voice speaks, the voice of Karen who was away all these years. "Three days after Christmas. That's when the world goes dark. There's nothing that can be done and there's no escaping. I saw it happen in 1979. By accident, some doors had been left open and I got a peek. I wasn't snooping. I just saw it at the right time. I thought I could sleep my way out of it—I wasn't sure of the date it was going to happen. I wanted to be asleep forever. It's not the same as death, but it's the only way we

167

have to escape time. That's what makes us different from every other creature in the world—we have *time*. And we have choices."

Jason is quiet. The camera still rolls. Richard, Pam, and Wendy watch. In the lull, they can hear Gloria's voice saying, "What am I supposed to do when she keeps shutting down and spouting claptrap. Does she not have the word 'retake' in her vocabulary?"

"Gloria, she's been in a coma for twenty years almost. People expect her to be odd."

"I can't believe we lost the tear shot."

Jason says, "Are there any details you can give, Karen. Places? Names? Is it a bomb or is it—?"

"It's sleep. Nearly everybody falls asleep and then they go. It's painless. Where do you live?"

"New York."

"You'll go. Gloria goes. Everybody there goes."

"And this doesn't make you sad?"

"It hasn't happened yet. I won't know until it's over."

"What about you and your family and friends. Don't you worry for them?"

"There's nothing I can do to help them one way or the other. All of this was decided a long, *long*, time ago. And I don't know *specifically* who lives and who doesn't. So I can't tell you people, really, I can't."

"And you?"

"Me? I get to live. I know that for sure." Karen seems to have no more to say on this subject.

Jason's face is thoughtful. "Thanks for telling me this."

"I might as well." And then Karen wakes up while still asleep. She startles: "Wha—?—I spaced out again there. I dreamed I was telling you the world was going to shut down."

"A dream?"

"No. Not really. I suppose not."

21 | YOUR DREAMS OF WAR ALARM YOU

Karen feels release and confusion. She knows that her words have annoyed the Americans and baffled—perhaps even slightly frightened—her friends.

She knows that she is in the center of some sort of mass transformation—one larger than just her mere reawakening. But how big will this change be? Miracles always have limits. When one is granted wishes, one is granted only *three* wishes— not four or five or ten. What will be the limits here?

Karen feels trapped inside the biggest déjà vu in the world. Her behavior seems preordained, like a queen who spends her day cutting ribbons, judging flower shows, and overseeing state dinners—all of these activities preordained. And she has decided, somewhere between her co-interview with Megan and the camera crew's taping the two of them hobbling down Rabbit Lane, that she'll try and play it dumb about her on-camera statements of impending doom. Already she is detecting that Richard and Wendy think her comments might be evidence of incipient madness. Oh *God.*

She misses running and she misses her hair and she misses being normal, being absorbed by the crowd. She has decided that the best way for her to go through life is for her to view even her smallest actions and gestures as coincidental, charged, and miraculous. It was the way she remembered life felt at the age of sixteen and it is a way she is determined to re-create.

Beef south/chicken north.

The night of the TV shoot, Karen goes to bed almost immediately, thus precluding any discussion of what she had told Gloria and then Jason. She is still asleep when Richard leaves for work the next day. During the day, when he calls home, there is no answer—Christmas shopping. He phones Wendy at her office and the two of them convene at Park Royal for coffee, where dispirited Christmas mall music serenades their baffled conversation. Wendy stirs the sugar in her coffee thirty times and says, "I think that Karen's memory and thought processes maybe aren't as clear as we'd hoped for, Richard. Are you scared—about going south?"

Richard, obligated to visit Los Angeles, says yes. He leaves on the twenty-seventh and returns on the twenty-eighth.

"Can't you go some other time?"

"No. We're behind schedule as it is. Besides, it's so preposterous. If I stay home, I'll only reinforce whatever fantasy or phobia it is Karen's going through." He bites a muffin. "It *is* fantasy, right?"

"Who's to say? It's like those cartoons of guys with long beards holding a sign on a street corner saying THE END IS NEAR; there's always a little part of you that wonders, *what if?* Yeah, it's spooky. Have you spoken about this with her yet?"

"No. It's been crazy. I will tonight. Holidays throw everything into a mess. But one question, Wendy, if you were me, would you go?"

"I'd probably go, too."

Later that evening, Richard and Karen have their first real fight, which colors the entire next week. "The twenty-eighth is *not* going to be a good day, Richard."

"Karen you can't just say, '*Oh, something awful's going to happen.*' You have to tell me *why*. You have to tell me what you know. And why."

Karen sighed. "What about trust?"

"Karen, whether or not I believe you on this particular issue has nothing to do with whether or not I love or trust you. Karen—look at it from my point of view."

"How do you explain what Wendy told us about Pam and Hamilton in the hospital—their stereo freak-outs?"

"I can't."

170

"Doesn't that note I gave you back before my coma mean anything?"

"Of course it does."

"The fact that I'm on TV on the twenty-seventh doesn't sway you? You can't stay here for moral support?"

"It's bad luck. I'll watch it down there. I'll watch it on speakerphone with you."

"So you're still going to go?"

"I will—unless you can get a helluva lot more specific about what's going to happen and when. The sleep thing doesn't cut it."

"Richard, I *want* to be able to tell you. I'm not being a cow and keeping something away from you on purpose. There are these background voices I hear. The only time they became clear was on film with Gloria."

Richard looks at her as calmly as he can, worrying that something is going wrong with Karen after her miraculous wake-up. "It's only for one day, Karen. One piddly little overnight; I promised the office I'd do it months ago. They're not going to be able to find someone to go instead of me during Christmas week."

"What are you doing there that's so important?"

Richard then feels he is arguing with a teenager. "I have to go over sets and budgets with the crew down there. It has to be done and it has to be done in person."

"Whatever."

"Please don't whatever me."

"Whatever."

In spite of tensions, a truce of sorts is called and Christmas and the engagement party continue as planned. It is a day of small gifts and gentle surprises. Megan hand-made a roomful of decorations using construction paper and silver hearts. The windows are slightly steamed and the air is tinged with eggnog. Pam and Wendy boo-hoo shamelessly over the toasts, and even crusty old Hamilton has a lumpy throat while Linus seems concerned about the structural integrity of the meringue cake.

One truly odd moment occurs halfway through the event.

Guests hear a galvanizing *crack crack!* on the living room window, where an ostrich pecks the glass with a cruel, hilarious beak. It is as though everybody fell into a deep warm dream. Then another ostrich appears and begins clacking its beak onto the living room window while the room devolves into guffaws and chaos. Karen loves it: "Oh, *Richard*, this is just the bee's knees. Did you plan this just for me? It's so *sweet*."

Mr. Lennox from the house around the corner scoots into view with a coil of rope. A small mustachioed man, he apologizes profusely. "They escaped from the garage. I was supposed to take them out to Abbotsford, but everything's closed for the holidays."

Megan asks, "What does anybody need with a pair of dorky-looking ostriches?"

"Why Megan—they're the meat of tomorrow. Lean as tofu and tasty like beef. They're my retirement fund. Please, can you hold onto that rope for me?"

A well-cheered ostrich rodeo ensues. Poor Mr. Lennox is petrified that his investment might be damaged. "Oh, Christ— just don't let them get into the forest. Then we're doomed. They'll break their legs or get eaten by coyotes. They're that stupid."

By late afternoon, the sky has gone black and cold and the core group of friends sit by the fire eating huckleberry muffins. Megan had asked for them specifically, unaware that it was her pregnancy and not her taste buds speaking.

Later, the doorbell rings. Linus answers. It is Skitter, but Linus doesn't know him by face.

"Megan here?"

"Megan, your friend's here." Megan and Jenny soundlessly gloss over to the front door, into their coats, and out of the house. Richard, looking at CD's by the Christmas tree, hears nothing. Minutes later, Linus asks, "Who's biker dude?"

"Huh?"

"The guy Megan just left with. The guy with the scar."

"Guy with a scar?" Richard clues in. "*Shit*."

*　　*　　*

172

Flying home from Los Angeles, the captain allows Richard to peek out the front cockpit window a few minutes after takeoff. Richard sees the view of God: a dappled sky like a baby's giggles, volcanoes stretching up the coast, the Earth's gentle curve at the horizon. Back in his seat, while idly flipping through a two-week-old *Newsweek* and rereading an article about Karen, Richard mentally reviews the past week only to find himself chilled. A drop of cool sweat crawls like a slug through his hairline and into his eyes.

Richard's plane ride continues—a cold ride: the airlines are saving money by not heating the cabins as they once did. Dinner service comes and goes. The sun, low on the horizon, is wan and colorless: a December sunset; even sunlight feels dark.

Richard thinks about last night in his hotel room, watching Karen's TV appearance on a speakerphone with the family. It was a tight little production and Gloria had managed to orchestrate a predictable level of syrupy rudeness.

Afterward, he and Karen spent nearly an hour on the phone apologizing to each other, whispering endearments, and feeling close in that special way that only phones provide. *I think this darkness stuff is all in my head, Richard. I'm not going crazy and I'm sure these voices and stuff will soon be gone.*

Afterward, Richard fell into a dreamless sleep.

Then this morning he drove to Culver City, but after ten minutes of work, he started to panic. He went to the washroom, rinsed off his face, breathed furiously, and then instinctively hightailed the rental car to LAX, catching the next flight up the coast, paying for full-fare Business Class, desperate to be aloft, the wheels no longer on the ground.

On the tarmac while awaiting takeoff, he looked out the window of his 2F seat just in time to see a blue-overalled airline luggage handler praying at the feet of another obviously dead luggage handler. The man from a fuel truck was screaming into a cell phone while an airline employee threw his blazer over the employee's head. An ambulance came, the body was sheeted, the stewardess closed the door latch, and the plane took off.

173

Now, five miles above Oregon, Richard continues trying to make sense of his rashness and his tangled feelings. He tries using the GTE Airphone, but service is out. "Good afternoon, this is your captain speaking. We're experiencing a delay on the ground at Vancouver. Traffic controllers there have requested we stay aloft for half an hour or so while the situation down there is rectified. I hope you'll understand our situation and continue enjoying today's flight. As a goodwill gesture, flight attendants will be serving complimentary beer and wines."

There are groans and cheers while the jet flies over Seattle and then follows I-5 up to the Canadian border. The traffic below looks jammed like he's never seen it before. Holiday sales. People everywhere burning leaves in bonfires.

Once near Vancouver, the plane circles the city then flies over the Coast Mountains and makes lazy eights over the pristine frozen alps and lakes behind, a flying tour of Year Zero. Another delay is announced, and then finally, after two hours of dawdling, the plane lands on the runway, but just before doing so, the runway lights that guide the way go black.

At Vancouver's airport, Richard's flight is the only moving plane on the tarmac. The captain announces another delay, and the passengers spend one more hour on the tarmac—a problem with ground staff, but not to panic, even though, as passengers can plainly see, half the building is without light and there's not a single ground person in view.

The passengers become increasingly crazed with the discovery of a seat-buckled dead salesman in 27C and then a dead teenager in 18E. Fear amplifies. Passenger can plainly see that there's no action at the airport—no trucks or luggage carts or other activity. Another whole section of the terminal's lights blink then fail, and finally the flight attendants pop open the door and the passengers slide down an inflatable yellow escape chute. To enter the airport, they pass through a utility door with quiet, orderly docility. Upon finding a dead stewardess propped against an access door, this soon devolves into anarchy. Outside it's raining and inside the building it's cold. There are almost no people present—at the immigration lineup there are no staff, save for one woman in the corner wearing a white paper breathing mask waving them onward. Bodies are strewn about the airport. Passengers scuttle toward the mild hum of the luggage carousel, which chugs and dies, never again to cough forth the passengers' luggage.

Something has gone dreadfully wrong. Richard is dazed. Karen's future had come true. An adrenaline fang bites the rear of his neck.

There are no staff at customs. The phones are blank and no taxis wait outside—only one or two cars speeding like mad through the main traffic corridor. Richard hears a voice calling his name—it's Mr. Dunphy, no, *Captain* Dunphy, a neighbor from West Van.

"Richard? Is that you, Richard Doorland?"

"Oh. Hey, Captain Dunphy. Hi. What the hell's going on here?"

"*Christ*. You wouldn't believe it. You on the Los Angeles flight?"

"Yes, but—"

"There was a real debate about whether they should let you land or let your fuel run out flying over the mountains." Richard is dumbstruck. "The tower operators thought that planes would bring in more infected people, but it turned out *every*body was dropping off. The moment you touched the runway they turned off the lights and went home. C'mon, let's scram."

They bustle through a labyrinth of metal corridors, ramps, and NO ACCESS hallways for which Captain Dunphy has a magnetic card. At the end of their jaunt, they stand on the runway's apron, where the rain has temporarily stopped and clouds blot the sky like sullied dinner plates. From a piece of yellow luggage that has fallen from the hold of a 737 and then split open, Richard takes a large winter coat. Captain Dunphy grabs an electric luggage wagon.

"Where are we going?" Richard asks.

"To the jetty at the runway's end. My brother Jerry's coming over from West Van in his sixteen-footer to pick me up. Called him on my cell phone—I just got in from Taipei. Fucking nightmare. We had three deaths onboard and the passengers were going ape-shit between Honolulu and Vancouver. Screaming, wailing—*Christ*. We had to bolt shut the cockpit door."

The two scan the horizon for a boat or a light. "I wouldn't have believed it possible in all my years flying. I'm just glad I was able to get home. Once we docked, all the passengers simply ran. They didn't even wait for their luggage. I don't even know where these people could have gone. Waiting relatives. No taxis then, too."

176

"The plague—what is it?" Richard asks, his mind spooling out plotlines from 1970s sci-fi movies. "Who's dying? Old people? Babies? Any one group?"

"No pattern. *Everybody*. It brought down planes everywhere. All the big cities are fucked up. Vancouver, too. Noon today people started dropping like flies. It's pointless trying to drive anywhere downtown. It's a parking lot clogged with desperate, freaked-out people. People who catch this thing—whatever it is—have this powerful urge to sleep, so they lie down wherever they are—in their cars, on the mall floors, in the offices. A minute later, they're dead."

The runway drive is far longer than Richard might have thought. North, toward the city, Richard can see the plumes of smoke of several fires and patches of the city with failed electrical grids. They park near the muddy water at the runway's end. They hop off the luggage cart and stand in the rain as Captain Dunphy blinks a flashlight. They can see a boat coming toward them in the distance, and soon they hear a boat's engine in the December wind. Captain Dunphy blinks the flashlight to signal his brother; the boat berths sideways against the shore onto which sloppy water laps feebly. Captain Dunphy sees Jerry's suspicious face and says, "He's with me, Jerry. This is Richard, my neighbor."

"Hop in. It's going to be dark soon. Christ, the city's a mess. Everywhere's a mess. This plague—it's speeding up."

They hop into the boat, which jolts away from the shore like a knife tugged from a magnet. As the boat slaps against the small whitecaps, its passengers goggle the fevered city. Richard tries to phone home to Karen on Jerry's cell, but something's not working.

As they near West Vancouver, binoculars reveal that Lions Gate Bridge is full of cars. Not one is moving. On the mountain, fires are burning—their gray plumes more reminiscent of autumn leaf burn-offs than of burning houses.

The boat travels up the shore and docks at a private dock a mile west of the Park Royal mall, currently in flames. Onshore, Mrs. Dunphy is in a Volvo. They weave throughout West

Vancouver's curves and hairpins. They see cars parked on the roadsides with dead drivers behind the wheels. A minivan stops at a stop sign and they briefly see four children looking out the rear window, chalky silent faces frightened out of their wits. At the corner of Cross Creek and Highland, two men try to stop them, but Mrs. Dunphy stomps the gas pedal as they race down the hill toward home. A shot is fired, which cracks the rear window.

On Rabbit Lane, the electricity still works, but Lois's and George's cars are gone. Karen is on the floor by the blank, snowstorming TV. Her knees are up to her chin, but her eyes are far, far away. She's shivering madly. Her forearms resemble a freshly-plucked chicken.

"Karen? Karen—*honey*?" Richard says, but there is no response. He picks her up in his arms and is about to stand up when Karen speaks.

"It's happening," she says. "It's here. What I saw back then . . ."

"I know, honey."

"I tried to run away from it so long ago."

"Karen— I know, but you've gotta tell me. Something big's going on—all over the world. And you know what it is. Tell me, please." Karen squeezes her eyes shut and says nothing. Richard is exasperated: "Jesus H. *Christ*, Karen, can you tell me what's going on! Speak to me!"

She says, "The world's falling asleep. But not me. I don't know about you."

"Who told you?"

"The voices—they came in clearly this afternoon. I could finally hear them. Him. Jared. *It*. I don't know."

Richard carries her onto the couch, smothers her body in blankets, and ignites the gas fireplace, which throws off considerable heat. He then cradles Karen in his lap and she calms down. Richard collects his thoughts. "Now tell me, Karen, what are we in for? Why us? Why here? Why you and me and . . . ?"

"Richard, I have a brain the size of a seventeen-year-old's. It's not always easy."

"Does anybody else live?"

"I don't know. I only know about me."

"What are we supposed to be doing?"

"I told you I don't know. Now stop this."

Richard thumps the sofa. "Jared! *Jared!* Can you hear me?"

"Don't scare me by thumping like that. Anyway, he, or whatever it is, can't hear you, Richard. He's busy."

"How obvious. I should have known."

"This is *not* a very good time or place for sarcasm, Richard."

"It's called irony these days."

"Whatever."

23 STEEL MINK BEEF MUSIC

She breathed deeply; the plastic-wrapped beef was cool on her cheeks.

The lucky people, thinks Lois, will fall asleep *inside* their sleep: blissful sleepiness followed with a visit to dreamland forever—*heaven*—the cold clear hills and alps that graced the world of her youth.

Lois was at Super-Valu in Park Royal, striding purposefully amid the store's glorious aisles of glorious food all gloriously lit, when the sleeping began. She was savoring the waves of admiration sent her way by staff and shoppers who recognized her from the previous evening's broadcast.

"You are so *strong*," said one young woman.

"A saint," said another. Lois's cheeks burned with pleasure.

Lois was the first shopper to notice a sleeper, a young woman in blue sweat clothing asleep beneath the cauliflower and broccoli bins. Lois bent down to gently tap her on the shoulder; a shank of hair fell from the woman's face revealing her peaceful death mask.

Paramedics were called, and no sooner had the young woman been moved into the back office when a shout came from down the mall outside the Super-Valu—news of another death. A nervous buzz began among the shoppers. "Just the *oddest* thing, isn't it?" said the woman in line in front of Lois. "Plastic bags please—I mean, you just don't see something like that too often and then—"

Lois's eyes flared wide open; behind their till the cashier was yawning, falling down onto her knees and taking a nap before them. "Hello?"

The cashier from the next till came over. "Susan? *Susan?*" The cashier looked up at Lois. "No," Lois said, "it can't be."

The woman grabbed the intercom and beckoned management down to the tills pronto. Another shopper fell asleep on the frozen foods aisle's cold white floor. With news of this, delicate pandemonium broke out. Customers abandoned their carts and dashed for the exits. A voice came over the speakers announcing that due to technical problems, the store would have to close for the day.

Lois watched the shoppers panic. The man behind her squeezed his full cart through the space behind the clerk and left the store without paying. Lois, like some shoppers, moved out of the checkout area and stood silently in one of the main aisles to watch the scene unfold. Two more shoppers keeled over; the mall's tiny first-aid post lost its ability to cope with trauma. From some unknown corner, a siren, dormant since the days of the USSR, woke up frightened and cranky.

At the end of the aisle Lois saw her neighbor, Elaine Buchanan, piling steaks and chickens into a cart. She walked down to say, "Elaine—"

"Lois. If you're smart, you'll do this, too. Whatever's going on is way bigger than any of us." Elaine lurched slightly, putting a Family-Pak of hamburger into the storage area on the cart's bottom. "That does it—I'm bailing out of here. Better for you, too."

"But Elaine—how do we know this isn't just a local thing?"

"Lois, listen to the sirens."

Lois had the strange sensation of being back in the 1960s, back when grocery stores had contests where a winner could keep all the food that could be crammed into a cart within sixty seconds. She had always wanted to win that particular prize.

Many shoppers had taken Elaine's strategy to heart; Lois stood and watched her world go random, shoppers pilfering the shelves as fast as tinned pyramids could topple. There was a scream, a shout, the sound of tipped carts and breaking jars. And then the main lights failed and emergency lighting kicked in. Lois saw panicked silhouettes, like visions of souls in the underworld, percolate over by the front entrance where lazy daylight chinked into the structure. Another body hit the ground.

The lights returned and the store was almost empty of patrons; a few lay conspicuously asleep on the floor. Rather peaceful looking, Lois thought. She bent down to look into their faces and said good night to them. She walked out toward the front of the store and nobody stopped her or prodded her onward. Shrill alarms continued flaring from unknown corners. Turning around, Lois saw that the store was all but abandoned. The lights failed once more and Lois calmly walked around the supermarket bathed in pale orange light. Nearby, Elaine lay asleep on the floor, a cartload of beef her tombstone.

The Super-Valu was her empire. Today is the twenty-eighth—the day her daughter had foolishly predicted some kind of end. Karen. *Who is this child of mine? What did I ever do to deserve her? What did I ever do that led us to this, this collapse of the world?* Lois rifled through her memories of Karen's youth, but found no particular incident that might lead her to believe Karen was special—marked for a strange destiny.

Lois thought of Karen and the children who grew up so wild inside the forest. She remembered what the realtor had said when they bought the Rabbit Lane house in 1966. George had asked him if there were any community centers for the kids to go to. The realtor laughed and pointed to the forest. "That's all you need." Lois has no doubt that the children did filthy, vile things in there. Drugging. Fucking. Drinking.

She yawns and looks down at the frozen meat section. So cool and comforting. Her upper skull is tingly, and she remembers photographs of Elizabeth Taylor with a bald, scarred head after brain surgery. *I think I've had just about as much of this world as I'm able to take. I'm pooped. I'm sleepy. I just want to go home.* She lifts her legs and climbs up onto the meat. She breathes deeply; the plastic-wrapped beef cool on her cheeks. She closes her eyes and goes home.

*   *   *

Linus and Pam are filming on location a few miles up the mountain in a vast, stuccoed bunker resembling a cross between a medical/dental center and the compound of a South American drug lord. It is a neighborhood of houses built in the early nineties designed solely to maximize floor space and ignore the outer world save for a postcard city view out the front windows. The view dictated that the neighborhood be free of trees. Even at the best of times, a drive through its unpeopled streets lined with blank white boxes was spooky; on a glum day charged with blood, it is outright haunting.

The job of the day is a cop-and-buddy film involving guns and betrayal with just about all the actors turning into what Linus calls "lawn sprinklers" at the end. The shoot is going slowly, and the star, hung over from a holiday binge, is forgetting his lines, walking into walls, ab-libbing dumb sight gags, and causing continuity issues that take an hour apiece to clean up while Linus and Pam refit the star with blood charges, makeup, hair, and fresh shirts and pants. As the day wears on and the number of takes multiplies, the minds of workers on the set begin to wander and look out at the view of the city.

Cut.

Pam walks around the living room, touching up the shooting victims who will spend most of their day lying in strange contortions on the furniture and floor, pretending to be dead. She smiles and is a good sport, but in the back of her mind she's thinking of Karen's broadcast last night. She came across as so . . . sugary gooey. Not Karen at all. Megan came across as an average-seeming teenager. Oh, if the audience knew the truth! And Lois came across as Belinda Q. Housewife. *Well, that's TV—that's what TV does.*

After lunch, the crew and actors are all in better moods. While setting the mock-dead actors back into place, Linus says, "Pam—look out at the city, the fire." Pam looks out, and rising from somewhere in the city is a smoke plume, pointy at the bottom and rising into a slippery triangle like a marzipan tornado.

"Office building fire?"

"I dunno."

183

The scene continues. The star, mistakenly thinking his enemies have been killed by the CIA, opens his front door calmly for perhaps the first time in his life, only to be assailed with machine-gun fire from which he escapes (of course). After this, he turns around to see black-sweatered armed thugs whom he promptly shoots dead in a series of quick takes. Only the star survives.

"You know, Linus, I wish movies could be filmed in sequence."

"Body number three needs spritzing."

Pam heads to body number three to freshen up the blood. "Wakey wakey, drug lord," Pam says, but the actor plays dead. Pam says, "Smart-ass," and returns to edge of the scene and through a side window notes that there are now several plumes over the city. She nudges Linus: 'Look."

The scenes requiring the bodies are finished. Pam helps them up and out of their mucky togs. "Hey smart-ass—the scene's over." Smart-ass doesn't move. "Oh God, you actors—do you *ever* get enough attention? C'mon, Gareth, you have to prep for the next scene."

Gareth still doesn't move. Hands on hips, Pam looks out the window at the city now covered with a score of plumes—columns, holding up the sky. She shivers and gets on her knees. In her bones, she feels the truth: "Gareth? Gareth? Oh, shit. Dorrie? Get Dorrie!" Dorrie, the production assistant, comes over. "He's dead."

"What's that?" The director, Don, comes over.

"Call an ambulance."

"Dead? Nobody *dies* during a shoot."

"Don, how can you be a prick at a time like this?"

There's a ruckus out by the catering truck; one of the servers, a plump fortyish woman, has been found dead at the feet of the lunch buffet table. Someone rushes in to say, "Sandra's dead. Call 911. Quick—who ate lunch here?"

A buzz passes through the workers: *food poisoning.*

"No. It can't be. Gareth's girlfriend made him a macrobiotic lunch. He never eats the catered stuff."

"You mean—well if it's *not* food poisoning . . ."

"Nine-one-one's gone dead. I can't get through to the States, either.'

'Phones are all dead, Don."

Shit.

Already actors and crew are evaporating from the set. Pam and Linus wipe the makeup and fake blood from Gareth. Outside, they can already see the city on fire, too many fires to count. They walk out onto the balcony. "Karen," Linus says.

"I know."

"We should go home."

Inside the house, the director is screaming at those people still remaining. Don comes out onto the deck, glowers at Pam and Linus, looks at the city, and then screams at nobody in particular.

"Let's wash up," Pam says.

Yet in the end, Pam and Linus stay longer than the others. Duty. Linus says, "My parents are visiting family out in the Fraser Valley, an hour away at the best of times. Pam, take a look through these binoculars—there's no traffic moving anywhere."

Pam looks. "My parents," she says, gently lowering the binoculars. "They're down in Bellingham with Richard's parents—after-Christmas sales."

"Hamilton?"

"At home. Wendy?"

"She's on double-shift at the hospital."

They turn around and their eyes catch: fear.

Gareth's body still rests on the floor as the sky darkens. A few of the crew members, unable to get anywhere in nightmare traffic and unable to think of anywhere else to go, return to the house. As a group, they wrap Gareth in a canvas tarpaulin and place him in a cool, animal-proof garden shed. And a few minutes later, as Linus and Pam pull out of the driveway in their car, the neighborhood's electricity fails and they drive down the hill under a soot gray sky.

*   *   *

185

Wendy's "day" had already passed the twenty-six-hour mark when her first sleeper arrived dead at the hospital just shortly into the lunch hour—a North Van housewife a neighbor had found sleeping on the steps outside her house, her Collie's leash in her hand, the dog whimpering. Wendy was examining this body when two more sleepers were brought through the door—an eight-year-old girl who had fallen asleep on a swing set and an elderly woman's husband who had fallen asleep on the passenger side of her car while driving to the pet food store. She thought he might have had a stroke.

And then the cord of normalcy snapped. Over the next several hours, Wendy helped catalog perhaps a hundred more sleepers, most of whom had been driven to the hospital by friends or family, owing to overtaxed ambulances. And for every body taken to the hospital there were hundreds if not thousands out there who didn't make it.

Later in the day, the radio broadcasts a plea saying that the hospitals are unable to process any further patients. Nothing is known about this new sickness, nor is any treatment available.

The hospital staff are confused and frightened beyond words, but they work on. Wendy reaches the thirty-four-hour mark and is dead on her feet and needs to sleep, yet at the same time she needs to go home—to check on Linus—*Linus*—as well as to ... as well as to ... *what*? Phones are out, cell phones, too.

What is happening is what *Karen* knows about. This also has something to do with Pam's and Hamilton's stereo dreams. The answer isn't at the hospital. The answer is back at Rabbit Lane.

Stepping over log booms of the dead, she is feeling almost as tired as the day's sleepers. She understands the sleepers and their complete lack of fear as they go groggy and lie down wherever the need hits them. Wendy feels the same way, but she knows it's only sleep she needs at the moment, not death.

Linus had dropped her off at work yesterday, her own car being in the shop. She finds that the only transportation alternative available now is walking: *Taxis gone; don't know how*

186

to steal a car. Walking will take a few hours, but she refuses to hitchhike—even out on Lonsdale all civil decency seems to have evaporated. In the dark, she walks up to the Trans-Canada highway, where cars are traveling at speeds she thought unimaginable. She spots two accidents—either sleepers or leadfoots—but no emergency vehicles attend the scene. Nobody seems to be slowing up, even for a juicy rubberneck, which strikes Wendy as most unusual human behavior. She considers this when, without warning, the Esso station by the Westview overpass explodes like a jet at an air show—bodies like ventriloquist dolls puked into the sky as though in a cartoon or an action-adventure film.

The traffic slows down and freezes, never to start again. *Is everybody going home? Will home be safe? Or perhaps home is only familiar. What do they expect at the other end that will make them feel safe? What will make them strong?*

Wendy walks over to the gas station, where seared bodies lie in the grass embankment just below: all six thoroughly dead, no survivors. Shards of a VW bus remain where the gas pumps once stood and the husks of shotguns and rifles. What can Wendy do? She's so tired she can barely think, let alone act.

From the grass below the station, Wendy picks up a twenty-four-pack of M&Ms and decides to walk onward; nobody can be saved here. And what other choices does she have? Only the electricity, perversely, seems to be intact: streetlights and the storefronts light the looted Westview Mall. Sleeping and dead bodies lie crash-dummied across the asphalt, sprinkled with broken liquor bottles and shop-front glass. How many people are dead? How many people will die? Why is this happening? Am I infected? Is Linus okay? Where was everybody and will they reach home safely?

Wendy looks onto the Trans-Canada, where many people like her, stranded without cars, are walking dronishly down the freeway's margin, shuffling inside the glare of the headlights stalled behind them. A middle-aged man in a yellow raincoat is asleep under the overpass. A multi-car pileup has plowed off the Mosquito Creek bridge and down into the ravine.

Wendy decides to walk overground, through quiet suburban streets, around the small commercial strip at Edgemont Village where the armed forces are guarding a Super-Valu. Even there she can see a dead soldier asleep in a Starbucks alcove.

In one of the smaller streets, she finds a ten-speed bike lying on its side for no discernible reason. She looks around—nobody near—then takes it and pedals toward the dam, where she crosses over and reaches home through the dark forest she knows by heart.

24 | THE PAST IS A BAD IDEA

Megan is keeled over a flower bed vomiting up the eel that writhes within her stomach; camouflaging her pregnancy is becoming increasingly difficult. In the flower bed's soil, she sees beer bottle caps and cigarette butts. *Ugh.* Skitter is no dream neighbor: shitty, oily car wrecks rust inside the garage; the lawn is a crab-grassed junkyard.

She feels her stomach giggle, as though the eel has left and a small bird is now fluttering insider her—this new piece of life. She wonders what personality her new child will have. Will it be condemned to loserdom with Skitter's DNA? Megan hasn't told Skitter about her pregnancy, nor does she feel likely to. Once she tells him, the child is no longer just her own; she'll have to share it. She doesn't want this. She was tempted to mention her pregnancy last week when the Americans were up taping the TV show, but pulled back.

The TV show: Megan can't believe how sucky she looked in it, but she thinks it was more good than bad. She's happy that she and Karen came across as pals rather than as a mother–daughter unit. And Megan's also happy that they only gave Lois a small amount of air-time. *Ha!*

Walking in through Skitter's basement door, she catches a reflection of herself in a scrap of mirror leaning against the wall. Last night her head looked fat, but Karen, so emaciated in real life, looked almost fashionably thin. So what they say about cameras adding ten pounds is true. More like twenty.

Back inside the kitchen, Megan finds a clean mug and makes instant coffee and turns on the radio to a local rock station, at which point she notices sirens in the background obscuring

189

the music. She looks down at her arms in the watery midday light: She is stronger now. She eats only good food. She exercises. She no longer does drugs, and she feels ridiculous being in Skitter's house—as though she's been forced back into the seventh grade. Stupid of her to end up here. She can faintly hear Skitter and Jenny making it in the bedroom.

The first sip of coffee burns her tongue, and she idly kills time melting a few undissolved coffee nodules on top of the coffee. She reads biker magazines for a while and time vanishes. She needs to vomit and again heads out into the flower bed. There, after a dry wretch, she lifts her head and sees a pair of plaid-trousered legs protruding from behind a corner of the neighbor's house. She walks over to investigate. It is an older man—sixty? He seems to have had a heart attack. She rings the man's doorbell, but nobody answers, so she returns to Skitter's to phone an ambulance. The phone is dead.

There is a song on the radio – "Blue Monday"—a rhythmic 1980s dirge. Then the radio signal goes blank. Megan goes to change the station, but the stations all sound foreign. The music has vanished. Just voices now: a crisis is occurring, but authorities are unable to be more specific. The gist is that people are dropping like flies all over town—a panic is gridlocking the city and causing untold violence. Megan looks out the window: small birds flittering in the firs; a touch of rain. Certainly no crisis could be happening *here*. Is this a *joke*?

The radio station has decided to cancel all music; other stations have done the same. Announcers everywhere are telling people not to panic or use phones or electricity unless their situation is critical. Megan decides that this news is important enough to tell Skitter and Jenny, and she knocks on the bedroom door and hears no reply. She knocks louder, to which Skitter yells, "Jee*zus*. I'm busy. Get the fuck away." Megan knocks once more. Skitter rips open the door and says, "*What?*" Jenny is in the background looking defiant, lighting a cigarette and showing off her breasts.

"There's a crisis going on."

"You got me up for a *that*?"

190

"Crisis. A plague. People are dying. Like in the movies."

"Go *away*, and that's a shitty joke." Skitter locks the door and Megan pounds it once more; Skitter returns and yells again for her to leave. At this point, Skitter's car-fixing friends, Randy and Scott, galumph in the front door, both looking pale.

"Hey, Megan. Skitter in there?"

"*Duh.*"

"Skitter," shouts Randy, "the city's all fucked up, man. The news is for real."

"Randy, I . . ." Skitter looks at the three faces outside his door. He throws a towel around his waist. "Okay. Crank the TV."

"Skitter," whines Jenny, "come back."

"Not now, Jailbait. Time for action."

Megan says, "You're such a pig, Skitter. You don't believe anything until a *guy* tells you."

Soon everyone is in the living room watching TV. The CNN footage they see tightly clamps their attention: helicopter shots of smoking downtown cores—Atlanta? Los Angeles? New York? All cities have embraced madness; all major bridges and tunnels are hopelessly snarled, accident-clogged roads everywhere resemble the contents of a child's Halloween sack spilled onto the pavement. A local news helicopter shows Vancouver's freeways and bridges rendered impassable. Pedestrians resembling evacuees trudge to suburban homes far away, occasionally having to gingerly step over bodies. Looting is kept to a minimum—people are too fearful of contamination to steal.

The five people in Skitter's living room stare out the window into the backyard greenery. Is this a bad dream for all of them? Randy and Scott take off to wherever they live. Skitter plays with his mustache and grins: "I'm going to do a bit of window shopping. Megan, Jenny. Coming along?"

"Give me a ride home," Megan says.

"What—to your *dad's* place?"

"Rabbit Lane, bozo."

Minutes later, as they drive out onto the larger roads of the suburb, bedlam reigns. Traffic lights are skipped; cars drive over lawns; cars containing sleepers are pushed off the roadside by more robust vehicles. A corner grocery-store owner stands outside his front door with a sawn-off shotgun, a weapon Megan recognizes from her lifetime of TV viewing.

Jenny is jack-rabbiting about the Satellite's front seat, swearing and bug-eyed at the dimensions of the crisis. Sleepers are everywhere—in cars, on sidewalks, in parking lots. "Oh, this is just too weird. Skitter, I wanna go home."

"Soon, enough. I want to do some shopping first."

"Everybody's heading *home*," Megan says to herself, and she wonders what will happen to these people once they *get* home. Will they wait to die? Will they sit still? She realizes that there is no tactical advantage to being home. At home all you can do is nothing. Even still, what other place can there be?

The car pulls up to a Shopper's Drug Mart in Lynn Valley, where the parking lot is now a crashing, squealing bumper car ride. All car windows are rolled up and many drivers are simply plowing through the landscaping to escape. The power is now out. Skitter leaps out of the car with his down jacket pockets brimming with handguns. At the mall's main entrance, Megan and Jenny can see an RCMP officer telling Skitter to leave. Skitter shoots him dead right there in the head and the two girls scream and hop out of the car. *Skitter has gone mental.*

Megan runs up to the officer and cradles his leaking head. She hears another blast from inside the mall and sees a few stragglers run outside clutching weird, stolen-looking objects: enormous cartons of cigarettes and boxes of appliances. "Jenny!" Megan turns around, but Jenny has fallen asleep on a bench not far away, her mouth open, a forgotten newspaper flapping under her tongue.

Another blast cuts the air. Megan runs to the other side of the lot, opposite the Satellite, and tries to collect her wits. Shortly, Skitter leaves the Drug Mart with cartons of prescription tablets. He looks around, more likely for other armed opponents than for Megan, and when he reaches the car, he hurls the boxes into the backseat and then—and then— *nothing.*

Megan walks over for a better look; Skitter has fallen asleep in the front seat. Megan is too confused to be terrified for herself. "Oh, God—oh *God*." The mall seems drained of people, and the parking lot has cooled down to near emptiness. Traffic on the road above is filled with speeders and horns and bumps and squeals.

How to get home?

The sky darkens. She can hear herself breathe. It's only a week past the shortest day of the year and it feels it. Looking at Skitter, she's too afraid of his death to rifle his pocket for his car's keys. She creeps into the mall, now lit only by emergency bulbs. From a sporting goods store she takes a mountain bike and from the drug store some Tylenol-3, two nine-volt flashlights, and Bubblicious gum. A lost springer spaniel behind her barks and startles her. Outside, back in Skitter's car, she takes two handguns then sets out to navigate her way home through the craziness of the highway.

The two miles from Lynn Valley to Westview are vastly more insane than she could have conceived. Nothing is moving save for motorcycles and crazy people driving down the shoulders and over the embankments, plowing whatever lies in their way. Three times, men try to stand in her way to take her bike; three times, Megan has shot them in or near their feet and feels a bit sicker with each *crack*. She realizes the next miles of highway leading up to the Rabbit Lane exit are going to be impassable. While planning her next steps, a motorcyclist pulls over in front of her—a big bruiser Yamaha. The driver kicks the kickstand, hops off, winks at Megan, and falls asleep face-first onto the pavement.

Megan instantly hops onto the bike and guns it up Delbrook Road, through Edgemont and across Cleveland Dam. By now it's fully dark. She takes the utility road up to Glenmore then bombs down Stevens and into Rabbit Lane. She is home.

What an ucking-fay aste-way of an ay-day.

Hamilton wakes up with a crashing headache and tumultuous hangover; his brain feels like a boxcar full of dying aliens being buried in the desert soil—an image taken from an old episode of Richard's TV show. Shortly before noon, he hobbles up for water, stubs his toe on a chair leg, curses, feels his head throb, and quickly snugs into the tangle of sheets and duvet that is his lair while he recuperates. The phone rings somewhere in the afternoon; he ignores it. Around three, he gets a glass of orange juice and the morning paper and tries to read the paper in bed, but he's still dizzy. He gives it up, turns out the light, and waits for Pam to return around six.

Wendy is lost in the forest. She is tired. She thought she knew the correct pathway home; now she has only the hushed roar of the Dam to the north to give her guidance. There is no moon or glow from the city—the clouds are too dense. The ten-speed is gone long ago, its wheels bent after snagging a root. She hears occasional explosions or booms down toward the city.

The path twists; trees that fell during last year's storms confuse her memory of the trails. Suddenly, there's a stream where there ought to have been soil and ferns where there ought to be stone. Wendy falls to her knees—she is beyond tired. She can't even begin to count the hours she has been awake. A half-formulated idea flits within her mind: She will build a nest of ferns to keep her warm until daybreak. This is only a foolish child's dream. She knows it.

She cuts her knee on a burl. She reaches down to hold the cut when in her peripheral vision she sees a pale yellow haze of light float down from the treetops, a shape and shade of green and gold, steadily falling down, down, down. She pivots her head to watch the light's steady downward sweep, steady and smooth like a glass elevator. It stops.

"Hello Wendy." It's Jared, standing before her, impossibly young, unchanged from the sunny day he threw a football to a startled Wendy eating lunch alone in the bleachers.

"Jared? Sweetie? Is that *you*?"

The light that is Jared holds his finger to his lips and shushes Wendy. He extends his hand and Wendy clasps its lightness—

there is no actual touch sensation, yet suddenly she is warm. This is all she'd ever wanted.

She says, "Jared, I've missed you so much. I've—we've all—" She begins to blubber. "I loved you and I miss you and the world has never been the same since you left. And now I'm lost and I'm frightened and the world seems to be closing down and dying. I'm a doctor now—I was at the hospital today. Oh Wendy, stop being so *emo*tional."

Jared kisses his fingers, flicks the kiss at Wendy, smiles, and makes a wanking off gesture. He nods his head to indicate that Wendy should follow. His long curly hair doesn't jiggle as his head moves. Wendy follows him, lit by his body's gentle sulfur color. Wendy's feet squelch in mud patches and her cheeks burn red, thwacked by damp salmonberry twigs. They wind through unfamiliar paths, and they reach a straightaway that Wendy recognizes. Jared stops. He moves his eyebrows the way he did two decades previously to indicate that he's leaving.

"You're leaving? No. Jared—*no*. Don't go. Please stay with me. Talk. I missed you so much. You were all I ever wanted. It's only half a world without you."

But Jared gently pulls away his hand and walks back three paces. He smiles and melts downward into the soil like a peg in a hole. Wendy is left behind. She grabs a small stone at the point where Jared's head left the path and crushes it so hard in her palm that her skin bleeds. For years, Wendy had thought the world was fine and complete—that she could make do with what she had worked for and with what life had handed her. Now she knows this has never been true.

She arrives out onto the sunlit street and sees her own house unlit, but decides not to go there. She sees candlelight down the road at Karen's, so she walks that way. Once inside, she looks around at the familiar faces lit by the flames. She says to them, "I'm going to sleep. I'm not tired—not *that* kind of tired—I'm exhausted." She tumbles into a warm clump on the couch. Linus places a mohair blanket over her, and Wendy flinches at his touch.

"The Queen is dead."

"Go on," Richard says.

Karen continues: "The two princes are wearing blackout sunglasses. The Queen's body is being lowered into a grave. Only a few people are looking through the palace fence. It's dark out—and raining. The grave is all muddy."

Silence.

"Karen, do you really have to wear that paper bag over your head?"

"It's not just *one* paper bag, Richard, it's *three* bags. I can't see my visions properly if there's even one speck of light hitting my face. Even candlelight. It's a recognized paranormal fact."

"You look like a joke wearing it."

"Yeah, a real triple-bagger, Richard."

"Richard," Hamilton says, "could you please shut up? Let Karen speak."

"Hamilton, stop being an alpha male for just one second and let Karen alone."

"Hey, Wendy, excuse *me* for being so interested in what is decidedly one great big dung heap of a situation. I thought you were asleep."

"I'm not going to sleep through this situation no matter how tired I am."

"He's right, Wen," Pam says, "this is an *extremely* not good situation."

"*Quiet*, everybody. If you want me to tell you what I can see, then be quiet. Could you all put your personalities on hold for just two minutes?"

Karen is trying to describe the collapse of the world to her terrified friends, who are masking their fear with funeral giggles—a protective, ironic coating. "Okay. Let me see— Pam, did I just hear you yawn?"

Pam jumps: "Yawn? No! Tired? Not at all." The group is entirely afraid of yawning, physical comfort, and anything that might make them restful or sleepy. Their coffee is strong.

"Karen," Hamilton says, "do you have a little list of who makes it and who doesn't?"

"You're being facetious, Hamilton. I don't have a list. And I don't know where my information comes from."

"Hmmm. I think Mr. Liver needs a drink."

"Can we get on with this?" Richard asks.

"Richard, please remove the paper bags from my head. I don't know if this is a good time for me to trance. You people have to stop thinking I have this huge scoreboard in my head with constant information spewing out that I'm not telling you. It's not like that. I tell you facts whenever I can."

The room goes silent. "I need a break. Linus, can you turn on the generator again? Let's scan the radio and watch that CNN tape again."

Linus activates the Honda generator and Karen's house on Rabbit Lane regains electric light. The radio squawks out only predictable news: Every human activity has shut down—hospitals, dams, the military, malls. All machines are turned off. Once again, they watch the CNN VHS tapes Karen recorded earlier that afternoon before the power failed. The tape plays and again Pam and Hamilton blanch as they see the images they witnessed in stereo last Halloween play themselves out on screen: Dallas; India; Florida . . . They have no idea what to make of them.

Sleep that night is dodgy. Helicopters buzz the trees; a military jet strafes the mountain then crashes somewhere down near Park Royal. Blankets and duvets are brought downstairs and the fire is stoked and everybody camps there. Unspoken is the agreement to not display fear. Yet in spite of the fear, Richard is excited by the fantastic changes of the day. They all are. Richard remembers a few years ago on the Port Mann bridge where he witnessed a five-car pileup coming the other way—that same combination of being special and thrilled. He remembers being the only child in his third-grade class not to get a flu one year.

Before lights out, Linus asks for helpers to collect water samples to check with the Geiger counter. Shadows of neighbors can be seen walking out in the rain while the quacking sound of ostriches can be heard down the block.

Karen remembers the exact point of the day when the Great Change began. She'd been sitting alone in the TV room waiting for the noon news rotation on CNN. She was feeling partially angry, restless, and bored, as well as somewhat silly over telling Richard not to go to California.

"Karen, stop beating yourself up over this," Richard had said during one of the many arguments on the subject. "Nothing's going to happen. If I *don't* go to Los Angeles, then I'm just enabling your paranoia."

"*Huh?*" Karen remembered that modern people occasionally lapse into a strange jargon of emotional claptrap and hooey. "Richard, I'm only telling you what I saw and heard in my heart."

"Please, Karen, don't make this any harder—*please*."

And so Richard went to Los Angeles. Lois had gone out shopping and George was down at the auto shop; Megan was out with Jenny; and the gang were all out in the world on the one day she knew they oughtn't to be.

Chilly, she wore three sweaters and a pair of Richard's gray work socks; her legs that morning were sore and hard to move. She was listlessly watching CNN while trying to unscrew a coffee thermos, at which point the TV screen fuzzed into snow and then flared a brilliant white. She looked up and dropped the thermos. Other lamps in the TV room as well as the kitchen pulsed brightly then browned out while the entire house bumped and wavered as though it were an improperly docking boat.

"It's *you*, Karen said. "*You*. You're finally here."

Yes.

To her right, the glass patio door jiggled as she watched its hook unlatch itself—*clack*. With a rusty dry squeaking, the glass slid across its floor runner and the rain blew a cluster of brown leaves inside. Karen began to caterpillar her body across the room, a throw rug caught on her numb senseless legs like sacks of potatoes strapped onto her waist. Brisk wet air and rain slapped her face as she neared the sliding door. *Oh God, the glass is so heavy. Go away.* A tug of war began between herself and the door's mass.

Show yourself, Karen said, her weak spindly hands aching as she pushed the door closed ever so slowly. *Why'd you do this? Why'd you take my youth? Go away. I know you're here. That should be enough.*

She was crying, her face wet, her hands red, feeling as though the tendons were peeling like ribbons from her bones. With a final jolt, the door slammed shut and she fell exhausted onto the linoleum's ancient daisies. *There.* And then came a crash from the outside, like a tackled football player, *oomph*, the sliding door's glass shattering into a spider's web lace, a million tiny shards in a fraction of a second—yet only a few tiny shards tinkling out from the middle, allowing the wind to whistle through the small remaining hole. Karen screamed and then went silent, laid back on the floor, stared at the ceiling, and waited for what could only be bad news. She grabbed a cool, soft cushion that had fallen from the couch and used it to calm her eyes, holding it over her face. The TV resumed its babbling in the background; Karen found the remote button and began recording a tape.

She thinks: I had so little time to enjoy the world and now it's soon to be over. I don't want to live in what this world is about to become. I yearn to leave my body. I yearn to leave this life quickly and cleanly, as though falling into a mine shaft. I want to climb a mountain—any mountain—and put the world behind me, and when I reach the top turn into a piece of the sun. My body is so weak and scrawny. I miss holding things. I miss wiggling my toes and I miss my period. I never held Megan as a baby.

She thinks: I used to ski once. The sky would be so cold it ached, but I was warm and I sped down the snow like a dancer. I used to jump and twirl. And I've never complained until now—not once. But I wanted to enjoy the world a bit more— just a little bit more.

She can hear a helicopter overhead and booms from downtown. *It's happening quickly, isn't it?*

She closes her eyes and she sees things—images of blood and soil mixed together like the center of a Black Forest cake; Grand Canyons of silent office towers. Houses, coffins, babies, cars, brooms, and bottle caps all burning and draining into the sea and dissolving like candies. There's a reason for this, she's sure. She sees a convenience store in Texas, and a black-and-white monitor camera shows two children lying on the floor covered in slush drinks. She sees a nerve gas explosion at Tooele, Utah, a yellow ghost rising to haunt the continent. She sees work cubicles—an office in São Paulo, Brazil, yellow sticky notes falling like leaves from a tree onto the carpeting.

This is the moment she's been waiting for and dreading. Now it's here.

26 | PROGRESS IS OVER

The next day, Richard and Megan drive through the water-soaked mountain, through ten-thousand ranch homes, some of them burnt or burning, past forlorn souls staggering through the landscape firing pistols at the horizon, their faces haggard and failed.

Few other cars are driving. Many houses have their doors wide open and the urban animals—the dogs and raccoons and skunks—have been quick to enter. A car is parked in the middle of a lawn; two dead dogs rest upon a driveway's end.

All the people we've ever known, think Richard and Megan, *the best-looking girl in high school; favorite movie stars; old friends; lighthouse keepers and lab technicians. Am-scrayed.*

On Bellevue, they find Richard's parents' condominium blandly indifferent to the world's transformation. Inside, the clocks still tick; two coffee mugs sit unwashed on the drain board; a calendar reads:

2:30 Crown fixed

olive oil

chicken stock

asparagus

Bellingham w. Sinclairs

They can hear the ocean outside the front windows. Upstairs in the main bedroom, the odor of Richard's parents is strong. Their bed has the feel of a memorial stone. Parents.

They were the engines and the rudders of suburban life.

201

Richard's and Pam's parents will never return from the States, nor will Hamilton's father return from Kauai or his mother from Toronto. Linus's parents and Wendy's father are sixty miles away, which might as well be a million. Karen's parents haven't come home, and Karen has given the impression they are not to be expected.

Megan sits on her grandparents' bed and sniffles, then hits herself.

"Why'd you do that, Meg?"

"For being too weak to cry like a real human being."

"Oh, honey . . ."

Richard puts his arm around Megan's shoulder and he allows her to blubber; he can do so himself later. Once she's cried out, Richard says, "Let's collect some things right now. Some to bury and some to keep."

Megan stands up and half-heartedly shuffles about. A pair of house slippers; a pearl necklace; a pipe; framed photos. Megan clutches a pillow so that she can remember her grandmother's smell.

They walk out onto the deck and look across the water to downtown. The sky is overcast and smoky, tinged with burning wood and scorched brake pads. As Richard looks at the view, Megan goes inside and returns shortly with one of Richard's mother's diamond clip earrings. "Here," she says, "bend down, Dad." Megan takes the diamond and presses it into the center of Richard's palm. He looks at the crackles of white light that glint from within it and he remembers a day long ago with Megan down at Ambleside Beach, a bright day. He was gazing at the sun and the light on the water and had thought that there is a light within us all—a light brighter than the sun, a light inside the mind. He had forgotten this and now he remembers, there on the balcony.

The roads are clear and silent as Linus, Wendy, Hamilton, and Pam drive up the slope of Eyremont Drive. Once at the top, the city lies before them, a glinting damaged sheet of pewter, with fires burning like acetylene pearls fallen from a broken

202

choker. Ropes of smoke rise from the ground as though teth-ered to the damage; in the harbor, oily gorp has spilled into the waves and burns a Bahamian turquoise blue.

"The ocean's on fire," Hamilton says. "Like a sea of burning whiskey." Linus captures the image on Hi-8.

As of yet, nobody shows signs of mourning; they are still shellshocked. *What exactly is a citizen to do?* they wonder. *What possible purpose or meaning could there be in this strange situation?*

"I was in a train once," Pam says, "in England, returning to London from someone's country house near Manchester." She lights a cigarette. "It was morning and I was deadly hung over and had to get back to London. At eleven o'clock, the train pulled to a stop—it was Remembrance Day morning— and all machinery stopped and all noises and voices stopped, and the world went silent. There was silence for one minute as everybody closed their eyes. A whole *country* shut its eyes. I felt as though the world had stopped. In my head I thought, *So this is what the end of the world is like.* I thought, *So this is what it's like when time ends.* I kind of feel that way now."

The breeze changes direction. "What's that smell?" Hamil-ton asks. Already they can smell—the *smell.* Hamilton says, "Uh-oh—*Leakers.*"

Pam screams and throws a camera at him.

Having returned from her grandparents' condo, Megan feels the need to do something productive. She walks to feed the ostriches at the Lennox house a few doors over. The birds' hungry quacking grows louder as she walks across the wet grass and through the Lennoxes' cheerfully wreathed front door. In the utility room, she finds sacks of corn piled on top of the washer and dryer. Through the opened upper half of the Dutch door leading into the garage, Megan is unable to see the big birds, and then from the side edge of the garage prance two angry, silly faces with Maybelline eyes. They cluck and bobble, making her smile. They're ravenous; she quickly slits open a sack, opens the door, and drags it into the garage. While the ostriches gobble their meal, she fills a bucket of water from the goldfish pond out back. On returning, the two ostriches peck at Megan's hands, eager to have the water for themselves. Megan is enchanted with these frantic, funny animals and she sits on the garage stoop to enjoy them.

The garage is so grotty, she thinks. These poor creatures haven't seen light for days now. She walks inside the garage to the door, wondering if she can open it just slightly so that light and air can come in through the bottom. *Bang!* The ostriches run through the Dutch door and enter the house, knocking over chairs and tables, quacking and hissing about the living room, and then head out of the front door, which Megan had forgotten to close. *Oh shit*, she thinks, *another rodeo*.

She storms out onto the lawn, where the two birds are joyfully bouncing about, fluffing their silly little wings. The ostriches vanish into the forest as surely as if they had fallen into a river with weights on their knotty legs.

That night the steady hum of Linus's gas generator offers a false sense of stability with its precise rhythms.

Karen places the paper bag on her head and resumes her visions of events around the world: "Skeletons sitting on plastic seats outside a Zürich Mövenpick restaurant."

"Skeletons? Already?"

"No. It's in the future. Oh—I see an Apple computer smashed on the floor of a Yokohama branch of a Sumi . . . Sumi . . . Sumitomo Bank. This is all random stuff. I see . . . morning glories growing out of an Ecuador sewer line and entwining onto a human femur. I see . . . five brightly-dressed skiers frozen asleep on their skis on the slopes of Chamonix; a Missouri railway car sidled off its tracks, with millions of scratch 'n' play lottery tickets spilled into an overflowing creek. In Vienna, two teenage girls are entering a bakery and filling their pockets with chocolates. And now . . . now . . . *there*. They've just fallen asleep."

"Can't you focus in on our own specifics, Kare?" asks Wendy. "What about my dad?"

"Give me your hand." Wendy grabs Karen's hand. Karen speaks: "He's asleep. On his bed. He had no idea what happened. He was napping and fell asleep while he was sleeping. Does that make sense?"

"Yeah."

The others want to know about their families and bustle toward Karen. Hamilton's father fell asleep on the beach and was pulled out with the tide. His mother in Toronto fell asleep in a downtown shopping arcade. Richard's parents fell asleep in a lineup trying to cross the border. Pam's parents got out of the car and walked across, but only got half a mile or so into Canada before sleeping. Linus's parents died in a car crash on the highway near Langley.

After a silence, Richard asks, "What about Lois and George?"

"Asleep. Mom in Park Royal and Dad in his shop."

"Oh."

The generator huffs and stutters and kicks out and then back in. The lights flicker. They now feel fragile, and the youthful sense of infinity that got them to this moment in their lives is utterly gone. "Richard, please remove the paper bags from my head. I want all of us to go out for a walk."

"But the rain—"

"What is your *point*? Get some flashlights and rain gear."

Minutes later, the seven walk through the street, where a rain of stunning proportion turns the sky into a sea. "Look," Pam says, "each drop is like a glass of water." Nobody can remember the last time it rained so hard. Water clobbers them on the head; water renders them deaf. Down the street they march, without lights, Karen in her wheelchair, soaked and sad, down the street until they reach the bottom. Richard says, "Karen, can you tell us what's going on—why we're here?"

"Richard—" In spite of the water that gullies down her hood, she looks him calmly in the eye. "The world was never meant to end like in a Hollywood motion picture—you know: a chain of explosions and stars having sex amid the fire and teeth and blood and rubies. That's all fake shit."

"So exactly what are you saying?"

"I'm saying, *shh*!" Karen whispers as they stand in the rain, drenched, on the pavement at the foot of Rabbit Lane bordering the entrance to the forest. "Listen: There is an older woman in Florida. She's in her kitchen and she hears her wind chimes tinkle. On the kitchen chairs are bags of groceries bought yesterday but never placed in their cupboards. It's cool out and she is wearing a nightie. She walks out of the kitchen door and down to a nearby dock where a warm wind sweeps over her head and through the fabric she's wearing. She sits down and looks at the sky with its stars and satellites and thinks of her family and her grandchildren. She's smiling and she's humming a song, one that her grandchildren had been playing over and over that week. 'Bobo and the Jets'? No—'Benny and the Jets.' Suddenly, she's sleepy. She lies down on the deck and closes her eyes and sleeps. And that's that. She is the last person. The world's over now. Our time begins."

PART THREE

27 FUN IS STUPID

Jared here, one year later . . .

. . . lock up your daughters. And your smutty magazines. And your sofa, for God's sake, because you never know, I may go and hump it like a Great Dane. Har *har*. Listen to my friends and you'd think I was the world's biggest perv. Right. And take a look at *them* now, will you—one year later: useless sacks of dung *they* are, slumped around Karen's fireplace watching an endless string of videos, the floor clogged with Kleenex boxes and margarine tubs overflowing with diamonds and emeralds, rings and gold bullion—a parody of wealth.

Between tapes what do they do? They have money fights, lobbing and tossing Krugerrands, rubies and thousand-dollar bills at each other; at other times they make paper airplanes from prints by Andy Warhol and Roy Lichtenstein and shoot them into the fireplace.

During one particularly long lull between videos, I, Jared, slip to the side of the house and turn off the Honda gas generator Linus has rigged up. The power dies and triggers a clump of groans amid the clan. It's at this point I choose to appear outside the window—across the lawn—a ball of white light. Wendy is the first to see me and she calls my name.

"Jared?"

"What's that, Wendy?" Megan asks.

"It's Jared. Look. He's back."

All eyes gaze rapt while I gavotte across the lawn in my old football uniform, the brown and whites.

In the silence I glow like a deep sea-creature, like a pale

moon, and I flow several feet above the ground, and then scoot through the one unsmashed pane of the glass patio doors as though catching a fumbled ball. I walk across the room as though on an airport conveyor belt and out the other wall. Hamilton runs out to the car port but I'm not there.

Wendy lights candles and a few moments later I enter the room from the ceiling, stopping with my feet above the fire-place, where I introduce myself:

"Hey guys. It's me—Jared. Fucking A—I'm so happy to see all of you."

"Jared?" Karen says.

"Hi, Karen. Hello everybody."

"Jared, what *are* you? *Where* are you? Are you *okay*?" asks Richard.

"I'm a ghost and I guess I'm blissed out, Richard. I'm high on life. It's the Hotel California. Yessiree."

"What are you *doing* here?" Megan asks, recognizing me from my old high school yearbook photo.

"I'm here to help you out," I say as I begin to dissolve through the floor.

"Wait!" Wendy shouts. "Don't go!"

I'm halfway through the floor: "*Man*, this floor feels good."

"You can feel the floor?" Linus asks.

"What's heaven like?" Richard asks.

"What happens when you die?" Pam asks.

"Show us a miracle, big boy," Hamilton says.

Only my head lies above the floor: "Oof!—you should try this sometime. This floor beats Cheryl Anderson any day of the week."

"Jared!" Karen's shout is urgent.

"All of you," I say, "—you're birds born without wings; you're bees who pollinate cut flowers. Don't pee yourselves. I'll return soon. Let's get weird."

It's the next day and Richard is growing impatient with Hamilton and Pam, dawdling as the two step out of the minivan, wobbly and silly.

210

"You go first, Barbara Hutton."

"No wayyyy, Mr Hefner. *You* first."

"Pals call me Hef."

"Listen you two freaks, can we just step to it?"

Before them is a wide, faded tar piazza strewn with skeletons, cars parked at odd angles, and rusted shopping carts. Beyond this is the faded and ratty looking Save-On supermarket. Its glass doors are like gums without dentures.

"*Ooh*. Miss Thing needs a drinky."

"Hamilton—I mean *Hef*—let's get in and out as quickly as we can."

"Okay, okay, *Rich*ard. Don't cack your nappies."

"Richard," Karen says, "I'm going to stay out in the van. You three go in. I need some sun."

"You want anything special, Kare?"

"Yeah, cotton balls . . . a hot oil treatment . . . some licorice if it's still any good."

"Gotcha."

Karen sits alone in the minivan's front seat, sifting through CD's and enjoying a freakish heat wave warming the remains of the city. I, Jared, become manifest.

"Hi, Karen."

"Jared! Where *are* you?"

"Out here." She swivels to see me standing outside the door atop a rusted shopping cart on its side. I'm hard to see during the day—like gas flames against a blue sky.

"Jared, what's the deal here? I've got a thousand questions I want to ask you."

"Ask away, Karen. You look good. How are you feeling?"

"Crappy. But my arms are getting pretty strong. My legs— they're kind of going downhill now. They're deteriorating. I can only barely walk around the house and stuff. What about you—do ghosts have pain? I mean, do you *hurt*?"

"Not the way you do."

"No. I imagine not." She changes gears: "So cough up the truth, Jared, because I'm really mad at you or whoever did this to me. You deep-freezed me for seventeen years and left me with a puppet body. And who smashed in the patio door last year when everything started falling apart?"

"Actually, that was *me* at the door."

"You?"

"Apologies, Kare. I screwed up—it was my first time back here. I was going to give you a speech. I decided not to—I was too embarrassed about wrecking the door. It was just like the night I walked into Brian Alwin's parents' patio door in tenth grade. *Duh.* I went and helped Wendy instead. She got lost in the forest coming here from the dam."

"You scared the crap out of me."

"Hey—it won't happen again. I've got good control of it now—my astral presence, I mean." I do a double flip there and land atop the rusted shopping cart. "Sexy or *what*?"

"*Ooh baby baby.* Shit, Jared, tell me, what exactly is the *point* of everything that's happened? And why did *I* go into a coma? I can't explain *any*thing. So maybe *you* can. Everybody treats me like I know the answers and that I won't tell them out of spite. I hate it."

"Well, Karen, you—how shall I say this—you accidentally opened certain doors. You were taking all those diet pills and starving yourself. Your brain did somersaults; you saw things; you caught a glimpse of things to come."

"For *that* I lost my youth? And for that matter, how come I was the one selected for coma duty? *Huh*? Did I ask? Who decided?"

"Mellow out, Kare—I mean, if you remember the note you gave Richard, you yourself wanted to sleep for 'a thousand years,' and avoid the future. *You* chose this, not me or anybody else. Worse things could have happened. I mean, you could have died completely. You could have had brain death."

"So why am I awake now instead of sleeping another 983 years?"

"You woke up from your coma because you'd be able to see the present through the eyes of the past. Without you there'd be no one to see the world as it turned out in contrast to your expectations. Your testimony was needed. Your testament."

"Jared, nothing *ever* turns out the way it was intended. Just look at me." Karen looks at her legs and grimaces. "Oh, God. This is so bizarre. This is *not* what I was expecting life to be like. Hey wait—Jared—how come it's you here and not anybody else? I want to see my parents."

"I can't swing that, Kare. *I'm* your Official Dead Person. I'm the only person any of you knew who died when you were young. Because of this I register in your heads as the, umm, the *deadest.*"

"The *deadest*? What a crock . . ."

"Karen, forget about that for a second. Tell me—I have to ask you this: What *is* the main thing you noticed—the major difference between the world you left and the world you woke up into?"

Karen exhales heavily, as though she's having a massage and her tension is dissolving. She looks into the Save-On's dark interior and says, "A lack."

"A lack?"

"Yes. A lack of convictions—of beliefs, of wisdom, or even of good old badness. No sorrow; no nothing. People—the people I knew—when I came back they only, well, *existed*. It was so sad. I couldn't allow myself to tell them."

"What's so wrong with that—just existing, I mean?"

"I'm not sure, Jared. Animals and plants exist and we envy them that. But in people it just doesn't look good. I didn't like it when I came out of the coma and I still don't like it— even with just the few of us remaining here."

"And?"

"God, Jared—you're relentless. I know. Tell you what— you tell *me* who you slept with and I'll answer more of your questions."

"Karen, I dunno . . ."

"Stacey Klaasen?"

"Okay, yeah."

"Jennifer Banks?"

"Yeah."

"Jennifer Banks' younger sister?"

213

"Guilty."

"I *knew* you two did it."

"No shit, Sherlock."

"Annabel Freed?"

"Yes."

"Dee-Ann Walsh."

"Yup."

"God, Jared—we should have come and hosed you down like a mink in heat. Who *didn't* you make it with?"

"Pam."

"I could have guessed that."

"Wendy."

"I *knewww* that."

"I was going to meet her after the football game. It was in the cards. And now you have to answer more of my questions."

"Fair n'uff."

"You were talking about what was different about people when you woke up. Spill."

"All right already. Let's see. Give me a second." She scratches her chin while a wild animal screams within the Save-On. "I know—I remember when I first woke up how people kept on trying to impress me with how *efficient* the world had become. What a weird thing to brag about, eh? Efficiency. I mean, what's the point of being efficient if you're only leading an efficiently blank life?"

I egg her on. "For example?"

Karen pulls a blanket around herself, speaking as she moves. "I thought back in 1979 that in the future the world would— *evolve*. I thought that we would make the world cleaner and safer and smarter, and that people would become smarter and wiser and kinder as a result of all the changes."

"And . . . ?"

"People didn't evolve. I mean, the world became faster and smarter and in some ways cleaner. Like cars—cars didn't smell anymore. But people stayed the same. They actually—*wait*— what's the opposite of progressed?"

"In this case, *devolved*."

214

"People *devolved*. Hey, Jared—how come you know so many words now?"

"How to best explain ... there's a certain aspect of the afterworld that's like English class and you're not allowed to skip. Anyway, forget that. You were talking about devolution."

"Yes. Megan—my daughter—she didn't even believe in the future before the world ended. She thought the future was death and crime and lawlessness. And as soon as the future actually *did* end, she took it in her stride. She had a daughter, Jane, born blind and brain defective—probably because of all the crap in the air these days—and she simply assumed that's the way life should be. Actually, nobody believed in the future: Richard, Wendy—it's like they expected the end."

"How?" My body temporarily flares orange with anticipation.

"Drugs. Pam and Ham did smack—still *do*—or whatever they can find that's all fresh after one year because the notion of forty more years of time was, and continues to be, too much for them. Wendy lost herself in grueling routine. Linus apparently went away for years trying to figure out the meaning of life and he never found it and so he curled up inside himself and became dusty and slightly bitter. Megan had the baby born blind and with mental problems and so now Megan's gone slightly autistic as a result. And *Richard*—Richard drank and placed all his hope in *me*. He thinks I don't know, but I do. You have to remember, Jared, I wasn't supposed to ever wake up. Richard could have spent his life mooning away about me and never have to deal with real life."

"All good points. But a bit harsh, wouldn't you say?"

"Jared, use your brain—*look* at me. I'm a monster. I'm like some UFO woman that Linus or Hamilton cooked up for TV movies. I gave up my body just so I could learn that the modern world was becoming sort of pointless and empty? A crappy trade."

"Okay, but answer me this: Would you have believed in the emptiness of the world if you'd eased into the world slowly, buying into its principles one crumb at a time the way your friends did?"

She sighs. "No. Probably not. Are you happy now? Can I have my body back?" Karen grabs Pam's cigarettes from the dashboard, lights one up, and then coughs.

"You smoke?" I ask.

"You jock. Yes, I'm smoking again as of now. *Ooh*. My head's dizzy. Hey—how's God?"

"Aw, Karen—don't be flippant. It doesn't suit you. This isn't social studies class."

"*Oops*—careless and stupid. But, how are *you*? I mean, you're dead. I don't want to be flippant. I'm really curious. Who wouldn't be?"

"Don't worry about me. I'm totally cool. But I *am* worried about you and the rest of the crew, though."

"Us? Forget *us*. We're losers. Who'd worry about us? Go find some winners and worry about them."

"Don't say that, Karen. It's just not true. It just *isn't*."

Karen stares at me as though I've made a lame joke. "I have to go now—into the Save-On."

"Well *I'm* not going anywhere with these chopstick legs of mine. I feel like one of those glass birds that dips its beak into a glass of water. By the way, if you go in to see the others, Hamilton and Pam are going to drive you nuts. They spend their days shooting up and watching biography videos about the Duchess of Windsor, Studio 54, and Hollywood stars. They're losing themselves back in time. They talk all crazy."

"I can handle it."

"Hey Jared, you haven't answered many of my questions. Don't go. Quick, tell me, what's the deal? What happens next? Ten more years of this? Twenty? Thirty?"

"I can't answer that, Karen. You know how the deal works."

"You *do* know something then."

"Come here, Karen—open the door." Karen opens the door. "Swing out your legs," I command, and she does. "Here—" I approach Karen and kneel before her. I kiss both her shins and then rise. "Stand up," I say, and Karen, coltish and unsure, steps down onto the parking lot. "Run," I say.

And she runs—around the van and then around the lot, whooping with joy. Her legs are whole again.

"I love you, Jared," she says, to which I reply, in words she can't hear because she is now so far away, "I love you, too."

Inside the blackened supermarket, scores of animals, birds, and insects have made the building their home. Shit of all types splotches the floor, as do tussles of feathers, fur, bones, and soil. Squirrels and raccoons have reduced the cereal aisle to fiber while the meat department's offerings have been entirely looted by wildlife. The smell of rot, a year later, is ebbing away, masked by the smell of shampoos and cosmetics fallen to the floor in a small earthquake six months prior. Birds rustle in the ceiling while down below flashlights carried by Richard, Hamilton, and Pam klieg their way across the store's floor. The trio daintily minuet above the muck and locate the pharmacy in the middle of the store. A white-smocked Leaker sits at the counter—a beef jerky skeleton.

"Lord, I am *sick* of these things," Hamilton says, draping the corpse with a spare smock. "I, Hef, last of the Famous International Playboys, have no time for rot. Agnelli, Niarchos, the Prince of Wales—all gone now. I alone must keep up their grand tradition. *Voulez-vous un Cadillac car?* I live solely for night clubs, hooch, and rides on the Concorde."

"Hamilton, f'Chrissake, shut up," Richard says. "Did you bring the awl and hammer?"

"Presto."

"*Thank* you."

Richard and Pam prod and jimmy a locked cupboard storing untold pharmaceutical gems. After some expert elbow grease, it flies open, causing plastic tubs to tumble onto the floor.

"Brush me, Daddy-O!"

"Just give me the rucksack, Hef," Richard says as a shadow runs across his feet. "Squirrel alert."

"Oh look! Look—it's so sweet," Pam says. "We can take it to Babe Paley's place in Bermuda for dinner."

"It's Jamaica, dear. Who's on the guest list?"

"Twiggy. The Sex Pistols. Jackson Pollock. Linda Evangelista."

"You two are driving me up the fucking wall with your fantasies," says Richard.

"If having a fantasy is a crime, I stand guilty as accused." Hamilton makes a big huffy sniff of the air and then quickly regrets it.

Richard ignores this. "Aye yi *yi*. Oh, look—*bingo!*—two thousand Vicodins." Something screams and scampers across the store down Aisle 3. "Oh, *man*, this place is a creep show. Let's grab and scram. Hamilton, go get a shopping cart for the loot."

"Roger." In the greeting card section, Hamilton finds an abandoned cart. It squeaks and rubs across the sludgy floor. Richard and Pam pile the pharmaceuticals into the cart.

"Oh, Christ. Karen wants some cotton balls and a hot oil treatment. Where are they?"

"Next aisle over."

The trio walks slowly through the store's cobwebbed, stinky carcass, and the farther away they get from the front, the blacker it gets. They pass two Leakers along the way, but of course, after all this time they are casual about such a sight. Slowly, slowly they move when suddenly they bump into three raccoons who hiss and try to escape, scaling a Matterhorn of soggy paper towels. "Oh shit . . ."

"Do I hear Karen calling us from outside?"

Koonk-koonk.

The lights in the ceiling pulse into operation, scorching brighter than daylight—the light all the more painful for its unexpectedness, illuminating the store and causing all of the wildlife into shrieks of panic, revealing the extent of devastation.

My friends scream and look up above, where they see me, Jared, in the rafters. "It's me," I say, and tell them, "I've come back to you to bring you light."

"You prick," Hamilton bellows, "—the light almost blinded us!"

"Whoopsy daisy, guys. I was trying to put on a light show for you. It fell kinda flat. See you later this afternoon."

"Light show?" Pam says.

"He's technically sixteen, Pam," adds Hamilton.

"Oh yeah," she muses, "he's younger than Karen."

Wendy is hesitantly meandering through the browning forest behind her house, armed with a twelve-gauge rifle should feral dogs attack. Her hair is washed and styled in a manner considered fetching by 1997, and, for that matter, 1978, standards and beneath her thick beige raincoat clings a saucy frilled lingerie getup fetched earlier that morning from a Marine Drive naughty shop. She's calling me: "Jared? *Jared?*" She's worried I won't hear her call—or that I won't respond—but I do.

"Hey, Wendy." I appear a stone's throw away, floating in the air, golden and light, weaving my way between the tall dwindling stands of firs and hemlocks on this steep canyon slope. I arrive and stand before her.

"You came."

"Fuckin' right, I did. How ya doing, Wendy? We never got our date, did we?" A silence passes between us. I let her be the one to break it.

"I've missed you. You helped me that horrible night last year when everything was falling apart—and then you went . . . away. Why?"

"I knew I'd be back."

She slowly walks nearer to me. "What's it like to be dead, Jared? I don't mean to be blunt, but I'm frightened and I'm also a doctor. In school and later at the hospital I looked at every corpse and I wondered the same thing: *Dead—what next?* And then the world shut down and all I saw—all I *continue* to see—are dead bodies. It's all we see down here—

220

dead bodies. We have a 'clean zone' around the houses, but everywhere else is one big pauper's grave."

"Death isn't death, Wendy—blackness forever—if that's what you mean. But it's not my place to say anything more to you beyond that. It's a big deal. I have to be quiet."

"What about heaven?"

"Okay, sure. I give you that."

Standing almost in front of me, she says, "Were you scared in the hospital? I visited you all those times. I brought you all those cookies I baked myself. You were sweet. And your eyes were far away. You never lost your beauty—even at the end when I think you maybe lost your hope."

"I was too young to be really afraid of death. But my cancer was my Great Experience, and I don't begrudge it."

"Bullshit."

"Okay, you're right. I was scared shitless. What else was I supposed to do? Everyone kept descending on me and kept making all these brave little faces and handing me muffins and teddy bears. No matter how scared you get you have to make that same brave little face back in return. It's like, the *law*."

"Jared—did you ever . . . you know, *think* about me?" Her arms are crossed protectively.

"Yeah. You know I did. We missed our date—I never showed you my candy."

"Were you in love with Cheryl Anderson?"

"*Wha*—Cheryl *An*derson?"

"Don't look so surprised. She had a big mouth."

"Hmmm. We liked each other a lot. But it wasn't love, no. I was a jock so everybody thought I had to be a sex machine— and so I became one. It was great. It's different now—totally different."

"How?"

"I'm no longer incarnate. But I can still—you know, get it on. In my own way."

She begins to whimper: "Jared, can you please just take me away? *Please*? Put me in your arms and drive me to the sun. I'm so lonely. And I can't kill myself, even though I think about it all the time. There's no point to the world now. It just erodes and becomes chaotic and poisoned. Look at the trees around us. Brown. Probably radiation from a North Korean reactor gone wrong. Or Chinese. Or Ukrainian. Or . . . Just take me away, dammit! You're a ghost, Jared. *Prove* it."

"I can't take you away, Wen. But I can make the loneliness leave you."

"No—I don't want that. I want to *leave*."

"Just imagine, Wendy," I say, "a world without loneliness. Every trial would become bearable, wouldn't it?"

She thinks this over. She's smart and she sees the truth. "Yes." She sniffles. "You're right. You win the Brownie badge. But why do we have to *get* lonely? It's so awful. It's so—wait—" Wendy's composure returns somewhat. She wipes her eye and her voice becomes still. "You're not going to take me away—are you?"

"Nope. I would if I could, but I can't. You know that, Wendy."

She sits on a fallen stump to collect her breath, her mind racing so quickly it almost seizes up. She takes several deep gulps, calms down, and then looks across the ferns and moss at me, a sixteen-year-old dead boy. As she does this, her raincoat opens slightly, exposing her lingerie beneath. She sniggers and takes the jacket off completely, revealing her pale thick body. "Ta da! Hey Jared, welcome to the new *me*. Doesn't this getup make me lovable? *Huh?*"

"You're a part of the world, Wendy, as much as daisies, glaciers, earthquake faults and mallard ducks. You were meant to exist. You've gotta believe me. You're lovable . . . and you're hot! You look so good."

"Could *you* love me, Jared?"

"Which way?"

"Any way that stops me from being lonely."

Her skin is goosebumped, her nipples are rigid. "Oh man, *could* I—"

"I'm here."

222

And so I remove the bulk of my spectral football outfit—cleats and pads and shirt—but I leave my shoulder pads on.

"Your shoulders," she says.

I walk toward her: "Just shush, Wen. Feel me walking through you."

"*Shhhh*—quiet, Jared."

"Oh, fucking A, man, this is *great*. Man, this is even better than Karen's floor." Wendy giggles and her voice drains. "Oh, Wendy—I don't get to do this all too often these days. Oh!"

I stand there inside her body while a flock of crows caws in the treetops, and then I pass through her and it's as if I'm receiving answers to questions I'd asked long ago—the same sense of being suspended in a moment of truth. As I look back, she is frozen with pleasure, eyeballs skyward and white. Her senses are still locked inside another realm.

I put my football togs back on and float in front of her, watching over her for a few minutes as her mind and body thaw. She looks at me and asks, "That's as good as it gets, isn't it?"

"Yep."

"I've been thinking of this since 1978."

"It was a powerful dream. You were great."

"You're going to leave now, aren't you?"

"I'm not leaving you, but I *do* have to cut out. And also—"

"*Shhh* . . . Let me guess—I'm pregnant now, aren't I?"

"Yep. How'd you know that?"

"It's this skill I have. I can always tell when a woman's pregnant." She pauses, her mind dreamy. "Thanks, Jared."

I float upward, up into the canopy of trees and into the sky. "Good-bye, Wendy."

Jane is papoosed onto Megan's back as she motorcycles slowly through the ghostly suburb, ever vigilant for fallen trees, angry dogs, or freak weather bursts.

I look into Megan's mind and I am fascinated by the things I see. Megan, being a teenager, had the least formed personality of the group as the world shut itself down, and she is also the

223

least affected by the catastrophe. She drives over a crunchy skeleton on Stevens Drive as though it were merely a fallen branch; lighting a cigarette, she throws the lit match into the nearest house, not even sticking around to watch it burn.

It's a sunny day and the air is clear—a rare day when the world doesn't smell like a tire fire, the endless reeking fumes that cross over the Pacific from China.

In the middle of driving down Stevens to Rabbit Lane, Megan endures a pang of loneliness so real and so strong that I can only compare it to a tornado or lightning. It dawns on her that she has never visited Jenny Tyrell's house in all the past year. She doesn't know what she will find there, but she knows she has to go.

Megan's hair is now long and falls to the side of her head like a bird lowering its wings as she pulls into the driveway of Jenny Tyrell's house. Its lawn, like all lawns, has turned into a scraggly meadow; the Christmas decorations have faded after a year of neglect; the shingles have begun to snaggletooth; the cars in the driveway are coated in dust, and the tires have gone flat—a fairly good indicator that there'll be Leakers inside the house, and indeed there are—Mr. and Mrs. Tyrell, mummified and serene on the living room floor surrounded by books of family photos, Mrs. Tyrell's wedding dress, a wine bottle, and two glasses. No odors.

"Yo! Mr. and Mrs. Tyrell—" Megan gives the parents a fond gaze. "Came to check out Jenny's stuff. She's over at the mall in Lynn Valley. Mind if I go upstairs? Thanks. Oh *look*, Janie—Jenny's room is a pigsty like always."

Megan unstraps a googling Jane and puts her on Jenny's bed. The room hasn't changed much; the door was closed, so there's little dust. Makeup and clothes are scattered about. There's a photo of Megan, Jenny, and the old gang on the grass hockey team; ski boots; several Alanis Morrisette posters on the wall; and on the desk a diary—Megan had no idea Jenny kept a diary. "Move over Jane—we're going to be here a little while." Her eyes moisten; her heart explodes.

September 28, 1997

Who does Megan think she is? Just because
she's dating an older guy she thinks she's Mrs.
Hot Shit. His name is Skitter and it's not like
he's a big catch or something. He's got nice legs
and he's buff, but he's so crude and he dresses
like a metal-head and a druggie. Please give me a
ten-foot pole.

Won our grass hockey game today. 5 to 3
against Hillside and I got a goal. We rock!

"Jenny, you *cow*. You were jealous from the word 'go,' and
you *know* it. You tried to worm your way into everything me
and Skitter did. Skitter's nickname for you was 'The Remora
Fish.' I pitied you."

October 13, 1997

Megan got dumped by Skitter, but she tries to
make it sound like she left him. As IF. She's
really far away in her head these days, so it's no
wonder she got the boot. I think it's because of
that loser school she goes to—the school for
losers down in North Van. I'm going to try and
think of a way to call Skitter without looking like
a slut. Maybe I'll call and ask him where I can
score some hash. I've still got his number.

"Now this is really too much. *Way* too much. *I* left *him*,
thank you. Because he was a cheating tightwad bastard and I
ended up buying everything he asked for and I realized he just
uses women—even having high school girls pay for his own
cigarettes." Megan finds herself missing Jenny dreadfully.

November 2, 1997

Wow! Megan's mother came out of her coma.
Wow!!! She's been in it as long as I've known
Megan, which is my whole life, which is a pretty

long time. It was in the papers and on TV and everywhere, but Megan's family won't let anybody take pictures so they keep showing that creepy high school photo Megan's dad keeps in the den. I guess this means Megan is going to be ignored even more by her family. Ha HA. Now she'll know how it feels to be left out in the cold like me. I tried to call, but the phone was busy all day.

Later on I went with Skitter to one of his friends, but they weren't there so he pried open the door and we made out for 3 hours and it was really sexy being in somebody else's house.

"Jenny, you are so crude. You take my mom's waking up and twist it into something about *you*. You had nothing to do with it, and as for Skitter and other people's houses, he was a real perv and went out of his way to do it in cool places like the changing room at Le Château, which, I have to admit, was a real turn-on."

December 26, 1997

Megan and I are friends again, and to show it she invited me to a party down at Lois's and I got to see KAREN for the first time close-up. She was so scary looking—like she was anorexic to the point of death and it's so sick to think of Richard and her making it. Ick-o-rama. Maybe Richard'll wait a few months until she puts some meat on. She looked at me like she knew my secrets or something. She's just really really creepy.

Returned most of my Christmas presents today. I don't want to seem ungrateful, but I could really use the cash to buy the tool kit Skitter keeps talking about. His birthday's next week.

226

"I'm not even going to dignify your comments about my sacred mother by replying to your adolescent filth. And as for Skitter, hey, it looks like you're falling into his 'buy-me-something-or-I-leave-you' act. Sucker."

December 27, 1997
Bought Skitter's tool kit, but it was so
expensive I nearly freaked out and I had to go sit
and hyperventilate for fifteen minutes afterward
in the subway and then I ate too much.
"The Remora" and her mom and Lois were
on TV and they looked way better than they do
in real life, and Megan looked like such a
goody-two-shoes and you never would have
known to look at her that she did Warren and
Brent on the SAME NIGHT last year at the
Burnside Park party.

"That does it, Jenny—you are no longer my friend. One of the best days of my life, and then you go and hang out with me the next day as if you hadn't put all this crap into your diary!" She pauses and breathes. "I miss you."

A wall glows golden, and then I appear from within a mirror.

"Oh," Megan says, "it's *you.*"

"Such a warm reception, Megan. Do you get many visitors from the dead every day?"

"Go away. You're probably not even a real ghost. You're probably something cheesy way down the food chain, like a sprite or a wisp."

"Me? A sprite? I think not."

"Go away. Go say 'boo' to people, Casper."

"What did I ever do to bug *you* so much?"

"If you're such a big ghost, why don't you take me away from this slag heap of a world and on to someplace better?"

"Because I personally can't do that."

"Just as I thought. You're a sprite. Go twinkle somewhere else. Don't bug me, transparent loser."

227

"Whoa, man! What's with this angry little stance? Don't you want to see a miracle or something?"

"I've had enough miracles for one lifetime, thank you."

I change subjects: "Your baby's pretty. How old?"

"Six months."

"Why did you name her Jane?"

"Jane seemed like the name of somebody who never has a damaged life. Janes are always calm, cool, and up to date."

"Nice eyes."

"They're Skitter's eyes—crazy eyes. They're blind. Hamilton said that looking at Janie's eyes was like looking at a full moon and then realizing that it's just one day short of being truly full. That was before we figured out she was blind."

"Hamilton's been saying stuff like that since kindergarten. I knew him and your father my whole life."

"You at least had some friends. I don't even have *one* anymore. I miss Jenny real bad." She hands me a wad of Jenny's CD's and says, "Want a CD collection? Lots of dance mixes."

"No thanks."

"Go away."

"What's wrong, Megan?"

"I said go *away*."

"Are you lonely?"

"No!"

"You can tell me if you are. Do you miss Jenny?"

"That treacherous scag bag."

"Yes, *that* treacherous scag bag."

Megan stays silent for a minute and I give her all the time she needs. "I miss her. I'm lonely. I want to change the subject."

"To what?"

"I dunno. You choose."

"Fair enough. Let me ask you a small question: Tell me, what is it like to be living in the world the way it is now?"

"That's a small question?"

"Well, it's a *good* question. Give it a shot."

"You sprites just never quit. Okay. Let me think." She closes Jenny's diary and leans back against the wall, Jane on the bed

228

by her side. "*The world right now*—gee, Jared, it's one party after another. Funzies. *Ooh.* I'm having so much fun it hurts." She feigns stitches. "What do you think, bozo? Every day is like Sunday. Nothing ever happens. We watch videos. Read a few books. Cook food that comes out of boxes or cans. No fresh food. The phone never rings. Nothing ever happens. No mail. The sky stinks—when everybody died, they left the reactors and factories running. It's amazing we're still even here."

"Were you surprised when the world ended?"

Megan pulls her body up into a more comfortable position on the bed. "Yes. No. *No*—I wasn't. It was kind of like the whole *world* went into a coma. I'm used to that. I'm not saying that to make you pity me. It's just the truth." She lights one of Jenny's year-old cigarettes. "Still tastes menthol fresh. Did you ever smoke?"

"Me? No. I was a jock."

"You're kind of cute. Did you ever make it with anybody?"

"Here and there. Why are you curious?"

"There's kind of a cute guy shortage down here."

I come closer and see Megan more clearly: pink windburnt skin, eye whites clear as ringing chimes. "Do you ever—" I say, not finishing the sentence.

"Wait," Megan says. "Are you hitting on me?"

"Me? What?" I've been caught.

"You are! I don't believe this—I'm being hit on by the dead." Jane squawks; Megan gives her a bottle of formula and yanks a small cotton bunny from the pack. "Look, Mr Ghost . . ."

"Jared."

"What*ever*. This isn't the time or place. I'm flattered, but no. I prefer real meat."

"I can take a hint."

Megan folds up Jenny's diary with a snap, then looks at me. "So how come we were abandoned here? Why us?"

"There's a reason."

"Which *is*?"

"Oh, God. I can't tell you right now."

"You're pulling a Karen. Stupid sprite."

"Oh, grow up."

"*You*, a sixteen-year-old telling *me* to grow up. Ha. So then tell me this—is there anybody else left down here besides us? Karen said there wasn't, but I'm not so sure."

"Karen's only allowed a few facts, but those she has are always true."

"I was right! Linus kept on trying to ham-radio weird places like oil rigs in the middle of the Indian Ocean and scientists at the South Pole. Now he owes me a bucket of Krugerrands."

"A bucket of gold?"

"It's a joke really. There's so much gold it's silly. We huck it off of bridges. We have money fights. Money's over."

"I guess so."

"Hey Jared, what's heaven like?"

"Heaven? Heaven's like the world at its finest. It's all natural—no buildings. It's built of stars and roots and mud and flesh and snakes and birds. It's built of clouds and stones and rivers and lava. But it's *not* a building. It's greater than the material world."

"Well. Isn't that something. Do people get lonely there?"

"No."

"Then it really is heaven." We're quiet for a second as I stand close to her. "Sorry I can't take up your offer, Stud Boy. It's not like I get many others."

"I know." I slap my forehead: "Hey—I need to go now. I liked speaking with you."

"No. Don't go—you're somebody new."

"Here," I say. "Hold Jane out to me."

"Why?"

"You'll see." Her arms are like a set rat trap ready to spring back in case I do something weird, which I don't. I breathe gently into each of Jane's eyes and then I touch my tongue to the space between her eyes. I am the first thing she sees on Earth. "Your kid is whole. She's more than whole—she's a genius: she'll be wise. And *you* are now her servant."

Speechless, Megan watches as I shrink into nothing and disappear.

29 | INFINITY IS ARTIFICIAL

There are things I miss about Earth. I loved the way my mother made a pork roast and I loved getting up in the mornings super early and being the first to see the sun, jogging around the neighborhood in nothing more than terry underwear knowing that everybody else was sleeping. Once in summer 1978 I ran my daily jog naked and if anybody saw me, they never phoned the cops. Even more than sex, that solitary jog remains my most potent body memory of Earth—the air and the sun and the pads of my feet landing on Rabbit lane. What else? Oh, there was an owl that lived in the tree behind the house. Its roost was bang outside my window and each night around sunset it came out and swooped its long floppy wings— like an Afghan hound's ears. It used to fly into Karen's yard on the hill below mine and catch mice. I used to watch Mrs. McNeil feed it meat scraps but she never saw me, but I know for sure Mrs. McNeil was watching me quite clearly the summer afternoon before eleventh grade when I was mowing the back lawn in my red Speedo. Saucy old broad! I popped a rod and I *know* she noticed it.

Regrets? I have no regrets about life. I didn't live long enough to make a mess of it. But then I never really had any pictures in my head of adulthood. Had I made it that far I probably would have floundered like the rest of the gang.

I've been watching my friends over the past year or so— ever since Karen woke up. Karen can't remember, but she was with me for much of the time she was in her coma. She receives her "extra" information in the same way I do—in fits and

231

snatches that make no sense at the time, filled with maddeningly blank stretches.

The technicalities of my visits are strict. My current appearances are only allowed to be brief—I'm allowed only X amount of time to visit the old crew and in these brief snatches I have specific goals that have to be met.

Goals—that word sounds like I'm crew chief at McDonald's or something. But you know, every second of our life we're reaching goals of some sort. Every single second of our lives we're crossing a finish line of some sort, with heaven's roaring cheers surrounding us as we win our way forward. Our smallest acts—crossing a street, peeling an apple, giving Miss January the one-hand salute—are as though we are ripping an Olympic ribbon to thunderous applause. The universe *wants* us to win. The universe makes sure we're winning even when we lose. I wish that I could have run naked through the streets every moment of my life.

But I think I'm ahead of myself now. Now I have to go see Linus, up on the highest point of the mountain suburb where one can see far over the curved ends of the Earth, the United States and over to the Olympic Peninsula. The sky is clear as a lens. To the east stands Mount Baker a hundred miles away— an American Fuji: solid as lead, white as light.

Linus is thinking about me, and he's thinking about time— about death, infinity, survival, and those questions he sought answers to back when he was so young. He was the only one of us who ever asked questions bigger than where the night's party was scheduled to take place. I've always respected his opinion.

He's sitting on the warm hood of his Humvee, which is parked at the top of the driveway of the film shoot location from a year ago. Some of the film trucks and trailers are still parked on the street. The silent city, pocked with burns and sores and rashes, is spread below him.

In the midst of this serenity comes a surf-like roar and then a catastrophic *bang*. An image flashes through his mind: his drunken father slamming the dinner table with a fist. The ground booms and Mount Baker in the east erupts with a fire pole of lava shooting up into gray, cabbagey Nagasaki ash clouds. A shock wave ripples across the land and throws Linus onto the ground with another boom. The glass in nearby houses shatters.

"Oh, *man*—"

The spectacle is gorgeous and voluptuous and *sad*. Sad in that so few people will ever even see it or know about it. Linus isn't even sure if an erupting volcano counts as news. "News" no longer exists, and Mount Baker might just as well have erupted on Jupiter. This is the point when I appear.

"Hey Linus."

"Jared—*hey*!—I mean, look at that! I mean—oh man, I sound like a cretin, but look at that vol*ca*no."

"I know. It's cool. So beautiful it almost hurts."

Mt. Baker stops shooting lava, but continues blowing staggering plumes of ash and steam that are now melting ever so slightly in the easterly winds, off toward Alberta, Idaho, Montana, and the Dakotas. Linus is torn between watching the eruption and speaking with me. "Jared! Man, I missed you so badly." Linus tries to hug me, but he ends up hugging himself around his chest. "Jared—let me look at you." I hover above the ground, shining and radiant as always. "You look so young, Jared. Like a puppy, so young."

"You were this puppy-young once, too."

"It was a long time ago."

"Yeah."

Linus looks me over more. "You missed so much that happened in the world after you died. Did you see any of it?"

"Enough, I guess. I've been busy, kinda."

"We threw your ashes out into the ocean. Your dad chartered a sailboat. The day was clear like today. We said prayers on the boat."

"I was there."

"Yeah. It was beautiful. Your parents were so nice." Linus scans the plume again. "We never got used to your dying, you know. Richard especially. And then Karen went into the coma

233

and I think it wrecked Richard's life. I guess there must be a connection between you and Karen. I mean, here you are now."

"Here I am."

"Can you tell me what that connection is? I mean, between you and Karen and the rest of the world going away."

"Blunt or what! Okay, Linus—I'm going to be telling you things soon enough, but not right now, okay?"

"Jeez—you and Karen. Why does everything need to be so mysterious? Me, I've tried to make sense of everything over the past year and haven't been able to descramble it at all."

"It's not anything you might expect. By the way, what *has* the past year been like for you?"

"Scary. Lonely. And quiet! So amazingly quiet. I keep on waiting for people to emerge around a corner or to see a plane fly or a moving car. But I never do. I'm still not used to it yet."

"From what I can see, the group of you are handling the situation calmly."

"Let's just thank the drugs for *that*, thank you. And the videos. And the booze and the canned goods. In some ways it feels as though the world is still the same. At the start, I used to think we'd all feel as if we were waiting to die. Instead it feels as if we're simply waiting—for *what* I don't know. Waiting for *you*? I miss so many things about the old world— the way the city used to light the clouds from below, making them all liquid pearly blue. I miss the smell of sushi. And electricity. Fridges. Shopping. New ideas. Oh—I'm married now, too, to Wendy. And I was working in TV."

"Yeah, I know about all that."

"Sometimes we all used to feel like a creepy Neil Simon play. Hamilton tried to think of a title and show tunes to go with it. His best title was *Five Losers*."

"Hamilton—always the witty fellow."

"He's so wacky."

"A real nut."

"He slays me. He really slays me." Linus gathers his breath

234

and looks out at the volcano. He sighs, then says, "Jared, tell me something: Is time over?"

"Huh? Meaning what?"

"I've been thinking about this so much. When I say time I mean history, or . . . I think it's human to confuse history with time."

"That's for sure."

"No, listen. Other animals don't have time—they're simply part of the universe. But people—we get *time* and *history*. What if the world had continued on? Try to imagine a Nobel Peace Prize winner of the year 3056, or postage stamps with spatulas on them because we ran out of anything else to put on stamps. Imagine the Miss Universe winner in the year 22,788. You can't. Your brain can't do it. And now there aren't any people. Without people, the universe is simply the universe. Time doesn't matter."

"Linus, you spent years roaming the continent looking for all sorts of answers, didn't you?"

"I did. In Las Vegas especially. It was a shithole, but it gave me space to think. And you're not answering my question, Jared."

"I will. Did you reach any conclusions in Las Vegas?"

"No. Not really. I thought I was going to see God or reach an epiphany or to levitate or *some*thing. But I never did. I prayed so long for that to happen. I think maybe I didn't surrender myself enough—I think that's the term: *surrender*. I still wanted to keep a foot in both worlds. And then this past year I've still been waiting for the same big cosmic moments, and still nothing's happened—except you're here and instead of feeling cosmic, it simply feels like we're cutting gym class and coming up here for a butt. Your arrival seems somehow appropriate; I wish I could feel more awe. I wish you could be here all the time. We're so bloody lonely."

Another smaller rumble tickles the ground and we can see lava flows treacling down Mt. Baker's slope. Linus wants to blurt words so I let him: "Jared, I *know* God can come at any moment in any form. I *know* we always have to be on the alert.

And I *know* that day and night are the same to God. And I *know* that God never changes. But all I ever wanted was just a *clue*. When do we die, Jared?"

"Whoa! Linus—it's not that easy. I don't have that kind of exact answer."

"Nobody ever seems to dish out the real answers."

There's a strangely uncomfortable pause, and I try and switch moods: "Look at Mount Baker," I say. "Remember that ski weekend there when we trashed the transmission in Gordon Smith's Cortina?"

"I kept the gear-shift knob as a souvenir."

The lava now burns gullies through the mountain's glaciers and steam rises as high as a satellite. Linus feels calm and his voice becomes gentle: "I guess this is what the continent looked like to the pioneers back when they first came here, eh Jared? A land untouched by time or history. They must have felt as though they were walking headlong into eternity, eager to chop it down and carve it and convert it from heaven into earth. Don't you think so?"

"Yeah. The pioneers—they believed in something. They *knew* the land was holy. The New World was the last thing on Earth that could be given to humankind: two continents spanning the poles of Earth—continents as clean and green and milky blue as the First Day. The New World was built to make mankind surrender."

"But we didn't," Linus says.

"No, we didn't."

"But time, Jared—is it over? You never said."

Linus knows he's on to something, but I'm unable to give him an answer. "Not quite yet."

"*Again*, nobody has full answers. Where's everybody else now—the people who fell asleep? What are *we* supposed to be doing now?"

"Linus—buddy—I'm not trying to dick you around. There's a reason for everything."

"Always these eternal mysteries," says Linus. "I don't think human beings were meant to know so much about the world.

All this time and all this exposure to every conceivable aspect of life—wisdom so rarely enters the picture. We barely have enough time to figure out who we are and then we become bitter and isolated as we age."

"Wait a second, Linus." I approach him and place my hands on top of his head, making his body jiggle like a motel bed. I say, "There." Linus goes rigid, grows limp, and then swoons to the pavement; I've shown him a glimpse of heaven. "You'll be blind for a while now," I tell him. "A week or so."

Linus is silent, then mumbles, "I've seen all I've ever needed to see."

"Good-bye, Linus." With these words I pull backward, up into the sky, smaller smaller smaller into a blink of light, like a star that shines in the day.

"Well, *Hef*, I grant you that these seats are comfy, but not *nearly* as comfy as being dragooned through the grottoes of Fez on a litter carried by four of Doris Duke's seven-foot Nubians."

"Babs, you sassy vixen—make me jealous."

"Shush, Hef—I need to make a transatlantic phone call to the Peppermint Lounge. '*Pardonnez-moi—est-ce-que je peux parler avec Monsieur Halston?*'"

"Sure—call Halston. Last week *I* had lunch with the Princess Eugenie, Joe Namath, and Oleg Cassini. Lobster Thermidor, Cherries Jubilee, and Crêpes Suzette. Ha!"

"You tire me, Hef. Please leave."

Hamilton and Pam lounge on the front seat of an unsold Mercedes 450 SE inside the dusty dealership showroom on Marine Drive. The car doors are shut, the tires are flat, and on the seat between the two sits a trove of bric-à-brac connected to their drug use as well as cartons of cigarettes and stray unopened tequila bottles. I appear outside the front window, hovering in the middle of the pane. I glow.

Pam shivers. "Umm—*honey*—I think maybe you should look out the window."

Hamilton is weighing various cones of powder and says,

"I'm busy, Babs. I'm hiding my stash of dental-grade cocaine inside Gianni Agnelli's leather ski boots."

"Hey goofball—look up!" I shout; Hamilton turns and I shatter the showroom window and float above the shards through the now-open air toward their car.

"*Ucking*-fay *it*-shay," Pam says.

"Oh man, it's *Jared*."

I lower myself down onto the dealership's floor and then walk across the showroom and into the engine so that my body is half inside the car. "Hi Pam. Hi Hamilton."

"Um—*hi* Jared," Pam says. The two feel slightly silly being surrounded by so much contraband. Pam giggles.

"Jared—*buddy*. This is so *Bewitched*."

"No Hamilton, it's real life. What are you guys doing inside the car here?"

"We wanted to smell the interior. We miss the smell of new things," Pam says with further titters. "There's nothing new anymore. Everything just gets older and older and more worn down. One of these days there'll be nothing new-smelling left in the world. So we're taking whatever newness we can get." She looks at the dashboard. "Older older older." She lapses into a child's song.

"Old old old," Hamilton adds. "Everything's *old*. We'd kill for a new newspaper, a freshly mowed lawn, or a fresh coat of paint on something. By the way, great light show this morning at the Save-On. It was like you lifted a rock and everything underneath scurried to burrow into the crap underneath."

They're high and not responding soberly. "Tell me, where else have you been today?" I ask.

"Just you come and have a look." Hamilton and Pam slither out of the car and we go to their pickup truck outside the building. The bed is filled with gems, gold coins, cutlery, jewelry, and other treasures.

"We raided the safety deposit boxes at the Toronto Dominion Bank in Park Royal," Hamilton says.

"It's not as treasure-ish as you might think," adds Pam. "There were things like locks of hair, Dear John letters, fishing trophies, blue ribbons, keys, garter belts—not pricey stuff. More like stuff you'd expect to find left over after a garage sale."

"*Oh*—here's a strange one . . ." Hamilton says, lifting a plaster casting of a large phallus. On its bottom is felt-penned a date, November 4, 1979, and no other information.

"Must have been a good day for somebody," I say as Pam starts pouring handfuls of diamonds back and forth between her hands and the occasional stray tinkles down onto the pavement, clicking like a camera's shutter. She tosses the diamonds onto the center pile, one at a time. "Pear-shaped, suncrest, radiant, marquise, baguette, my little best friends." She looks toward me: "You're *real*, Jared, aren't you—it's not just the drugs?"

"I'm real. I'm like a biology test come back to haunt you."

"Oh, *wow*," Hamilton says.

"Oh *wow*? I come back to life and all you can say is, 'Oh *wow*'?"

"Jared," Hamilton says, "Mellow out. I seem to remember *you* were the one who had fourteen people toking their brains out inside your parents' Winnebago the night Elvis died."

"Exposing hypocrisy in itself doesn't make you a moral person," I say.

"Huh?" Pam says.

"Oh, don't be so thick, Pamela," Hamilton says. "He never *did* have a sense of humour. Jocks never do. Listen to what Jared's saying . . ."

"Don't so-thick *me*, Heffy-Weffy. I'm the one who cracked the safe today."

"Hurt me, *hurt* me—"

"Oh *Lord*. You guys want a miracle to make you go '*oh wow*' for real?"

"Deal us in, big boy," Hamilton says.

"Very well." I approach them and tap them each on the head.

"You touch us on the head? That's a miracle? Jared, I—" Pam stops, touches her cheeks, and looks at her body. Hamilton puts his hands to his ears and then falls down on his knees. "No. No. Oh, *my*. It's—it's real, isn't it, Jared?" Pam asks.

"It's real."

The two go silent; Hamilton crawls across the pavement and lowers his head to the ground, inspecting the dust.

Pam bursts into tears and grabs Hamilton's shoulders and tries to lift him up. Hamilton looks both lost and found at the same time. "Is it what I think it is?" he asks.

"Yes."

He moans. "You mean—we're *clean*?"

"Yes, you are clean. Your addictions are gone. No withdrawal. No pangs. Nothing." The two unclasp and then come over to me and try to touch me, but as with Linus earlier on that day, they end up batting each other's arms. After this, they stand and do leg squats and stretches and run around the parking lot and spin and look at the cellophane sky.

"It *is* a miracle. I can think! I'm clear! So clear! I haven't been this clear since—*ever*. The six wives of Henry VIII! The Fibonacci number sequence! How to make a smooth non-lumpy cream sauce . . ."

"It's so clean!" Hamilton echoes. "My head inside is clean as a lake! Hydrogen, Helium, Lithium, Beryllium, Boron, Carbon; August, 1969—American talk show host, Merv Griffin launches his late-night CBS show in direct competition with Johnny Carson. Opening night guests include Woody Allen and Hedy Lamarr, but scheduled athlete Joe Namath is a no-show."

"Oh Hamilton—look at the world!"

"It's . . ."

"Yes . . ."

The two fall silent; their bodies slacken as though they've realized a friend has betrayed them. Sitting down on the truck's lowered tailgate, they swat diamonds from underneath their bottoms and sit limp.

"Well, *well*—here we are," Pam says.

"Clean," Hamilton says. "And I don't feel like getting high. You?"

"No," replies Pam. "I like being inside my own skin again."
A seagull shrieks above them and they look up. "There's still
birds," Pam says.

"But no people."

"No people. The world's over, isn't it, Jared?"

"Pretty well."

"You're real, aren't you?"

"Yep."

Silence falls where in other days traffic would have hummed
and honked. "This is life, then, isn't it? I mean, this is *it*."

"Basically."

Hamilton and Pam hold hands. Pam says, "What do we do
now, Jared? Is this it forever—silence? It's so quiet down here.
Lonely. You're the ghost. *You're* the expert."

"Your brains are as tender and fresh as a baby bird's. Walk
home. Enjoy your clarity. Go romp in a hot tub. You count;
you were meant to exist. I'll be seeing you again."

And with this I vanish.

Richard was my best friend growing up, although we did grow apart over the years. He was one of the people I missed most when I died, so I'm kinda choked to see him again. But there are severe limits on how much I'm allowed to reveal to the living, so I can't be as gooey with Richard—or the others—as I'd like.

Richard is huffing up Rabbit Lane with a shotgun, so I slide down the hill to meet him. "Hey, Jared—thanks for fixing Karen's legs. That was beautiful."

"It was the least I could do."

"We came home and played splits on the front lawn with a steak knife for an hour. She's just so high on life now. Good trick with the lighting system down at Save-On, too."

"You flatter me shamelessly. Where are you walking to?"

"Out for a stroll before the sun sets to get a good view of Mt. Baker. And the weather—it's so beautiful today. It's the end of December and it might as well be June. But then again there could be a snowstorm in three minutes. Weather's random these days."

"So I've heard." I walk alongside Richard.

"Were you alive when Mount St. Helen erupted, Jared?"

"No. Missed it."

"That's right. It was huge. And you missed new wave and alternative rock. Rap. Grunge. Hip-hop. People wore some pretty stupid clothes. Cars got really good, though."

"I didn't miss out on earthly things entirely, Richard. Check this out—I can do the 'Moonwalk.'"

"No way. This I've got to see."

"Just you watch me now . . ." I slinkily Moonwalk up the road while Richard belly-laughs. "Am I doing something wrong?" I ask.

"The opposite. It's perfect."

"Thank you. I'd like to see *you* do it."

"Oh please, *no*."

I float back beside him: "So you see, I'm somewhat up to date." We continue our walk. "Fucking A. The neighborhood's one big mess, don't you think so?"

"I don't think you ever get used to the silence, Jared. Back before the plague or whatever it was, the neighborhood looked almost identical to the way it did the year you died. But now—" We survey dead trees, rangy vines, an occasional charcoal stump where a house once stood, a bird resting on a skeleton's ribcage. Pavement is crumbling and cars are stopped in the strangest places.

We pass a dog's skeleton, bleached clean by sun and acid rains. "Pinball, may he rest in peace. The Williams' Doberman. It tried to attack Wendy, but Hamilton shot it in time. It was only hungry. Poor thing."

"Sad."

"So Jared, tell me: What about when you were dying back in 1979. What was that like? I've always wondered. I mean, were you scared near the end, when you were dying in the hospital? You seemed so calm—even at the end when all those machines were pumping gorp in and out of you."

"Scared? I was scared shitless. I didn't want to leave Earth. I wanted to see the future—the lives of people I knew. I wanted to see progress—electric cars, pollution controls, the new Talking Heads album . . . Then my hair fell out and I knew I'd crossed the line. After that I put a good face on it because my parents were falling apart." Richard is lost in thought. "Do you think about death much?" I ask.

"Pretty much all the time. How could I *not*? I mean, look at this place."

"And what do you think?"

"I don't worry about dying. I figure that I'll just meet up with everybody else in the world wherever they went. But if I'd been *you* back in high school, I don't think I'd have been able to put as good a face on death as you did. I'd scream and yell and beg for more time, even on this clapped-out hulk of a planet we live on now."

"You like it here?"

"No, but I'm alive."

"Is it enough—being alive?"

"It's what I have."

"Richard, tell me the truth—and you have to tell me the truth, because, um, I'm a heavenly being."

"Shoot, buddy."

"Did you use Karen and me both as an excuse for you not to continue your own life? Did you bail out of life?"

Richard looks hurt, but then makes a dismissive "nah—why not?" gesture. "Sure. I pretty much withdrew, Jared. But I was a good citizen. I put the trash out every Tuesday night. I voted. I had a job."

"Did you feel kinda hollow inside?"

"A bit. I admit it. Does my answer make you happy?"

"Hey man. I need to ask. I need to know how you are."

"But I stopped withdrawing when Karen woke up."

"Fair enough."

"Do we have to discuss this, Jared? Let's talk about the old neighborhood. People. Friends."

"I've visited all the others today. You're the last. I save the best for last, my oldest friend."

"I'm honored, you stud."

We continue walking and cut down into St. James Place and approach my old house, a slightly shambled split-level rancher, baby-blue. On the right hand side there are cinder burns from when the house next door burned down. "The fire was three weeks ago," Richard tells me. "Lightning." We stand at the end of my driveway. "Here's your house. You wanna go inside, Jared?"

"Could we? I've wanted to go in there, but only with

somebody else. It'd make me nervous to go in alone."

"You? A ghost? You get nervous over bodies?"

"Yes. So I'm a wuss on this one issue."

"You get used to them. Trust me. Hamilton calls them Leakers."

My old front lawn is knee-high; all of the ornamental shrubs have browned and withered. Green ivy has persisted, over-growing onto the front door, which is unlocked. It opens silently as Richard tries it. A whoosh of warm air comes out, as does a foul, ammonia-like stink that makes Richard grimace at me: "You still want to go through with this, Jared?"

"Please."

Time has stood still inside. "Oh *boy*, Richard. It's almost identical to the last day I was here—my final day pass out of the palliative care unit. I wasn't supposed to eat meat, but Dad cut my turkey up into bits the size of peas and said to hell with it. I puked my dinner and then some blood and then the paramedics had to come. My parents and sister were so frightened. It was such a bad scene."

Richard stands in the front area and waits as I float through the house. A new TV here, a microwave oven there, some fridge magnets, but otherwise the house remains as it was when I left it. I approach the staircase, but Richard looks at me. "Are you sure you're okay with this, Jared?"

"I'm fine. As long as you're here. Let's go up."

He walks behind me and we enter my old bedroom, now a sewing room. Then I look in the old bathroom, my sister's room, and finally my parents' room. "Let me look first," Richard says. I tell him it won't be necessary, but he's adamant. He nudges the brown door open, peeks in, blanches, and then tiptoes out. "Leakers. I guess I have to tell you it's pretty gruesome in there."

"I need to see." I walk in, Richard behind me, and I see my parents' remains mummified into their bedsheets and mattress. "Sorry, man," Richard says.

"It's okay. It's nature's way." I walk through the room— my photos are on the wall, they never took them down—and

245

I see the hand mold I made in kindergarten. "Where are your own parents, Richard?"

"They're in their Camry at the Douglas Border Crossing. Linus and I made an overnight mission down there last summer and found their car. We were going to bury the remains, but it just wasn't, um, *possible*." I look around the room some more. "It's darkening outside," Richard says. "I have to go now—to see Mount Baker. You want to come?"

"I want to stay here with my folks a bit more. I wish there was something I could leave you with," I say, "a gift—a small miracle I can perform for you. Is there anything you want or need?"

Richard, now standing in the driveway, says, "No. It sounds ridiculous, but I've got everything I need. Are you sure you want to stay here?"

"I'm sure. Good-bye, Richard. Thanks for coming in with me to see my folks."

"It was nothing. Thank *you* for fixing Karen's legs. When are you coming back again?"

"In two weeks."

"See you then, buddy."

"Bye guy."

31 ONE IDEA WILL WIN

I was never a good "talker" when I was young and alive. Usually, a shrug and a smile carried me through most social situations. And to meet girls all I had to do was have a stare-down contest with them and make sure not to blink. It never failed. But now I've got the gift of clarity and directness.

What's clarity like?

Try to remember that funny feeling inside your head when you had math problems too difficult to solve: the faint buzzing noise in your ears, a heaviness on both sides of your skull, and the sensation that your brain is twitching inside your cranium like a fish on a beach. This is the opposite sensation of clarity. Yet for many people of my era, as they aged, this sensation became the dominant sensation of their lives. It was as though day-to-day twentieth-century living had become an almost unsolvable algebraic equation. This is why Richard drank. This is why my old friends used to spend their lives blitzed on everything from cough syrup to crystal meth. Anything to make that sloggy buzz make a retreat.

It's been two weeks since my last visit. The sky is clear but smoky smelling and a fine ash falls from no identifiable source. In the house's kitchen, both Wendy and Pam are playing soli-taire on personal computers electrified by the Honda gener-ator. Their hair is dirty. Linus, still partially blind, can't get the water pump fixed—and their voices are raspy from uneven weather and from colds, which still seem to appear even with-out a population base to spread them. Their bodies are swaddled inside down coats adorned with hundreds of Bulgari jeweled brooches.

"Did Richard say he'd have the heater and the water fixed by the afternoon?" Pam asks, and Wendy says no. "Oh *pooh*. My hair feels all matted like a wad of Slim Jims. I'm getting a club soda. You want one?"

Wendy declines and strolls onto the patio where Linus is bundled up as though in a Swiss tuberculosis sanitorium. "Hey, Linus, are you sure you're wearing enough white terry robes? You look like Bugs Bunny in Palm Springs."

"Tee *hee*." Linus is still recovering from a wicked cold garnered from the three-day-long blind walk home from up on the mountain where I gave him pictures of heaven.

"*Brrr*. It's cold out," Wendy says. "But the sky looks pretty."

"I can tell by the sound of your voice," Linus says, "you're hiding something. Wait—let me guess. Yes, you've checked the Geiger counter, haven't you?"

"Guilty as charged. Chattering like maracas."

"Some surprise."

They stand silent for a second, then Wendy says, "Jane is starting to reject her food. I'm not feeling so hot, either."

"You sound fine," Linus says. "Jared's back tonight. He'll tell us what to do."

From the living room they can hear Hamilton cursing the cold, throwing a Yellow Pages into the fireplace for a meager dollop of heat.

"Oh—look!" Wendy says. "Up there—a bald eagle—still alive. Flying."

"I'll take your word for it. This pesky blindness, you know."

"I mean, it's so large—the big white head, the yellow beak. It's so big I can see the color from here."

"I'll live. I'm going inside now." He has difficulty finding the latch.

Inside the living room, Linus feels his way past Hamilton, asking, "What are you reading?"

"I'm taking my minty fresh new brain out for more test drives. *Industry and Empire* by Eric Hobsbawm—about the English Industrial Revolution. Also, *One More Time* by Carol

Burnett. The funny lady of television and films remembers her beginnings. The coast-to-coast bestseller that warmed the hearts of millions."

"Well it's *cold* in here. We should find a smaller house that's easier to heat."

"No. Maybe we can just start putting bits of this house into the fire, and when we run out of this house we can find another big house."

At that moment, Megan's bedroom explodes with a top-forty hit from 1997. "Bloody hell.' Hamilton sits bolt upright then stomps down the hall to Megan's door. "Turn down the bloody boom box, Megan. We can't think out here." Megan makes no response, so Hamilton nudges open the door and finds Megan and Jane sitting on the bed where they've stationed themselves for the past two weeks—a landscape of half-used Gerber jars, cigarette butts, CD's, and batteries. Hamilton turns the music down to a low level. Hamilton glowers at Jane, who gawps right back at him. Hamilton has the spooky sensation that Jane is far more aware of the world than any of the others. "Are you coming out for dinner tonight?" Hamilton asks. "It's a Sunday dinner. A good one."

"Maybe. How do you know it's Sunday?"

"Wendy's PowerBook."

"Right." Megan turns off the stereo and picks up Jane. The two look out the window onto the driveway, where Richard has parked the car and is carrying cases of tinned foods into the house. "Oh goody-goody," says Megan, "more canned food. No, excuse me—I see a few boxes there, too. Lucky us—such variety." Richard sees Megan and suddenly Megan feels badly for Richard, who is the one person trying hard to maintain civility and comfort during the entire fucked up and crazy year. She calls out the window, "Dad, do you want me to help you with those?"

"They're nearly all in, Sweetie. Thanks anyhow."

Richard places the final box down on the garage floor. Walking into the house, he sees Karen by the small pool, which in the course of a year has converted itself into an enormous science project on algae. "You okay down there?" he asks.

"I'm fine. I went for a small run. Now I'm just taking in the air. It turned warm a few minutes ago."

Richard goes inside and Karen resumes her sentry over the gone-to-seed backyard. The sky is oranging and she is sad because her voices have departed. She can no longer see into the future or even try to explain the unexplainable. She is merely mortal, and a frail mortal, too. *But we've all had our hopes returned,* she thinks. *Jared will know what to do next.*

From somewhere in the house comes the sound of rattling paper. It's Linus feeling his way back out to the patio carrying a bag of charcoal briquettes. "It's gotten warm out all of a sudden," he shouts, "let's barbecue, methinks." Within minutes, the ball barbecue is opened, the briquettes lit, the embers are glowing, and spirits are raised.

The darkening sky is becoming a warm, dead Xerox and the winds blow forcefully as though aimed from a hair blower. Yet there is no sound—a warm river flowing over the skin; the amplified sound of the Moon. It is summer in mid-winter.

My old friends are seated on the back patio, toasting marsh-mallows and joking around. They know that my two weeks are up and I'll be returning shortly.

Richard asks Linus, whose eyesight is just now returning, to count how many fingers he's holding up. Karen darts about serving drinks and flaunting her new legs ("Shirley MacLaine in *Irma La Douce*"). Hamilton and Pam sit calmly, their facial muscles loose, their crow's-feet vanished. They listen to the voices of the others with the peace of small children. Wendy helps Linus guide his stick near the flames; she is silent about her pregnancy by me, having kept details of our encounter hush-hush. Megan, seated on a fading folding chair, beams as baby Jane gurgles and clicks with her continuing enchantment with the gift of sight, not crying once since her encounter with me. Richard, bearing a marshmallow-clumped trident at his side, is simply pleased to see his friends so jolly.

"I can smell the skins burning," Linus says. "Carbon."

"Isn't it just the prettiest thing?" Pam adds. "Hey, King Neptune—start toasting your prongs."

As I look down at them from the sky, their barbecue is the only speck of light on Earth for hundreds of miles save for the lava that oozes down Mt. Baker's slope and a small forest fire north of Seattle. I become a star in the sky and grow until Megan sees me and says, "Look. I bet that's Jared now."

Seconds later, I appear at the patio's edge and Megan smiles, saying, "Jane, say hello to Jared," making Jane twitter birdishly.

"Are you able to eat, Jared?" asks Karen. "Marshmallows—a bit stale, but they plump the moment they burn."

"Hey Kare, no food, thanks, no."

"A dance, perhaps?" She sweeps around the patio, her dress twirling and her eyes flashing because she is in love with the world.

"How about some lemonade?" asks Hamilton. "Num *num*. Made from a powder, of course, but lemony fresh nonetheless."

"Thanks again, but no, Ham." I move a bowl of potato chips and sit down on a stump Karen's father once used as a chopping block. Linus, semi-blind, holds up his glass in my general direction and says, "A toast to Jared." The others join in with a cloud of hear-hear's. "Our miracle man."

I blush. Wendy, who's heavily dolled herself up for the night, sugars moonily, "Hello*ooo* Jared."

"Hey Wen, looking good." And then there's a pause as in the old days when we made bonfires down at Ambleside beach, a bonfire's flames and embers hypnotic and silencing. "Guys—I need to speak with you all," I say, and I receive seven smiling faces in return—eight, now that Jane, as well as Linus, has vision. "Please listen."

The fire spits as insects kamikaze inward.

"It's hard for me. It's hard stuff. It's about all of you."

"Us?" Karen asks.

"Yup. All of you. And just because I'm able to speak more clearly than when I was alive doesn't mean I feel any more

251

comfortable doing it. Cut me some slack. I'm here to speak to you about transforming your lives and yourselves. Making choices and changing who you are.

"You've all been wondering why it was only the eight of you who remained to see the world's end. It's because you've all been given a great gift, but a confusing one, too."

"Confusing? *Duh*," Karen says.

"Gift?" Hamilton doesn't believe me.

"Uh huh. You've all been allowed to see what your lives would be like in the absence of the world."

Silence while everybody bites their lips.

"This is like that Christmas movie," Pam says. "The one they used to play too many times each December and it kind of wore you down by the eighteenth showing. You know: what the world would have been like without you."

"Sort of, Pam," I say, "but backwards. I've been watching over the bunch of you ever since Karen woke up, to see how different you'd be without the *world*."

"Why us, Jared?" Linus asks. "I mean, why not a syphilitic middle-aged rice trader in Lahore, India, with, um, um, a collection of taxidermied squirrels." He pauses. "Or a five-year-old Nigerian girl who communicates to the world, um, um, only through a green-painted Barbie she found in the alley behind the Finnish Embassy. I mean, why *us*?"

"Why you? People never asked that question of Jimmy Stewart's character in *It's a Wonderful Life*."

"*That's* the name," Pam says.

"Just go with it," I recommend.

Richard harrumphs.

"You were spying on us?" Megan accuses—these modern kids—so paranoid.

"Nope. Just watching. And caring. And worrying. And freaking out."

"What was so wrong about our lives that we had to go through the past year?" Linus asks. "At least Jimmy Stewart was having a life crisis. Our lives were going along pretty smoothly, actually."

"Were they?" I ask. "I mean, were they *really*?"

"Hey, Jared," Hamilton says, "it's not as if you were out there selling Girl Guide Cookies when you were down here. Who are *you* to watch over any of us and tell us what our lives should or shouldn't be?"

"For starters, Hamster, I'm a ghost, so that gives me a few extra course credits. No, I didn't get to stay on earth for an extra few decades, but I did get so see—oh, good *God*, Hamilton—what do you want me to have—wings and a halo?"

"For sta—"

Karen interrupts: "Will you testosterone cases clam up? *Shush!*"

Wendy says, "Jared, I get the impression that we were supposed to have been doing something else down here this past year—and that we've failed some kind of test."

"Yeah," Richard adds. "And what if we had done the right thing, Jared? What would we have won—a trip to Rome on Sabena airlines? A year's supply of Rice-a-Roni? Maybe you haven't noticed, but Earth is a big slag heap these days. There's not much we could alter even if we wanted. What—we're supposed to start a new race of human beings? A new civilization? Assemble some new Noah's Ark? Build a legacy? We don't even know what we're going to be able to eat in a year or two. Tang? Each other?"

Wendy adds, "Jared, there's radiation here now. And the weather isn't weather anymore. We can't plan for five years when we're unable even to plan for a week."

"Wendy, you're carrying our kid," I say . . . *oops*. "What kind of life do you expect him to lead?"

Wendy replies, "Him? You know the gender already? If you

254

know the future, Jared, *you* ought to have thought of that beforehand."

"Wait wait wait wait wait," Linus says. "You two *made* it?" Wendy's sigh is a confirmation. "You bastard!" he shouts at me, throwing a patio chair at the spot where he roughly imagines me to be floating. One of the chair's legs knocks over the barbecue's dome and the embers fall onto the ground, missing Richard by inches.

"You pinhead!" Richard shouts. "You could have brained me."

Linus ignores Richard and turns on me. "You couldn't even keep it in your pants when your dead, you dumb jock." He swivels toward Wendy. "Very well. Where'd you do it? *How'd* you do it? Now I know why you've been so moony lately."

"In the canyon. Two weeks ago. It wasn't *sex* sex," Wendy says. "It was a soul-to-soul thing. I didn't even remove my clothes."

"Don't soul-to-soul *me*."

"*Linus*," I say, "cool down. I simply made her stop feeling lonely."

"Yeah. Sure."

Wendy and I sigh. "Linus—do you want me to make *you* pregnant, too? It's not impossible. I can arrange it."

Richard is sweeping the embers into a small pile with a stray brick. Linus is confused. He wants to be angry but now he isn't sure what should be the anger's focus. Karen says, "It's not bad like you think, Linus."

Linus sulks and the group stands silently and looks at me. Surprisingly, it is Richard who breaks the quiet, saying, "Jared's right to be worrying about us." He puts down his marshmallow trident. "We really *don't* seem to have any values, any absolutes. We've always maneuvered our values to suit our immediate purposes. There's nothing large in our lives."

Hamilton snaps in, "These past weeks are the first time I've felt good in years, Richard, and you're starting to bring me down. Do we really need to analyze our shortcomings so thoroughly?"

255

"Yes, I believe we do," Richard says. "Jared's here to ask us to take a look at ourselves, Hamilton. I mean, *look* at us: instead of serving a higher purpose we've always been more concerned with developing our 'person*alities*,' and with being 'free.'"

"Richard?" Karen asks.

"Karen, let me say what I feel: This has been on my mind ever since Jared first appeared. I think we've always wanted something noble or holy in our lives, but only on our own terms. You know, our old beefs: *The World Wide Web is a bore. There's nothing on TV. That video tape is a drag. Politics are dumb. I want to be innocent again. I need to express the me inside.* What *are* our convictions? If we *had* any convictions would we even have the guts to follow them?"

Marshmallows broil then slime through the grill and into the embers. Papery carbon husks above are blown away in the breeze like used black cocoons. "It's true," Linus says, and all eyes move to him. I let him speak because he's saying the right things. "Our lives have remained static—even after we've lost everything in the world—shit: the world *itself.* Isn't that sick? All that we've seen and been through and we watch videos, eat junk food, pop pills and blow things up."

Hamilton says, "*Okay* Helen Keller, get to the point. And if you get any more depressing, I'm rearranging the furniture and not telling you how."

"Hamilton," Richard says, "tell me—have we ever really gotten together and wished for wisdom or faith to come from the world's collapse? No. Instead we got into a tizzy because some Leaker forgot to return the *Godfather III* tapes to Block-buster Video the day of the Sleep and now we can't watch it. Have we had the humility to gather and collectively speak our souls? What evidence have we ever given of inner lives?"

Karen perks up: "Of course we have interior lives, Richard. I do. How can we *not* have one?"

"I didn't say that, Karen. I said we gave no *evidence* of an interior life. Acts of kindness, evidence of contemplation, devotion, sacrifice. All these things that indicate a world inside us. Instead we set up a demolition derby in the Eaton's parking lot, ransacked the Virgin Superstore and torched the Home Depot."

"Aren't *we* holier than thou?" Wendy snipes at Richard, her arms tight around young Zygote Junior inside her stomach.

"Actually, Richard," I say, "the demo derby looked like a lot of fun. And I like the way you spray-painted names on your cars. I thought your 'Losermobile' would win in the end."

"Me, too. I—"

Megan ignores Richard and looks at me: "Jared—stop talking about cars. What are we supposed to do now?" she asks. "How can we change? You arrived saying you would teach us things that would allow us to change. So tell us."

My friends go calm—quiet. "Okay, guys, I think you want me to tell you that the world is a moral place. It is. But you're right to be thinking about your souls—the better parts of you—they're all desperate to climb from your bodies and leave you far behind. You're going to have to lead another life soon; a different life. The choice will be obvious when it arrives. You can get the world back yet."

A salvo of questions follows: "But you didn't tell us how to—" "What do we do to—" "What happens next?" "When do we—?"

"Hold your horses. A few squabbles ago Wendy asked what it was you were supposed to have been doing here this past year. The answer is that you ought to have been squabbling twenty-four hours a day for all of this time—and asked a million questions about why the world became the way it did. If you'd done that, you'd have been returned to the world the way it was and you'd be smarter and wiser. But you didn't— arson, looting, cocktails, videos and demo derbies—so now we move to Plan B."

The barbecue hisses. "I'll return when the lightning ends. I'll meet you on Cleveland Dam in seven days—at sunset."

"What lightning?" Hamilton asks.

Lightning cracks; the sky ignites.

"*That* lightning, goofball."

257

When I was alive on Earth I always noticed how events in the night sky had such a powerful capacity to alter human moods. One fall night in the 1970s, I was at a BC Lions football game. Just after sunset and directly over the cheap-seat bleachers to the east, a full moon, amber and veined, pumped itself upward and seemingly hovered over the stadium's edge. At this point, the announcer said, "Ladies and gentlemen—let's have a big round of applause for . . . the *Moon*!" and everybody went nuts and the rest of the game felt like a Super Bowl.

Around that same time, I was in a soccer tournament and the team and I had to fly to Manitoba on a red-eye flight. Somewhere over Saskatchewan I looked out the plane's window and saw the aurora borealis spritzing and jitterbugging up to the north—I felt as though I'd seen God singing along with the radio at a stoplight. We won the tournament. Fuckin' right we did!

And then one night, shortly before I got leukemia, a thinly sliced crescent moon rested high in the south sky over Vancouver; the planet Venus, white and hot, was also in view, and I watched the two bodies veer ever closer until Venus finally hit the unlit portion of the lunar edge. Just before Venus disappeared, it looked as though there was a light directly on the Moon's surface. And shortly afterward, as I said, I got leukemia. So there.

I mention events in the sky to help make sense of lightning and thunder and their profound effects on the soul. My friends have so far endured six days of continual storms and my old neighborhood and its surrounding forest are bursting in flames from untold numbers of lightning strikes. My friends are scrambling madly for cool air and sanctuary, having piled what few things they've been able to save into minivans in which they hightail up the charred stubble of the nearby golf course's pampas.

Below them, the fire on the sloping neighborhoods burn like a million Bic lighters held up in the dark at some vast, cosmic Fleetwood Mac concert. There is nothing remaining on this mountain slope save for the foundations of houses, tree roots beneath the soil, and a swirling maze of roads that lead from nowhere to nowhere.

Soon, two miles up the hill, the gang reaches a stone clubhouse surrounded by links of ashes. From within its solid interior they watch the lightning continue unabated, like watching a car crash that never stops, ripping and grinding and chewing and burning for day upon day upon day, sickening and dull.

The night is chilly; the fireplace is stuffed with burning chairs, yet their room feels only slightly warm. Dinner was a few cans of chicken broth and tinned green beans found in the kitchen. Tablecloths and towels are used as bedsheets as a freak Arctic cold front lands upon them pre-dawn. They cluster together like January blue jays roosting inside a stump, and still they wake up freezing. But for the first time in seven days the sky is silent. Across the Capilano Canyon they see the snow-crested mountains of our childhood reduced to black cinders and stone.

The day is spent driving lazy-eight's through the old neighborhood's tangled lariat of roads, seeing only charred stumps, melted patio furniture, and metal globs that were once sportscars. My friends cry and make fruitless attempts at salvage. Wendy finds the skeletons of the two ostriches and hands Linus the femurs. "It's nearly sundown," Karen says. "Let's hit the dam."

Their minivans hairpin down the black streets, the interiors smoky with the scent of itty-bitty salvaged mementoes—a pair of Adidas ROM shoes; a Snoopy trophy; a framed photo of

Liam Gallagher; a Becel margarine tub full of emeralds and Richard's asbestos astronaut suit.

On Cleveland Dam, they park at the west end and walk to its center, as promised; I hover invisibly above the silent spillway. The reservoir behind the dam is slightly below runoff level and algae within the water has loaned it an otherworldly shamrock sheen. The dam's road is smooth and glistening from a freak rainstorm and is seemingly paved with diamonds.

Quietly, everybody follows Karen onto the dam. For the first time in weeks she hears voices. "It's almost sundown," Karen says. "Kneel."

"I'm not kneeling," Hamilton says.

"Then *don't*," Richard says, and the group ignores Hamilton and kneels.

Hamilton stands with his arms crossed, watching the group and feeling like Noël Coward at a gauche cocktail party, and then he remembers his past year of madness with Pam, the drugs, the mania, his rebirth as the Last of the Famous International Playboys—Petula Clark, Brasilia, Le Côte Basque, Jackson Pollock, Linda Bird Johnson, and gimlet martinis— the ideas and images of a clean, sophisticated, and plausible future long vanished. *My head is now clean*, he thinks. *My veins are clean, but the world is soiled.*

Pam watches him from the corner of her eye. *Poor Hamilton*—Hamilton who has always felt unsophisticated having grown up so far away from the centers of metropolitan glamour. But Pam knows of the blankness at the core of that world, and she's aware that through her, Hamilton has learned this, too. She thinks back on the past crazy year on drugs and then the miracle of becoming clean. She looks at the city's skeleton through the charred forest. If this is the world, then take it. *I hated Milan. I hated catwalks. I hated my face for taking me the places it did. Let the insects fight for the remains.* "Hamilton, get over here," she calls.

Hamilton shakes his head. "I can't."

"You knelt at Jared's memorial service, didn't you?" Hamilton nods. "Then you can bloody well kneel here." Hamilton comes, kneels beside Pamela and looks up at the sky. This is their moment of surrender.

Linus clacks together the ostrich femurs and the noise rattles comfortably across the spillway and into the canyon below. Jane squeals and then falls silent.

And so it's here, on this dam, where this group, for the first time since the beginning of their lonely year, align their thoughts on the Great Beyond. This is where I enter. Linus clacks the femurs together: *clack clack.*

"I'm back." I appear before them, hovering slightly above the spillway.

"Jared!"

"What are we going to do, Jared?" Megan wails.

"Guys—hey—don't freak out. You think you've been forsaken—that the opportunity for holiness is gone, but this isn't true. Time *is* over; the world *is* gone.

"You've got just one option left. You blew it this year, but you can make good. As I said, there's still Plan B."

STOP BREATHING

I want to squish my friends into my heart, as though they could help me grout a troublesome crack. They wonder, *How did life ever come to this?* They're not bozos; they know everything's over. They're naked parachutists waiting to be pushed out of the plane and into the sky. Such is birth.

A warm sooty wind blows up the dam's face, its dark dead confetti floating through me, then shining. I'm a wall of light. "Guys! Feel the *air*," I say. "Across your skin. It's like icing sugar. So sweet. And feel the charged wind in your lungs—it *does* feel like the end of the world, doesn't it? Come on—drag your butts up. *Huddle!* And while you're at it, look at all the water pouring down the spillway—it's like melted lime Jell-O. And hear the water growl—like a cougar inside an unlocked cage. Oh! And remember that night at Linda Jermyn's party? Remember when we found that TV set in the alley and brought it here and hucked it off the edge." My friends stand up and circle around me as I hover above the commotion.

"Correction, Jare," Hamilton says. "*I'm* the one who did the actual hucking. If I remember correctly, you and Richard were off on the sidelines sniveling."

"You *wish*, Hamilton," Richard says. "*I* sweet talked the RCMP into thinking you'd thrown a half-melted ice swan off the edge. I mean, they saw you throw *some*thing. Jared and Pam were horking in the rhododendrons over by the parking lot."

"It was that home-brew of yours, Jared," Pam says. "It was like Liquid Plague. It's the absolute sickest I've ever felt. Even worse than methadone. And you were so *sick* that night, Jared—so sick that you couldn't even hit on me."

Ping! At this moment, a phenomenon in the sky captures my friends' awe and attention—a web of shooting stars now visible through a parting hole in the sky—a crosshatched ceiling of shooting stars as hasn't been seen on Earth since 1703 in the southern part of the African continent.

"Look at the sky," Linus says. "This is so *Day of the Triffids*."

"Everything's a light show for sixteen-year-olds, isn't it?" Richard says.

Even with all the hoo-haw and thunder of the past week, my friends find wonder and *ahhh*s in the spectacle. Young Jane reaches up to the sky as though it were a wise and generous person and not merely light. Jane, the planet's newest genius, is counting stars, her brain already advanced beyond mere numbers.

Warm, slightly stinky air, like air pushed forward by a subway car, sweet and full of adventure, whooshes over us. "And here we are all these years later," I say, "at the end of the world and the end of time."

"How fucking ironic," Hamilton says.

"Oh, come on, Hamilton," I say, "get *some* drama out of this. I mean, *all* of you noticed how 'time' feels so different here at the world's end—how weird it is to live with no clocks or seasons or rhythms or schedules. And you're all correct, too—time is a totally human idea—without people, time vanishes. Infinity and zero become the same thing."

"Gee," Hamilton says.

"Why just before all this happened," I say, pointing out the brightly lit black suburban dust, "nobody we knew had a second of free time remaining. All of it was frittered away on being productive, advancing careers and being all-round efficient. Each new advance made by 'progress' created its own accelerating warping effect that made your lives here on Earth feel even smaller and shorter and more crazed. And now . . . no time at all."

"Hey—" Wendy says.

"What?" I ask.

263

"Nothing. I just wanted to stop Hamilton from making some cynical crack."

"It's okay, Wendy," I say. "It's nice to think back on old times and be with old friends. I mean, we were all so *lucky* living when and where we did. There was no Vietnam. Childhood dragged on forever. Gasoline, cars, and potato chips were cheap and plenty. If we wanted to hop a jet to fly anywhere on Earth, we could. We could believe in anything we wanted. Shit—we could wear a San Diego Chicken costume down Marine Drive while carrying a bloody rubber head of Richard Nixon if we wanted—that would have been just *fine*. And we all went to school. And we weren't in jail. *Wow*." The stars are suddenly stained pink as a tiny waft of chemical residue from a long exploded Yokohama paint factory passes over.

"I remember running through the neighborhood in little more than a jockstrap. I remember being able to read *Life* magazine and making up my own mind on politics. I remember being in a car and thinking of a road map of North America and knowing that if I chose, I could drive anywhere. All of that time and all of that tranquility, freedom and abundance. *Amazing*. The sweet and effortless nodule of freedom we all shared—it was a fine idea. It was, in its own unglamorous way, the goal of all human history—the wars, the genius, the madness, the beauty and the grief—it was all to reach ever farther unclouded points on which to stand and view and think and evolve and understand ever farther and farther and, well, *farther*. Progress is real. Destiny is real. *You* are real." The pink passes on.

"And so that's why we're all here tonight—today—whatever day it is: Thursday—six weeks from now—1954—three days ago—one million BC. It's all the same. I mean, I *know* you're wondering what was wrong with the way you were living your lives in the first place—what your Jimmy Stewartesque crisis was—and I know you're wondering why you had to spend the past year the way you did. You say your lives weren't in crisis, but you know deep down they were. I was up there hearing you."

264

"You narked on us?" Megan asks, ever alert.

Richard darts in, "Megan, drop it, okay?"

The water behind the dam is luminous Day-Glo green. It looks electric. Radioactive. "So, yes, here all of us were, living on the outermost edge of that farthest point. People elsewhere—people who didn't have our Boy-in-the-Bubble lifestyle—they looked at us and our freedoms fought for by others, and these people expected us with our advantages to take mankind to the next level . . . newer, smarter, innovative ways of thinking and living and being. They looked at us and hoped we could figure out what comes . . . *next.*"

Wendy sneezes three pistol-crack snorts. "Bless you," I say. "And bless all of you, too." The light in the sky is so bright it's like daylight. "And weren't we blessed, too, with options in life—and didn't we ignore them completely?—like unwanted Christmas gifts hidden in the store room. What did life boil down to in the end? . . . *Smokey and the Bandit* videos. Instead of finding inspiration and intellectual momentum there was . . . Ativan. And overwork. And Johnny Walker. And silence. And—I mean, *guys,* just *look* at the situation. And it's not as if I was any better. I never looked beyond the tip of my dick."

"Get to a point," Richard says. He knows we're close to an answer.

"This past year—if you'd have tried, you'd have seen even more clearly the futility of trying to change the world without the efforts of everybody else on Earth. You saw and smelled and drank the evidence of six billion disasters that can only be mended by six billion people.

"A thousand years ago this wouldn't have been the case. If human beings had suddenly vanished a thousand years ago, the planet would have healed overnight with no damage. Maybe a few lumps where the pyramids stand. One hundred years ago— or even fifty years ago—the world would have healed itself just fine in the absence of people. But not now. We crossed the line. The only thing that can keep the planet turning smoothly now is human free will forged into effort. Nothing else. That's why the world has seemed so large in the past few years, and time so screwy. It's because Earth is now totally ours."

"The pioneers—they conquered the world," Linus says quietly.

"They did, Linus. The New World isn't new anymore. The New World—the Americas—it's over. People don't have dominion over Nature. It's gone beyond that. Human beings and the world are now the same thing. The future and whatever happens to you after you die—it's all melted together. Death isn't an escape hatch the way it used to be."

"Well fuck *me*," Hamilton says.

"Your destiny's now big enough to meet your jaded capacity for awe. It's now powerful enough for you to rise to the task of being individuals."

The meteorites disappear and the pulsing white sky goes black as though unplugged. Richard asks me, "Jared, wait a second—wait wait *wait*. You're going too quickly. Way earlier you said we could return to the world. What did you mean— the world as it was before—all this?"

"Exactamundo, Richard. You can return to the world the way it was—back to the morning of November 1, 1997. There'll have been no Sleep, and your lives will continue, at least in the beginning, as they were."

"Bull," Wendy says.

"I shit you not."

"Jared—are we gonna forget all this past year? The Sleep?" Linus asks. "Will I lose the pictures of heaven you gave me?"

I say, "You'll remember every single thing, Linus: everything that was lost and everything that was gained."

"Jane," Megan says. "What about Jane?"

"Jane will be whole."

"My—*our*—baby . . ." puffs Wendy.

"Born," I say. "And Hamilton and Pam, you'll be clean."

Eyes are wide before me—all save for Karen's. Karen has pulled back from the group, biting her finger, sucking in breath, closing her eyes and standing with her arms and legs pulled in as tightly as possible—as though she wished to become a thin line, so thin as to be invisible. The gang doesn't notice this; they're riveted by my words.

"You said that in the beginning our lives will be the same," Wendy says. "I sense there's some kind of deal happening here. We have to change somehow. There's a catch. How *will* our *lives* be changed. What's your Plan B?"

"Plan B is this:

"You're to be different now. Your behavior will be changing. Your thinking is to change. And people will watch these changes in you and they'll come to experience the world in your new manner."

"*How?*" Richard asks. "How do we change?"

"Richard, tell me this: back in the old world, didn't you often feel as if the only way you could fully *truly* change yourself in the powerful way you yearned for was to die and then start again from scratch? Didn't you feel as if all of the symbols and ideas fed to you since birth had become worn out like old shoes? Didn't you ache for change but you didn't know how to achieve it? And even if you knew how to do it, would you have had the guts to go forth? Didn't you want your cards shuffled a different way?"

"Yeah. Sure. But didn't everybody?"

"No. Not always. This feeling is specific to the times we live in."

"Okay . . ."

"And Richard, haven't you always felt that you live forever on the brink of knowing a great truth? Well that feeling is true. There *is* the truth. It does exist."

"A*ha!*"

"Yes. Well, now it's going to be as if you've died and were reincarnated but you stay inside your own body. For all of you. And in your new lives you'll have to live entirely for that one sensation—that of imminent truth. And you're going to have to holler for it, steal for it, beg for it—and you're never going to stop asking questions about it twenty-four hours a day, the rest of your life.

"This is Plan B.

"Every day for the rest of your lives, all of your living moments are to be spent making others aware of this need— the need to probe and drill and examine and locate the words that take us to beyond ourselves.

"Scrape. Feel. Dig. Believe. *Ask.*

"Ask questions, no, *screech* questions out loud—while kneeling in front of the electric doors at Safeway, demanding other citizens ask questions along with you—while chewing up old textbooks and spitting the words onto downtown sidewalks— outside the Planet Hollywood, outside the stock exchange and outside the Gap.

"Grind questions onto the glass on photocopiers. Scrape challenges onto old auto parts and throw them off of bridges so that future people digging in the mud will question the world, too. Carve eyeballs into tire treads and onto shoe leathers so that your every trail speaks of thinking and questioning and awareness. Design molecules that crystallize into question marks. Make bar-codes print out fables, not prices. You can't even throw away a piece of litter unless it has a question stamped on it—a demand for people to reach a finer place."

There's silence. The water's white noise is invisible now. The sky has cleared and the stars are timidly reappearing, point by point.

"What do we ask?" Wendy asks.

"Ask whatever challenges dead and thoughtless beliefs. Ask: *When did we become human beings and stop being whatever it was we were before this?* Ask: *What was the specific change that made us human?* Ask: *Why do people not particularly care about their ancestors more than three generations back?* Ask: *Why are we unable to think of any real future beyond, say, a hundred years from now?* Ask: *How can we begin to think of the future as something enormous before us that also includes us?* Ask: *Having become human, what is it that we are now doing or creating that will transform us into whatever it is that we are slated to next become?*

"Even if it means barking on street corners, that's what you have to do, each time baying louder than before. You must testify. There is no other choice.

"*What* is *destiny? Is there a difference between personal destiny and collective destiny?* 'I always knew I was going to be a movie star.' 'I always knew I was meant to murder.' *Is Destiny artificial? Is it unique to Man? Where did Destiny come from?*

"You're going to be forever homesick, walking through a cold railway station until the end, whispering strange ideas about existence into the ears of children. Your lives will be tinged with urgency, as though rescuing buried men and lassooing drowning horses. You'll be mistaken for crazies. You may well end up foaming at the mouth in a central Canadian drug clinic, magic-markering ideas onto your thighs which are bony from scouring the land on foot. Your eyes will always feel as if you've been staring at the sun, your bodies seemingly aching to cool them by staring at the moon. There aren't enough words for 'transform.' You'll invent more."

"We'll go crazy!" Hamilton shouts.

"No. You'll become clearer and clearer."

"No—we'll go totally effing crazy."

"Haven't you always known that, Hamilton? At the base of all of your cynicism across the years, haven't you always known that one day it was going to boil down into hard work? Haven't you?"

Hamilton and the rest imagine their new lives.

"And you're going to care about what people think? As if *they* care! And *you* know the truth—or at least you'll always be headed in its direction. It doesn't matter how stupid or crazy or extreme you become. There is no other meaning. This is it."

Hamilton closes his eyes and specks of mica dust fall from the sky, making his face glint.

"In your old lives you had nothing to live for. Now you do. You have nothing to lose and everything to gain. Go clear the land for a new culture—bring your axes, scythes and guns. I know you have the necessary skills—explosives, medicine, engineering, media knowledge and the ability to camouflage yourselves. If you're not spending every waking moment of your life radically rethinking the nature of the world—if you're not plotting every moment boiling the carcass of the old order—then you're wasting your day."

The water flowing beneath us and over into the spillway has stopped, but nobody notices. One by one I come face to face with my friends.

"Pam, you have hard work ahead of you. Every moment of your life from now on is going to be work, and no excuses. It's as though you've had to dig up a massive tree and untie the roots which have been tied into complex knots by dark forces beneath the soil. Could you do that? Are you capable?"

"Yes."

"Hamilton—no more pretending to be a child trapped inside an aging body. No avoiding the enormity and responsibility of being an adult. Could you do that? Are you capable?"

"Yeah."

"Wendy, no excuses: no drugs, no sleeping, no booze, no overworking, no repetition or insulation or efforts to make time disappear. You're in for the long haul. Could you do that? Are you capable?"

"I am. But what about the baby?"

"You may not be able to change the world on your own, but our kid *will*—as will Jane. You'll be their teachers and then they'll teach *you*.

"Linus—the world is *not* going to end in your lifetime once you return. That form of self flattery is gone. But too much freedom won't swamp you anymore. Are you ready to change—to join—to become part of what's Next?"

"Yes."

"Megan—if necessary, you're going to need to reject and destroy the remains of history—kill the past—if it hinders truth. Most of the past can only hold back what needs to be done. An astounding weight of history hangs around your shoulders. But in so many ways, it'll be useless to you. Too many things are too new. Rules have to be made up as you go along. Are you ready, along with Jane, to change—to join—to become part of what's Next?"

"Yes."

"And Richard: will you go undercover? Will you destroy information? Cut wires? Sever links? In an efficient, adult and professional manner will you dismantle and smash everything that stops questioning? Will you cut your hair? Will you infiltrate systems? You had no trouble thinking of dinosaurs and Ice Ages as pre-historic. Will you have just as little trouble thinking of your new epoch as post-historic?"

"I will."

Nobody notices that I don't speak to Karen. Richard asks me, "Jared—."

"Yes, Richard."

"What if we don't want to go back? What if we don't mind the way things are? What if we choose to stay here?"

"I was wondering when you'd ask. The answer is, if you want to stay here and continue the life you've been leading, you can. No strings attached. But I want you to think about that for a second." Richard and the others mull this over and the implications of this quickly become obvious. "No, I didn't think you'd like that option. You had another question, Richard . . ."

"Yeah, Jared—what happens if we go back and we stop asking questions? What happens if we stop looking and asking?"

I look at Karen; everybody's eyes turn to Karen. "Karen— you remember now?" I ask. "Don't you, Karen?"

"I do."

"What?" Richard shouts. "What are you talking about?"

"I remember now. It's all coming back to me. I can't believe I didn't remember. Richard—Beb . . . I have to go back into my . . . *coma*."

"Oh no—"

"Yeah," she says, "I do. I have to go back," she says.

272

"What do you *mean* you're going back? You can't. Stay here. I won't let you."

"It's not your choice to make, Richard—it's mine. And unless I make it, none of you can go anywhere. That's what I saw, Richard. Back in 1979. This. Here. Me—I'm your Plan B."

"Jared, you demented psycho—what gives you any right to do this?"

"Richard, buddy, *bro*—I wish I *were* psycho, but I'm not. And neither's Karen. I'm not even *doing* anything, Richard, I mean, *you're* the ones who need to do the choosing."

Richard is flailing and it's not cool—it reminds me of when we were younger and he never got picked for teams. He says, "What happens if Karen and I—all of *us*—don't go along with your deal—what then? What if we all *like* it here and want to stay here? We *could* build a new society—the planet could be our ark. I've been thinking of this—we've all thought about it at some point during the year. Earth isn't heaven and it isn't hell but it's *some*thing."

Karen's breathing is stiff and pump-like, similar to latex lungs I once saw in a high school guidance film on smoking. "Richard, Beb, that's sweet. But it's too late. This was decided a long time ago." She looks toward me. "You can't stop it. It's a done deal. Sacrifices need to be made. This is mine."

Megan breaks the silence: "How do we go back?" she says.

"Megan, at least defend your mother," Richard says.

"Dad, you *never* listen to me. She's going, okay? She's *leaving*."

"Megan," I say, "getting back is easy, a real no-brainer. All you guys have to do is each return to the place you were at the moment Karen woke up—that point in time and space where the world banged off of its old foundations. Just before dawn, November 1, 1997. Walk to the places where you were at that moment. All of you standing in your correct spots will

274

be like notches on a key in a tumbler—you'll unlock the world—reopen its doors. Megan, I believe you and Jane, then eight cells big, were in the Emergency waiting room with Linus that morning. Wendy was with Pam and Hamilton in intensive care. Richard was down there," I say, pointing to the canyon just down around the bend from the dam's spillway.

"Oh excuse me, Glenda, Good Witch of the North," Hamilton interrupts, "you mean all this time we've been marooned on this slag heap all we had to do was go stand around the hospital?"

"No, Hamilton. The offer's only good as of now. C'mon, Karen, it's time to leave."

"But wait, Jared," Richard says. "You didn't fully answer my question—okay, so Karen goes back into her coma. I repeat my question—what happens if we stop questioning—what happens if we stop looking for good questions and good answers?"

"Then you come back here."

"Yeah?"

"And you *stay* here." I let this sink in. "Ready to go, Karen? It's almost dark out."

"Wait!" Linus shouts. "We've lost something—and I don't know what it is we've gained in the process."

The lights above us dazzle. I say, "Linus, there are three things we cry for in life—things that are lost, things that are found and things that are magnificent. You've got all three this evening."

The lights, dazzle as they will, are silent. "Karen," I repeat, "it's game time."

"Go *where*?" Richard asks, his voice sandpaper dry with desperation. "*Now* what?"

"Karen needs to walk up the mountain," I say, "and she needs to take Jane with her. When she reaches the top, the world will return and Jane will be born on the same date as before."

Richard says, "Jared, shit, *no*. You can't—her legs—"

"My legs are fine, Richard. Stop treating me like porcelain.

275

I'm strong. The die's cast." One-by-one Karen bids good-bye to the others as Richard stands beside her, trying to catch her eyes.

"Pammie—Hamilton: we'll have drinks some day. Okay? With the Duchess of Windsor and Jimi Hendrix—and we'll laugh at this past year. And Pam?—always speak your mind, and Hamilton—always say whatever's truest. Don't be afraid of being kind." Hamilton and Pam look grief stricken. "Please guys—it's for the best. I'll always be dreaming of you and maybe you of me." Hurried hugs, as though a train is leaving, which it is. She moves along: "Wendy—Linus—you know this is true—this is all for the better. And I'm counting on you guys to change the world."

"Karen—"

"This is odd," Karen says. "I feel like I'm an astronaut before take-off. Maybe you guys can think of it that way. Look at this as glorious and exciting. It's a launch—think of it that way, each of us reaching a new world once again. Megan?" She approaches Megan whose eyes are overflowing into Jane's wool sweater. "You're a good daughter, Megan. You're a smart kid. You're a good mother. You're a good friend. I wouldn't have wanted anybody else to be my kid."

"Mom?"

Karen kisses Jane. "She's beautiful. I'm glad you can know how much I love you."

"She—she goes with you now?"

"Sorry Sweetie. Just for the time being. You'll meet again come September."

"But."

Karen holds Jane and comes to Richard. "Richard—Beb, I'll still love you, even in my sleep, and in my dreams I'll—" She pauses. "We never did get married, did we?"

"No. We didn't."

"Well then, in my dreams we'll be married."

"No—"

"Yeah. Yes. *Yes*, we *will*." A final kiss. "Bye." She turns to me: "Hey, Jared. I think you made the cut."

276

I touch my heart and remove a glowing spark from it. I take the spark and place it inside Karen's chest and say, "Touchdown."

Karen turns and walks away from the group, across the dam toward the mountain's base, her body like a doodle on a telephone book. "I'm *glad* I woke up," she shouts. "The world is so pretty and the future was so interesting. But I'll be awake inside my dreaming. I'll be dreaming of you all. Good night everyone!"

Then there's silence. I look at those who remain, frozen by the speedy sequence of life and its action. "The rest of you, it's time for you to go. Wendy, Linus and Megan, Ham and Pam—you walk to the hospital. Richard, you walk down into the canyon. Once you reach your places, please sit and stay. Once Karen reaches the apex you will have your world again."

I pause. "Good-bye, men. Good-bye women. Think of me."

"Good-bye, Jar—"

And then I'm gone, sunk down into the dam's concrete, leaving their lives for the time being. But I have my own secret job. I'm a part of Plan B, too. My job is to stay here on this blank and now empty earth and traipse its unholy carcass for years and years—decades, even—for as long as Karen remains in her coma. That's the choice I had to make. I'd do it again.

God.

So it looks as if I'll be running the streets here naked for the next fifty years. Reading a bit of porn; watching a few tapes. Tomorrow it may rain spiders or it may rain battery acid—I'll still be here. And no dates for a few decades except for Miss Fist; don't blame me if I crack.

I can see the others now as I feel my own life pulling away from theirs. Megan and Linus are sitting in the waiting area as the outside sky flickers hot and white. The hospital lobby is littered with countless leathery skeletons, but neither these bones nor the clanging silence bothers them.

"I still feel pregnant," Megan says. "Jane's still here. Four hours old. She's a clump of cells now, like a basketball, like bread dough—imagine that, Linus."

Down a hallway, something clanks.

"Look at all these people," Linus says. "They'll be *real* people soon."

Megan's face relaxes. "Funny how used to them we got—Leakers, I mean. I don't think of them as monsters anymore."

"Me neither."

"We're friends now, aren't we, Linus?"

"Yup."

"Are you scared about our new lives?"

"Yup."

"But there's no other choice, is there?"

"I don't think there ever was."

Over in the ruins of the intensive care unit, Wendy stands beside both Hamilton and Pam, who are resting on two gurneys. They're silent. What is their fate? How will their lives be changed?

"The room's a bit dark," Pam says.

"Do you want more flashlights on?" Hamilton asks, reaching over to swat one of a dozen emergency flashlights placed on their bottoms, shining up into the dusty air at the trolley's end.

"No. It's okay. It doesn't scare me anymore. Darkness, I mean."

"I know what you mean," Hamilton says.

"And look at the beams," Pam says, "the way they cut through the dust. They're like pillars, aren't they? Aren't they, Wendy?"

A catafalque of skeletons encircles the room; Wendy nervously taps steel forceps onto a stainless steel tray and she feels extremely old. "Yeah," she says. "They are."

Karen meanwhile limps and hobbles up the rock mountainside lit by the sky which is committing suicide above. She'll reach the top. The walls of her heart are as thin as rice paper and her breath as frail as dandelion puffs. From there she'll once more leave the waking world.

She speaks out loud to herself, unaware that the others will

278

also hear the words. She looks down from the slope at the burnt forests and the lost suburbs.

"You guys just wait and see. We'll stand taller than these mountains. We'll bare open our hearts for the world to grab. We'll see lights where before there was dimness. We'll testify together to what we have seen and left.

"Life *will* go on—all of us—crawling; stumbling, falling perhaps. But we *will* be the strong ones. Our hearts will shine brightly. We will forever be crossing the goal line."

Down in the canyon, Richard's heels sink into mud and loam and fungus and mouse holes as he crumbles down the hill. His body falls and lunges the same as always, like the times as a child he carried sockeye salmon sandwiches down to the salmon hatcheries for lunch. The soil is soft and warm, like an old shirt, like moist wedding cake. *Focus ahead, Richard: jettison everything. Leap forward. You have a mission.*

A bird's trill . . .

Quartz . . .

A green leaf . . .

A bruised knee . . .

His breath is a small wisp—a thought of a thought of a thought.

On the river he locates the spot where he sat on the rocks that strange November morning. He sits and rests his head on a smooth boulder. He lies there as Karen reaches the apex, where she finds a dusty rock onto which she hoists herself and Jane. The air is cool and scratchy. She breathes in deeply.

Richard resumes his vigil on the rocks under the sky gone insane. He shivers and his legs are numb with cold. Richard gets to thinking—he gets to thinking there must be all of these people everywhere on earth, eager, no *desperate* for just the smallest sign that there is something finer or larger or more miraculous about ourselves than we had supposed. *How can I give them a spark?* he wonders. *How can I hold their hands and pull them all through flames and rock walls and icebergs? With our acts we will shock and captivate them into new ways of thinking.*

He hears Karen's voice once one last time; she has climbed the mountain and she says, "*You* are the future, and the eternity, and the everything. You're indeed what comes *next*. I'm going now. It's my time to leave. Yes—I can feel myself leaving. You'll change the world. Good-bye, guys."

In London the supermodels wear Prada and the photographers snap their photos. The young princes read their *Guinness Book of World Records*. In California, meetings are held and salad is picked at. Across the globe hydro dams generate electricity and radio towers send powerful signals out into the heavens advertising Fiat Pandas and creme rinses. Golden lights oscillate wildly. Giant receiving dishes rotate and scour the universe for voices and miracles. And why shouldn't they? The world indeed awakens: the Ginza throbs and businessmen vomit into Suntory whisky boxes to the giggles of Siberian party girls—the excitement and glamour and seduction of progress—cities shine: cities of gold and tin and lead and birch and Teflon, molybdenum and diamonds that gleam and gleam and gleam.

Near dawn, he feels the tremors—the world resuming. There is an enormous camera flash. He can feel it happening— the world returns.

And suddenly it's almost sunrise. A final flash of light alarms a school of spawning salmon huddled in the water—a maroon, collective brain huddled underneath the rocks. Richard tries to imagine their collective thinking—the one idea they want to put forth.

Richard thinks of his life and his world once more: no, my daughter is *not* confused and angry and lost on drugs. No, she *doesn't* hate me for all that I've forgotten or neglected or failed to do for her. No, the woman I love is *not* a papery husk of a woman, breathing shallow thimbles of air as her gray hair crackles and her body turns to leather and bone. My friends are *not* lonely and tired and dried-up and sad. And I'm not just fooling myself, either. That's all over—we made the trade.

Richard thinks about being alive at this particular juncture in history and he can only marvel—to be alive at this wondrous

280

point—this jumping-off point toward farther reaches. The things he'll see and feel—even the tiny moments like the Moon mural in Karen's old bedroom or satellite weather maps—it's all such a tiny bit of what comes next.

His mind races: Think about all those crazy people you can see on the streets. Maybe they aren't crazy at all. Maybe they've seen what we've seen—maybe those people are us.

Us.

You'll soon be seeing us walking down your street, our backs held proud, our eyes dilated with truth and power. We might look like you, but you should know better. We'll draw our line in the sand and force the world to cross our line. Every cell in our body explodes with the truth. We *will* be kneeling in front of the Safeway, atop out-of-date textbooks whose pages we have chewed out. We'll be begging passers by to see the need to question and question and question and never stop questioning until the world stops spinning. We'll be adults who smash the tired, exhausted system. We'll crawl and chew and dig our way into a radical new world. We will change minds and souls from stone and plastic into linen and gold— that's what I believe. That's what I know.

P.S.

Ideas,
interviews
& features...

MEET

What is your idea of perfect happiness?
Right now. Where I am. At home.

What is your greatest fear?
That God exists, but doesn't care very much for humans.

Which living person do you most admire?
Vaclav Havel.

What objects do you always carry with you?
Earplugs.

What single thing would improve the quality of your life?
Everybody I like and love all living in the same city.

What is the most important lesson life has taught you?
We have time and we have free will. Otherwise, we're just animals.

Which writer has had the greatest influence on your work?
Jenny Holzer, an American artist whose work is text-based (what a dismal term). How tightly can you compress an idea? Where do ideas end and you, as a person, begin?

Do you have a favourite book?

Non-fiction, *The Andy Warhol Diaries*. Fiction, it's either Truman Capote's *Answered Prayers* or Margaret Drabble's *The Ice Age*.

Where do you go for inspiration?

Four-hour drives in my car, usually into the interior of British Columbia, into the desert cordillera that stretches from BC down into Mexico. Believe it or not, Canada has cactuses/cacti.

Which book do you wish you had written?

***The Age of Extremes: The Short Twentieth Century 1914–1991* by Eric Hobsbawm.**

What do you think of literary prizes?

They're wildly engaging, and they get people who normally don't discuss books discussing books. That's a hard thing to do.

What are you writing at the moment?

A new novel, *Eleanor Rigby*. ●

BRIEF

NAME
Douglas Coupland

BORN
30 December 1961, on a
military base in Baden-
Söllingen, Germany.

EDUCATION
Coupland graduated
1979 from Sentinel
Secondary School,
West Vancouver.
Graduated 1984 from
Emily Carr College
of Art and Design,
Vancouver. Went to
European Design
Institute, Milan, and
the Hokkaido College
of Art and Design,
Japan. Completed
course in business
science together with
fine art and industrial
design in Japan in 1986.

CAREER
The first exhibition
of Coupland's sculpture
took place at the
Vancouver Art Gallery
in 1987. He has won ▶

HEADLINING

For many of the critics, *Girlfriend in a Coma* was the moment where Douglas Coupland got 'metaphysical'. His fifth novel was, according to **The Times**, 'a dark, prescient book, a meditation on the mystery of life, the next step in a continuing search for meaning'. The **Sunday Times** identified the book as 'a fusion of cautionary tale and morality play', and the **Mail on Sunday** was bolder in calling it 'an extraordinary, enthralling moral fable'.

Yet despite the soulful gear change, Coupland's media literacy remained a talking point. Prompted by the swiped Smiths song title, critics tallied the pop culture references. '*Girlfriend* is a richly associative novel,' began the **Independent**.

'It ranges from the dysfunctional teendom of Twin Peaks *to the chilly metaphysics of* The Sweet Hereafter, *en route to winding up as a post-apocalyptic version of* It's a Wonderful Life.'

The **NME**, on the other hand, swallowed 'a heady, schizophrenic brew of a book: part *It's a Wonderful Life* and part *OK Computer*.' *Girlfriend* is, it continued, 'Coupland's wake-up bomb before we, as a culture, reach a critical mass of spiritual vacancy'.

BBC2's **Late Review** was vocal in its admiration for *Girlfriend*. Tom Paulin described it as 'visually brilliant, full of extraordinary imagery, fresh like new paint'. Fellow panellist Mark Lawson confessed to being 'amazed by it. The dialogue is some of the most brilliant I've ever read in a novel. It's a great wake-up call to young Americans everywhere.' And the **Guardian** was left in no doubt:

'Coupland directly tells us to pull our socks up and look at the world afresh… He is becoming extraordinary.' ●

BRIEF *(continued)*

◄ two Canadian national awards for excellence in industrial design, and you can still buy the baby cribs he designed in JC Penney stores. By 1988 he was a contributing journalist to *Vancouver* magazine. St Martin's Press, New York, asked him to write a guidebook to Generation X, a theme he had been exploring in his articles. Instead he went to California and wrote a novel – **Generation X**. This was published in 1991.

Subsequent fiction includes:
Shampoo Planet (1992)
Life After God (1993)
Microserfs (1995)
Girlfriend in a Coma (1997)
Miss Wyoming (1999)
God Hates Japan (2001)
All Families Are Psychotic (2001)
Hey Nostradamus! (2003)

Non-fiction includes:
Polaroids from the Dead (1996)
City of Glass (2000)
Souvenir of Canada (2002)
School Spirit (2002)

BACKSTAGE

In July 1984, 39-year-old Terry Wallis of Arkansas was involved in a horrific car crash. The vehicle he was in plunged into a creek, and the driver was killed. Terry was found a day later. He had survived, but had fallen into a coma that would last nineteen years.

In June 2003 Terry Wallis's brain decided to rejoin the world. His first and third words on waking were 'Mom' and 'Milk', which seemed lyrically appropriate for someone who had undergone something of a rebirth. His second word would no doubt have sent Douglas Coupland into raptures – 'Pepsi'. Perhaps Terry was still thinking about the slogan Pepsi had unveiled to the world in 1984: 'The Taste of a New Generation'.

We all hope that our last words on this earth will be epic and, wherever possible, memorable. But people like Terry Wallis, who are obliged to conjure up some famous first words upon emerging from a coma, sometimes find it difficult to hit the top notes. Take 50-year-old Annie Shapiro. For most of 1963 she ran two apron shops in Toronto. Then came 22 November, and Annie suffered a stroke while watching news coverage of President Kennedy's assassination. She fell into a thirty-year coma, only to snap out of it in Florida in 1992 with the following message from the mysterious shadowlands of her slumber: 'Turn on the television. I want to see the *I Love Lucy* show.'

The problem with famous first words for coma victims is that they often wake up not knowing that they have been out of the game. The word coma finds its root in the ancient Greek word for heavy sleep, and kneejerk requests for Pepsi and an *I Love Lucy* rerun sound not unlike the sort of startled non-sequiturs one sometimes blurts out after being jolted out of a snooze. Indeed, the relationship between comas and sleep could go much deeper than the word's linguistic roots. A medical study in 2002 suggests that a coma can result from damage to the portions of the brain that under normal circumstances would help you wake up in the morning. For instance, the thalamus and upper midbrain help us to wake up when we are disturbed from sleep by a noise. And the seriousness of the coma is thought to be dictated by which particular portions of the brain have suffered injury. A blow to the cerebral hemisphere may be the precise cause of vegetative states.

But what exactly is a coma? It is best described as a state of deep unconsciousness. Illnesses such as kidney infections or even diabetes, together with strokes and poisoning, can cause a person to slip into a comatose state. There are two main types of coma. The first type results from brain tissue damaged as a result of severe head injury. The second occurs with damage to the brainstem, and this latter type tends to result in fewer recoveries. Within the duration of a coma, there tend to be two identifiable periods. The first looks like typical unconsciousness – the victim's eyes remain closed, there is no speech and even motor responses to pain can be absent. This type of coma rarely persists for more than four weeks. But it can then drift into a second period, known as a persistent vegetative state. The eyes open, but the victim remains unable to exhibit conscious behaviour. Around 10 per cent of coma victims progress to this second state, which can last for months and even years.

To observers, comas have a particular eerie sadness about them. Patients appear to be supernaturally suspended between life and death, but recoveries often take place in

' Karen's dramatic sequence of coma, childbirth and recovery in *Girlfriend in a Coma* has real-life precedents. '

equally extraordinary circumstances. Terry Wallis suffered his car crash on Friday 13th, and began talking nineteen years later on Friday 13th. What's more, Karen's dramatic sequence of coma, childbirth and recovery in *Girlfriend in a Coma* has real-life precedents. In the US in 2003 a 26-year-old dental receptionist called Amanda Thomas fell into a coma after contracting pneumonia while pregnant. Doctors were considering whether to risk a Caesarean section when Amanda's body kicked into action and gave birth to a baby boy called Charlie, who was fifteen weeks early. A month later Amanda came out of her coma to meet the child she didn't know she had. ●

COVER STORY

Art Director Lee Motley has overseen the jacket design for the paperback *Hey Nostradamus!*, as well as the other Coupland reissues. She says: 'Douglas does a lot of his own sculpture and his own art, so he always has really interesting suggestions.'

Coupland liked Motley's starting-point, to draw inspiration from *The Virgin Suicides*, Sofia Coppola's 2000 film about five doomed teenage sisters living and dying in American suburbia. Mock-ups were made with stills from the film which seemed to evoke similar themes to Coupland's work. Lee Motley says: 'The whole film was very teen-American, and a lot of Douglas's books are set in the Eighties. We wanted to create a specific atmosphere.'

'Douglas does his own art and has really interesting suggestions.'

In particular, the lens-flare effect on the final cover of *Hey Nostradamus!* (a visual theme across the covers of the reissued Coupland paperbacks) was inspired by the film's cinematography. 'There's something very Seventies and Eighties about that,' says Motley. 'It was something put onto the images after they were shot.'

The image on the front of *Girlfriend in a Coma* takes artistic licence with the story. Motley says: 'We wanted some ambiguity there. The girl could just be lying innocently asleep on the grass. It's the hospital band around her wrist that adds the elements of darkness and doubt.'●

ON LOCATION

IN THE STUDIO WITH DOUGLAS COUPLAND

Mutation Garden *Squeeze bottles, ikebana vases and poured resin forms*

Spike Sculptural installation

Gorgon 2003 Aluminium and fibreglass, approx. 1.25 x life size
Kneeling Figures Plastic, life size

HAVE YOU READ?

● **HEY NOSTRADAMUS!** (2003)
Pregnant and secretly married, Cheryl Anway scribbles her last will and testament – and eerie premonition – on a school binder shortly before a rampaging trio of misfit classmates gun her down in a high school cafeteria. *Hey Nostradamus!* tells the story of Cheryl's death and the knot of alienation, violence and misguided faith from which her family and friends must untangle their lives.

'A pleasure to read: clever, affecting, effortlessly conceptual. The current landscape, the mindless and endless landslide of mass culture versus individual vulnerability – no one sees these or gets to the heart of them quite like Coupland.'
ALI SMITH, AUTHOR OF *HOTEL WORLD*

● **ALL FAMILIES ARE PSYCHOTIC** (2001)
In a cheap motel an hour from Cape Canaveral, Janet Drummond takes her medication and reflects on her children. Wade has just been in jail, Bryan's suicidal, and Sarah's an astronaut waiting to board the shuttle this Friday. Where did it all go wrong?

'Heartbreakingly bitter-sweet…This book will make you want to phone your own psychotic family and tell them how much you love them.'
DAILY TELEGRAPH

❛ Coupland continues to register the buzz of his generation ❜

● **MISS WYOMING** (1999)
Meet Susan Colgate – Miss Wyoming. Winner of a hundred teen pageants, child TV soap star, daughter of a hideously pushy mother. Now she's reduced to small, brainless parts in small, brainless movies. She is also the sole survivor of Flight 802. If she were to walk away from the wreckage now, before the

emergency crews get here, she could disappear and nobody would ever know…

'Astonishing…Coupland creates concepts that allow us to get to grips with our unimaginable, real-life, end-of-the-world news.'
LITERARY REVIEW

● MICROSERFS (1995)

Young Microsoft workers in Seattle ride the internet wave, all thanks to their Fearless Leader, Bill Gates. Then they decide to fly the nest and join a start-up in Silicon Valley. A snapshot of the digital dream before the internet bubble burst.

'Rather than reading it as an indictment of another lost generation, see it instead as a primer in the Jurassic stage of digital Darwinism, when nerds were becoming geeks and climbing the first evolutionary steps towards their eventual deification as life-style engineers of the 21st century.'
GUARDIAN

'Douglas Coupland continues to register the buzz of his generation with a fidelity that should shame most professional Zeitgeist chasers'
NEW YORK TIMES

● LIFE AFTER GOD (1993)

This collection of 8 entwined short stories showcased a starker style to Coupland fans reared on the freewheeling prophecies of *Generation X*. Characters search for meaning and chinks of spiritual value within the mundane routine of everyday life.

'Plainly, even beautifully written, in an achingly nostalgic present tense.'
THE TIMES

> **❛Beautifully written in an achingly nostalgic present tense❜**

The Sweet Hereafter
by Russell Banks
Chilly metaphysical tale
probing a small town's
response to the loss of
its children in a school
bus accident.

**The Diving Bell and the
Butterfly**
by Jean-Dominique
Bauby
Diary of a man who,
with his left eyelid (the
only surviving muscle
after a massive stroke),
dictated a remarkable
book about life locked
inside his body.

Diary
by Chuck Palahniuk
A woman keeps a
'coma diary' after her
husband's failed
suicide attempt. Dark,
funny and poignant
storytelling from
America's favourite
populist nihilist.

Awakenings
by Oliver Sacks
Classic account of
survivors of
encephalitis lethargica
and their return to the
world after decades of
'sleep'. The inspiration
for the 1990 film (see
Films).

HAVE YOU READ? *(continued)*

'A wizard at cataloguing our lives.'
THE OBSERVER

● SHAMPOO PLANET (1992)
Tyler Johnson, 22, shampoo collector.
Resident of a rundown town on the Pacific
Northwest, he's burdened with a hippie
mum, a drunk stepfather and a love-life
split between his girlfriend and a French
summer fling. Only one thing to do – escape
to Hollywood. Coupland's X-files continue...

'A snappy analysis of modern consumer
culture in all its paradoxical surreality'
MAIL ON SUNDAY

● GENERATION X (1991)
Andy, Dag and Claire reject the fast-lane
pressures of modern life, moving to Palm
Springs for a life of minimum wage McJobs
and disillusioned storytelling. In *Generation X*,
the book whose title gave a name to the
sons and daughters of the baby boomers,
Douglas Coupland unleashes an entirely
new vocabulary for modern living.

"'A new age JD Salinger on smart drugs'
TIME OUT

'Fiercely comic'
SUNDAY EXPRESS

THE WEB DETECTIVE

www.coupland.com
*The author's own site, with information
on his books, art and furniture design.*

www.heynostradamus.com
*The book's official site with a promo video
about all the characters.*

http://oliversacks.com
*Informative site detailing the life and work of
Oliver Sacks.*

http://www.waiting.com
*Support site for people whose lives have been
changed by brain injury.*

www.braininjury.org
*Medical, legal and information resource for
brain injury patients and their families.*

www.thepests.com
*Sassy site sporting a Douglas Coupland
dictionary of neologisms.*

http://www.geocities.com/SoHo/Gallery/5560/
Coupland fan site.

http://www.coupland.dk/
Another good tribute site.

BOOKSHOP

Now you can buy any of these great paperbacks from HarperCollins at **10%** off recommended retail price. **FREE** postage and packing in the UK.

Hey Nostradamus! Douglas Coupland 0-00-716251-0	£7.99
All Families are Psychotic Douglas Coupland 0-00-711753-1	£6.99
Miss Wyoming Douglas Coupland 0-00-717982-0	£7.99
Microserfs Douglas Coupland 0-00-717981-2	£7.99
The Corrections Jonathan Franzen 1-84115-673-6	£7.99
The Restraint of Beasts Magnus Mills 0-00-655114-9	£6.99
The Subject Steve Sam Lipsyte 0-00-713366-9	£6.99
The Gift David Flusfeder 0-00-714078-9	£7.99
The Nineties: When Surface was Depth Michael Bracewell 0-00-712802-9	£7.99

Total cost _____

10% discount _____

Final total _____

To purchase by Visa/Mastercard/Switch simply call **08707 871724** or fax on **08707 871725**

To pay by cheque, send a copy of this form with a cheque made payable to 'HarperCollins Publishers' to: Mail Order Dept. (Ref: BOB4), HarperCollins Publishers, Westerhill Road, Bishopbriggs, G64 2QT, making sure to include your full name, postal address and phone number.

From time to time HarperCollins may wish to use your personal data to send you details of other HarperCollins publications and offers. If you wish to receive information on other HarperCollins publications and offers please tick this box ☐

Do not send cash or currency. Prices correct at time of press. Prices and availability are subject to change without notice. Delivery overseas and to Ireland incurs a £2 per book postage and packing charge.